A Fear of Dark Water

Craig Russell

W F HOWES LTD

This large print edition published in 2011 by
W F Howes Ltd
Unit 4, Rearsby Business Park, Gaddesby Lane,
Rearsby, Leicester LE7 4YH

1 3 5 7 9 10 8 6 4 2

First published in the United Kingdom in 2011
by Hutchinson

A CIP catalogue record for this book is available
from the British Library

ISBN 978 1 40748 880 6

Typeset by Palimpsest Book Production Limited,
Falkirk, Stirlingshire

Printed and bound by CPI Group (UK) Ltd,
Croydon, CR0 4YY

For Jonathan and Sophie

WM

A Fear of Dark Water

Stirling Council Libraries

Und das Meer gab die Toten, die darin waren

Offenbarung, Lutherbibel

And the sea gave up the dead which were in it

Revelations, King James Bible

Thalassophobia is a fear of large and deep bodies of dark water, such as seas or lakes, where the bottom cannot be seen. As a specific phobia, it is not related to aquaphobia or other water phobias but is more akin to agoraphobic conditions.

It is not a fear of water itself. It is a fear of the void: of what lies beneath the surface.

The Klabautermann is a traditional figure in the superstitions of Northern German seafarers.

There were two views of the Klabautermann: one as a friendly, helpful sea-elf who helped repair leaking ships or guide them to safe waters; the other as a malevolent demon who played cruel tricks on sailors and guided ships to their doom. One thing was common to both versions: that the Klabautermann was invisible to almost everyone.

If you did manage to catch sight of the Klabautermann, it meant only one thing: that you were going to die.

PROLOGUE

CHAPTER 1

FIFTEEN YEARS BEFORE
THE STORM

Too deep.

Korn hit the *Pharos One* comms link again. He heard Wiegand's voice but the transmission was breaking up. No crackle or hiss: the digital communications system had no degrees of function; the signal was either there or it was not. Wiegand's anxiety came to Korn in severed syllables and silences. Shards of words. Sharp-edged.

Korn looked at the submersible's depth meter. Oh Jesus, too deep, too deep. And still dropping. Dropping faster. Three thousand metres. Three thousand, two hundred. Three thousand, six hundred. No sense of falling, of descent. Just the relentless plunge of the reading on the depth meter.

Beneath him the trench. Around him the water: chill, dense, crushing. Black.

It was a different universe. A different reality.

Pharos One had travelled the shortest of distances. A journey of three and a half kilometres. On land, you could walk it comfortably in three-quarters of an hour. Yet Korn was now in a place as remote to mankind as space. As the moon.

1

Four thousand metres.

Now Korn was on the edge of the abyss. Literally. This was where the abyssopelagic zone began. The water outside was now beyond any normal understanding of the concepts of water, of a liquid. This was deep in the aphotic layers of the ocean, where all life was blind in a lightless universe. The readings showed that the water temperature outside was near freezing, yet it remained fluid because of its intense salinity. It was a liquid, yet had an unimaginable, crushing density. Korn knew that already the pressure was four hundred times that of the atmosphere at sea level, and it increased by one atmosphere for every ten metres that the *Pharos One* submersible sank.

'I've lost control,' he shouted into the comms. 'The control desk is completely dead. You have to try to bring me up remotely . . .'

More sharp shards of speech came through the comms. Korn knew that that was how he would have sounded to the mother ship on the surface. If basic communications were not working, then there was no chance of them establishing a reliable remote-control link. And, even if they could link in, there was no guarantee that whatever system failure had robbed him of control had not also severed the link with the remote-navigation computer.

Another shatter of syllables.

Korn didn't attempt to answer. He tried to think. Or more accurately he tried to slow his brain, to clear it of panic, so that he *could* think. Why had *Pharos One*'s main motors cut? Why had he no control from the helm? And why had the submersible experienced such a catastrophic loss of buoyancy? It was as if the whole system had collapsed. He was sure that the engines were okay, the steering gear. It was an electronic fault, rather than mechanical. Why didn't he know? He had helped to design the *Pharos One*; planned its electronic management himself; designed fail-safe systems with Wiegand. How had this happened?

And having helped design the *Pharos One*, Korn knew that, unlike a bathyscaphe, it did not have ultimate buoyancy. Its mix of gasoline and electromagnet-capture ballast was limited. Korn had insisted on a submersible capable of reaching significant depth, but which could 'fly' through its environment. Without motive power its weight would, ultimately, sink it.

Korn stared out through fused quartz into the dark water, the beams of the iodine floodlights picking out an upward snowstorm of particles. Then something pale was caught in the external navigation lights. An intricate basket star, like a lost lace doily, drifted up and past the window; the only life he could see. If you could call it life. Bloodless, capable of regenerating parts of itself, even of reproducing a complete new creature from a lost tentacle. A being with a sixty-five-million-year-old pedigree.

I should not be here. The thought hit Korn as he

watched the basket star drift up and out of sight. Not a passing thought; a revelation. A rejection of years of study; of millions in investment. Of a lifetime's devotion. I should not be here. Suddenly it struck Korn that his presence in this place was as preposterous as the basket star he had just sunk past exploring the heights of Mount Everest. I have no right to be here. This is not our world. He thought of the time, the effort, the money he had poured into the Pharos Project. Millions.

Void. Korn heard Wiegand's one complete word before the comms went completely dead. Void. Void what? It was a word well suited to the black, crushing emptiness around him. But Wiegand had been trying to tell him something. Korn tried to raise the mother ship again, but there was no response. He hit the main motor control. Nothing. The desk was still dead. I am going to die here, he thought. I'm going to die and no one will ever find my body and I deserve it because I should not be here.

Creaking.

It was a low, rumbling groan, like a sea creature moaning in the abyss. But Korn knew it was the ribs of the pressure hull protesting. He looked desperately around the cabin; at the tightly, claustrophobically confined space of reinforced steel that surrounded him; at the thick quartz of the portholes. Maybe it would be quick. He had imagined himself coming to rest at the bottom of the trench, trapped and motionless, going claustrophobically insane as he waited for the one hundred hours of oxygen to run out. Screaming and clawing. But he realised that the *Pharos One* would soon exceed its safe operating parameters. Maybe it would be a rivet that would kill him; fired, bullet-like, from its socket by the intense pressure of crushing water. Or maybe, and more likely, he would be squeezed to death, like a bug between fingers, by the implosion of steel as the hull yielded.

Wiegand's voice again. This time clear.

'Dominik!'

Korn stared at the depth meter. Four thousand, eight hundred metres. Five thousand. Oh God, no. Too deep. Too deep.

'Dominik!'

'I'm here,' he said and was surprised at how dull his voice was. There was a sound. Not loud, but constant: a soft, mechanical whirring. The engines.

'We've overridden the controls, Dominik. Dominik, can you hear me?'

'I'm here,' he said. 'I shouldn't be here.'

'Dominik, listen to me. Concentrate. Put on your evac suit.'

'Evac suit?' Korn suddenly felt alert. A voice from five kilometres and a universe away woke something in him. 'What the hell use is an evac suit? I'm down nearly five thousand metres.'

'We've got the readings on your power levels. Something's damaged the cells. We can get you up, we think. Maybe all the way, maybe not.'

Korn looked at the depth gauge again. For a

second that seemed to last for ever it stayed static. Then, unbearably slowly, it started to indicate ascent.

'Do you hear me, Dominik?'

'I hear you.' Now fully alert, and suffering. The unbearable pain of hope. 'I'll do it. I'm doing it.' Korn fumbled furiously at the restraint belt. He struggled in the coffin confines of the cabin to pull the suit from its housing behind the command chair; wrestled himself into it. Neoprene and rubber cuff seals strangle-tight, the bright orange evac suit loose-tented around him. A second confinement.

'You're going to have to hurry, Dominik . . .' Wiegand's voice over the comms was tight and even. Forced. Artificial calm wrapped around panic. 'Listen, Dominik, when the power fails, we're going to void all the ballast. It'll be explosive. We're hoping the momentum will topside you. But you're going to come up fast. Too fast. Do you understand?'

'I understand,' said Korn, his voice muffled through the plastic screen of the suit's hood.

'You may lose comms again. You've got to keep watching the depth gauge. If your ascent stops, you've got to get out and come up in the evac suit. We may get you all the way up to the surface without evac, but if we don't, you've got to act fast. You'll drop like a stone again otherwise. Have you got that, Dominik?'

'Got it. Just get me out of here, Peter.'

'We're going to kill all power except the engines and comms. Hold tight until we bring back the control-panel lights.'

Darkness. A darkness beyond any night. To begin with he could see nothing; then something drifted past the quartz porthole. Something glowing in the distance. A single bright pinpoint. Bioluminescence: an angler fish or cookie-cutter shark creating its own distant speck of light in the abyss, like a distant lighthouse. A beacon. For a second, Korn fixed his full attention on that small, faint glimmer and it seemed to him to have a profound significance he could not quite grasp.

The control board before him lit up again. The few blinking buttons and the LED display of the depth gauge suddenly blindingly bright after the abyssal dark. Three thousand metres. There was an alert light on the suit. When he switched it on, its flashing exploded in the cabin. More creaking. The sea still wanting to crush him out of existence.

'Dominik . . .' Wiegand's voice again.

'Go ahead.'

'We have to get you up to at least one-eighty metres. The evac suit's tested to that depth. Just relax and let it bring you up. The suit's designed to ascend no faster than three metres a second, so don't worry about decompression sickness. But you must get out if there's any sign that the module isn't going to make it to the surface.'

One thousand, five hundred metres.

'I shouldn't be here,' Korn said to himself. 'We shouldn't be here.'

'Repeat, Dominik . . .'

'I said we shouldn't be here. We have no right. We shouldn't have the presumption, the arrogance—'

'I need you to focus, Dominik,' Wiegand's voice cut across him. 'Stay focused. Got it?'

Nine hundred metres. Eight.

'I'm focused, Peter. I'm more focused than you think . . .'

The water outside became less dark. Not lighter; less dark.

'Keep your eyes on the gauge, Dominik . . .'

The constant, reassuring whirr of the motors stopped.

'Peter . . .'

'Brace, Dominik!' Wiegand's voice over the comms was urgent. 'I'm going to vent the tanks. Brace!'

Something thundered around Korn. Deafening. Uncompressible petroleum ballast being voided from the stabilising tanks. Steel ballast released from the *Pharos One*'s electromagnetic grip. Now he felt movement. A surge upward pinning him to his seat. He clung tight to the armrests, trying to control his breathing, his pulse pounding in his ears.

'Peter?'

The comms system was down again. He was

alone once more, but surging up to the environment he belonged in. His true place in the world. Out of the depths. *De profundis.*

Five hundred metres. Four. Three. He snapped the red cover off the emergency explosive-bolt release and pushed back the trigger guard. He had to time it right. Exactly right. Two hundred and eighty metres. Just a little more.

He knew what he was seeing, but didn't want to see it. His ascent was slowing. Two hundred forty . . . twenty . . . Even slower now. Two hundred. Too deep. Still too deep. The gauge held for an eternity at one seventy.

Now. Do it now. His reason screamed at him: he knew that the impetus given by the explosive voiding of the tanks was spent. There was only one way to go now: back down into the abyss. Yet something froze him: an irrational hope that the submersible would somehow overcome the universal laws of physics.

One hundred and eighty.

He had lost ten crucial metres and gained one atmosphere of extra pressure. He checked his restraint harness was fastened and pulled the switch. The explosive bolts fired, releasing the hatch.

It was like being hit by a car: the water did not surge into the cabin, it rammed into the back of the command chair like a solid mass. An intense steel-sharp pain shot through his arm and into his shoulder. He knew his forearm had been broken, but when he checked his arm it wasn't to examine the extent of the break but to make sure the sleeve of the evac suit hadn't ruptured. It hadn't.

Slamming the fist of his uninjured arm into the release buckle, Korn undid the safety harness. Ignoring the sharp pain in his other arm, he scrabbled around behind his chair and pushed himself out of the *Pharos One*'s only hatch, at the rear of the vessel. He was going to be coming out of a fast-sinking submersible; he needed to get out and clear fast. A snagged sleeve or belt, or becoming tangled in the robot arm, and he might end up trapped there, dragged back down to the bottom. As it was, he reckoned he'd have lost another ten, maybe twenty metres. Suddenly he was outside, in the open water. Pushing away. The survival suit insulated him against the cold, swelling up with captive air to resist the worst of the pressure, but its buoyancy pushed him upwards against the rear hull of the sinking submersible.

He braced his legs against the bright yellow hull and pushed away with his feet. He was free. Free and rising.

He watched the *Pharos One* sink beneath him. Silent. Fading fast in the gloom; becoming smaller, then gradually invisible in the dark of the water. He looked at the depth gauge on the wrist of his suit. One sixty and rising.

Survivable. Dangerous, but definitely survivable. He was going to make it.

He continued to rise at a decompression-safe

rate for another ninety-seven metres. He could see, vague and distant above him, the attenuated bloom of day.

The surface.

It was at that moment that the material of his evac suit – which, unknown to Korn, had been caught on a hull rivet and stretched to tolerance when he had been evacuating the *Pharos One* – split open and exploded into a constellation of escaping air bubbles.

CHAPTER 2

TWO WEEKS BEFORE THE STORM

Meliha made her way along the street, hugging the wall as if the red brick had been magnetised. They were after her. They were after her and they would find her. They always found everyone. And when they found her, they would probably kill her. Maybe not there and then. Maybe not even in the way most people would think of a killing. They could kill someone's mind, destroy their personality, and leave the body living, walking, breathing. But as a person, as a being, you would be just as dead.

It was cold. So cold. And wet. And dark. And her feet hurt. She had walked so far. Most of all, Meliha was afraid. She was afraid of the people who were after her because she could no longer see them as people. Somehow they had achieved what they had always wanted to achieve, what they claimed they could achieve, and had become something other than human. She found that she didn't even think of them as individuals, but as a collective, single being. Corporate.

A singularity.

Meliha tried to push the fear out of her being.

Fear was an emotion she had never really had much time for. She had been a clever, brave, inquisitive child. A bold little girl who faced the world pugnaciously. Fearlessly. *'Benim küçük cesur kaplanim'*: that was what her father had always called her: 'My brave little tigress'. She thought back to the times, the hours, she would sit and talk with him, asking bold questions about the world. Whatever the question, he always had an answer. Not always *the* answer to her question, he would tell her, but *an* answer. He had once showed her a crystal paperweight that he kept on his desk. Something he had picked up during his many years and countless travels as a geologist. He told her that beautiful things like crystals and jewels lay scattered all around the world, waiting to be found; sometimes buried deep in rock, sometimes lying scattered near the surface. There were times, he had told her, when you simply found them by chance, other times when you had to work hard – looking carefully and digging deep – to find them.

Answers, he had explained, were exactly like that. They lay scattered throughout the fabric of the world. And they were never more precious than when you found them for yourself.

And that had become how she would live her life. She had searched for answers, for the truth. And now she was here, in a strange city in the cold north, being hunted because of the answers she had found.

Meliha was in Hamburg's Speicherstadt, a city within a city: the old bonded warehouses looming above her and the dark waters of the canal at her side. A light mounted high up on one of the warehouses cast a puddle of light and the Hamburg rain danced as little silver explosions on the cobbles. She tried to get her bearings. The warehouse she sought was somewhere near here. If she could make it to the warehouse, maybe they *wouldn't* find her. At the very least, she'd have time to think through her next move.

Meliha went through her pockets again. No cellphone. She had left it behind in the café she had had lunch in. She had left it on the table, switched on, and had placed her napkin over it. Then, when she had walked out of the café, she had left it behind.

One more check. Illogical: she knew she'd left it in the café, but she had to check her bag and pockets again. Just to be sure.

It could be that the staff in the café had found the phone and had put it to one side for her to claim it later. But the café had been in a rundown part of Wilhelmsburg, and Meliha guessed that it was more likely that someone had pocketed the phone on finding it. She thought about the obese pig of a man who had sat at the next table, making disgusting noises as he ate. It hadn't been his eating habits that had most caught her attention, though: it had been the smartphone or hand-held PDA he had constantly tapped at with a stylus between overfilling his mouth.

Maybe he had taken her phone. Or perhaps another café customer was walking around Hamburg with her phone in their pocket.

Which was exactly what she wanted. Because when Meliha had rechecked her pockets, it had been to reassure herself that her cellphone was *not* there. Now it was out there somewhere, like a message in a bottle cast out on the sea. Maybe someone would understand the ringtone's significance and decrypt the phone's content. At the very least, it would send her pursuers on a false trail.

She took the street plan from her pocket. A booklet: print on paper, not a hand-held satnav device or GPS navigator. She plotted her position from where she had come into the Speicherstadt, across the bridge and along Kibbelsteg, then into Am Sandtorkai. The warehouse was near. If she had calculated it right, it was just a block away and around the corner.

The warehouses in the Speicherstadt were vast red-brick cathedrals of commerce dating back to the nineteenth century. But now it was all changing. They had extended the original Speicherstadt with a very twenty-first-century version of itself: the vast Kaispeicher A, the Speicherstadt's most westerly warehouse which had once housed massive stores of tea and tobacco, was being built upwards and outwards and into the shape of a vast sailing ship that dominated the skyline. A building project that had lasted years

15

and was transforming the storehouse into a massive concert hall, hotel, apartments. Like the Speicherstadt before it in the nineteenth century and the Köhlbrandbrücke in the twentieth, the Elbphilharmonie would become the landmark to define Hamburg in the twenty-first century and beyond, as distinctive as the Sydney Opera House, while reminding everyone of the city's maritime past.

Even this part of the original Speicherstadt was changing: ad agencies and trendy bar-restaurants were making inroads, mainly to be near the stylish new HafenCity development that extended to the old bonded-warehouse city.

But the row of buildings outside which Meliha now found herself had remained largely unchanged. Just as there had been for two centuries, the cobbled canalside path was lined with huge storehouses containing imported rugs and textiles from Turkey, Iran, Azerbaijan, Kazakhstan, Pakistan.

She moved out of the puddle of light cast by the warehouse lamp and checked up and down the cobbled canalside path. No one. No sign of them. But, she knew, that meant nothing. It was their function to follow, to shadow you unseen. To find you without you knowing they were there until the last moment.

And, of course, they had the kind of technology that you normally only expected the intelligence services of some superpower to have. Maybe they were watching her right now, able to see her in the dark. Maybe she was a bright infrared beacon in the cold dark of the Speicherstadt.

So close. Meliha ran. Her feet hurt even more with every footfall. She had walked for kilometres to get here. No taxi. No public transport. Nothing that was connected to a computer system or radio network. She had crossed a city without crossing a circuit, without connecting with a technology: even avoiding the few parts of the city that had CCTV, taking circuitous detours to avoid the spots marked in red pencil on her map.

She stopped suddenly, realising she was at the right block. The signs on the warehouse were in Turkish, English and German. This was the one. There was no alarmed keypad entry, just an old-fashioned brass keyhole in a sturdy, traditional German warehouse door: robust, dense wood, reinforced with brass plates. Reassuringly low-tech: a door that had protected the contents of the warehouse for more than a hundred years. She took the heavy key from her bag and unlocked the door. She slipped through it and into the warehouse's darkness, with just one last check of the canalway outside.

Maybe she was going to be all right, after all.

Meliha took a small wind-up LED torch from her handbag and scanned the warehouse. She was in an entry foyer and a sign listing the tenants told her that what she was looking for – Demeril Importing – was on the third floor. She pushed through the glass-panelled doors and into the main warehouse. Over to one side of the warehouse was a large goods lift, but Meliha decided it was better to take the stairs and make as little noise as possible.

When she reached the door of Demeril Importing, she took a second key from her bag and let herself in through an ornate *Jugendstil* door. She shone her torch around the warehouse. Textiles piled high: rugs, carpets, kilims. Rich Turkish designs revealed on the folded edges. Tags revealed names she knew so well: Kayseri, Yeşilhisar, Kirsehir, Konya, Dazkiri . . . Somehow the familiarity of the names gave her comfort. There was a robust, ornate wooden desk and a kilim-upholstered chair near the door; the desk was piled high with paperwork and ledgers, bills and orders impaled on two spikes. Business was done here as it had been done in the last century and the century before that. No computers. No websites. No electronics.

Moving across the warehouse Meliha continued searching until she found an alcove at the back of the main storage area, filled with less carefully stacked carpets. She chose a lowish pile of carpets right over in the farthest corner of the alcove and lay down on them, switching her torch off. She could rest. She could rest, but not sleep. Sleep would be dangerous. She would be safe here until the morning. Then . . . well, then she would try to get in touch with Berthold. How she could do so without using a phone or any other electronic medium she had not yet worked out. But she must get to Berthold. Tell him what she knew. But now she could rest, but not sleep.

She fell asleep.

It probably had been the quietest of sounds. Maybe it had been the main door, three floors below: an indistinct, dull clunk that had fired into her sleeping brain like a bullet. Whatever the sound had been, she had been asleep and now she was totally, nerve-janglingly awake. For a sliver of a second she wondered if she had slept all night and if what she had heard was the arrival of the warehouse staff; but it was still dark. She lay still on the pile of rugs, only her head raised. She didn't breathe; straining to hear any further sound. A few seconds passed, stretched intolerably long by the adrenalin surging through her system. Silence. Then she jumped as she heard another sound. Faint and muffled. Voices. Two, three, maybe more. The floor below. Far apart from each other but talking calmly and quietly.

Meliha couldn't make out the words, but she knew they would be communicating in English. They always spoke English. Her heart pounded. Of course they didn't need to speak any louder. They would be *enhanced*: able to communicate at a distance, to see in the dark, to locate the slightest sound.

They would be working their way through the

floor below. Systematically, methodically. The way they did everything. A single consciousness. A groupmind. An egregore.

Taking her torch, Meliha shone it into the darkness to search her surroundings for concealment or escape. The LED light was dim, but she dared not wind up the torch again in case they heard the sound.

There was a storage cupboard further behind her, right at the back of the alcove, barely visible behind a stack of carpets, some lying loose on the floor next to it. If she could get in there, perhaps ease a carpet roll across in front of it, maybe then they wouldn't see her.

She slipped off the shoes from her aching feet and eased herself off the stack of rugs. She crossed the rough wooden floor to the storage cupboard. It was much bigger than she had thought and empty except for a stack of sample books in one corner and, leaning against the wall, a metre-and-a-half-long roll of a textile that was too lightweight for carpeting but too heavy for curtains. Easing herself in behind the sample books, Meliha rearranged them to offer meagre concealment. She started to move the textile roll over for additional cover, but it was heavier than she expected and started to slip from her grasp. She made a desperate grab for it and only just stopped it from crashing into the wooden side of the cupboard and alerting her pursuers to her hiding place. Muscle-achingly slowly, she eased the textile roll diagonally across in front of her, like the bar of a gate.

Shrinking back as far as she could in the store cupboard, Meliha switched off her torch and was immediately plunged into dark. As her eyes became accustomed to this new depth of darkness, she peered through between the top of the sample books and the angle of the leaning textile roll. She could see only a narrow section of alcove and nothing of the main area of the carpet warehouse.

And she could hear nothing. No movement. No voices.

It was like a shadow passing.

Right in front of her. Someone or something passed swiftly and silently across her narrow view of the alcove. Right to left. A dark flutter you could not identify as a person. She gave a start but instantly contained it, not moving, not breathing. They were there. On her floor. Now she could hear faint sounds of movement. Something spoken quietly in English.

The shadow crossed again, this time left to right. Closer.

Meliha didn't move. She still held her breath, afraid they would hear even that. A tear welled up and ran down her cheek, the agony of waiting for the moment when they would tear away her makeshift camouflage becoming unbearable. More sounds. Then silence. Minutes passed, still nothing. Meliha concentrated so hard on the silence that she gave a small start when it was broken. But this time the sounds were even more muted. And above her. The next floor up.

She let go her breath, slowly, quietly. They were definitely above her now. They were not as good as they thought. They still had very human fallibilities.

It was difficult for her to tell how long had passed: her fear stretching every second immeasurably. But Meliha guessed it had been at least an hour since they had finished checking the floor above. No sounds of searching, no quiet, calm, measured voices in English. She peered into the gloom. Nothing. Carefully, slowly, making sure not to touch anything, she turned her wrist but, as it lacked a luminous dial, she still could not see the time on her watch. Her legs began to cramp but she didn't move them. The pain grew and grew, the fibres of her muscles knotting in spasm. But she ignored it. She concentrated once more on driving out her fear.

'*Benim küçük cesur kaplanim.*' She focused on remembering her father's voice as he had said it. The gentle tone; the pride. '*Benim küçük cesur kaplanim.*'

She waited for another hour. Meliha perceived a faint brightening of the light out in the warehouse. A hint of morning. She had not heard anything more.

They had failed. Or perhaps they had not known

but merely suspected that she had been in the building. There were other places they perhaps knew about and were searching there. She decided that, from now on, she must not go anywhere she had been before. But she had to keep moving. Their failure had presented an opportunity for her to open up the distance between her and them. She could get out of the city, out of the country. If she acted now.

Meliha eased the textile roll back as gently as she could, making no sound. Edging herself out from behind the sample books, she paused and searched all she could see of the storeroom before taking tentative steps out of the alcove.

There were four of them waiting for her. They were standing, motionless, in the centre of the main floor of the warehouse. Four dark shapes, shadows. Genderless, ageless. They were silhouetted against the vague milky bloom of the large warehouse window. Two of them had something bulky around their eyes. Night-vision goggles. None made a move as Meliha appeared; no hint of reaction. They had been standing there for two hours, waiting for her to come out of her hiding place. It was more efficient, quieter that way.

They were what Meliha knew had been pursuing her. They were what she feared most.

Consolidators.

The Consolidator closest to Meliha slowly raised its dark arm as if pointing at her. There was a popping sound and she felt a sharp pain in her chest.

As she fell backwards onto the same stack of carpets on which she had slept, she thought she heard her father's voice call to her.

'*Benim küçük cesur kaplanim.*'

CHAPTER 3

THE NIGHT OF THE STORM

There was no storm.

All there was, was a vast expanse of open, dark sea. No land, no ships; no one there to witness the storm's night-time birth. But there *was* syzygy: the perfect alignment of sun, moon and Earth, with the moon at its closest to the Earth, and the yearning sea heaved and arched its back under the moon's compelling pull.

Above the sea the air was cool. Dry. And higher above it was a colossal mass of even colder air that had been born somewhere in the north and far to the east, and had drifted south-west, over the Baltic Shield. And as it had done so, it had climbed higher into the troposphere. Its Siberian chill had become even colder with altitude. And now, superchilled and super-elevated, it slid silently and disdainfully over the Atlantic.

But it would not be allowed to pass.

Something moved low across the arching back of the sea; something equally as colossal as the cold above it. This mass of air had been born in the tropics and carried warmth and moisture with it. And just as her counterpart above was colder than normal, she was three full degrees warmer than the usual drift.

Warm air rises, cold air sinks: a simple fact of physics, of meteorology.

The storm was born. It sucked the warm, moist air upward in a violent convective mesocyclonic vortex, the torn air reaching speeds of 180 kilometres an hour. A waterspout formed, joining sea to sky. Condensing water vapour from the warm air fizzed and crackled with electricity and clouds bulked and boiled and fumed. A vast supercell stormcloud, like a titanic anvil, formed above the Atlantic, turning the night darker.

Filled with millions of tonnes of water, it rotated slowly, malevolently, and began to shoulder its way towards the land.

CHAPTER 4

Kreysig recognised the fluttering in his chest as a rush of adrenalin and felt guilty about it. This was a catastrophe: buildings had been damaged, people had been injured, perhaps some had even lost their lives. Kreysig's home city had been assaulted; violently, relentlessly, without mercy.

But as he stood there, surrounded by tumult and clamour, Lars Kreysig felt a thrill. This was what he had been made for.

The night was filled with the roar of heavy equipment and machines, of mobile generators, the piercing, insistent bleeping of reversing fire trucks and the relentless churning of the water pumps: man-made thunder competing against Nature's tempest of wind and rain. Everything was glossed wet and sparkled under the arc lamps and the red, blue and orange flashing lights of the firetrucks, emergency vehicles and heavy caterpillar-tracked bulldozers. The worst of the storm had passed, and the ebb had begun, but a contemptuous Nature still wind-tugged at Kreysig's yellow protective suit and angrily drummed pellets of rain on his hard hat.

Like the neck of some improbable nocturnal dinosaur, the massive arm of a Liebherr LTM 1130-5.2 lattice-boom truck swung overhead, heavy cable and chains swinging and clashing. A team of firemen fastened the chains around a tangle of wood and metal that had been swept up onto the wide expanse of flooded ground beside the Fischmarkt. The lattice boom hoisted the debris up and clear of the flood area, lowering it onto the back of a flatbed. A second, smaller crane lowered a section of armoured evacuation pipe into place and the same fire team rushed forward and snapped shut the camlock couplings to connect it to the rest of the pipe. As soon as the connection was made, Kreysig shouted into his radio and another two pumps came on line.

And still Kreysig felt the thrill of battle. This was Man against Nature. And he was the man.

Kreysig had known well in advance that the storm had been coming. It had wrought devastation across France and England; the North German Climate Bureau and the German Weather Service had tracked its progress. They had also tracked another cluster forming in the North Sea, one hundred and eighty kilometres south-west of Jutland. It was like two armies gathering before attacking at once, combining their strengths before the onslaught on the Netherlands, Denmark and Northern Germany. Kreysig had seen Hamburg devastated by flood before. The 1953 flood had been before he was born, and he had been a baby when the '62 storm had hit and killed more than three hundred and left sixty thousand homeless in the city; but he remembered '76 and had been a senior fire and rescue officer in 2007. Each time the water had hit higher, but each time Hamburg had been that little bit readier, that little bit more protected.

And this time, before the flood hit, millions of euros' worth of flood barriers had paid for themselves in a single deployment: blocking and channelling the storm surge. But some flooding was inevitable, and they had known where to be ready, where the battle lines would be drawn, including here, at the Fischmarkt, where St Pauli met the city centre.

Tramberger, Kreysig's deputy, came across to him and leaned his weather-beaten face in close, shouting to be heard above the combined clamour of storm and machine.

'That's all the electric submersibles and all the diesels on line. We've got an ebb and the water level is dropping. We're down to plus three metres.'

Kreysig grinned and slapped his deputy on the shoulder. They were winning. He looked around at the teams he had deployed; all were still working full tilt: hard, muscle-tearing work against a far stronger opponent, but no one showed any sign of the fatigue that must, by now, be adding lead to every movement. It was a good team. A bloody good team. He had put it together himself, picking the best from the Hamburg Fire Service, from the

Hamburg Harbour Police, from the Hamburg City and State Engineering Department.

He checked in with his other crews, further to the west on Klopstockstrasse and Königstrasse. Same news. He checked his watch: it was nearly five a.m. They had been fighting the flood for twelve hours. Looking up at the still-dark sky, Kreysig saw the heavy clouds scud malevolently over the city. It was like watching a fleet of bombers pass overhead, laden with potential destruction. But these clouds, he knew, would wreak havoc elsewhere. Hamburg's turn was over. For now.

It was then that he noticed one of the teams had stopped working. The firemen stood in a circle looking down at something on the newly exposed tarmac of Elbestrasse. The team leader looked across to Kreysig and Tramberger and beckoned, urgently, for them to come over.

Something, Kreysig could tell, was wrong.

PART I

CHAPTER 5

Jan Fabel awoke. Gradually. He had been dreaming: a dream about sitting in the house he'd grown up in in Norddeich, in his father's old study, talking with a young man whom Fabel knew was dead and who knew it himself. Fabel wanted to leave the dream behind, where it could be forgotten.

He surfaced slowly from the depths of his sleep and became aware of the sound of voices. The radio alarm. NDR Radio. A debate. One of the voices vaguely familiar.

He lay staring at the ceiling for a moment, mustering the sleep-scattered pieces of his consciousness and trying to work out what the voice on the radio was talking about. And *who* the voice belonged to: Fabel realised that he recognised the male voice from somewhere in his fully awake world but, for now, he was too sleepy to concentrate on locating it. He rolled over onto his side; Susanne had her back to him. He shook her shoulder and she made a sound somewhere between sleepy contentment and irritation.

'It's time to get up,' he said.

Another low, sleepily discontented muttering.

He swung his legs out and sat on the edge of the bed. Berthold Müller-Voigt. That was whose voice he recognised on the radio. He had been sure he had heard it before somewhere. Müller-Voigt was the Environment Senator in the Hamburg Senate and someone with whom Fabel had had dealings in the past.

Fabel frowned and pushed his blond hair back from his eyes. He shook Susanne again: another grumpy response. Switching the radio-alarm off, he rose and stretched and made his way through to the shower. Susanne and he had lived together in this flat for more than two years, but he still found that he had to think about its early-morning geography. He shaved and showered. Dressed. Roll-neck sweater, expensive English tweed jacket, chinos, brogues.

He had just made the coffee when Susanne came into the kitchen, still in her bathrobe. Her thick dark hair a tumbling statement of her unwillingness yet to face the day.

'You'll be late,' he said. He meant *they* would be late. Susanne usually worked from her office in the Institute of Legal Medicine in Eppendorf, but two days a week she worked out of the police Presidium. On those mornings they took one car. And on those mornings Fabel was always rattled by Susanne's tardiness. This morning, he was even more tense: Susanne was attending a seminar at the Federal Crime Bureau in Wiesbaden and he

34

had agreed to run her to the airport to catch her early-morning flight to Frankfurt.

'I'll be ready.' She took the cup of coffee he offered and leaned on the kitchen counter. 'Did you sleep okay?' she asked. 'That bloody storm kept me up half the night.'

'I think it woke me up.' He lied. It hadn't been the storm that had woken him in the middle of the night; but they didn't talk any more about Fabel's dreams. The bad dreams.

Susanne switched on the small TV they had in the kitchen. It was one of the compromises Fabel had accepted: he was no great television watcher and never had understood why people needed more than one in their homes. But one day he had come back from work and had found it sitting on the counter. A new and gleaming intrusion into his world. A cohabitational *fait accompli*; another indication that his space, his life, was now shared.

'Look at this . . .' she said. The report on the TV was of serious flooding all along the banks of the Elbe. There was footage of the flood defences down by the harbour and the Fischmarkt being deployed. The reporter did his piece to camera with practised gravity.

'It's good we're not travelling along the Elbchaussee this morning,' she said.

'We may have problems getting to the airport anyway. I would imagine that there's going to be more traffic, what with the diversions and every-thing. We'll have to leave that bit earlier,' Fabel replied, looking pointedly at his watch. Susanne made a face and went back to a leisurely enjoyment of her coffee.

'I'll phone the airport just to check the flights are on time . . .' Fabel made to lift the phone.

'Why phone in?' asked Susanne from behind her coffee cup. 'Just check it online.'

'You never know when these things are updated,' said Fabel. 'At least if you talk to a human being . . .'

Susanne snorted. 'A human being? We're talking about someone who works in an airport. Trust me, use the computer – it's less robotic. I tell you what, I'll do it when I'm dressed. I just don't get why you're so technophobic.'

'I'm not technophobic,' muttered Fabel. 'I'm *traditional*. Anyway, I fully admit that I'm not too keen on the digital age. Look at this so-called Network Killer we've been chasing for the last six months . . . or at the havoc that reliance on computers causes. We've had all kind of memos about this Klabautermann Virus that's been hacked into the Hamburg State email system.'

Susanne laughed. 'You don't *hack* a virus. Tell me, how come you survived when the meteor hit?'

'What meteor?' Fabel asked irritatedly.

'You know, the one that wiped out all the other *dinosaurs* . . .' Susanne emphasised the word and laughed at her own witticism. 'Anyway, as far as I can gather, the Klabautermann Virus hasn't breached the Polizei Hamburg's security. We've got it at the Institute for Legal Medicine, though.

36

It's a pain, I'll give you that. But we were able to back-up all our emails before it hit.'

'I've got a simpler solution. It's called print on paper.'

'Oh yeah?' Susanne put her cup down and sauntered past him, letting her hips swing as she walked. 'Then we wouldn't have to worry about Klabautermann Viruses or system crashes . . . all we'd have to worry about would be little bookworms like you, wouldn't we, honey?' She ruffled his hair as she passed. Fabel frowned.

It had stopped raining by the time Fabel and Susanne made their way to where Fabel's BMW convertible was parked, but the sky was glowering and heavy, the colour of ship steel. Fabel sighed as he put Susanne's suitcase and attaché case in the trunk.

'Another shitty day,' said Susanne gloomily. She closed the car door and cursed when a trail of rainwater from the roof dribbled into her hair. 'This thing's leaking – you know that, don't you?'

'It never used to be a problem,' said Fabel in an almost-mutter. 'I had covered parking at my old place.'

'You really should think about trading this in.' Susanne ignored his comment. 'It must be ten years old now. You're always banging on about the environment; this can't be that fuel-efficient or environmentally friendly compared with what you could get now.'

'It does me fine,' said Fabel, manoeuvring the car from its parking space. 'I don't see how adding another car to the roads could be considered environmentally friendly. And anyway, if you're so green, why are you flying to Frankfurt? You could have asked to go by train.'

'You're the tree-hugger, not me.' She grinned maliciously. 'It must be because you hardly saw a tree when you were growing up in the good ol' flatlands of East Frisia. I suppose all that wind blew them down.'

'We had trees. Maybe not as many as you had in darkest Bavaria, but we had trees.'

'We had trees, all right,' said Susanne. 'Forests full of them. And mountains. You know what a mountain is, don't you Frisia Boy? It's like a really, really, really big dyke.'

'Very funny.'

'I'm surprised you moved here to Hamburg. We must be all of two metres above sea level. Don't you get nosebleeds?'

Fabel laughed. 'If people like you keep taking domestic flights then we'll be below sea level soon enough.'

'Then I'll travel by boat. Or U-boat.' Susanne started to hum the tune of 'Yellow Submarine', smiling contentedly.

Rather than battle through the city, Fabel headed out along Behringstrasse and onto the A7 autobahn. As they approached the ramp, Fabel noticed a huge poster by the side of the road: a picture of a tumultuous sea beneath a stormy sky, a small, distant lighthouse casting a beam of light across the waters. Beneath the image was a logo of sorts: the words THE PHAROS ENVIRONMENTAL PROJECT in English, next to what looked like some kind of stylised eye. The slogan below stated in German: *The Storm is Coming*.

'D'you think it's real?' Susanne asked abstractly, watching a huge four-by-four Mercedes thunder past them.

'What?'

'Anthropogenic climate change.' Susanne repeated the question while tilting the rear-view mirror in her direction as she applied lipstick. 'Do you think it's real? That we're responsible for screwing up the climate. Creating storms like last night?'

'Of course it's real.' Fabel snapped the mirror back to its correct position, pointedly sighing his irritation. 'All the evidence points to it being real. You're a scientist, you've seen the data. You saying you don't believe it?'

'No . . . I'm not saying that. But maybe it's not all us. Maybe there's a natural shift. It's happened before. And as well as natural shifts, a single volcano can do more damage than we've done over our entire history. Just look at the impact of all that Icelandic ash belched out into the atmosphere. If that baby or one of her bigger brothers really blows, then it could be winter for years. Mass starvation. Maybe even total and irreversible climate change. That's not us. That's Nature.'

'Maybe there is a natural shift, but we're defin-itely adding to it. It makes sense: releasing millions of years' worth of stored carbon energy in a century and a half.' Fabel sighed and looked at his watch. The road was even more congested than he had predicted. Luxury congestion: from the number of Range Rovers and battleship-sized Mercs and Lexuses, Fabel guessed that most of the usual commuter traffic from the affluent suburb of Blankenese, a little further upriver and upmarket from his Ottensen flat, had been re-directed away from the Elbchaussee, the main route running along the side of the river.

'Maybe I should think of trading up, after all,' he said dully, watching the slow procession of luxury marques.

'I hope we're still talking about cars . . .' Susanne grinned at him. 'I'll phone you tonight from my hotel, after the seminar.'

'I'll probably still be in the Commission.'

'This Network Killer case?' asked Susanne.

'Yep. I'll be chasing electronic ghosts until midnight,' he said gloomily. He was about to say something else when the buzzing of his car phone interrupted him.

'Hi, *Chef*, it's Anna . . .'

'Hi, Anna. What's up?'

'You on your way into the Presidium?'

'No . . . or, at least, not yet. I'm dropping Susanne off at the airport, then heading in. What's up?'

'You maybe want to make a diversion down to the Fischmarkt. We've got a wash-up.'

'Shit . . .' Fabel paused for a moment and sighed. Not another one. 'Does this look like the Network Killer?'

'Actually, no. Not this one. Not unless he has completely changed his modus. This is a partial body. Dismembered.'

'But female?'

'Yes. She doesn't fit with the other Network Killer victims, but it still looks like it's one for us.'

'Okay,' said Fabel. 'I'll come straight there from the airport.'

CHAPTER 6

The man behind the desk sat with his back to the view. The wall behind him was completely made of toughened glass strengthened with pale steel: an edgeless window looking out across an edgeless expanse of sodium-grey water beneath a sodium-grey sky. It created the impression that the office was unconnected to anything; just suspended, untouched by gravity and removed from the environment around it.

In his late forties, with a stocky build and powerful shoulders, the man behind the desk was shaven-headed but his jaw was framed by a dark, trimmed-close goatee beard. He wore rimless glasses and a black suit with a dark grey, Nehru-collared shirt beneath. There was an unnatural neatness to him, to the order of his desk, to the layout of his office. Even his movements seemed unnaturally methodical, as he inserted the memory stick into the laptop computer and clicked his way through the images stored on it.

'There is no doubt about this, then?' He spoke to the tall, thin, grey-suited man, pale-faced under short but starkly black hair, who stood in front of the desk.

'I'm afraid not, Herr Director.'

'How the hell could we have missed this? How could an outsider uncover all this . . . this *chaos*, and our own Consolidation and Compliance Office be totally unaware of what was going on?'

'I'm sorry, sir. Obviously, this is beyond anything we could have imagined. I mean, this behaviour is so extreme, particularly from one of our own members. I know it's no excuse, Herr Director, but we weren't looking for something like this, whereas the woman infiltrated the Project specifically to find something she could use against us. I'm guessing that even she didn't expect to uncover something of this magnitude. But I can assure you that the instant this came to light . . . when I realised who it was in the file, and knowing his position in the organisation, I put my best security and surveillance officers onto tracking his every move, twenty-four hours a day. Ever since then we have been monitoring all his internet, email and cellphone activity, as well as tracking his movements and contacts. Our surveillance confirms what is in the USB stick we found on the woman.'

'And there is no way she could have communicated any of this to someone on the outside?'

'I cannot say with certainty, Herr Director, but I believe not. It's my opinion that she intended to sell this information to the press, or to expose it on a website. She would not have told anyone who might have compromised her scoop. And she would be aware of our reach, so she would not risk exposing herself until publication.'

'She was a journalist, you think?'

'I can't say. And she wouldn't say. She was *unresponsive* to questioning. However, there is, we believe, a cellphone unaccounted for.'

'What do you mean, "unaccounted for"?'

'Simply that we can't find her cellphone. A Nokia 5800. But we've got a tracker on it. It'll be found, Herr Director.'

'I sincerely hope so. I don't need to tell you how much data can be stored on a hand-held.' The man behind the desk paused meditatively, then nodded towards the image on his laptop screen. 'What about him?' Does he know he's been found out?'

'Absolutely not, Herr Director. I get the feeling that he believes he is immune from detection. His actions suggest a certain arrogance. And my Consolidators are expert at covert surveillance. He doesn't know he's being watched, that I'm sure of.'

'Have you heard of the Observer Effect, Bädorf?'

'I can't say I have, Herr Director.'

'It comes from quantum mechanics, from the observation of subatomic particles. The act of observation itself changes the behaviour of the observed particle.' The Director examined the image on the screen for a long time. 'It is imperative that he does not know we are onto him. And no one outside your immediate team must know about this. You realise the danger his actions have placed us in, don't you, Bädorf? The danger they have placed the entire Project in?'

'Of course. I have told the Consolidators involved to destroy all records of the surveillance, other than those you now have. But I do believe we got to the woman before she could pass on any of this information. And we could deal with . . . with our *problem* . . . before he does anything else to compromise the Project. What are your instructions?'

Wiegand stared at the images again, clicking through them. 'Nothing rash. This takes planning. He has to be stopped, all right, but not in a way that links with us.'

'If I may suggest, Herr Director: perhaps *Mister Korn* should be advised.'

'You are talking to me, Bädorf. It's the same thing. What I want you to do is to come up with something discreet and effective. Something *innovative*. Can you manage that?'

'Of course, Herr Director. We have various resources at our disposal that cannot be linked directly to us. I will examine our options and report back to you.'

After Bädorf left the office, the Director swung his chair around to face the glass wall. The sky's colour had shifted subtly to a more glaucous grey and now hinted at turbulence. Perhaps there was another storm coming.

CHAPTER 7

A moment's calm before the storm.

Sitting quietly in his car, Fabel listened to his music and watched the rain through the windshield as it eased to a drizzle. He knew what was coming.

This was his business. His job. Looking at death. Trying to understand it. But it didn't matter how often you saw death – violent death – it still stirred a turmoil in you. Maybe not as big a turmoil as it had ten, fifteen years and countless cases ago, but it was still there: the vague churning in your gut triggered by an irrepressible human instinct. A natural fight-or-flight reaction firing somewhere in the oldest evolved part of your brain. Especially if there was a lot of blood. When there was a lot of blood something instinctive kicked in and over-rode your reason. And, later on, long after you had left the scene of crime, the images of the dead would come back to you. Unbidden and at the most inappropriate moments: eating a meal, during sex, relaxing with friends.

So Jan Fabel took a moment and sat in the car with the wipers switched off, watching the viscous rain burst maliciously against the windshield. The day outside was grey: the sky, the water, the buildings – all tonal shifts of graphite. It was a grey peace, this moment.

The music seemed to fit his mood – and the weather – perfectly: the Esbjörn Svensson Trio, played through the mp3 player he had plugged into the BMW's sound system. *From Gagarin's Point of View*. A great title. A great piece for a Hamburg morning in graphite tones. Pleasantly melancholic in the way only the Scandinavians seemed able to master.

Cold, wet knuckles rapped on the passenger window and snapped him out of his grey peace. He opened the window and chilled pinpoints of rain prickled against his cheek.

'Are you going to join us, *Chef*?' Anna Wolff leaned over into the window, frowning against the cold and wet. Impatient. Anna had always been youthful-looking and pretty: dark eyes and dark hair cut short. Girlish. But standing there in the rain there was a hint of a future, older Anna: an Anna with the edge of her typical energy blunted. Fabel noticed the subtle change and felt bad. He also noticed her slight limp as she stepped back from the car and felt worse. His team had taken more than its fair share of casualties over the years.

'You look full of the joys,' she said as Fabel stepped out of the car.

'So what have we got, Anna?'

'Like I said, a wash-up. And be warned: it's a

stinker. It was found by the flood-defence team working here. The boss is a guy called Kreysig.'

'Lars Kreysig?'

'You know him?' asked Anna.

'More know *of* him, but I have met him. He's a bit of a legend in the Hamburg Fire Service. A lot of people are breathing today who wouldn't be if Kreysig hadn't been there to pull their fat out of the fire. Literally. He still here?'

'We asked him to hang about until you arrived. What was that crap you were listening to in the car?'

Fabel stopped and turned to face Anna. 'You have no soul, Commissar Wolff, do you know that? No appreciation of the finer things in life. Leave me alone, Anna . . . Susanne's been having a go at me all the way to the airport about my car.'

'Really? Personally, I like antiques. Anyway, Susanne's good for you. You're less grumpy these days. You ready for this?'

They made their way across to where a white forensic tent had been set up, stepping over pipes and hoses and avoiding the dark rainbow puddles of oil and water and the black tangles of flotsam washed up from the flood.

'I've already had the pleasure,' said Anna when they reached the tent. 'If you don't mind I'll wait for you here.'

Fabel nodded: Anna was tough, and she had seen more than her fair share of violent deaths, but her Achilles heel was dealing with a messy corpse. And

Fabel knew that there was nothing messier than a body that had been in the water for anything more than a few days. In water, the processes of decomposition are greatly accelerated: the flesh softens and the body swells with trapped gases, rising and bobbing on the surface like some putrid buoy.

There was a table with forensic kits set up outside the tent. Anna handed Fabel a white paper oversuit, latex gloves, blue stretch overshoes and a cup-filter face mask. She took a perfume atomiser from her jacket pocket and sprayed a puff into the inverted cup of the mask.

'You'll need it,' she said. 'This one's ripe. And keep your forensic suit zipped up. If that stink gets on your clothes, you'll never get it off.'

'I've dealt with floaters before, Anna. I know the drill.' Fabel smiled as he said it: he had noticed Anna's pale face grow paler, obviously as she recalled her time in the tent.

Fabel looked up at the sky, still steel-grey after the storm, then around the clean-up site with its temporary village of generators, cranes, trucks and fire engines. He took a long deep breath, tried to play in his head a few bars of *From Gagarin's Point of View* to ease the flutter in his chest. Then, putting the strongly perfumed face mask over his nose and mouth, he stepped into the white forensic tent.

Even with the mask and the strong scent of the perfume, the stench hit him as soon as he entered the tent. He recognised the smell immediately; there was no other odour in the world like it: at once rancid and sour and sickly sweet. Fabel had come across it with a couple of other water-recovered bodies and a black-stage corpse found in the woods. Black was the fourth stage of putrefaction, between ten and twenty days after death. And the smelliest. Despite an extractor fan working full tilt, the air in the forensic tent fumed with the stench of putrid flesh.

Fabel often wondered how the Hamburg Harbour Police could put up with dealing with so many floaters. There was a demarcation of responsibility for discovered corpses between the Harbour Police and the ordinary Polizei Hamburg: the high-water mark. Any body found above the water mark was the responsibility of the City Police; below, it belonged to the Harbour Police. Rumour had it that more than a few bodies washed up along the shore had been given a nudge by the boot of a squeamish City Police officer and rolled back below the high-tide mark and into the Harbour Police's jurisdiction.

'Hi, Jan, how are you?' Holger Brauner was a shortish, powerfully built man in his forties. From behind his mask, the head of the Polizei Hamburg's forensic squad greeted Fabel gleefully as he entered the tent. Brauner, it seemed to Fabel, was irrepressibly cheerful. They had been friends for years and Fabel had never been able to square the *joie de vivre* of the friend with the grim task of the colleague.

Fabel did not answer at once. All his attention was focused on an effort not to vomit. The source of the odour lay on the wet asphalt: a torso, the skin puckered and greenish-black in patches, violet and greenish-white in others. It had no head, no legs, no arms. The flesh where the amputations had taken place was puckered and fluffed; nauseatingly pink and raw-looking. The torso looked as if it belonged to someone morbidly obese, the belly stretched taut and the breasts pushed out sideways, but Fabel knew that it was the pressure of the gases within that had distended and bloated the body.

'I'm doing better than she is. How can you stand the stink?' asked Fabel between controlled breaths.

Brauner mimicked taking a deep appreciative sniff. 'I love the smell of putrescine and cadaverine in the morning. Did you know that cadaverine is also what gives semen its smell? It's there at the beginning and end of life.'

'You need to get some hobbies, Holger.' Fabel nodded towards the torso. 'Washed up by the flood?'

'Well, I don't think she swam here ...' Somewhere behind his mask Brauner gave a small laugh.

'The loss of the head and limbs ... no chance that's accidental? A boat or something?'

'No. Clearly done deliberately. And reasonably expertly. Disarticulative amputation of the arms, transfemoral amputation of the legs. Neat job, actually.'

'When we catch her killer I'll pass on your appreciative critique of his work.' Fabel's voice was tight

51

as he unconsciously tried to keep his breaths short and shallow. 'Whoever it was, he clearly doesn't want us to identify her. Or at least wants to slow us down.'

'Yeah . . .' said Brauner absently, tilting his head as he examined the severed neck. '*Soooo* last century. Who needs fingerprints these days? We can match her to a missing person through familial DNA.'

'*If* she's reported missing and we can trace a relative.' Fabel noticed what looked like a network of tattoos and then saw where some of the skin had burst, exposing slimy fat and flesh that looked like overcooked chicken. He felt a sudden strengthened surge of nausea and looked away.

'We have *anserita cutis*. Goose skin,' said Brauner. 'And there is some evidence of skin maceration. But no significant adipocere in the subcutaneous layer. So I can tell you that this body has been in the water for more than one or two weeks but less than six.'

'Are those tattoos on the skin?'

'No, those lines are the work of our old friends *bacillus prodigiosus* and *bacillus violaceum*. Nature's tattooists . . . chromogenic bacteria that pigment the skin red and purple respectively. It's a sign of lengthy immersion in water.'

'Any idea of the cause of death?' asked Fabel.

'Having her head cut off would have done it,' said Brauner. 'Didn't they teach you anything at murder-detective school?'

'Very funny. I'm guessing that the removal of the limbs and head were post-mortem. Any signs of violence on the body?'

'Sorry, Jan, you'll have to wait for the autopsy. With a ripe floater like this, it takes close examination to sort out what's been done pre- or post-mortem. There could be bullet holes in there, but closed up and hidden by the swelling. And water corpses like these get buffeted about, hit by boats and nibbled at by all sorts in the water. The autopsy will also establish if decomposition is exclusively due to aquatic bacteria, so we'll know if she spent any length of time on land after she died.'

'Thanks, Holger. Give Anna Wolff your report when it's ready.' Fabel turned to leave the tent.

'How is Anna, by the way?' asked Brauner. 'I mean, how is she coping?'

'Fine. She's fit and she's been back on duty for six months. You know Anna.'

'What d'you reckon?' asked Anna when Fabel emerged from the forensics tent. 'Dismemberment like that suggests an organised killer.'

'Could be anything,' said Fabel. 'It *could* be our guy, but it could also be an organised-crime killing, a sex murder . . . or just a disgruntled husband with a meat saw and a rowing boat.' He paused and they both turned to look back at the tent: there was the sound of whistling from inside.

'He was at *The Lion King* last night, apparently,' explained Anna. 'A sucker for a catchy tune, he tells me. Brauner's a friend of yours, isn't he?'

'Yep,' said Fabel. 'Holger's a good guy.'

'Yeah . . . but you have to admit he's a bit weird.

53

You know that if he wasn't a forensic specialist I'd probably have him on a list of potential serial-killer suspects.'

Fabel gave a small half-hearted laugh. Then, looking up at the sky, took a long breath. The air felt cool and clean and fresh, but the sickly-sweet smell of death lingered in his nostrils.

'Awful in there, wasn't it?'

Fabel nodded. 'I hate floaters. You smell them for a week. You and Henk take this one. Let me see the forensics and autopsy when they come in. Like you say, it's not the Network Killer's MO. That's all we need – someone else dumping bodies in Hamburg's waterways. It'll do the tourist industry no end of good. Talking about the Network Killer, how are you getting on with possible contacts?'

Anna shrugged. 'We've nailed down another thirty identities on social-network sites that the victims visited. We've got a court order to get the IP addresses from the site administrators. We should have them by lunchtime.'

'Okay, good – we'll talk about it in the office. Where's Lars Kreysig?'

Anna pointed to a group of men at the far side of Elbestrasse, leaning against a fire appliance. Even at this distance, Fabel could see the weariness in their posture. As Anna and Fabel approached, one of the firemen straightened up and smiled weakly.

'Principal Chief Commissar Fabel?' The man who spoke was taller than Fabel. Lean, with lines engraved deep in a long face topped with unruly prematurely grey hair.

'Yes. Herr Kreysig?'

'Call me Lars. I expect you want to talk to me about the floater?'

'You've given Commissar Wolff all the details of when you found the body; I wanted to ask you if you could hazard a guess as to where it came from. The direction in the river, I mean.'

'I'm not the one to ask.' Kreysig called over his shoulder to the group of men leaning against the fire appliance. 'Sepp . . . could you come here a minute?' Kreysig turned back to Fabel. 'My deputy, Sepp Tramberger, is one of your colleagues. Or, at least, he's from the Harbour Police. He's on attachment to this special flood-response unit. I tell you, *no one* knows the way the Elbe works better than Sepp. When he's not *on* the river in real life he's on it virtually.'

'I don't get you . . .' said Fabel.

'He's created a "Virtual Elbe". In his free time. A computer model of the river and its currents. He's put it together with some boffin from the university. You can see it on the internet. Or a version of it, anyway. It's really very impressive.'

Tramberger joined them and, after introducing him to Fabel and Anna, Kreysig repeated Fabel's question. Tramberger was a shortish, stocky, scoured-looking man with blond hair buzz-cut to a stubble and a face that looked like it had been beaten by more than weather. Fabel knew that most Harbour Police officers had their master's tickets, meaning that the Harbour Police was largely made up of ex-sailors who had seen a fair bit of the world before patrolling the wharves and quays of Hamburg. Tramberger looked off somewhere in the indeterminate distance and screwed up his leathery face in the contemplative expression that Fabel associated with plumbers about to deliver an open-ended estimate.

'Hard to say . . .' Tramberger rubbed his chin. 'It depends on how long the pathologist says she was in the water.'

'More than two weeks, less than six, according to our crime-scene specialist,' said Fabel.

More chin rubbing, more frowning into empty space.

'The thing about floaters is that they don't start out as floaters. They sink. Sometimes to the bottom, or they hover a metre or so above it. If the water temperature is low then they stay there. Sometimes for good. But if the water temperature is warmer, and if they're unruptured, then they come back up to the surface and bob along. If your girl was in the water for more than a week, then my guess is she was dumped somewhere upstream. But not far. The body wasn't too churned or chopped-up. And it didn't look as if it had been scavenged much by fish and eels. Maybe just the other side of the river and a little upstream.'

'Thanks,' said Fabel.

'When you get more info from the pathologist,' said Tramberger, 'why don't you let me know? I could run the data through the computer and see if we can back-trace it. I'd be able to give you a more accurate location for her being dumped in the river.'

'Okay,' said Fabel. 'I'll do that. Thanks.'

'Is this another victim of that internet killer you're looking for?' asked Kreysig with dull curiosity. He looked exhausted to Fabel.

'Maybe,' said Fabel. 'But I doubt it. Our guy doesn't dismember his victims – but who knows?'

'It's quite apt, isn't it?' said Kreysig.

'What?'

'The name they've given this storm.' Kreysig's weary expression suggested that his comment should have been obvious. 'The storm . . . the federal weather bureau has given it the name Störtebeker.'

Fabel made a puzzled face.

'It's apt that a storm named *Störtebeker*,' said Kreysig, 'has given up a headless body.'

'Oh . . . I get you. Yes, I suppose it is.'

'What was all that about?' asked Anna as they left the firemen and headed back to the scene of crime. 'All that gobbledegook about Störtebeker.'

Fabel stopped and turned with an expression of mock shock. 'First you call my music crap and now you tell me you don't know who Störtebeker was?'

'Of course I know. Klaus Störtebeker, Hamburg's

57

Robin Hood of the sea and all that crap. What's that got to do with the floater?'

'You obviously don't know the legend of Störtebeker's execution . . .'

Anna made a couldn't-care-less face. 'So demote me.'

'Klaus Störtebeker was the greatest-ever thorn in the flesh for Hanseatic Hamburg. He and his fellow *Victual Brother* pirates robbed only Hanseatic ships and shared their booty equally. Simon of Utrecht was made Bürgemeister of Hamburg, built a fleet of new warships and hunted Störtebeker down.' Fabel waved his hand vaguely towards the east. 'You know where the new Elbphilharmonie is being built? Well, it was down there that they executed them. Back then, long before the Speicherstadt was built, that was all just one long stretch of sandbank. That was where they executed all Hamburg's captured pirates.'

'Anyway . . .' said Anna impatiently.

'*Anyway*, when Störtebeker was due to be executed, by beheading, along with seventy-odd of his men, he asked for a last favour: that the Hamburg Senate would release as many of his men as he could walk past *after* his head was cut off. The legend is that after he was beheaded, his headless body stood up and walked past eleven of his men before the executioner tripped it up.'

'And did the Senate release the eleven men?'

'No. The Senate were all politicians, of course, and businessmen first and foremost . . . so naturally they didn't keep their promise. Everyone got the chop. Mind you, after all seventy-plus were dead, the Mayor asked the headsman if he wasn't exhausted after so much axe swinging. He made a joke to the effect that he still had enough strength to behead the Mayor and the entire Senate if necessary. Not famed for a sense of humour, either, are politicians or business types, so they had the executioner beheaded on the spot as well.' Fabel smiled. 'So, all in all, it's appropriate that the German Weather Bureau has called this storm Störtebeker. And, like Kreysig said, it's ironic that *Störtebeker* has delivered up a headless corpse.'

'What can I say, *Chef*?' said Anna dully. 'It's always an education . . .'

CHAPTER 8

It was shortly after lunchtime when Fabel sat down with his team.

Just before he went into the briefing, he got a message on the Presidium's internal email system that Criminal Director van Heiden, chief of the investigative branch and Fabel's boss, wanted to see him at around three-thirty. After several years working with van Heiden, Fabel knew that *around* three-thirty meant three-thirty on the dot. As he was only too willing to admit, Fabel himself had a tendency to be punctilious about punctuality, but his boss's timekeeping made the average atomic clock look sloppy. Fabel could guess what van Heiden wanted to see him about. The Criminal Director was as scrupulous about being kept informed of every development in every case that was remotely in the public eye as he was about timekeeping; he would no doubt have already been briefed about the body down by the Fischmarkt.

By the time Fabel walked into the main conference room at the end of the Murder Commission's corridor, his team had already assembled. The conference room was large and decorated in neutral tones, clean but bland and somewhere between linen white and beige. In contrast, striking, vivid colours leapt from the two large frameless canvases on the side wall. The two abstract paintings were what Fabel described as 'corporate art': the kind of stuff you found in the reception areas of banks, insurance companies, ad agencies and accountancy firms in an effort to convince you that they were actually 'quite edgy'.

The conference room's large windows looked out over the treetops of Winterhude Stadtpark. A jug filled with iced water, a white vacuum coffeepot and cups, all of which looked as if they had come from Ikea, were neatly arranged on the cherrywood table. The officers sitting around the table had all set down their clipboards with notepads in front of them, like table settings.

Sitting there at the top of the conference table, an electronic whiteboard behind him, Fabel felt as if they were about to discuss monthly sales targets, or the launch of a new product line or ad campaign. It seemed to Fabel that the whole world was becoming *corporate*. Politicians, medical professionals, now even policemen, all looked as if they were about to sell you something. The *business* of policing.

Fabel was only forty-eight but sometimes he felt he'd been born a decade or two too late. Everything seemed to be less *real* than it had been when he had started his career. He noticed that even edgy Anna Wolff was beginning to dress more conservatively. Every rebellion, it seemed, ended in resigned conformity. In addition to Fabel's regular team, there was a tall, thin man sitting at the far end of the cherrywood table. He would have been in his early forties but had a demeanour of seriousness that, along with his conservative tailoring and a thin face that was all bony angles, made him seem older. Fabel had nodded to the visitor as he had entered the room and took his seat.

'Will you work this thing for me?' he asked Anna, dodging having to operate the electronic whiteboard himself. Technology was something else that had crept up on Fabel: somewhere along the way, murder had become digitised.

'Okay . . .' Fabel stood up. 'The so-called Network Killer. We've got three victims and you all know the background to the murders so far. Each investigation team has been allocated a case file. But, before we get started, I have to tell you that this morning we recovered another body from the water. Or, more correctly, the water delivered up a body to us this morning: she was swept up onto the Fischmarkt by the storm.'

There was a low groan from the team.

'Great . . .' It was a thickset bull of a man sitting hunched with his elbows resting on the conference table who spoke. He was in his late fifties with grey hair cropped tight to his skull and he had the look of a boxer. Senior Commissar Werner Meyer – Fabel's deputy. 'Another one.'

'Probably not,' said Anna. 'The stiff this morning was a dismembered torso. No head, legs or arms. If our guy is anything, he's consistent.'

'*Perhaps* not . . .' Fabel fired a meaningful look at Anna. 'The body found this morning certainly looks like something different, and that probably means *someone* different. So there's no point in us including this body in this case until we get a full forensic and autopsy report. My main worry is that maybe we have a copycat killer. Or it *could* be our guy and he's simply experimenting with his art. But, as Commissar Wolff has so helpfully pointed out, so far our guy has been completely consistent. And he doesn't strike me as the type to play with his food: he stalks his victims, traps them, rapes them and strangles them. That's the main event. Anything he does afterwards is house-keeping. Disposal. He's never felt the need to dismember the bodies before. So, for the moment and until we get the reports, let's leave this one out.'

Fabel nodded to Anna, who hit a key on the wire-less keyboard. Four photographic panels appeared. In three, the usual flash-stark scene-of-crime pictures of the young female victims. In the fourth, a sequence of photographs, all of young men, flashed rapidly on the whiteboard. Scores of them. Hundreds. In fast succession.

'We're in a whole new area of offending here,' continued Fabel. 'Our killer has a familiar modus for anyone who's worked a multiple sex-murder case before. Everyone in this room has experience in the investigative process of identifying and locating a murderer. We work with the forensic detail, the chronology of the homicide and the connections between witnesses, key events and locations. We can visit the places, we can trace witnesses, find physical evidence, gain background intelligence; and from all that we can build a picture, even get a description of our suspect. But in this case, we are not dealing with the physical world. Our killer locates his victims in cyberspace. Three women, to date completely unconnected, each of whom was lured to their death by one of these men . . .' Fabel indicated the still-flickering procession of photographs.

'These are the men with whom we *know* the victims had contact on the internet through social networking sites. Could you slow that down a bit, Anna?' Fabel asked. Anna Wolff held a key down and the images changed less frequently. All of the photographs were amateur shots of men in their twenties or early thirties, some taken with a phone or a digital camera into a mirror. Several of the faces were indistinct: blurred or partially masked behind the reflected camera flash. There was a variety of the usual grimaces and postures, some muscled torsos shirtless, and most made the predictable, inane 'hanging loose' or 'throwing horns' hand gestures. 'The problem we have is this. In the real world we could pinpoint a single person out of this selection who has had contact

64

with all of the victims and put a face to him. But here, on the internet, he could be *several* of these faces. Or none of them. It is almost certain that he uses a different identity for each woman he "meets" on the internet, and that none of these identities are his. For all we know, he isn't even posing as a man. It could be that he has arranged to meet his victims while posing as a female, or even a representative of an organisation.

'The one thing we have to bear in mind about this environment is that, like I said at the start, none of the rules we've learnt over the years apply here. This is a place where anyone can be anybody or *anything* they want to be. Even if we find the face of the person our victims agreed to meet, it's almost certain it isn't the face he has in real life.'

'What about forensics? There's nothing more real-world than being raped and strangled. Don't we have DNA from semen, hair or skin he's left on the victims?' asked Dirk Hechtner, a small, dark-haired detective who hadn't been on Fabel's team long.

Fabel shook his head. 'Our guy is fastidious. He wears a condom and we think he may have shaved his pubic region. To date we haven't found a single trace of non-victim DNA. His dumping the bodies in water works against us forensically, too.'

'So where do we start?' asked Werner Meyer.

'This is a good point at which to introduce Chief Commissar Kroeger, here . . .' Fabel indicated the man who sat at the far end of the table. 'Herr

Kroeger heads up the Presidium's specialist information-technology team. Herr Kroeger?'

Kroeger nodded his long bony head. 'As Principal Chief Commissar Fabel has pointed out, information technology has, in law-enforcement terms, presented as many challenges as it has opportunities. One of the biggest problems we face is those who exploit and abuse children. And, unfortunately, it has been in this area of offending that we have had to go through a steep learning curve; because it has been this group of offenders who were first to recognise the advantages the internet offered them. It changed the whole way they found and trapped victims, exchanged images of abuse and, most of all, developed a way of communicating with each other and exchanging information without exposing their identities. At one time, before the internet, these people acted alone and were generally isolated. On a very few occasions they would encounter like-minded individuals, more often than not meeting them in prison. Occasionally, in the pre-internet world, you would get an organised paedophile ring. But communication, far less collaboration, was reasonably rare; and when it did occur, it was within a specific geographical area. The internet changed that. All of a sudden these people could, for the first time ever, gain a sense of *community*. They were no longer isolated from each other and could exchange information and images, across the country and across the entire world. They could persuade each other that, because there were so many others who shared their perversions, then they *weren't* perversions. That their behaviour *wasn't* aberrant, sick, twisted.' Kroeger paused. Fabel had noticed that the internet-crime specialist's long thin face remained impassive, the bony angles lacking animation, as he spoke. The grey eyes stayed dull and sluggish. Maybe, thought Fabel, that was what happened when you worked with technology, with machines all the time: maybe you became less vital, less human.

'That's what the internet can do: offer an environment of normality for the sickest and most twisted minds,' continued Kroeger. 'The most important thing about the internet is that it gives these people a sense of security, of impunity. And that's where we come in. There is no such thing as anonymity on the internet. Herr Fabel drew a comparison with real-world investigations: where you can track an offender across an environment, interview eyewitnesses, etc. The truth is that it's wrong to think the internet is any different. It's just that it's a *virtual* world instead of a physical one. You still leave tracks everywhere you go. And no matter how hard you try to disguise yourself as somebody else, there are always clues to your identity left behind.'

'How can that be?' asked Fabel. 'If someone claims to be a fourteen-year-old girl instead of the forty-year-old man that they really are, how can you see through that?'

'Okay, let's start with the basics. A lot of browsers offer private browsing, where nothing is logged in your internet history and your computer doesn't pick up cookies or other traces of your excursions on the net. The truth is there is no such thing as private browsing. Your internet provider keeps a record of every site, every page you visit. And the administrators of those sites you visit similarly store your IP address. Every time you connect to the internet, you leave a trace. And if you're dumb enough to use a computer at work or at home, then we're just one court order away from having your name and address.'

'But our guy isn't dumb,' said Anna.

'No . . .' Kroeger reached into his pocket and produced a USB stick. 'This is a *dongle*. This particular type of dongle allows you to access any WiFi spot. Obviously, you still have an IP address, but if you have paid cash for a pay-as-you-go broadband dongle, then your name and address aren't listed anywhere. My guess is that your Network Killer, if he's smart, is using one of these. But even if he is, he's still traceable. Whenever he is online he can't disguise his location. Or at least he can't without some pretty sophisticated software. We can identify the general physical location of the connection. If it's a pay-as-you-go dongle, then he has to top it up somewhere. And that means resurfacing in the real world. The person behind the counter in the newsagent or mobile-phone store who sells him the credits is the witness that Herr Fabel talked about earlier. My point is this. My *beat* isn't that dissimilar to yours. There are always tracks left behind, always something to follow. How much effort has been made, and how much skill has been employed in covering up those tracks depends on the intelligence and expertise of the offender. Just like in the real world.'

'But that still doesn't answer the question about how to see through a fake identity,' said Werner.

'I don't know how many of you are members of a social networking site, but those of you who are will be aware of the rather disturbing phenomenon of seeing ads for things that are particularly relevant to you, right at the exact time they're relevant to you ... ads for wedding photographers just after you've become engaged, a restaurant ad just before an anniversary, sports stores offering you deals in your particular sport ... It's like there's some kind of cyberpsychic reading your mind. The truth is that you have left so many details of yourself scattered all around. Because you think in terms of normal space, you think that all of these little scraps of information are so scattered that they can't be put together. They can, and instantaneously. And you're not even aware of having left some of that information behind: your personal data and browsing behaviour have been analysed, sometimes automatically. Nothing you do is random in the internet. You think it is – you think you jump from one site to another, from one page to another spontaneously, impulsively – but there is always an underlying logic or psychology to everything you do. The truth is that the more relaxed and free-roaming your internet exploration is, the more it reveals about your psychology, your identity. In the Cybercrime Unit we have access to all kinds of experts – IT specialists, sociologists, psychologists, criminologists. We even use linguistic experts who can analyse your vocabulary, your syntax and grammar, and who can profile your educational standards, age, etc. And, as well as the experts, we have analytical software that can give us a breakdown of a user in seconds. So, to answer your question, Herr Meyer: yes, it can be difficult to see through a carefully constructed avatar identity on the web, but we do have an armoury of weapons at our disposal and it's much more difficult to hide behind an invented identity than you would think.'

'Thanks,' said Fabel. 'Chief Commissar Kroeger will be working alongside us on this and provide the liaison with the other specialists in his unit. Anna has provided him with the full list of possible convergent identities from the social-network sites. What's narrowed it down is that each of the victims seemed to favour a different site. We've found it difficult to find any points of convergence in their day-to-day real lives, and it's proving tricky in their online activities, but we do know that all four women made regular use of social networking sites to meet men.'

'One thing I didn't mention,' said Kroeger, 'is that we have a distinct advantage in being in possession of the computers used by each of the women. We have technology that enables us to retrace their steps. We may even be able to recover a good part of their chatroom messages. And that could point us in very specific directions.'

'Where are we with that?' asked Fabel.

'Not that far away. I reckon another day or two and we'll potentially have a lot of leads from what was keyed into the computers. It's painstaking work, of course.'

'Of course,' said Fabel and smiled. Kroeger was all numbers and no personality. This was no game nor some kind of professional challenge. In two days another woman could be dead. She could be planning to meet her killer right now: chatting, flirting, making arrangements with an electronic fiction of a human being. 'But, as I'm sure you appreciate, time is of the essence here.'

'Naturally we will treat this case as an absolute priority.' When Kroeger spoke he always said the right things. But whatever sentiment was in it never made it into his expression or his grey eyes. He was himself almost a machine, thought Fabel.

Fabel had worked with Kroeger once before, on a child-murder case involving an internet-based paedophile ring; Kroeger had all but come right out and said that he thought Fabel's technological illiteracy compromised his efficiency as an investigator. But what had riled Fabel most of all was the way Kroeger had remained so detached from the human suffering involved in the case. Kroeger seemed as uninterested in and as uncomprehending of the fact that a child had been murdered and a family ripped apart by horror and grief as Fabel was about the difference between a kilobyte and a gigabyte. The result was a lingering mutual distaste.

But Fabel needed Kroeger on this case. There was no denying that if they stood a chance of catching the Network Killer, then Kroeger's expertise was the most important tool they had. It was, as Kroeger had said himself, his beat.

'Unfortunately my team is unusually stretched at the moment,' continued Kroeger. 'We've been given the responsibility of tracking down the source of this Klabautermann Virus that's been wrecking e-comms within the state government. But, like I said, this case will naturally take priority.'

'I appreciate that.'

Fabel spent the rest of the briefing with the usual mechanics of a major investigation. Each team of two detectives gave a report on their corner of the investigation, followed by a group discussion and the allocation by Fabel of further investigative tasks.

'That guy Kroeger gives me the creeps . . .' Werner came up to Fabel after the others had gone. 'I'm sure I saw him in that science fiction film – you know, *The Matrix*.'

'He's good at his job,' said Fabel. 'One of the best in Europe, I've been told. That's all that counts. And god knows we need him on this one.'

'Maybe it wasn't *The Matrix* I saw him in. I used to watch a lot of Westerns when I was a kid,' said Werner. 'You know . . . when the cavalry are in hostile Red Indian territory but they have to rely on a native tracker from the same tribe to get them through. Why do I get the feeling Kroeger is as likely to take scalps as the bad guys?'

'He's an odd one, that's all, Werner. As far as I can remember I've never seen Kroeger wear feathers in his hair.'

'Suppose not.' Werner rasped a shovel of hand across his stubble-cut scalp. 'But I have to admit to being out of my depth with all of this electronic stuff, Jan. I have never been able to understand these social networking sites. Why do people need to use computers to connect with each other, piling all of their personal stuff out there on the internet? Yet if you sit next to one of them on the S-Bahn, you can't have a conversation with them because they're plugged into their mp3 players.'

'That's the technological society for you,' said Fabel. 'All technology and no society.'

Most of the officers working in the Presidium took lunch in its huge canteen. Fabel frequently used it himself but often preferred to take three-quarters of an hour in the middle of the day to get out of the Commission. Thinking time, he liked to call it.

He was just about to leave the building when a bleep from his cellphone alerted him that he had received a text message.

Arrived safely Wiesbaden. Weather crap. Hotel soulless. Phone tonight. Sx

He sighed. Fabel could never understand why Susanne sent him texts: she knew he wouldn't reply to them. It took him too long to fiddle around with the phone keys and even then it was all wrong or he would accidentally delete the two-sentence reply it had taken him fifteen minutes to compose. Why didn't people simply *talk* to each other any more? The thought hit him and he remembered Werner saying pretty much the same. Fabel resigned himself to Old Farthood.

One of the places Fabel favoured for lunch was a café on one of the dozens of canals that criss-crossed the city. This particular café was on the Alsterstreek canal, next to the Winterhuder Fährhaus, where tourists and locals would catch the red and white water buses that criss-crossed the Alster. Sitting below the city that surrounded it and tucked in tight to the bridge, the café gave Fabel an odd sense of safety. Its location made it handy for the Presidium and if the weather was half decent he could sit out at one of the tables by the railings that ran along the side of the Alsterstreek and watch the swans patrol the waterway. Being beside the water, too, comforted Fabel, calmed him; which was strange, because, as a boy growing up in Norddeich, Fabel had been just a little afraid of the water; specifically of the sea. He had always put it down to the fear of flooding that was instinctive in East Frisians and their neighbours, the Dutch. Fabel's boyhood home had been behind a dyke and there had been nights in his childhood – not many, but a few – when he would lie awake thinking about the dark mass of sea held back by a simple man-made earthwork.

A waiter came over to wipe down the table before taking Fabel's order. He greeted him with a smile and asked him how he was. It was a ritual of recognition: Fabel was a known face here, but he knew that none of the staff would have any idea what it was that he did for a living, and that somehow added to his sense of comfort. It was something he had often wondered about: what people assumed about him, not knowing that his daily business was all about violence and death. Did he look like an academic, which is what he would prefer them to think, or did they take him for some kind of businessman? The latter thought depressed him.

Fabel had given a lot of thought to how people perceived him, and how they perceived each other; mainly because it was something that came up so frequently when interviewing the family and friends of murderers. Not, of course, in the majority of homicides where the murder was committed by people known to the police and to their victims as habitually violent and potentially dangerous. Most of the murders Fabel dealt with occurred within a certain *milieu* and were fuelled by drink or drugs; but there were cases – particularly with sex killings – where everyone stood open-mouthed on discovering that the murderer was someone they knew. The *I-would-never-have-guessed* killers. The bloated body washed up at the Fischmarkt, head and limbs removed, could well turn out to be the victim of just such a killer.

Over the years Fabel had become accustomed to the shock and disbelief of others: how, in so many of these cases, people who knew the killer well had to adjust their perspective on everything; had to learn to view everyone with a new element of mistrust.

We all have a face we show to the world; and we all have a face that we only allow ourselves to see. It had been Uwe Hoffman, Fabel's first boss at the Murder Commission, who had told him that. Maybe, thought Fabel, this Network Killer case wasn't that different after all; maybe the internet was just a further extension of the way things had always been.

He ordered a salad and a mineral water and was watching the swans, thinking about nothing in particular, when his phone beeped again.

He read the text. It didn't make much sense. It didn't make any sense at all.

CHAPTER 9

The house was on the boundary between the Schanzenviertel and St Pauli. It had its back to a railway line and had, at some distant point in its history, faced the world with some dignity. Now, however, that face was tattooed with a continuous, swirling band of graffiti, two metres high, and the ground-floor windows the graffiti half-framed were dark with soot and grime.

The young man who hesitated on the other side of the road, near the corner, carefully checking the street in both directions, was Niels Freese. He was checking for any hint of a police presence, uniformed or otherwise, before crossing over and knocking on the heavy door of the squat. The grimy glass of the window shadowed darker for a moment as someone inside checked out the approaching figure. They would, he knew, recognise him by his limp.

The door opened on his first knock and he slipped inside, into the dark cavern of the house. He instantly recognised the man who admitted him, a tall gangly male who was a little older than

Niels, maybe thirty, and who had the kind of tough look that attracted police attention. But he did not know the man's name. Then he realised that he had never met the man before, nor seen him. The thought flashed through Niels's mind that the man at the door was actually also Niels, but in disguise, but he dismissed the thought by applying, as he had been taught to do by the doctors at Hamburg-Eilbek, reason and logic to an unreasonable and illogical perception. No, the man at the door was real and he was not another version of Niels. And the house was real, and not an exact replica in a carbon-copy of Hamburg created to beguile him.

He would not have known the man's name, anyway: that was one of the rules, that you didn't know the names of anyone outside your immediate cell. The fascists of the Polizei Hamburg or the BfV could not torture the information out of you if you did not have it to give. Niels nodded wordlessly to the man as he passed. Niels did not trust him, because Niels trusted almost no one older than himself: it had, after all, been they who had done what had been done to the world. And trust was something alien to Niels in any case. He might have got his delusions under some kind of control, but he still did not entirely trust the world he perceived around him.

Inside it was all gloom. Whereas the exterior had been run-down, the interior of the house was positively dilapidated. Large scabs of plaster had fallen from the walls and the floorboards were coated with plaster dust, grime and general filth.

A girl of about twenty, with lank blonde hair and bad skin, waited for him at the end of the hall, by the foot of the stairs.

'He's waiting for you.' She tilted an acned chin up the stairwell. 'Second door on the right. Go straight in. Were you followed?'

'I wasn't followed.'

'Are you sure?'

'I'm sure.'

The fact was that Niels did not only follow the protocols of the Guardians of Gaia regarding security, he had a routine that was ten times more elaborate than that which the Guardians demanded. He never explained his routines, because his need to defend himself against impostors sounded bizarre to others. The girl nodded and Niels made his way up the stairs. Despite having been told to go straight in, Niels knocked on the door before entering.

It had, at one time, been a bedroom. A pretty grand one. Now the windows had been boarded up from the inside, making the room a large, sealed box. But there was more light in here than anywhere else in the derelict house: artificial light from the desk lamps placed around the room. It did not have the clutter or detritus evident in the rest of the house: the floorboards had been swept clean of dust and cables taped to them; there were three workstations set against the wall to Niels's right, each with a large computer monitor, and he could hear the distinct monotone hum of the five large hard-drives. The sight of the technology made Niels want to vomit. It represented everything that the Guardians of Gaia were fighting against, a complete negation of the organisation's eco-anarcho-primitivism. But Niels knew, for he had been told by the Commander, that such technology, abhorrent as it was, was essential in carrying out the war against the forces of pollution and globalisation.

The theory did not help Niels with the reality: the irony was that, had it not been for the scruffy walls and boarded-over windows, this room could have been an office for any Hamburg business.

But it wasn't. Straight ahead of Niels as he entered was a large desk at which sat the Commander, a heavyset man in his late thirties with a head of thick, curling black hair. To the Commander's left, to Niels's consternation, sat a couple dressed in grey business-type suits. Both the man and the woman looked as if they had walked out of a bank or insurance company and Niels noted that they shared the same expressionlessness.

'Sit down, Freese,' said the Commander.

'Who are they?' Niels nodded towards the couple.

'Friends.'

'Are they members of the Guardians?'

'This is a war with many armies, Niels. Our

friends here are allies. They fight for Gaia just like us, on the same side as us, but on a different battlefield. More than that need not concern you.'

Niels stared at the couple. They stared back, but without aggression; without *anything* in their expression. Why were they dressed like that? Niels did not like their suits in the same way that he did not like the computer hardware in the squat. For a start, where had it come from? Where had the money to pay for it come from? There again, he thought, it could be that the Commander had had it stolen to order. The idea cheered him a little.

'The Globalist-Polluters are creating their own doom,' continued the Commander. '*Our* doom. Even their own scientists are talking about a Malthusian Cataclysm, about the Great Die-Off . . . so they are not blind to the catastrophe that they are shaping every day by chasing the Myth of Progress. They cannot say they don't know the consequences of their actions.'

'A Malthusian Cataclysm would not be a bad thing, Commander,' said Niels, eagerly. 'Humanity is a pestilence that needs to be controlled if Gaia is to survive.'

'Mmm . . .' said the Commander. 'In the meantime we have to do all we can to wage this war. Our fight is the greatest battle in the history of mankind. While we sit here, Freese, our world, our ecosystem, is being raped. In the time it takes us to have this conversation, four million barrels of oil will have been pumped from the Earth. And all that carbon will just as quickly be pumped into the atmosphere.' The Commander paused to allow Niels to process the information. He knew that you *had* to allow time for Niels to process information. He had noticed Niels's limp again as the younger man had come into the room. He knew that the neurological damage behind the limp came from the same cause as Niels's *unique* intellectual architecture. Oxygen deprivation at birth.

'This is a war,' said the Commander. 'A real war. And a war needs good soldiers. *I* need good soldiers. And you, Freese, are one of my very best. And that is why I am entrusting you with one of the most important missions we have ever undertaken.'

Niels felt the pride bloom in his chest. All he had ever wanted to do was to be a good soldier for Gaia.

'I'll do whatever it takes to protect Gaia,' said Niels proudly.

'You have to understand, Freese, that I am asking you to take this war to a new level. Burning cars in the Schanzenviertel is not enough. The stakes are higher.' The Commander nodded to the man in the grey suit, who pushed an envelope across the table to Niels. Niels opened it; it contained two photographs, one of a man in his early forties and the other of a car: a huge Mercedes cabriolet. There was also a piece of paper in the envelope with a time and an address written on it.

'Who is he?' asked Niels.

'All you need to know is that he is an enemy of Gaia. A real enemy. His activities have got to be brought to a halt. You have carried out a number of successful car-burnings with Harald. I want you to team up with him again and torch this car . . .' the Commander tapped the photograph of the Mercedes. '. . . while it is parked outside the café at this address. Do you understand?'

'I understand what I have to do, but I don't understand why burning his car will stop him doing whatever it is he has been doing.'

The Commander turned to the silent grey-suited couple. The woman reached into her handbag, brought out a clear plastic bag and handed it to the Commander, who slid it across the table to Niels.

'When his car goes up, he'll be inside the café. He meets a woman there. You wait until they're both inside, then torch the car. And make it spectacular. I want you to bring him out of the café. Then I want you to use that.' The Commander nodded to the plastic bag and its contents, which Niels had not yet lifted.

'*Can* you use that?' asked the Commander. 'It will be the first mission of its type.'

'This man is an enemy of Gaia?' asked Niels, still staring at the bag.

'More than that, he is threatening the whole success of the movement. He has done things . . . well, like I said, his actions could be disastrous for all we stand for.'

Niels picked up the plastic bag, opened it and removed the automatic pistol and ammunition clip from it before placing them in the patch pocket of his combat jacket. As he did so, he had the feeling that he had seen and held the weapon a dozen times previously. But he knew he had never held any gun before.

'I'll do it,' he said.

CHAPTER 10

Horst van Heiden was a man of middle height, stockily built and with a brooding face framed by a grey-white continuum of hair and beard. When he walked into van Heiden's office, Fabel was struck by the same impression that he always had on seeing the Criminal Director: that he wore an expensive suit as if it were a uniform. It fitted, because most of van Heiden's career had been spent in the uniformed branch, including some time on attachment to the Harbour Police, and even after ten years in the post he did not look suited to the role of chief of detectives.

Van Heiden looked at his watch as Fabel entered. The Criminal Director wasn't making a point: it was simply a habit he had of time-checking the beginning and end of each meeting, or segment of a meeting, or time between meetings. Time was important to van Heiden. Fabel had worked with him for seven years and the relationship had become as relaxed and close as a relationship with van Heiden could become. Fabel had no doubt that van Heiden respected him, even liked him, but the Criminal Director was a hard man to read. Distant. Closed-off.

There were two other men in the office, sitting facing van Heiden's desk. They both turned in their chairs when Fabel came in. He recognised one of them instantly – a medium-height fit-looking man in his mid-fifties with receding greying hair swept severely back and a neatly trimmed beard. As he had the first time they had met, he gave Fabel the impression of a successful film director, artist or writer. Fabel was taken aback by the synchronicity of it all.

'Ah, Jan . . . thanks for coming at such short notice,' van Heiden said and indicated the chair between the two men. 'You know Herr Müller-Voigt, I believe?'

'Indeed I do.' Fabel shook hands with Müller-Voigt. 'How are you, Herr Senator? I heard you on the radio this morning.'

'Oh, that?' Müller-Voigt looked as if the memory of it was vaguely irritating. 'I don't know why they put me in with that idiot . . .'

Fabel made a vague 'mmmm' noise of agreement, hiding the fact that he had been too sleepy even to take in who *that idiot* was, or indeed anything other than the sketchiest impression of what was being discussed.

'And may I introduce Herr Fabian Menke, of the BfV?' Van Heiden indicated the other man. Menke was in his late thirties, Fabel reckoned, and had thinning fair hair and blue eyes behind frameless spectacles. His suit was several hundred euros downmarket from Müller-Voigt's designer casual-chic. The BfV was the Bundesamt für Verfassungsschutz, the Federal Office for Protection of the Constitution: Germany's main internal security service. The agency's brief covered anything that was considered to endanger German democracy: skinheads and neo-Nazis, left-wing extremist groups, Islamic terrorism, destructive cults or anti-democratic groups, foreign espionage. More controversially, the BfV had a unit devoted to the monitoring of the activities of Scientology in Germany. Even the Interior Ministry of the Hamburg State Government had a Scientology Task Force and, although Fabel had not met Menke before, he had heard of him and knew he was the main liaison between the BfV and Hamburg's law-enforcement agencies. Van Heiden turned to Menke: 'This is Principal Chief Commissar Fabel, who heads our special Murder Commission team.'

Fabel shook hands with Menke and sat down.

'I've heard about your unit, Herr Fabel,' said Menke. 'I believe you now assist other Murder Commissions across the Federal Republic with complex cases.'

'When we can,' said Fabel. 'I'm afraid that, at the moment, we have too much of a workload of our own to deal with.'

'Ah, yes, this Network Killer case?' Müller-Voigt

cut in. 'I believe there was another body found this morning.'

'We found a body, yes, Herr Senator. But we have not established whether or not it is linked to the other murders.'

'You think it may be unconnected?' asked Müller-Voigt. Fabel remained silent for a moment, fighting back the instinct to tell the politician that such information was a police matter and none of his damn business.

'Our investigations are continuing,' said Fabel blankly. He turned to his boss. 'You wanted to see me about something, Criminal Director?'

'Em, yes. Yes, I did.' Van Heiden had clearly sensed the tension between Fabel and Müller-Voigt. He reached across the vast plain of his desk and handed a file over to Fabel. We have a major environmental summit, GlobalConcern Hamburg, about to take place in the city. As Environment Senator, Herr Müller-Voigt here heads up the organising committee. But of course you already know about it, because you said you heard the debate on the radio this morning.'

'I only caught part of it . . .' Fabel was beginning to seriously regret having mentioned hearing Müller-Voigt on the radio. But it was true that he did know something about the GlobalConcern Hamburg summit.

'This is an unusual conference,' said Menke, the BfV man, 'insofar as the focus is not just on saving the planet, it is about the commercial opportunities that environmental technologies offer. There are now a lot of major corporate players involved in environment-related activities. The difference is that these operators aren't motivated by revolutionary zeal but by the same old imperative of turning a profit. Not that there's anything wrong with that, if, at the same time, they're making a positive contribution to the environment.'

'I see,' said Fabel, then looked at van Heiden with a confused *so why am I here?* expression.

'I'm sure you're aware that there is almost a tradition of the disaffected of the Free and Hanseatic City expressing their disaffection by setting other citizens' cars on fire?' continued Menke.

'Like the first swallow or the blossom on the trees,' said Fabel. 'You know it's summer in Hamburg when you smell the scent of boiling automobile paint in the air.' No one got the humour and Fabel moved on. 'What's that got to do with the Murder Commission?'

'Last year there were thirty-four thousand politically motivated crimes in Germany,' said Menke. 'A significant proportion of these crimes is made up of arson attacks on cars and business premises in Berlin and Hamburg.'

'I can quote the figures, Jan,' said van Heiden. 'Two hundred cars burned out in Hamburg over the last year. Ten in a single night in Flottbek, a dozen over a one-week period in Harvestehude. And then, of course, there was the attack on

89

the police station in the Schanzenviertel. Unbelievable. One patrol car burned out and a police station in the heart of the city under attack by masked thugs . . .' Van Heiden shook his head in genuine disbelief. Fabel knew that no matter how much you tried to explain it to van Heiden, the chief of detectives would never be able to understand how there could be so much anger in Germany's most prosperous city, his beloved Hamburg.

'All of these have been down to extreme-left or anarchist groups,' continued Menke. 'And that is a worrying trend. The vast majority of the politically motivated crime we investigate at the BfV is skinhead/neo-Nazi. In fact, twice as many offences are committed by the radical right as by the radical left. But there is a shift taking place. We are seeing more and more *envy* crimes being committed. We have mounting evidence that extreme environmentalist groups are becoming involved.'

'I don't think it's fair to describe these groups as exclusively extreme environmentalists,' said Müller-Voigt. 'These people are just as easily described as anarchists or extreme leftists.'

'Well, it wouldn't be the first time there's been a *crossover* between the two philosophies.' Fabel kept his tone even and conversational, as if making a general observation. The truth was that everyone in the room knew that Müller-Voigt, a contemporary of Joschka Fischer and Daniel

90

Cohn-Bendit, had been involved in radical-left politics in the 1980s. And there had been some question marks over how far his involvement with some of the more extreme groups had gone.

'The point is . . .' Menke continued to address Fabel '. . . that our intelligence suggests there are elements who are promoting ever more aggressive levels of direct action.'

'In short, Jan,' said van Heiden, 'it's only a matter of time before someone gets killed. We believe things may escalate during the GlobalConcern Hamburg summit. Violence and property destruction. We also have reason to believe that we may see delegates at the summit targeted.'

'But that doesn't make sense,' said Fabel. 'These people are trying to *help* the environment, aren't they?'

'Like I say,' said Menke, 'this summit is about the *business* of environmentalism. Making a green buck, as it were. And there are those who believe that corrupts everything the environmental lobby stands for.'

'But others,' interrupted Müller-Voigt, 'believe that it is a natural evolutionary stage: the belief or value that was once the preserve of the minority becomes the accepted truth of the community at large. But I have to say that I know from personal experience that there are some in any political belief system who love being proselytisers so much that they don't like it when their message eventually becomes accepted. It deprives them of their feelings of moral superiority; it takes away their exclusivity. There is nothing more bitter than a rebel without a cause.'

'And,' said Menke, 'there is also evidence of a growing consensus between the extreme left, extreme environmentalism and anti-globalisation. And GlobalConcern Hamburg, in many ways, represents everything they hate.'

'So do we have any definite intelligence that someone in particular is going to be targeted?' asked Fabel.

'No one specific, but we are anticipating *vigorous* protesting and organised street violence. And the word is that there is some kind of *showcase* one-off action being planned.'

'And you think that may be an assassination?'

'It's possible,' said Menke. 'The BfV and the Polizei Hamburg's anti-terrorism branch are working together on this, but it was suggested that you should be briefed on the situation; that your particular perspective and experience may be useful.'

'Oh? Who suggested that?' Fabel looked pointedly at van Heiden. He had enough on his plate at the moment and was surprised that his chief hadn't appreciated the fact.

'I did.' It was Müller-Voigt who spoke. He read Fabel's puzzled expression. 'That business a few years ago. The Mühlhaus thing. I was very impressed by how you dealt with . . .' He struggled for the right word. 'With *things*. Very efficient but also very sensitive.'

Fabel nodded his thanks. He noticed that Müller-Voigt, who was normally uniquely composed, seemed less sure of himself.

'I have already explained to the Senator that you have a rather pressing workload, as you mentioned earlier. We have set up a task group with officers of our own anti-terror unit, the BKA federal crime bureau and agents of the BfV. At the moment we just want you to acquaint yourself with the contents of the file. But we may want to call on your services later.'

There goes my evening, thought Fabel, looking at the thickness of the file.

'There's no need to take that with you,' said Menke. 'I can email it to you.'

'Email? Is that safe?'

Menke gave a patronising laugh and earned Fabel's instant dislike. He indexed the BfV man in a mental file next to Kroeger, the Cybercop. 'Yes, Chief Commissar, it's safe. We only use secure servers and systems. Just as the Polizei Hamburg do.'

Fabel shrugged. 'Well, the State Government's email system was also meant to be secure. That didn't stop it from being infected by this Klabautermann Virus. If you don't mind, I'll hang on to this hard copy. Means I can read it quicker.'

They spent the next few minutes going over the logistics of the summit. As well as business leaders, GlobalConcern Hamburg was going to be attended by some senior politicians from across the Federal Republic and beyond. Including, of course, Müller-Voigt, who would be chairing the conference. Fabel could see that there was cause for concern, as there would be with any major summit held in the city, but he couldn't quite understand why his presence was needed. He was an investigator. A murder detective. His job was after-the-fact, not preventative. He was even more puzzled that it had been Müller-Voigt who had requested his involvement. Fabel caught himself involuntarily glancing at his watch. Van Heiden caught him too, but watch-checking was very much part of the Criminal Director's routine and he didn't seem irritated.

'Listen, Jan,' said van Heiden. 'I think we've got you as much up to speed as you need to be. I don't want to hold you back – I know you've got a lot on your plate.'

'Thanks,' said Fabel. He lifted the file and bounced it in his hand, as if assessing its heft. 'I'll look this over tonight.' Fabel rose and shook hands with the three men and took his leave.

'Actually . . .' Müller-Voigt looked at his watch and frowned. 'I'm afraid I'm already late for another appointment. I think I'll have to slip away too.'

'Fine, Herr Senator,' said van Heiden, also frowning: the idea of someone being late for an appointment was distressing. 'I hope we haven't kept you . . .'

'No, no . . . not at all. It'll be fine. Herr Fabel, could you see me out? I'd like a word, if I may.'

'Sure . . .'

Hamburg's police Presidium was designed as a cylinder, with an atrium in the centre and wings radiating out from it. The design concept had been to mirror a police star. As Fabel and Müller-Voigt walked along the curving hallway to the elevator, the politician made the usual small talk. Fabel was only going down two floors and they got into the lift together. As they did so, Müller-Voigt's entire demeanour changed. It became agitated. Something that Fabel would never have associated with the Environment Senator.

'Listen, Fabel. I need to talk to you. Urgently.'

'What about?'

'It's a long story, but it is very *very* important. I really do need your help.'

'I don't understand. You mean professionally?'

'Yes . . . no. Perhaps. But it is a matter of life or death. It's something that, for the moment, I'd like to keep between ourselves. You'll understand when we talk. Can you come to my house tonight? Around seven-thirty?'

Fabel held up the file. 'I had planned to do some reading . . .'

'This is more important, Fabel.'

They reached the Murder Commission's floor and the doors opened. Fabel stepped out but

95

placed a restraining hand to prevent the doors closing again.

'If this is official business . . .'

'Humour me, Fabel. I really need to talk to you. There's no one else . . . Can you make it or not?'

Fabel looked at the Environment Senator for a moment. 'I'll be there.' He let the doors close. As he walked along the corridor towards his office, the expression on Müller-Voigt's face haunted him. He had never seen the politician ruffled before. Even on the occasion when Fabel had interviewed him as a potential murder suspect.

What bothered him was that Müller-Voigt hadn't looked ruffled: he had looked downright scared.

CHAPTER 11

Niels Freese waited under a tree at the corner of the street, looking across at the café. He stood with a black sports holdall in one hand, his grip tight around its handle. He was dressed in a baggy dark combat jacket and jeans, with a black woollen hat perched on the top of his narrow, long head. The hat was actually a rolled-up ski mask, ready to be pulled down over his thin features when the moment came.

And the moment was coming.

He made a quick check that Harald was still in position, the engine of the stolen motorcycle ticking over. Then he closed his hand around the loaded automatic in his pocket and turned his attention back to the approaching Mercedes.

Niels Freese was twenty-eight and as angry as it was possible for a young man to be. Anger wasn't really a big enough word, a broad enough concept, to describe what he felt as he stood there, waiting for the luxury car to park. He was a sighted man in a land of the blind. The wilfully blind. But there again, all his life, Niels had had a different way of seeing.

It was Niels's anger and frustration that the Guardians of Gaia had been able to harness and give form and function. He was a walking – or limping – example of what Man's arrogant abuse of the environment had done. The doctors had tried to tell him different, but he knew – he just *knew* – that it had been the chemicals in that factory where his mother had worked that had caused the problems with his birth; that had left him brain-damaged.

It was not that he was a simpleton: the damage had been neurological and had caused a slight palsy that had left him with his slight limp. But it was the other symptoms that had caused the problems. All of his life, he'd had difficulty processing information and reacting to his environment with immediacy. It had given him subtle 'developmental problems', as the doctors had described them. There was the déjà vu. Everyone experienced déjà vu sometimes but Niels experienced it every day of his life, sometimes as many as twenty times in one day. It was as if his wiring had all become entangled and short-circuited daily; at one stage his déjà vu had blossomed into full-blown reduplicative paramnesia. As a young teenager, Niels had experienced depersonalisation episodes in which he had believed that he did not really exist. He also had experienced delusions that he was no longer living in his real home but in an exact replica of it, and that the replica was actually millions of light years distant from reality. He had been taken away for a while and treated in Hamburg-Eilbek Hospital's psychiatric department. He had been treated with lithium and then with immunoglobulin and corticosteroids. The delusions faded without entirely disappearing, but Niels learned to cope with them. The déjà vu remained as severe.

Niels's mental illness had separated him from the others in his school and he had ended up friendless and isolated. Or almost friendless: there had been Roman, the fat boy who had also been a loner and had seemed weird even to Niels. They had not really liked each other, but there was some kind of recognised commonality.

It was after school, working for the forestry department, that Niels had become obsessive about the environment. He started to see his different way of perceiving the world around him not as a disability but as a gift. It was then that he realised that he, and perhaps only he, could see what was really happening to the world.

Niels looked up for a moment through the bare branches above him and at the sky beyond. The leaves had been late in coming out on all the city's trees that year, but this specimen was not yet even showing signs of budding. It didn't stand a chance here, thought Niels, its roots hemmed in by asphalt, its foliage strangled by fumes. The sky he looked at through the lattice of naked branches seemed to match exactly what Niels was feeling inside: an emotion even he would find almost impossible to describe. There was hatred and anger, and, greater than either, there was a colossal sense of frustration: frustration that others were oblivious to that which was so painfully, urgently obvious to Niels. But most of all, at the core of the emotion that burned inside him, was a raw grief: a mourning for a death he could foretell but seemed powerless to prevent. But if it was an emotion that was impossible to describe, it was possible to articulate. And he was seconds away from that articulation.

He turned his attention back to the Mercedes convertible. New, maybe only weeks old. Shiny. It pulled up and parked across the street. The man who got out of the car looked exactly like the kind of person you would expect to see parking an expensive status-symbol car outside a self-consciously trendy, artificially alternative café in the Schanzenviertel: he was in his mid-thirties, tieless and dressed in a designer suit that fitted with the car yet would look out of place in a traditional boardroom. He was all dot-com, right-on, designery, sunrise-businessy. Ten years ago he would have had a ponytail.

Niels despised these people even more than he hated the old guard. At least the old guard did not try to hide what they were. The old guard made it clear that they were about making money and keeping it from everyone else; they were visibly exclusive and conspicuously fuck-the-planet arrogant. These bastards – bastards like trendy

Merc-Man – were much worse. They had exactly the same obsession with money and status, but they dressed it all up in a right-on, socially committed, environmentally friendly guise. They were fucking the planet just like the others, but they were doing it surreptitiously. Hypocritically.

Niels did not know the man who had parked the Mercedes. The Commander had not told Niels his victim's name nor anything about him, but Niels hated him. Hated him with every fibre of his being. And soon he would get to vent that hatred: soon, Merc-Man would come to understand that every decision, every choice you made had consequences, no matter how ignorant you were of them.

Niels watched as a woman pulled up behind the convertible in an equally new, boxy, ugly Alfa-Romeo Giulietta. Everything about her, her look, her clothes, her hair, told Niels that she was a female equivalent of Merc-Man. She greeted the Mercedes driver with a kiss and a laugh and they both went into the café together.

This was it. The next phase. Until now, the group had restricted itself to torching cars like this at night. But it was almost a tradition for the cars of the rich to be sporadically targeted in the Schanzenviertel and it was never clear which group was responsible. Often it was down to individuals simply protesting about the gentrification of the Schanzenviertel and the erosion of its edgy, individualistic character. But that was not what Niels was about, what the group was about. They were the Guardians of Gaia. Protectors of the Earth. Soldiers in a war to defend the air, the sea, the soil.

He looked up again towards the end of the street where Harald waited, ready with the motorbike they had stolen the night before. That too would be torched. Afterwards. Harald, on the Commander's orders, knew nothing about the automatic in Niels's pocket, nor that this daylight arson attack was, in fact, an execution.

Niels put the holdall on the ground and unzipped it. He didn't take anything out; he was just getting it ready. He picked it up again and walked purposefully across the street. As he approached the Mercedes, he stayed on the road side of it, pulling a hammer with a spiked head from his combat jacket with his free hand. As he passed the car, he heard the angry buzz of the motorcycle engine as Harald gunned it up the street behind him. Niels smashed the driver's window with the hammer and the car's alarm exploded into an urgent whine. Pushing the holdall through the window, he walked on, repocketing the hammer. Once he was a few metres clear of the car he turned to see Harald, his face hidden by his helmet, pull up alongside the Mercedes and toss in the lighted Molotov cocktail before accelerating away and screeching to a halt alongside Niels.

'Get on!' Harald shouted at Niels and held out an arm.

The couple were now out on the street, having rushed from the café on hearing the Mercedes's alarm. Niels could see the flames inside the car increase in intensity, but it was still just the Molotov cocktail that burned: the five litres of plastic-bagged accelerant hadn't ignited yet.

'Get *on!*' Harald shouted even more urgently. But Niels was hypnotised by the flames licking at the inside of the windshield. The fabric of the soft-top now burned and flapped. Merc-Man and his girlfriend were now out at the car, but were too focused on what was happening to the Mercedes to look in Niels's direction. Merc-Man looked distraught and tugged at his hair, doing a little dance of decision/indecision, towards the car and back from it. He hadn't a clue what to do. Niels guessed that there was something he wanted to rescue from inside the car.

Niels closed his hand around the butt of the pistol still hidden in his pocket. But for some reason he hesitated. There was something about this situation, this environment, this event, that suddenly seemed overpoweringly familiar. Niels felt himself enter a fugue of déjà vu. He felt he had taken the pistol out of his pocket but knew he had not.

But then, Niels realised he knew what was going to happen before it did happen, and that this realisation had nothing to do with déjà vu. Merc-Man pulled the sleeve of his jacket down over the palm of his hand in an improvised glove and snatched at the handle of the car. The door swung open and the man stepped forward. It was at that exact moment that the five litres of accelerant that Niels had dropped in through the shattered window ignited. It was like watching a flower blossom: a huge, curved, beautiful ball of flame burst out through the open door and up through the burning soft top. For a couple of seconds, Merc-Man disappeared into the flame, was consumed by it. Then Niels heard screaming. The girlfriend screaming. Onlookers screaming. He even heard a strangled, guttural cry, helmet-muffled, come from Harald behind him. But above it all, shrill and inhuman, he heard the screams of Merc-Man. The ball of flame surged up into the sky and Merc-Man was revealed again. His entire body was burning. All of him. A single walking, screaming flame. He staggered forward and fell onto the paving. A couple of onlookers ran forward and threw their coats over the burning man. Two men in the crowd suddenly noticed Niels and Harald and pointed at them.

Niels remained static, staring at the burning man and trying to remember if he really had seen him burn before, so many times that Niels couldn't count them. In that moment, he realised that none of what he was seeing was real. That everything they had tried to convince him of at the hospital had been lies. This was *not* reality. This was a fiction; an imitation. He did not really exist and what he had just witnessed had not really happened.

'For Christ's sake, Niels . . .' He heard Harald's voice urgent behind him. 'Get on the fucking bike. Now!'

It took the men in the crowd a second or two to work out the chronology of events, to apportion the blame for what they had witnessed. By the time they had started to run towards Niels, he was already on the back of the stolen bike. Harald accelerated away, not stopping at give-ways and causing a couple of cars to come to a screeching halt.

Sitting on the pillion seat, Niels still had the image of the screaming, burning man bright in his mind as they made their escape through the Schanzenviertel's narrow streets. And he heard the strangest sound. Laughter.

His own laughter.

CHAPTER 12

'Where are you now?'

'In the car. Hands-free.'

'I'm impressed,' said Susanne. 'Welcome to the twenty-first century.'

'This isn't the twenty-first century,' said Fabel. 'I distinctly remember on TV back in the 1970s they promised that by now we'd all be scooting about on hovercars, wearing silver jumpsuits and taking our holidays on the moon. How's Wiesbaden?'

'Bourgeois. More bourgeois than Hamburg, if you can imagine that. Where are you going? Are you taking advantage of my absence to have a tryst with some lithe blonde?'

'Hardly. I'm off to see Berthold Müller-Voigt. At his domicile, don't you know?'

'Since when did you hobnob with the *Schickeria*? What do you have to see him about?'

'Don't know yet. He asked me. Funny thing . . .'

'In what way funny?'

'Just that he's usually so cool and in control. Something's shaken him up. What, I think I'm about to find out. You missing me?'

'Terribly, but the young Italian waiter from the

restaurant is keeping my mind off it. I'll be back the day after tomorrow.'

'By the way, what did you mean, *"Poppenbütteler Schleuse"*?'

'What?'

'The text you sent me. Enigmatic, I'll give you that.'

'Jan, I haven't the slightest idea what you're talking about.'

'Earlier today,' he sighed. 'I was having lunch at the Fährhaus café and I got a text from you. It said *"Poppenbütteler Schleuse"*. Nothing else.'

'And I thought you never drank at lunchtimes.'

'I'm not joking, Susanne. It came from your number.'

'Well, I didn't send it. Definitely. Maybe you *do* have a blonde stashed away somewhere and she's telling you where to meet for that tryst. I believe there's a really good restaurant there.'

'I'm being serious, Susanne.'

'So am I,' she said emphatically. 'I didn't send you that text. Oh, Jan, you know what you're like with technology. It took me ages to show you how to work an mp3 player and now you'd be lost without it. That message *can't* have come from me. You better check with work. Maybe it was Anna Wolff. You know something? I sometimes get the feeling that Anna would like a little tryst with you up at Poppenbütteler Schleuse herself.'

'Anna?' Fabel snorted. 'You're way off there. For a psychologist, your insight stinks. But I will check with the office tomorrow and see if it was someone there who sent the text.'

Fabel realised that he was already approaching Stade. He hated talking on the phone while driving; even with hands-free he felt you were taken away from the road you were travelling. Particularly when trying to puzzle out who could have sent you a cryptic text message and why they had sent it.

'Got to go. I'll talk to you tomorrow,' he said. 'Sleep well.'

The sky had cleared a little and the sun was already low, painting the town of Stade red as Fabel approached it. He reflected that it was probably the only thing that had painted that particular town red for a long time: Stade was a sleepy, picturesque small town of canals, cobbled streets and gable-ended medieval buildings on the edge of the Altes Land – the Old Land – on the south side of the Elbe, about forty kilometres to the west of Hamburg. It was the kind of place that gave Fabel a sense of comfort. It appealed to the historian in him: Stade was over a thousand years old and one of the oldest settlements in Northern Germany. During the Middle Ages this small provincial town had been, in turn, a Swedish city, a Danish stronghold and a Hanseatic city-state in its own right. Now Stade was part of the Greater Hamburg Metropolitan Area, but nothing much seemed to change it and it stood, quiet, pretty and sedate on the banks of the River Schwinge, watching the passing of time and human follies with stately detachment.

Fabel cursed as he found himself passing through the town's ancient centre. He had been to Müller-Voigt's home, on the outskirts of the town, before and had not had to drive through the town to get there. Fabel had been sure he would have been able to find it without any trouble and had not bothered to key the address into the satnav. The truth was that Fabel hardly ever programmed the satnav. Something told him it was the most human thing to find your own way, and that quite often some of the best things happened to you, the best discoveries made, when you had lost your way.

Which was all well and good on a philosophical level, he thought, but not when you were late for an appointment with one of Hamburg's most influential politicians.

He made his way through Stade's pretty centre, out into the countryside and found his bearings, driving along a narrow, straight ribbon of road beside the high banks of a canal. The sun was filtered through the tops of the trees, squeezing through a letter box of clear sky between the flat landscape below and a parallel bank of dark cloud above. The trees thickened into a dense wedge at the side of the road and Fabel swung into the long drive that he knew led up to Müller-Voigt's home.

It was just as Fabel remembered it: massive, imposing, modern, all angles and glass. And what wasn't glass seemed to be faced with blue marble, although Fabel knew from his last visit that it was actually a façade made up entirely of solar panels.

It was the kind of place that the architects would use on all their publicity. A mixture of master-piece and pension fund.

Müller-Voigt was dressed in chinos, a blue long-sleeved corded shirt with a white T-shirt underneath and canvas deck shoes. It was the most casual of outfits, but Fabel reckoned it had cost more than some of Fabel's best suits.

'Thank you for coming,' the politician said as he opened the door. Fabel had the same feeling that he had had when the Senator had spoken to him in the Presidium's elevator: that he was looking at a troubled man. Which was a discon-certing sight: Fabel had never seen Müller-Voigt troubled. In fact, he'd never seen him anything other than calm and relaxed. And totally in control.

Like a million other Germans, Fabel had seen and heard Müller-Voigt in many stressful situations. Hamburg's Environment Senator was the kind of guest live TV and radio producers loved: he had an innate knack of being able to make statements that were both provocative and combative while maintaining a relaxed outward calm. It was a style that was simultaneously nonchalant and aggressive. And it made for great media interviews. Müller-Voigt seemed to thrive in an environment of conflict and

110

his value to broadcasters was the adroit way he could light the fuse of other politicians. Interviews would end with his opponent seeming to lack self-control and self-assurance. Müller-Voigt made full and effective use of the truism that whoever loses their temper loses the argument. Müller-Voigt never lost either.

But tonight Fabel was seeing something different. Someone different.

Müller-Voigt showed Fabel into a huge living room, pine-lined with a double-height vaulted ceiling and a banistered gallery above. Just as he had the last time he had been here, Fabel was annoyed at the vague pang of petty jealousy he felt looking around the politician's elegant home. Elegant but totally environmentally friendly. The house was making a statement: it was cool to be green.

They sat down on a large corner sofa facing the two-storey picture windows. The sun seemed tinged a different colour through the glass.

'I can adjust it at will,' said Müller-Voigt, as if he had read Fabel's mind. 'It's the latest technology: energy-capture glass. It doesn't just insulate and prevent the escape of warmth from the house, it actually captures solar power and converts it to energy.'

'I see,' said Fabel. 'Very impressive.'

'I know that many people – and I don't know if you're one of them – think this is all a bit of a gimmick with me. That I'm really more interested in the political than the natural environment. Normally I wouldn't care what you or anyone else thought, but I need you to understand something, Herr Fabel: I am genuinely, completely and irreversibly committed to changing how mankind treats the environment. It's more than a political belief; it's how I see life.'

Fabel shrugged. 'I have no reason to doubt that.'

'Well, as I said, some do.' There was a hint of bitterness in Müller-Voigt's tone. 'As a race, as a *species*, we've lost our way, Herr Fabel. And it's going to be the end of us. In fact, we've lost our most basic capability to read Nature, the geography and climate around us. Take where we are right now.' He waved a hand vaguely at the landscape beyond the windows. 'I built this house on a geest – an island of sand and gravel dumped as moraine by the last ice age, in the middle of a flat sea of heath, marsh and moor. If you look around this whole area you'll see that almost every town is built on a geest, Stade included.

'When these settlements were first created, our ancestors were connected to Nature and to the landscape. They could read the signs and learn from experience of changing weather patterns. And that meant they knew where to build their homes. Do you know something? These geests have provided the perfect protection against storm surges for a millennium of settlement. The marshes around them work like huge sponges and the geests themselves are natural flood barriers.

Giant natural sandbags. And you see all the Knicks that run alongside the canals and rivers here?' Müller-Voigt referred to the turf embankments, topped by trees and bushes, that criss-crossed the Altes Land and much of the rest of the Northern German landscape. 'Some of those Knicks are older than the pyramids of Giza, built by our ancestors more than five thousand years ago. And do you know something, they remain the best protection against aeolian and fluvial erosion this landscape has.' Müller-Voigt gave a small laugh. 'Look at the millions and millions of euros spent on flood defences for Hamburg. Don't get me wrong, they're needed to protect people and prop-erty – but if you look at the historical flooding patterns of Hamburg over the last century or so, you'll see all of the areas that have remained immune. And guess what? They're all the oldest settled parts of the city, on the Hamburg geest slopes. That's what we've lost, Fabel. *Connection.*'

'I understand, Herr Senator, but I assume that's not why you called me out here.'

'Isn't it?' I want you to remember what I have said because, believe it or not, it *is* relevant to what I have to talk to you about. There is a lot of discussion in the media about the environment, and it has slowly climbed the ladder of political priority, but it's still not high enough. There *is* a disaster waiting for us, Herr Fabel, and it's just around the corner. There are a lot of people who believe that extreme action has to be taken now. Very extreme action. Drink?' Müller-Voigt asked, making his way to the cabinet.

'No, thanks,' said Fabel.

'Of course. Never on duty . . .' Müller-Voigt smiled a half-hearted smile.

'Never when I've got the car. Anyway, I'm not on duty. This is, so far, unofficial.'

'I appreciate that, Herr Fabel. You don't mind if I do?'

'Go ahead,' said Fabel. It occurred to him that Müller-Voigt was not the kind of man who would normally need fortification to face anything.

Ice tinkled against expensive crystal as Müller-Voigt brought his malt whisky over and sat opposite Fabel. 'I really am grateful that you came to see me at such short notice.'

'Well, it was pretty clear that it's something urgent.'

'Urgent, but, as you said, at the moment unofficial,' said Müller-Voigt. He leaned back in the sofa and contemplated his whisky glass for a moment. 'Obviously, I am kept fully up to date on all developments when something as major as the recent storm hits Hamburg. Storms and related damage lie within my purview, as you probably can imagine.'

'I suppose so . . .'

'So you'll understand that any consequential fatalities and injuries are reported to me as a matter of urgency. Such as the body that was washed up at the Fischmarkt. The one I asked you about earlier today.'

'As we already discussed, Senator, the woman washed up at the Fischmarkt wasn't a *consequential* fatality. She wasn't killed by the storm or flood.'

'I see. How do you know she didn't die as a result of the storm? And what makes you think she wasn't a victim of this Network Killer?'

'Listen, Herr Senator, I understand your interest, but all I can tell you is that the victim did not die as a result of the storm. The rest is a police matter at the moment.'

'A Murder Commission matter, you mean . . .'

'Herr Senator . . .' Fabel infused a warning in his tone.

Müller-Voigt put his whisky glass down. 'I want to see the body,' he said decisively.

'What?'

'I want to see the body of the woman washed up at the Fischmarkt. I think I may be able to help you identify her.'

'I doubt it. The body is in a condition that would make that difficult. There's clearly something you want to tell me, Herr Senator. What is it? Why did you ask me to come here?'

Müller-Voigt took another swallow of whisky. 'You know my reputation, Herr Fabel. With women. The Hamburg press would have everyone believe that I am some kind of unprincipled sexual adventurer. Well, my private life is

115

my private life. I am unmarried and I am fortunate enough to enjoy the company of beautiful and intelligent women. I always have. And for some reason that I have never been able to grasp, they enjoy mine. But I am not married and never have been, so I am betraying no marriage vows. Unlike, it must be said, more than half of my upright married colleagues in the Hamburg Senate. Nor do I trick doe-eyed ingénues into bed or pay for cheap and nasty dalliances in the Reeperbahn. I'm not cheating on anyone and I treat the women with whom I am involved with respect and dignity.'

'Why are you telling me this?' asked Fabel. 'Your personal life is your own affair.'

'Of all of the women with whom I have been involved over the years there have been only three for whom I had deep feelings. Genuinely deep feelings. One died a long time ago, while the second affair withered on the vine, as it were. The third is the woman with whom I was involved up until just two weeks ago.' Müller-Voigt stood up, crossed the room to a bureau and came back holding a framed photograph. He fiddled with it for a moment before handing it over; Fabel realised that it was a digital photo frame and Müller-Voigt had been selecting the image he wanted to show him. It was a photograph of a young woman with dark hair and strikingly blue eyes. She was flashing a white-toothed grin at the camera but looked a little uneasy. Shy. She was also, Fabel could see, very beautiful.

'This is Meliha,' said Müller-Voigt. 'I've been seeing her for the last three months. As you can see, she is considerably younger than me.'

'She's a very attractive woman,' said Fabel and held the frame out to return it to Müller-Voigt. The politician made no move to take it.

'Look at her very carefully, Fabel. She's disappeared.'

'Missing? How long?'

'Not missing. Disappeared. Like I said, I was involved with her until two weeks ago, and then she disappeared without trace.'

'And you think she might be the body washed up after the storm?'

'I don't know . . .' Müller-Voigt shrugged, but there was nothing dismissive in the gesture nor in his expression. Fabel could see that he was a man in pain. 'She could be.'

'So you last heard from her two weeks ago?' asked Fabel.

'Yes . . . no . . .' Müller-Voigt made an exasperated gesture. 'It's complicated. I got an email from her two days ago. Breaking it off with me. Or that's what it seemed to be.'

'Listen, Herr Müller-Voigt, I'm getting confused. You say this woman has been missing for two weeks, and now you're telling me that you received an email from her two days ago.' Fabel frowned. 'One thing is for sure, she's not the body washed up after the storm. That woman had been in the water for at least two weeks . . .'

'Which is exactly how long Meliha has been missing. Listen, Fabel, I choose my words very carefully. When I say Meliha has disappeared, I mean exactly that. I know you think that I'm approaching you because I'm trying to pull strings to have this looked into discreetly and so avoid scandal. But that's not it at all. Someone has, systematically, erased all trace of Meliha ever having existed. And I can't report her missing if she doesn't exist any more. And as for that email, I know it's fake.'

'Can I see it?' asked Fabel.

Müller-Voigt gave a bitter laugh. 'No. It doesn't exist any more, either. I didn't print it out because I never print anything out unless it's absolutely essential. Environmental grounds, obviously. You'll have heard of the Klabautermann Virus, I dare say?'

Fabel nodded. 'Of course. I know the officer who's been tasked with finding the people behind it.'

'I have absolutely no idea what these people get out of destroying other people's data,' said Müller-Voigt. 'Probably just the challenge of proving they're even smarter nerds than the smart nerds who design the software . . . but, sadly, there are people out there who devote their time to developing ever more virulent, ever more destructive computer viruses. This latest one, the Klabautermann Virus, has been specifically targeted at official intranets and secure government email servers in the north of Germany.

Now what is the point of that – other than to disrupt ordinary people's lives? And the little bastards behind it may not even be anywhere near the north of Germany. They could be in San Jose or Mumbai or Beijing. Or just some spotty pubescent nobody in a back bedroom in Bönningstedt. Whoever they are and wherever they are, they infected the City and State government email. Because I'm logged into it, it got into my laptop and wiped all of my email folders – but not before sending itself to every contact in my address book. In short, thanks to the Klabautermann Virus, I don't have the email any more.'

'What makes you convinced it wasn't her? asked Fabel.

'I just knew it wasn't her. You can tell. Everyone has a . . . I don't know . . . a *style* when writing an email.'

'And that's it?'

'And, I know this sounds mad, but it was too grammatical. Meliha is Turkish. I don't mean Turkish-German, she's a Turkish national. Her German was excellent but she made mistakes, like all non-natives. This email was . . . well, too *perfect*. And, in any case, email just wasn't our medium.'

'Mmm . . .' said Fabel. He remembered what Kroeger had said at the briefing about identifying fakes on the internet. Maybe Müller-Voigt could have seen through a phoney email. 'I have to say I don't know what I can do, Herr Müller-Voigt.

119

It doesn't sound like a homicide to me. And, to be frank, not much of a missing-person case, either. But I can get in touch with the local police and get them to look into it.'

Fabel stood up.

'Listen, Fabel . . .' Müller-Voigt stepped forward, as if to block his exit. 'I don't know what you think of me, but I do know that you don't take me for the hysterical type. If anything I'm well known for being the opposite. I am telling you that I am absolutely convinced that a woman I was involved with has been abducted or murdered. I am also telling you that not only can I not offer objective evidence that this has happened, I can't even offer objective evidence that Meliha existed in the first place.' Müller-Voigt stood back and indicated the sofa. 'Please, Fabel, I need your help.'

'You must know where she lives,' said Fabel, but he remained standing.

'I was never there. I had an address for her, but when I called there the flat was empty. I don't mean she wasn't in, I mean the flat was unoccupied. I asked a neighbour about her and only succeeded in making the woman suspicious. I left before she called the police. But she did say that the apartment had been empty for more than a month.'

'You say Meliha was a foreign national?'

'Turkish, yes.'

'And she was here in Germany legally?'

'As far as I am aware.'

'Then there will be a record of her entering the country. What is her full name?' asked Fabel, taking his notebook and pen from his inside jacket pocket.

'Meliha Yazar. She was from somewhere just outside Istanbul. I think it was Silivri.'

Fabel wrote it down.

'Is there any reason she would lie to you about where she lived?'

'None that I can think of. I know this sounds insane, but I don't think she was lying. I think she lived in that apartment. You see, I met Meliha at an environmental conference. At the Hamburg Congress Center.'

'She was involved with the environmental movement?'

Müller-Voigt nodded. 'She was a campaigner, an activist, or at least said she was. From what I could gather, she had some kind of Earth-sciences degree from Istanbul. She told me that she worked as a researcher for an environmental protection agency but she was always pretty evasive when I asked which one. The truth is, I suspected she might be some kind of investigative reporter and I was pretty guarded around her at first. I definitely believe that she was into stuff that placed her in danger.'

'What kind of stuff?'

Müller-Voigt looked at his half-empty whisky glass and put it down on the table. 'I'm going to make some coffee,' he said decisively. 'It's a long story . . .'

CHAPTER 13

Roman Kraxner stood behind the door of his flat, head tilted close, ear angled, his sweat-freckled brow furrowed in concentration. He tried to keep his breathing quiet and shallow so he could hear as much as possible of what transpired downstairs. It was a difficult task: Roman's obesity squeezed each inhalation into a protracted snort through fat-compressed airways.

A deep male voice resonated outside in the stairwell, one floor down. The voice was quiet, too quiet for Roman to make out exactly what was being said, but it was calm, controlled, strong. Authoritative.

Another voice made Roman recoil slightly from the door. This voice was louder; angry and harsh. Accented.

'I bet it was that fat pig of a paedophile upstairs!' The voice was clear and Roman imagined the Albanian leaning into the stairwell, over the banister, shouting up in the direction of Roman's flat.

Of course it was me, thought Roman. *I* called them. And I'll be sending an email to the landlord, you can be sure of that.

'You should go up there,' the Albanian shouted for Roman to hear. 'I tell you. I tell you that what you should be doing. That what you should do . . .You should finding out what he got on all those computers. Little boys, little girls, I bet.'

Roman felt something between fear and fury surge up from someone deep inside. How dare he? How dare *those people* say these things about him?

The other voice: slightly louder now, but still calm and even more authoritative. A hint of warning in the tone. Leaning closer into the door, Roman still couldn't make out what the policeman was saying. A few words. An injunction against bothering Roman. A warning to keep the music down. A mention of Hamburg city ordinances. All voices lower now. Calmer.

The deeper voice laughed at something that the Albanian said. Laughing at what? Laughing at whom? Were they laughing at *him*? Why was the policeman laughing? He was supposed to be there to shut them up. Stop that stupid music. That was why Roman had called him here.

Roman couldn't hear the policeman's voice any more. He heard the outer door at the bottom of the apartment block's stairwell slam shut. Something muttered, loudly, in Albanian and then the slamming of a second door: the downstairs apartment.

He stood at the door for a moment, straining to hear footsteps on the stairs; the Albanian coming up to confront him. Nothing. Roman turned and leaned his back against the door. He felt something high in his chest, almost in his throat. A fluttering. He knew he would feel it again, every time he had to pass the Albanian's door. And, although Roman did everything he could to avoid leaving his flat, when he did go out it took him a breathless age to pass the Albanian's apartment.

God, how he hated living here. He was better than this. Better than the people around him. Better than this shitty little flat. Better than living in Wilhelmsburg.

Most of all, he hated living above the Albanians. Their country of origin was immaterial to Roman: he hated living above anyone, because what he loathed most of all about this flat was the climb up the stairwell. Since he had lost his job in the computer store, it was an effort that Roman had to make less and less. His flat was only two floors up, but the climb was enough to completely rob him of his breath and leave him white-faced and sweating, his lungs screaming for oxygen. There were times, frequent times, when his meal would be cold by the time he had brought it up the stairs: Roman never cooked. Occasionally he would reheat food in the microwave but he had never so much as made a cup of coffee in the apartment's tiny kitchen. Everything he ate or drank came from a can or a box or a styrene container.

The flat itself comprised three rooms. Four, if

you counted the bathroom. The apartment building was reasonably new and was well maintained by the landlord, and when Roman had moved in the decor had been fresh and clean. But now the inside of Roman's flat was untidy and grubby. He found doing housework tiring; not tedious – literally exhausting, sapping every ounce of energy from him. Ten minutes of moving trash from one corner of a room to another drained him; made him sweat until he dripped and was wheezing for breath. And ten minutes would make no difference to the piles of magazines and books, the detritus of convenience meals, the empty soft-drink cans.

Not that Roman cared that much about the look of his apartment. No one ever came here. No friends, no women, nobody. And it didn't carry any great significance for him personally; he did not attach the concept of *home* to this place. If fact, Roman Kraxner didn't really have much of a concept of *home*. Or at least, not in the physical world. He did have a sense of belonging, but it was not anchored in any tangible physical reality; for Roman, there was another universe of opportunity, of freedom from the constraints of his body, that was his true medium. *That* was where he truly belonged. Where he truly existed.

After he was convinced the Albanian had in fact gone back into his apartment and was not coming up the stairs to challenge him, Roman shuffled across the messy living room, past the bank of monitors, speakers, hard disks and keyboards arrayed on the table against the far wall, and made his way to the toilet. His gut was aching as it always did when he was stressed – as it did most of the time – and he felt the urge to void his bowels become more than vague. Plugging his iPod earphones into his ears, he dropped his tracksuit bottoms and lowered the one hundred and eighty kilograms of his bulk onto the toilet. As he listened to music and played computer games, Roman strained until his breathing became even more laboured and his face even more livid than usual. Nothing.

It was, as his doctor had explained, the inevitable result of Roman's diet, devoid as it was of anything that looked remotely like it had grown in the ground. What Roman had not explained to his physician was that he despised anything that smacked of the natural world; he relished artificiality, the semblance of synthesis. The more processed, the more manufactured the look of the food, the more Roman liked it. He preferred his meat ground, pulped, *extruded*. Any fibre he consumed lay hidden as a paste for bulking his hamburgers and hot dogs, his meat patties and battered chicken pieces. The bread buns and subs that his meat came in had to be white and smooth with no hint of a cereal origin or texture. His preference for vivid unnatural colours in the desserts, the ice creams and the beverages he consumed allowed him to place a conceptual distance between himself and anything resembling a dairy. It was the main reason Roman favoured American fast-food outlets over local Schnellimbiss or Würstchenbude snack stands: there was a science and an art to making food look as if it had little or nothing to do with the natural world; and it seemed only natural to Roman that it had been perfected by the same nation that had put a man on the moon.

After twenty minutes the urge to defecate remained undimmed, but the spasms in Roman's bowels had still failed to produce anything. It had been over a week since he had had a productive bowel movement. Sighing, he pulled up his tracksuit bottoms and made his way back through to the lounge-cum-diner and to the table where he had his computers set up. It was a gateway to that other universe, to those other identities. It purred at him: the soft whirring of internal cooling fans in the two 8-core MacPros, the massive HP, the five external drives that, between them, gave him seven terabytes of data storage, the blade server unit he had built himself. Thousands of euros' worth of computer technology purred a soft invitation to another life.

This small area of shining technology was the only part of his apartment that was clean and tidy. Roman kept this part of his environment dust-free, ordered, illuminated in the otherwise darkened room. It was also where he had his most expensive pieces of furniture: the sturdy table on which he had his equipment arrayed, like the command desk of a space-programme mission-control room, and the chair that Roman had had specially made for himself. It was the most expensive thing he had ever purchased; more expensive even than any single piece of his computer hardware. The chair moulded itself into his body, or his body moulded into it; it swivelled, tilted, glided in response, it seemed to Roman, to his will. It was the ultimate computer chair, the brochure had assured him. But where the real expense had come had been in having it custom-built to support Roman's mass. The manufacturers in Munich had sent someone all the way to Hamburg to visit Roman in his apartment. The technician had, at first, looked suspicious when he had seen the modesty and semi-squalor of Roman's home, but the suspicion had evaporated when he had done a quick mental calculation of the value of the computer-related technology arrayed on the desk. It had almost been as if he had understood Roman; that he had met others like him.

Roman remembered that when he had first sat in the chair the comfort had been sublime. It seemed to support every square centimetre of his body, making him feel, ironically, almost weightless. Now, as he eased himself into the chair, he still experienced some of that sense of relief, of sublime comfort, but less so than before. He knew the reason: the chair had been crafted to fit him perfectly when he had ordered it. Now, three months and seven kilos later, the fit was no longer perfect.

Roman drew as deep a breath as his obesity-hypoventilation syndrome, which compelled him to sleep each night with an oxygen mask, allowed him to draw and switched on his four flat-screen monitors, which had been configured to offer a continuous display. A single window.

Roman loved this moment: immersion. He could disconnect from the mass of his body, from the mass of the world. Like a beached whale swept suddenly back out to sea and into a natural environment of grace, Roman became weightless, formless, in a world where his mind and his mind alone was all that mattered. Here he communicated with other beings without form. Here he could be anyone, anything. Here there were no noisy Albanian neighbours, no colic spasms, no disgust at what looked back at you from the mirror.

Roman would spend the next seven hours, late into the night, in the cybernetic world. He would chat, play, be someone else. He would spend most of that time in *Virtual Dimension*. He had been a member for nearly a year. In *Virtual Dimension* he was slim, attractive, successful. Officially, his job was as a private detective and he had a string of mistresses, a penthouse apartment that looked out over the lagoons of New Venice, and he drove a 1962 Ferrari 250 GT convertible. He had dozens of friends and attended e-drugs parties.

In *Virtual Dimension* he had no weight problem, no grubby Wilhelmsburg flat, no Albanian neighbours. He ached to be back there.

But first, Roman had work to do.

The truth was that although Roman hated living in Wilhelmsburg, he could have easily afforded to move out at any time. The only thing stopping him was the questions that would be asked about how he had managed to amass such a fortune. He had a powerful electromagnet, weighing five kilos, permanently plugged into the power supply, ready to be switched on with a flick of his thumb and swept across his hard drives, destroying the data inside. The evidence.

If they came.

He would play *Virtual Dimension* soon. But first, he had to attend to business. He sat before thousands of euros' worth of technology which required constant updating, maintaining, expanding. And the way Roman paid for it all was to divert large sums of money from all around the world into accounts that he had all around the world.

But Roman was more than just a fraudster. He was an artist. No one was looking for him yet, because no one knew yet that the money was missing. Every institution, organisation and company that he had defrauded was hit immediately by a computer virus that erased data, destroyed records, wiped clean all traces of his visit. Each virus was different. Each was an individual, unique creation. A work of art.

And the greatest virus of them all – the Trojan

of all Trojans – was the Klabautermann Virus. His masterpiece of destructive programming.

Because obese, reclusive, Roman Kraxner – twenty-eight, one hundred and eighty kilos, with no university degree but an IQ of 162 and an Abitur result of 1.0, living in a grubby three-room apartment in Wilhelmsburg – was one of the most successful internet hackers and fraudsters in the world.

And it was time for him to go to work.

CHAPTER 14

Müller-Voigt came back into the lounge from the kitchen, carrying a tray with a coffee pot and two cups on it. Fabel noticed that the pot and cups were made from a very fine white china and were of an elegant, restrained modern design. He had seen exactly the same set in the Alsterhaus store down on Jungfernstieg and had wanted to buy it, but had decided he could not justify the expense. His East Frisian providence had triumphed over his Hamburg *savoir faire*.

While Müller-Voigt had been in the kitchen, Fabel had picked up the small piece of sculpture that had sat in the centre of the coffee table. It was a modernist piece. Some kind of stylised dragon. It had a beauty to it, but there was something about it that also disturbed Fabel. It was an inanimate lump of bronze but looked as if it was writhing as he watched. He put it back on the table when Müller-Voigt came back in.

'Like it?' asked Müller-Voigt as he set the coffee tray down. 'I had it specially commissioned. It's a representation of *Rahab*, the ancient Hebrew sea daemon. The creator of storms and the father of chaos.'

'Strange choice,' said Fabel, his eyes still on the bronze, still half-expecting to see it twist and writhe.

'It represents my enemy, if you like,' the politician said. 'A monster we are creating out of Nature.' Müller-Voigt paused to hand Fabel his coffee. 'Anyway, as I was saying, I checked with the organisers of the conference I met Meliha at. I asked them to go through their records of delegates and attendees. It wasn't open to the general public and everyone who attended did so by invitation and registration. They had no record of Meliha whatsoever. I saw her delegate badge, Fabel. We all had to have our photographs taken for those and we had to supply all kinds of information for security. As a foreign national, she would have had to show her passport as proof of identity. By the way, that was one of the reasons why, when you asked if she could have been an illegal, I said no. In today's security climate they would not have let her into the Congress Center otherwise. In fact, I would go so far as to say that there is absolutely no way Meliha could have been there if she hadn't been registered for the event and her details checked.'

'Administrative errors happen. Maybe her details have been accidentally wiped,' said Fabel.

'Mmm . . . just like her email to me has disappeared from my computer.'

'That was because of a computer virus that we all know about.'

'It's a hell of a coincidence, though, isn't it?'

'I suppose it is,' said Fabel. And if there was one thing Fabel didn't believe in, it was coincidences.

'And who's to say that the Klabautermann Virus isn't targeted? That it is a tool for deleting carefully selected information and hiding it in plain sight in a mass deletion?'

Fabel laughed. 'I'm sorry, Herr Senator, but I think we're wandering into the area of conspiracy theories.'

'You think?' Müller-Voigt poured more coffee. Fabel accepted it but knew he would regret it later. He had a low tolerance for caffeine and he knew that a second cup would keep him awake that night. Susanne habitually teased him about it, saying it was because all he had ever drunk while growing up in East Frisia was tea. But somehow Fabel didn't think the coffee would be the only thing to keep him from sleep.

It was now dark outside and Fabel noticed that the lighting in the lounge increased automatically to compensate.

'Look, Herr Müller-Voigt,' said Fabel. 'I have to ask you this. Did you give any money or gifts or anything of any value to Meliha? Maybe even information that may have some value or be of use—'

'I see,' Müller-Voigt cut across him. 'You think that I've been honeytrapped. No fool like an old fool, is that it?'

Fabel started to protest but the politician held up his hand.

'I don't blame you. I have to admit that the thought had gone through my head, but the answer is no. I can honestly say that nothing of any material, commercial or political advantage ever passed between us. We became lovers. It was as simple and as complicated as that. And now she's gone and I'm struggling to convince you that she ever existed. I'm beginning to struggle to convince myself of that.'

'People either exist or they don't, Herr Senator. And if they do exist then they leave material traces.'

'That's what I believed, too. But when I'd run out of all other ideas I used a contact I have in the education department. I got her to run a check with *her* contact in the University of Istanbul and gave her the rough span of years during which I reckoned Meliha would have been a student.'

'And she drew a blank as well.' Fabel made it a statement rather than a question.

'That's why I said to you that Meliha wasn't missing, but that she has *disappeared*. Not just physically but, as far as I can see, from any form of public record. It's almost as if someone has hit a button and deleted Meliha from existence.'

A silence fell over the two men. Fabel studied his coffee cup and considered what Müller-Voigt had told him. Fabel had heard stories like this before. People deranged with anxiety over a missing person elaborating their disappearance into some huge conspiracy, just to make sense of it. But Fabel knew this was not one of those cases. What Müller-Voigt was telling him made absolutely no sense at all, and Fabel believed every word of it.

'If what you say is true . . . No, let me put that better: if what you suspect is true, then it would take massive resources and organisation. Are you saying the government, or *a* government is behind this? You said that you thought Meliha was into something that might have placed her in danger. What, exactly?'

Müller-Voigt regarded Fabel for a moment, as if assessing him.

'Do you remember what I said about how we used to be more connected to Nature?' he said. 'That we could interpret our environment?'

Fabel nodded.

'I need you to keep that in mind for a while. Have you heard of the Pharos Project?'

Fabel remembered the poster he had passed when running Susanne to the airport: the over-done symbolism of the lighthouse in the storm.

'Not really,' he said. 'Heard *of* it but I don't know anything much about it.'

'The Pharos Project is purportedly an environmental organisation. It has a massive corporate conglomerate, headed by its founder, behind it. The European headquarters of the Pharos Project is, believe it or not, just a few kilometres from here.

There's an old disused lighthouse out on the coast, just to the north of Hörne: they've renovated the original lighthouse and added this massive building beside it. They call the building itself the Europa Pharos. You should see it – it is actually a beautiful piece of architecture and, of course, environmentally self-sustaining. It projects out on stilts over the water. There's another one, apparently, on the coast of Maine, called the Americas Pharos. Anyway, the Pharos Project uses its status as an environmental research and pressure group to avoid being classed as a religious or philosophical movement, or an out-and-out political organisation.'

'You're saying they're covering up being a cult?'

'You met Fabian Menke from the BfV earlier today,' said Müller-Voigt. 'I've been talking to him about the Pharos Project and he admitted to me that it is a group that his people are monitoring. Closely.'

'Doesn't that, well, *concern* you? That the BfV is investigating an environmental organisation? After all, you are Hamburg's most outspoken environmentalist.'

'Let's get one thing straight: the Pharos Project has nothing to do with anything I believe in. The Pharos Project *is* a cult. But more than that, it is a dangerous, malignant cult. You should talk to Menke about it.'

'So what was Meliha's connection to it?'

'She was very guarded about her work but, like I said, I got the impression that she was some kind of investigator for whatever organisation she worked for. Or maybe an investigative journalist. But, again, I've searched for her on the internet and can find no trace of her ever having contributed to any journal, press or TV. In any case, I know she was gathering as much information as she could about the Pharos Project. She even asked me what I knew about it, which turned out to be a lot less than she did.'

'And what *do* you know?'

'Well, I've done quite a bit of research since Meliha disappeared. And I was able to get a fair bit from Menke. None of it is good. The Pharos Project meets all the criteria for a dangerous cult. It is highly dictatorial and its leaders, particularly Dominik Korn, are venerated as demigods; it demands that all its members donate all their wealth to it; it has some kind of doomsday agenda; it exerts total control over its members and has an incredibly hostile and aggressive attitude towards any critics.'

'And you think that aggression has been directed towards Meliha?'

'Remember what I said about us not engaging with our environment any more? Well, that kind of disengagement is exactly what the Pharos Project, specifically its leader, Dominik Korn, positively encourages. He believes that the best way to save the environment is for humankind to be removed from it.'

'And how do they propose that is achieved?' asked Fabel.

Müller-Voigt shrugged. 'Most cults believe in some epiphanic moment. A Judgement Day, or Ragnarok, or Apocalypse. The Pharos Project is no different. They believe in an event they call the Consolidation. I don't know any more than that. But I suspect that Menke will be able to give you more details. There was a limit to how much he was willing to share with me, but you're not a politician, you're a policeman.'

'And you think that Meliha's disappearance is connected to the Pharos cult?'

'They don't like people investigating or criticising them. And Meliha did seem to be looking into their activities before she disappeared.' Müller-Voigt paused. 'I'm going to get to the bottom of this, Fabel. I'll do it without your help if I have to. It will make it difficult, but I'll do it. The question remains, Herr Fabel: will you help me?'

'As you've said yourself, there's no evidence of a murder. There's not even evidence that Meliha ever existed, from what you've told me. I simply can't launch an official Murder Commission inquiry based on what you've given me.'

'So you're saying that you won't help me?'

'I didn't say that. I'll look into it. God knows I've got enough on my plate with this Network Killer case. But I'll see what I can find out. But there's no point in you looking at the washed-up body we found. It was a torso: no head, legs or arms.'

Fabel saw the colour drain dramatically from

behind the politician's tan. For a moment he thought Müller-Voigt was going to throw up.

'Listen, Herr Senator, I think it's unlikely that it's Meliha. We believe the body was dismembered to avoid identification. According to everything you've told me tonight, Meliha doesn't seem to have any kind of recorded identity. Give me a few days and I'll see what I can find out.'

'Thank you, Fabel. I appreciate it. Can I ask you one more thing? Can we keep this between ourselves . . . for the meantime at least.'

'Okay, Herr Senator,' said Fabel. It wasn't an official investigation after all. Yet.

'You have to admit, though,' said Fabel, 'that you haven't really given me much to go on. Is there *anything* you can tell me about Meliha that might help me?'

Müller-Voigt's small laugh was both bitter and sad. 'After Meliha disappeared, I thought about how little I really knew her. Every time I thought about talking to you – or someone like you – about her disappearance I realised how little I really had to tell you about her. But I *did* know her. I knew her as well as if we'd spent our whole lives together. If you like, I knew the *essence* of her.' He thought for a moment. 'She was a Kemalist. You know, Mustafa Kemal Atatürk, the father of modern Turkey. Atatürk is a massive figure for a lot of Turks because he created something so totally, radically different to everything that went before. He simply *rethought* the concept of Turkey and shaped a secular,

140

progressive republic. He convinced an entire nation to put the past behind them and embrace a future that they had never considered. I can understand why he is so inspirational to Turks. As I said, Meliha was also deeply passionate about the environment. And that was her big thing: she believed that the world needed an "environmental Atatürk". Someone who was capable of rethinking our entire way of life. She used to accuse me and others like me of being "pop-environmentalists". Dilettantes.'

'I don't see how . . .'

' "*Hell hath no fury like a woman scorned*",' said Müller-Voigt in English. 'Do you know your Shakespeare, Herr Fabel?'

'Congreve,' said Fabel. ' "*Heaven has no rage like love to hatred turned, Nor hell a fury like a woman scorned*" is from a play by William Congreve, not Shakespeare.'

Müller-Voigt grinned. 'Of course, I was forgetting you're a very *learned* policeman, aren't you, Herr Fabel? Anyway, I think Meliha felt a little of that fury. Not that she had been scorned romantically, more *philosophically*. She was a great admirer of Dominik Korn, of his environmental views. At least when he set out his original vision for the Pharos Project. I think she saw him as the great hope for the future of the environment.'

'Her "Atatürk of the Environment"?'

'Exactly. But Korn had some kind of accident – a diving accident, I believe – after which he became increasingly reclusive. The Pharos

Project, which had started off as a genuinely innovative environmental research organisation, became a weird cult driven by Korn's increasingly bizarre philosophies. Meliha really had a bee in her bonnet about it. She felt it was more than a lost opportunity. It was a betrayal.'

'So you think she was on some kind of mission to expose Korn and Pharos?'

'I think that is entirely possible. If you're asking me where to look for Meliha, then I suggest you start with the Pharos Project.'

'By the way, the picture you've got in the digital frame – can you give me a hard copy of that?'

'I can email it to you. I have a new laptop and a private email that are not connected to the State's system so they haven't been exposed to this bloody Klabautermann Virus.'

'If you don't mind, Herr Senator, I'd rather have a hard copy.'

For a moment Müller-Voigt looked surprised. 'Okay . . . I think I've got a print in my office. I'll have it couriered over to the Presidium tomorrow morning. If not I can print it out again when I get my old computer back. They're de-virusing it or whatever the hell they do to get the data back.'

As Fabel drove away from the politician's house all kinds of nagging thoughts worried away at the edges of his mind. The simplest explanation of the woman's disappearance, and of the fact that there was no trace of her identity, seemed obvious to Fabel: that, for whatever reason, she had given Müller-Voigt a false name. That would explain the thing with the conference: she probably *did* have an official delegate's badge, but it had been under a different name and, once she had introduced herself as Meliha Yazar, Müller-Voigt wouldn't have thought to check her name tag. Maybe she was an investigative journalist or maybe she was a member of one of those extreme environmental groups Menke had mentioned, and she had simply been trying to get close to an influential member of the Hamburg government.

Yes . . . that was what made most sense. That she had used a false name. But for some reason, as he drove back through the dark alongside the canal, its high bank topped with the type of Knick that Müller-Voigt had talked about, Fabel couldn't quite believe it.

Maybe it was possible that someone, somehow, had been able to erase all traces of the woman who had been Meliha Yazar.

CHAPTER 15

The next morning, Fabel felt tired and irritable when he arrived at the Presidium. He had been right about the coffee: it had kept him awake half the night. Or, more correctly, the coffee, the absence of Susanne in bed beside him, and the ceaseless flashing picture show running through his head – featuring the woman in the photograph Müller-Voigt had shown him – had kept him awake half the night.

'Well, you look like crap . . .' was Werner's greeting as Fabel came out of the elevator. 'Hangover?'

'I wish,' said Fabel. 'Sleepless night. How's everything going with the Network Killer case? Have we got warrants yet?'

'Anna says we've got four addresses to hit this afternoon. She suggests we muster at three p.m. and hit them simultaneously. It would be good if we could have a few uniforms at each address.'

'I'll arrange it.'

Anna Wolff came out of the office she shared with Henk Hermann and greeted Fabel.

'You look terrible . . .'

'We've done that,' said Werner. 'He claims it was

the burden of his intellect that kept him awake last night, but my money's on a bottle of malt.'

'When you're quite finished . . .' said Fabel. 'Did you send me a text yesterday?'

'Me?' Werner frowned. 'No . . . not me.'

'You, Anna?' asked Fabel.

'Not me either, *Chef*. Is it important?'

'Don't know. No . . . probably not. All it said was "Poppenbütteler Schleuse".'

'Sounds like it was sent to you by mistake,' said Anna. 'Do you know anyone who lives in Poppenbüttel?'

'Can't say I do. Can I have a word with you both?'

Werner and Anna followed Fabel into his office.

'I know we're pushed at the moment but I need to check out a couple of things this morning,' said Fabel. 'You can reach me on my cellphone if you need me. Before I leave I'll arrange the uniform cover for the raids this afternoon. If I get bodies in at two-thirty can you brief them, Anna?'

'No problem. Here are the four addresses. I'm afraid they're spread out all across the city. By the way, Criminal Director van Heiden was trying to get hold of you. He phoned down about fifteen minutes ago.'

'Okay,' said Fabel, although the thought *what now?* flashed through his brain. 'There's something I'd like you both to check out for me. I have to say this could be unconnected to anything, but I need information on an organisation called the Pharos Project. Like I say, at the moment this is not entirely official, but there's a chance there may be a link to the wash-up from yesterday. I have a new best friend in the BfV, so I'm going to ask him if he can give me some info on Pharos. Either of you heard of it?'

Werner, who was still writing in his notebook, shook his head. 'Is that *Faros* with an *F* or with a *Ph . . .?*'

'Ph . . . the Greek way,' said Fabel. 'And it's headed up by some guy called Dominik Korn.'

'I've heard of them,' said Anna. 'I thought they were just some kind of environmental group like Greenpeace.'

Fabel laughed. 'Nothing like. I'm a member of Greenpeace but you wouldn't get me within a mile of the Pharos Project. It started out legitimately enough but it looks like it may well now be a manipulative cult.'

'I'll check it out,' said Anna, grinning at Werner. 'At least I can spell it.'

'Anything else I should know about before I go out?' asked Fabel.

'Just that we've got a potential homicide in the Schanzenviertel. We're waiting to hear if the guy pulls through. Poor bastard has sixty per cent burns.'

'What happened?'

'One of these car torchings went wrong.'

'A car torching?' Fabel's mood darkened as he thought back to his conversation of the previous day with Menke, the BfV man. 'And you say someone might die?'

'The owner came running out when he saw his car on fire,' said Werner, 'but the attackers had dumped containers full of kerosene inside. They ignited when the poor schmuck was beside the car. Human-torch stuff, from what I can gather.'

'Great,' said Fabel. 'I can guess why Criminal Director van Heiden was on the phone first thing. I'd better get back to him. I'll see you back here about one-thirty and we can brief in the raids on these addresses.'

After Werner and Anna were gone, Fabel took the list of addresses Anna had given him and contacted the Presidium control room to have resources allocated to each raid. Fabel explained there would be at least two Murder Commission detectives at each address, and asked that they have a couple of uniforms from each local police station as support.

Van Heiden took Fabel's call right away. It was exactly as Fabel had thought: the Criminal Director's reaction to the news about the car-burning. Fabel sensed that his boss was taking a little pleasure from reminding everyone about how prescient he had been about 'someone going to end up dead'.

Of course, the main thrust of the conversation was to remind Fabel how important it was, if the victim died, that the perpetrators were caught quickly. Fabel could never understand why van Heiden felt the need to emphasise the importance of a particular case: as if Fabel did not regard the taking of a human life seriously unless it was given management-team emphasis. For Fabel, the act of murder was emphatic enough, no matter who the victim was.

'There's perhaps more to this than meets the eye, Fabel,' said van Heiden. 'And another reason to give this case some priority. The victim, the owner of the Mercedes, is one Daniel Föttinger. He's a very important figure in environmental technologies. So much so that he is one of the organisers of the GlobalConcern Hamburg summit.'

'So you think this is political?' asked Fabel. 'That he was deliberately targeted and this is attempted murder?'

'It could be. At the very least, I don't like the coincidence. I think this is where your special talents may come into play. And if we can prove aforethought, which may be difficult, then I doubt it will be *attempted* murder.'

'He doesn't look good?'

'According to the hospital, he'll be lucky to make it through the next twenty-four hours.'

After he had hung up, Fabel did a search in his computer for Daniel Föttinger. As he went through the results he felt his unease grow. Fabel desperately wanted this not to be another homicide, attempted or not. The Commission was stretched as it was with the Network Killer case. Then there was the torso found at the Fischmarkt and its possible connection to the woman Müller-Voigt claimed had disappeared. But the more he read about Föttinger Environmental Technologies and its chief executive and principal shareholder,

Daniel Föttinger, the less convinced he was that the arson attack had been random.

There was something else that troubled Fabel: there were several photographs of Föttinger and Berthold Müller-Voigt at various functions, looking particularly chummy. But, there again, Fabel told himself, it was no surprise that Hamburg's Environment Senator and a leading light in environmental technologies should have frequently crossed paths; especially when Föttinger was an organiser of the GlobalConcern Hamburg summit.

But it still did nothing to lessen the gut feeling he had about it. A *bad* gut feeling.

Fabel drove out to the address Müller-Voigt had given him for Meliha. It was in a 1960s apartment block with galleries looking out over the trees and the small lake of the Wandsee. Fabel found the apartment on the third floor and, as Müller-Voigt had said, the windows were shuttered. He knocked at the door of the next apartment and a small woman in her forties with dark roots to her unnaturally butter-coloured hair answered. She eyed Fabel suspiciously and muttered something about not buying anything at the door before he showed her his police ID. Her expression shifted from suspicious and hostile to just plain hostile.

'I'm looking for the lady who lives next door. Meliha Yazar. Do you know where or when I would be able to find her?'

'There was already someone here a few days ago,

asking the same thing. He wasn't a policeman, though. I'll tell you what I told him: that apartment hasn't been occupied for a couple of months. And it was a family – a *German* family – who lived there.'

'Who's the landlord here?' asked Fabel.

'This block is all public. No private landlord here. Just the City and State of Hamburg, mister.'

Fabel thanked the woman and left. On the way back down to the car he called in to the Presidium and asked Henk Hermann to get in touch with the City and get hold of the rental records for the address.

He had just got back to the car when the phone rang. He saw it was the Murder Commission.

'Hi, Henk, that was quick—'

'*Chef*, it's Anna. You better get back here. It looks like the Network Killer has chalked up another one. A female body dumped in a city waterway. Werner's already out at the locus.'

'*Shit . . .*' said Fabel. He looked at his watch. 'You'll have to do the briefings for the raids this afternoon yourself. I'll meet Werner at the scene. Where was the victim discovered?'

Anna paused before answering. Fabel could have sworn he heard her take a deep breath.

'You're not going to believe this, *Chef*,' she said at last. 'Werner's up in Poppenbüttel. The Network Killer dumped his latest victim in the Alster canal lock at the Poppenbütteler Schleuse.'

CHAPTER 16

As he had been ordered, Niels had not gone back to the squat.

After the firebomb attack on the Mercedes, Harald had sped through the city on the stolen motorbike, ignoring Niels's demands to slow down: going too fast could attract the attention of the police. But Niels knew that Harald was panicked, and that made him a liability. He had ignored Niels's screaming in his ear to pull over until Niels had jabbed the muzzle of the automatic into his cheek. Once they were stopped, Niels had told Harald to ride slowly down to the river, making sure he did nothing to cause the police to pull them over. The original plan had been to ride out of the city and to dump the bike in woodland, setting fire to it to destroy any forensic evidence. But Niels had worked out that the police would soon have an alert out with a description of two men on a motorbike, so he had ordered Harald to head down to the docks, to a quieter section of waterfront, where a stone pier jutted out into the Elbe.

When Harald had dismounted and ripped the

151

helmet from his head, he had thrown it down onto the concrete of the pier with such force that it had bounced.

'He's dead!' Harald had screamed at Niels. 'I mean, he's fucking *dead*. They'll send us down for life for this, Niels. And where did that fucking gun come from? Were you going to kill the guy anyway?'

Niels had not answered. Instead, he had looked around, at the pier, at the cobbled road leading to it, at the city behind it. He had been here before, doing exactly the same thing. And when he had been here before, he had had exactly the same feeling. In fact, Niels knew he had been here many thousands of times. But he also knew that he had never been here before.

Still without answering Harald, Niels had wheeled the motorcycle to the end of the pier. Tipping it over the edge, he had watched it sink into the dark water. He had then taken the helmet from his head and had swung his arm as hard as he could, like a discus thrower, sending it hurtling as far out into the river as he could manage. He had repeated the action with Harald's scuffed helmet, which he had picked up from the ground. This time the effort had wrenched his shoulder and he'd cursed as pain stabbed deep into the muscles. He knew the helmets would float, but hoped that they would drift midstream, perhaps never being found.

'If we get caught I'm going to tell them I knew

fuck-all about the gun. Or that he was meant to be killed.' Harald had shaken his head emphatically. 'That's all down to you Niels. I joined the Guardians to protect the planet, not to murder people.'

Niels had returned to watching where the motorbike had sunk into the Elbe. The water would only be two or three metres deep, but it was dark enough to conceal the bike. When he had turned back, it had been as if he had not heard, or had not been listening to, what Harald had just said. Niels had stared at Harald and tried to work out who and what he was. The very moment that the Mercedes's owner had burst into flames, an epiphany had burst with equal violence in Niels's brain. Now he understood the truth about everything. He had been shown in an instant that the environment he cared so deeply about was, in truth, some kind of projection of another, distant reality; and that it wasn't Niels who had the disability. He realised that it was absolutely everyone else who did not experience the universe as Niels did. They were the deluded ones, not him.

Harald had looked stunned when Niels had pointed the gun at him and told him to stand at the end of the pier, at exactly the same point from which Niels had just pushed the motorbike into the water. It was evidence in itself, Niels had thought, that Harald did not exist, or at least did not exist in any *real* sense. He was bound to have known what was going to happen to him, standing there at the end of the pier, yet he had made no move to resist.

Niels had heard himself laugh again. He had never used a gun before so the first three shots had completely missed Harald, who now cowered and cried like a child. Niels had sighed and walked up to Harald and had pointed the gun at his head from less than a metre's distance. Then he had fired four times into Harald's skull.

Niels had stood and watched as Harald's crouched body toppled backwards off the pier and into the Elbe. He'd sighed as he'd watched the dead ecoterrorist float away, a plume of dark crimson from his head blooming in the murky water: it had been a waste of effort throwing the helmets so far out and wrenching his shoulder. There was clearly a current here close to the pier that would have swept them upstream.

That was the thing about this false reality: you could never count on the logic of its physics.

CHAPTER 17

Poppenbüttel lay to the north of the city
centre in the Alstertal district of Wandsbek
and marked the border between Hamburg
and Schleswig-Holstein. This was yet another
place that, at various stages of its career, had been
German or Danish. It was now one of the less
densely populated parts of Hamburg where the
city landscape was broken up by large green spaces
of park and woodland. The Poppenbütteler
Schleuse had, for two hundred years, provided the
city with two services: its primary function, as part
of an integrated system of sluices and locks, had
always been to control the flow of the Alster river
into the centre of Hamburg, ensuring a constant
water level in the city. But people knew it best for
its secondary role: behind the sluice gates of the
Poppenbütteler Schleuse, something between a
deep pond and a small lake had formed; almost
a miniature version of the Small, Outer and Inner
Alster lakes in the city centre. Each weekend and
on holidays, people would swim or hire a boat
to take out onto the lock pond's placid water. It
was sheltered by a thick curtain of trees, and

155

green-cocooned by the Henneberg Park. It was, Fabel reflected as he parked his car, the ideal place to dump a body: conveniently within the city and connected to a network of roads, yet offering seclusion.

By the time Fabel got there the uniformed branch had sealed off the scene with tape, but Holger Brauner and his team had not yet arrived to set up a forensics tent. Fabel parked off Saseler Damm, next to a canoe-hire stall. As he walked along the water's edge he passed a couple of uniforms talking in calm tones to a pale-faced middle-aged man who clutched a fishing rod as though it was a lifeline.

Werner Meyer was waiting for Fabel on the towpath beside the lake. Behind him, twenty metres along the path, the naked body of a young woman lay face down. Her head was turned to one side and her wet hair streaked across her face. Unlike the torso washed up by the storm, this was a body you would have had to take a close look at to ascertain that she was in fact dead. If it hadn't been for the inclement weather, you could have mistaken her for a sunbather.

'I take it our chum with the rod found her?'

'Yep,' said Werner. 'Where have you been? I was trying to get you on your cellphone. I couldn't get through.'

'Really?' Fabel frowned. 'I had it on all morning. Who fished her out?'

'A couple of local uniforms. The guy fishing

called it in with his cellphone. The uniforms thought she might have been a suicide but then they saw the marks on her neck and throat. And, of course, the Network Killer is pretty much front of mind.'

'Let's have a look.' Fabel took the latex gloves that Werner handed him and snapped them on. They lifted the barrier tape and stepped through. Squatting down beside the body, Fabel eased the wet strands of dark hair from the face. She was about thirty, Fabel reckoned, and looked like she had kept herself in good physical shape. He examined her hands, starting at the fingernails, checking the fingers for breaks and the palms, backs and wrists for abrasions. Nothing. From what he could see, there was no evidence of any defensive injuries. Just like the others.

Fabel rolled the body onto its back. Gently, as if he was afraid to hurt someone who was clearly far beyond hurting. Her skin was bright and pale against the wet asphalt of the towpath. He again eased back a wet cable of hair from the face. Her eyes were closed and her lips, faintly blue-tinged, were parted. She had been pretty in life. Fabel eased back her eyelids: the white of the eyes were red with ruptured blood vessels – petechial haemorrhages, a sure sign of strangulation. He examined her face and worked his way down to her neck. There was another petechial haemorrhage, this time a diamond of livid skin on her throat, just above the jugular notch where her collarbones came together to meet her sternum. He could see that there was only a little bruising on her neck, where her killer had gripped with his fingers before digging his thumbs in to crush her larynx. The bruising was limited, Fabel reckoned, because death had been quick and she hadn't had time to bruise.

'He does it clean, I'll give him that,' Fabel said to Werner, straightening himself up. 'He leaves us nothing to go on.'

'Except he looks like he's playing games now,' said Werner. 'And that's what will get him caught. These nut-jobs always end up doing stuff like that. It's like they *want* to get caught.'

'What are you talking about, Werner?'

'Well, I'd say it was pretty obvious that he's trying to open up communication. That text, I mean. The one you asked me and Anna about. That must have been him.'

'But why now? Why does he suddenly change his pattern? He's never tipped us off before. Anyway, the weird thing about that was that the message seemed to come from Susanne's number.'

Fabel took out his cellphone and flipped it open. 'See?' he said and scrolled through his text messages. 'Wait a minute, I'll get it . . .' He frowned.

'What's up, Jan?' asked Werner.

'The damnedest thing—'

'Oh, shit . . .' Werner interrupted Fabel's thought by tapping him on the arm with the back of his

158

hand and nodding in the direction they had come along the towpath. Fabel turned to see Horst van Heiden striding purposefully towards them.

'God,' muttered Fabel. 'How did he manage to get here even before the forensics team? He must have an always-on line to the ops room.' He pulled a fake smile over his irritation and nodded a greeting as van Heiden drew near. 'Herr Criminal Director, it's not often we see you at a scene of crime.'

'Do we have a name?' asked van Heiden, nodding to the figure lying on the towpath.

'We don't even have any clothes, far less ID. It will take time to get a name for her.'

'But she's a victim of this maniac who uses the internet?'

'Again, I can't confirm that yet, but yes, my guess is that there's a high probability that she is. The MO in dumping the body in an inner-city waterway fits.'

'And, of course, he sent you that cryptic warning about where to find the body. I have to say, Fabel, it's a pity you didn't realise it was an advance notice of where the next body would be dumped. Not that I blame you . . . no one would have guessed.'

'How did you . . . ?'

'I spoke to Frau Wolff.' Van Heiden looked at the body again and frowned.

'I take it you didn't come down here to check up on my scene-of-crime skills?' asked Fabel.

'Quite,' said van Heiden 'We've got to get this lunatic, Fabel. I hear you're going to execute those search-and-seizure warrants this afternoon.'

'Well, Anna is. I'm going to have to oversee things here. We won't be able to hold anyone, but the warrants mean we can get their computers into Kroeger's department. We might just get lucky. I'm also going to give my cellphone to Kroeger.'

'So he can trace who sent you the text?' asked van Heiden.

'Not quite . . .' Fabel sighed. 'I can't find the text any more. I think I may have deleted it. Accidentally. But I don't see how.'

'I see . . .' said van Heiden. It was a habit of van Heiden's to drop an elliptical *I see* into conversations with his officers. It was up to you to interpret what lay in the ellipsis: *I see . . . that I've got the wrong man for the job; I see . . . that you've really screwed up this time.*

'And we're just assuming that the text is significant,' said Fabel. 'It could be a pure coincidence.'

Van Heiden gave Fabel a look: the kind of look he would have given someone who walked into the Presidium and claimed to have been abducted by aliens.

'Okay,' said Fabel. 'It would be a hell of a coincidence. I'll get Kroeger onto it. You said you were looking for me this morning . . . why?'

'It was just that, after our discussion this morning, I thought that I should update you on

160

that car-burning attack in the Schanzenviertel. I've just had word that Föttinger died during the night. So we've got an unlawful killing, Fabel, which makes it your baby. But we may have a real job pursuing it as homicide, given that Föttinger was inside the café when the arson attack was carried out. He came out to the fire that killed him.'

'That was maybe part of the plan – to set light to the car to draw him out into the street,' said Fabel. 'But I'm guessing that that's not the only the reason you came all the way down here to see me.'

'No – or, at least, not entirely. I wanted to ask you if Berthold Müller-Voigt said anything to you when you left the meeting together yesterday.'

'What do you mean? Why?'

Van Heiden placed a hand on Fabel's elbow and steered him a few steps further up the towpath, away from the crime scene and out of Werner's hearing.

'Listen, Jan. You know the rumours about Müller-Voigt's past. The press accusations about his possible involvement with extreme leftist terrorists in the early eighties.'

'I don't think he had anything to do with that. I believe his involvement was never anything than purely political,' said Fabel. He didn't want to tell van Heiden that he had delved deeply into the politician's past as part of the investigation that had first brought him into contact with Müller-Voigt.

'Whether he had or not, I am uncomfortable with some of the information I have to share with him as part of the GlobalConcern Hamburg security committee. Whatever his background, Müller-Voigt is a conniving, manipulative swine. I know that you and he have had dealings in the past – I was just concerned that he was perhaps trying to get information out of you.'

'Information about what?'

'I don't really know. All I do know is that, before you arrived, Müller-Voigt had been very persistent with Menke. He kept asking him about what extreme environmental groups the BfV were watching. Naturally, given Müller-Voigt's *colourful* history, Menke wasn't keen to share anything more than he had to.'

'But Müller-Voigt is a senior member of the Hamburg government,' said Fabel. 'Whatever he was or wasn't in the past, he is an elected and appointed public official. I would have thought we should be cooperating as much as possible.'

'Of course . . .' Van Heiden looked a little taken aback. 'Of course we are cooperating. But Müller-Voigt's questions were . . . I don't know . . . they were irrelevant.'

'Well, I can promise you that Müller-Voigt didn't discuss anything like that with me in the lift. I got out at the Murder Commission, so we didn't get a chance to talk much.'

'Right . . .' said van Heiden absently, rubbing his chin for a moment. 'Right . . . I just wanted to ask. Müller-Voigt can be quite the slippery customer.'

Fabel didn't know why he hadn't told van Heiden what had really passed between him and Müller-Voigt. He just felt he had to keep it to himself, at least for the moment. He had, after all, promised the politician to keep everything unofficial and strictly to himself.

After van Heiden had left, Fabel supervised the management of the crime scene as he had before with so many crime scenes over the years. Holger Brauner arrived with his team and with his usual inappropriate good cheer examined the body, Tesa-taped anything extraneous on the victim's skin, placed numbered tent cards, took photographs, zippered the remains of the young woman in black vinyl and removed her from the scene. The uniformed police kept the growing crowd of rubberneckers at bay. Thomas Glasmacher and Dirk Hechtner turned up at the scene, took statements from the fisherman and started a door-to-door in the immediate area.

It was the carefully rehearsed choreography of the beginning of a new murder enquiry. And Fabel directed the dance in the faint grey drizzle. No horror this time; no dismemberment or stench of putrefaction. Just the sadness of a young life lost.

Another thing Fabel had never learned to get used to.

CHAPTER 18

Fabel made it back to the Presidium just in time to catch the start of Anna Wolff's briefing. He and Werner had left Glasmacher and Hechtner dealing with the follow-up at the crime scene.

Henk Hermann was also just on his way into the briefing room.

'Hi, *Chef*,' he said as he saw Fabel approach. 'I checked out that address with the housing authority. There's no record of any Meliha Yazar as a tenant and it's only been vacant a month. If she exists, she was never there.'

'She exists, all right,' said Fabel. 'And that means she has to have lived *somewhere*. Thanks, anyway, Henk.'

'By the way, you know that wash-up on the Fischmarkt . . . the torso?'

'What about it?'

'I didn't know Schleswig-Holstein have an interest in it too,' said Henk. 'What's their involvement?'

'Henk,' said Fabel impatiently, looking through the open door to the conference room, which was already filling with officers, 'I don't have the slightest clue what you're talking about.'

'There was someone from the Polizei Schleswig-Holstein – Kiel division, I think – up at the mortuary to look at the Jane Doe torso. A Commissar . . .' Henk frowned for a moment as he forced the name into his recall. 'A Commissar Höner, I think. He showed them his ID and said he'd cleared it with you.'

Fabel stared at Henk for a moment as he processed the information. 'Get a uniform unit up there right now to get a description or better still a shot from CCTV. I gave no one the okay to view the body, Schleswig-Holstein or not.'

When Fabel walked into the Murder Commission briefing room it was packed with uniforms and detectives and Anna had started to match teams with addresses.

'I thought you could do with an extra couple of bodies,' Fabel said to Anna. 'Your show, though.' He turned to address the rest of the room. 'Just to let you all know that the ante's been upped. We have just found another body. This one really does look like it's the Network Killer's work.'

A collective groan.

'Okay, okay . . .' said Anna over the voices. 'Listen up. If we've got another vic then it means we're going to be under even more pressure to get this guy. We're working on four addresses specifically. These aren't the ones we had originally planned to hit . . .'

'Oh?' interrupted Fabel.

'Chief Commissar Kroeger's been back in touch,' explained Anna. 'His team are still working on the victims' computers and cellphones, but they've been able to recover some partial exchanges with four males common to them all. And all on one website. Well, more than a website . . .'

'What do you mean?'

'You know, these weird sites where people have a kind of alternative existence. A virtual life, really. Run a farm without the smell, build a business empire in a fictional world, that kind of crap.'

'I know of them, yes,' said Fabel. He knew of them but couldn't understand them; why people would want to waste so much of their time living in a fiction.

'Well, this one is called *Virtual Dimension*. It's part social networking site and part real-time virtual-life site. It claims to "consolidate realities".'

'What the hell does that mean? Why can't these people speak plain German?'

Anna gave a don't-shoot-the-messenger shrug. 'According to the *Virtual Dimension* site, it deliberately merges this wacky virtual world with the real world. How it does that, I don't know. It all sounds pretty flaky to me. Anyway, at least two of the women have interacted with a number of men, if they are men in real life, on *Virtual Dimension*. And of these men, four have had

166

chatroom conversations elsewhere with one of the other victims.'

'Mmm . . .' Fabel nodded thoughtfully. 'It sounds promising.'

'Oh.' Something had clearly just occurred to Anna. 'Talking about virtual realities, that river cop we met down at the wash-up scene was looking for you.'

'Kreysig?'

'No, the other one, his deputy. Tramberger. He's been in touch asking if we still want him to run the data through his "virtual Elbe" computer model.'

'It can't do any harm. Could you check with Holger Brauner and get the weight of the body plus a ballpark on how long it was in the water? Send that off to Tramberger and see if he can do anything with it.'

'That'll keep him happy. He's very proud of his toy. Funny, he doesn't strike me as the computer type.'

'Who isn't, these days? Anything else?'

'Yeah. I made a few enquiries about the Pharos Project and I've got people coming back to me. But I've had my hands full with organising these raids. You say you're happy to take one?'

'Sure. What have you got?'

Anna handed Fabel a file and a warrant from the State Prosecutor's Office. 'It's an address out Billstedt way. Between Horn and Schiffbek. The IP address belongs to a Johann Reisch.'

'Because he pays the bills, it doesn't mean he's the only person using the computer.'

Anna shook her head. 'According to the census, Johann Reisch, forty-five, is the sole occupier at this address. And this . . .' she handed Fabel a printout of a web page, '. . . is Herr Reisch's online persona.' Fabel looked at the picture. A young man two decades away from his forty-fifth birthday, wearing sunglasses and with his muscled torso summer-shirtless, smiled at the camera under a foreign sun. The information on the page gave the name *Thorsten66*. 'You happy to take this one?'

'Okay,' Fabel took the paperwork from her. 'This is your show . . . *Chefin*.'

Schiffbek lay to the east of the city centre. The address Anna had given Fabel and Werner was in an immaculate street of terraced houses near the cemetery.

Fabel parked at the end of the street, having ordered the marked police car to pull in behind him: there was no point in giving advance warning of their presence. The two uniforms followed Fabel and Werner up the street towards the house. As they approached, Fabel noticed that the tiny garden at the front was neat but had the minimum of plantings in it, as if to keep it as easy to maintain as possible. He also noticed that a ramp ran up the side of the steps.

Werner rang the doorbell. A short woman with spiky blonde hair and glasses answered. She had a name badge pinned to the protective tabard apron over her clothes; it was a Hamburg State ID that told Fabel that she was an accredited care worker. She looked from Fabel to Werner and then to the uniformed officers behind them with a distinct lack of interest.

'Yes?'

'Polizei Hamburg,' said Fabel. 'We have a warrant to enter these premises and interview Herr Johann Reisch.'

'Herr Reisch?' She frowned. 'What on earth can you want with Herr Reisch?'

'I take it you're not Frau Reisch?' Fabel said, looking at the ID badge.

The woman laughed. 'There is no Frau Reisch. There hasn't been for years. Cleared off. I think you better come in.'

She led them into the house and along a short, bright hallway and into a living room with French windows that opened up onto a small patio at the rear of the house. A man sat behind a table that had a laptop computer sitting on it. He looked up slowly, his head moving stiffly. Fabel noticed that there was no expression of surprise or shock. No expression of any kind.

'Herr Reisch?' said Fabel. 'I am Principal Chief Commissar Fabel of the Hamburg Murder Commission. I have a warrant here to seize any computer equipment.'

'You can't take his computer,' the woman in the tabard protested. 'It's all he's got.'

169

'This warrant says I can.' Fabel held up the paperwork. 'Please stay out of this, or you could . . .' The sentence died on Fabel's lips. He noticed that Reisch was sitting in a motorised wheelchair, and that his head was held up by a neck brace. He returned Fabel's gaze with watery eyes and the same lack of expression.

'It's all he has . . .' The care worker continued to protest. 'It's his entire world.'

'Can he speak?' asked Fabel.

'Yes, I can speak,' said Reisch. His voice was thin and he seemed to gasp for breath between words. 'For now, anyway. But that will go soon, too. But I can speak and I *am* here. So you don't need to refer to me in the third person.'

'I'm sorry, Herr Reisch. Is this your only computer?'

'Yes. Why do you have to take it away? Frau Rössing's right, I'd be quite lost without it. There must be some kind of mistake . . .'

'No mistake, Herr Reisch. It's just that you're one of many people who have . . .' Fabel paused and turned to Werner, who nodded and steered Frau Rössing and the two uniformed officers out of the room. 'You have been in a chatroom and have interacted with two women who were subsequently murdered.'

'This Network Killer thing?' Reisch's speech remained punctuated by gasps, which robbed his question of any intonation of surprise or shock.

Fabel showed him the printout of *Thorsten66*. 'Is

this the . . .' Fabel struggled for the right word. '. . . the *persona* you use on the internet?'

'On that particular website, and a couple of others, yes.' Reisch paused. 'You must think me pathetic.'

'I don't make judgements like that, Herr Reisch. I can't begin to understand what it must be like to be in your situation. May I ask what has caused your condition?'

'Amyotrophic lateral sclerosis.' Again, small gasps between words. 'It's a form of motor neurone disease.'

'Is it treatable?'

'There are so few things doctors can tell you with any certainty, Herr Fabel, but I'm in the fortunate position to have been given some absolutes about my condition. It is one hundred per cent untreatable and one hundred per cent fatal. My neural system is shutting down, bit by bit, function by function. Within the next year I will be unable to speak any more. Six months after that I will no longer be able to swallow my own spit or breathe unaided. I will suffocate to death. And do you know the laugh? The sweet irony of it all? I will still be fully mentally alert. A healthy mind trapped in a decaying body.'

'I'm sorry,' said Fabel.

'Must you take my computer?' asked Reisch. 'I think you can understand that it means more to me than to most people. I spend hours on it each day. It's my only window on the world and I won't have it for much longer.'

'How do you operate it?' asked Fabel. 'I mean, given your condition?'

'I still have some movement in my hands, but not much. My computer is set up for voice recognition. I can control it by giving it spoken commands. Eventually, when I lose my ability to speak articulately, I will lose that too.'

Fabel looked down at the printout. Reisch's alter ego. Fantasy self.

'You're wondering why . . .' said Reisch. 'Why do I pretend to be young and healthy? It's simple: when I am on these sites, on the web, that's who I become. I picked that photograph because he looks a little like I did at that age. He has the insolent look to him that I had. Once.'

'I understand.'

'No, you don't. I'm not criticising you, but you can't even begin to understand. Not until you've spent a minute in this body.'

'You had contact with two of the four women who have been murdered. You even suggested meeting one of them. Why would you do that? *How* could you do that?'

Reisch made an odd rattling sound that took Fabel aback. Then he realised it was the disabled man's attempt at a laugh. 'I *did* meet with these women. I met with dozens of women. Sometimes partied all night. But not here. Not in the real world. When you read messages where we were arranging to meet, all of the venues are inside *Virtual Dimension*. It was all part of the fantasy.

Of course I know that I could never go out into the physical world and meet the women I talked to on the internet, but for as long as I was there, in that world, I believed anything was possible.'

'But you never asked any of them to come here? To visit you at home?'

'Never. Now you're proving that you don't understand. I exist in two universes. Distinct and separate. I would never bring them together.' Reisch paused again. A pause of short, shallow breaths. Listening to it gave Fabel a feeling of tightness in his chest.

'Do you know,' continued Reisch, 'that in the near future people like me will probably be plugged into a virtual world for as long as they wish? An alternate reality where they will be able to live a normal life.'

'But it wouldn't be real life,' said Fabel. 'I think I'd rather be disabled in the real world than live out some kind of fantasy surrounded by people who don't exist.'

'But that's the thing,' said Reisch. 'It wouldn't be like that. It would be populated by others like myself: all escaping whatever was wrong with them and interacting with each other. Real people in an unreal world. But, of course, that will be too late for me. But that's why I was signed into *Virtual Dimension*. It was as close as I could get to that type of alternate reality.'

'Does anyone else have access to your computer?' asked Fabel.

'No one.'

'What about Frau Rössing?'

'Never. It is password-protected. And I don't think Frau Rössing would know how to work one anyway. She's very old school.'

'I see,' said Fabel, and for a moment he did not know what to say next; what to do next. 'I'm sorry we disturbed you, Herr Reisch. I don't think it's necessary to take your computer away. But one of our technical experts may have to come out and have a look at it. There may be messages from these victims that have some relevance to our investigation.'

'I understand,' said Reisch, his voice still coming between breaths; still devoid of intonation. 'I will cooperate in any way. I just want to keep my computer.'

It was going to be a late night. Fabel tried to get Susanne first at her hotel and then on her cellphone but was put through to her answering service. He left a message, telling her she might have to take a taxi from the airport the following day. He frowned, pausing for a moment, then said, without really knowing why: 'That text message didn't come from work. Anyway, I think I've accidentally deleted it. I'm going to have to hand this phone in to have it checked. I'll phone you later to give you the number of the replacement.'

Glasmacher and Hechtner were back from the crime scene in Poppenbüttel and Fabel asked them to start writing up the report. He called Müller-Voigt at his home, but the politician was clearly out and again Fabel found himself talking to a machine.

'Hello, Herr Senator. I'm afraid I haven't had a lot of time to look into that matter we discussed last night. But she's definitely not at the address you gave, just like you said. I've made some other enquiries and I'll get back to you as soon as I have anything worth reporting.'

After he hung up, Fabel called Kroeger in the Cybercrime Unit and explained about the missing text on his cellphone; Kroeger said that his people would check it out if he sent it straight down. Fabel went to the canteen, first picking up a replacement cellphone from the technical division. He decided to sit and drink his coffee in the canteen: he was going to be at his desk for half the night and the idea of a few minutes outside his office appealed to him. He had not had any food since lunchtime but decided against taking the time now to eat; he'd grab something on the way home.

'Do you mind if I join you?'

Fabel looked up and was surprised to see Menke, the BfV officer standing there, holding a styrene cup of coffee and holding Fabel in a steady pale blue gaze from behind the rimless spectacles.

'No . . . no, not at all.' Fabel frowned. 'It's late for you to still be here, Herr Menke.'

'Yes.' The agent sat down opposite Fabel. 'I've

been in meetings all day with the chiefs of the MEK units.' Menke referred to the special-weapons and rapid-response wing of the Polizei Hamburg. 'You know, planning for GlobalConcern Hamburg.'

'I don't envy you,' said Fabel. 'I think there are more than a few nutters out there who are going to try to make the summit a spectacle to get themselves noticed.'

'You're right there,' said Menke emphatically. 'Lots of world press there to see it all. There will be mass protests and there will probably be further acts of violence such as the arson attack the other day. That was the thrust of my meetings with the MEK chiefs: to establish a strategy of containment.'

'Kettling?' said Fabel with genuine surprise. 'It wasn't legal in eighty-six and it's not legal now. I don't see Herr Steinbach giving his approval to that.' He referred to Hugo Steinbach, Hamburg's Police President.

Menke was silent for a moment, holding Fabel in his insipid blue gaze while he took a sip of his coffee. Expressionless. Fabel thought back to the man in the wheelchair whom he had interviewed earlier in the day. He idly wondered if Menke had the emotional version of Reisch's ailment.

'Of course I'm not talking about kettling,' said Menke eventually. 'We live in a highly sophisticated time, Herr Fabel. Technologically. That means we have certain advantages that we didn't have before. Our approach is more precision surgery than blunt-force trauma. When I say our strategy is containment, I mean we intend to isolate and excise those extremists who would hide themselves among genuine protesters. Our intelligence is good and getting better all the time. We don't intend to contain the fire, we intend to prevent its ignition.'

'I see,' said Fabel, swirling the dregs of his coffee and examining them. 'In other words, you've got people on the inside. Infiltrators.'

Menke approximated a smile. 'Like I said, we have very sophisticated technology at our disposal. But at the end of the day, intelligence is and always has been a matter of human agency.'

Fabel excused himself, explaining that he had to get back to the Commission. Another body had been found, bringing the total to four.

'What about the dismembered torso that Herr Müller-Voigt seemed so keen to discuss with you at our meeting? Have you definitely ruled that one out?'

'Not definitely. But it doesn't feel right,' Fabel said, standing up and draining his coffee. 'And murder investigation, like intelligence gathering, is a matter of human agency.'

'Have you seen the Senator today?' asked Menke.

'No. Why should I have?'

'No reason. It was just that he was supposed to be at our meeting today. In fact, it was exactly the kind of meeting I would have expected him to make a priority . . . he sees himself very much as the guardian of the people's right to protest and, to be frank, I don't think he trusts us that much. I'm very surprised he missed it. He sent us an email to say he couldn't make it.'

'Oh, I see,' said Fabel. He chose not to mention that he had met with Müller-Voigt the night before, nor that he had tried to phone him that afternoon without success. 'Well, I'll no doubt see you again soon, Herr Menke.'

Menke remained seated and stretched his lips in a perfunctory smile. 'No doubt, Herr Fabel.'

Fabel had already turned his back when Menke added: 'Oh, by the way – I understand that Commissar Wolff is gathering information on the Pharos Project . . .'

'Yes, she is.'

'May I ask why?'

'Because I asked her to.'

'And may I ask why you asked her to? Is this connected with these murders?'

Fabel sighed. He had not wanted the BfV man to know of his interest in Pharos until he had found out something more about Müller-Voigt's mysterious Meliha Yazar. But now that he did, there was no one better than Menke for Fabel to ask about it.

'I'm looking at a lot of things. It's just that the Pharos Project came up. I like to check everything out.'

'You could have come to me.'

'I intended to. My guess is that given the nature of the Pharos Project – I mean that it's generally accepted that it is a cult – I guessed that the Bureau has an interest in Pharos, that you have a file on the organisation.'

'Oh yes, we have an interest in Pharos . . .' Menke gave a sardonic laugh. 'We don't have a file on them. We have a full-time five-man team . . .'

Fabel pulled out the chair and sat down again.

CHAPTER 19

R oman Kraxner had spent two hours in *Virtual Dimension*. More than two hours. He was angry with himself for his lack of discipline. But something was not right. He hadn't seen Veronika534 for days and she had agreed the exact time they could meet by the Moon Pools at the far side of New Venice lagoons. There again, it was true that that happened all the time: people were suddenly sucked back into real life and sometimes never returned to *Virtual Dimension*. But Veronika534 had not seemed the type to skip out like that. There again, she had been spending a lot of time with Thorsten66; maybe they had hooked up in the real world.

The truth was that Roman was paranoid that the others he interacted with on *Virtual Dimension* would see through the façade: that he would do or say something that would reveal something of his reality. Roman was a conceited man: he was supremely confident in his intellectual abilities and looked down on the entirety of mankind as something inferior. But that was his mind. The part of him that connected with technology. As for the rest of his being, his physical presence, he knew that as far as everyone else was concerned he was just a fat loser. An obese computer geek who sweated and smelled and snorted and wheezed.

And that was what he was afraid of the others in *Virtual Dimension* seeing. There would never, ever be any real-world hook-up for Roman.

There had been a girl, once. In the real world. The only girl he had ever had a relationship with. Elena had been funny and very clever. Obviously not as clever as Roman, but very, very intelligent. They had met when she had brought her laptop back for repair. While he had worked on it, Roman had pried into every corner of her life, accessing all the personal information, the photographs, the online purchases she had made. It had revealed a person almost as lonely as he was. Somehow, without the mediation of any kind of technology, Roman had somewhere found the courage to ask her out. They had recognised a kinship in each other and they had seen each other for a few weeks.

But the truth, the cruel irony, was that Roman had found her physically repulsive. Because she, too, had been fat.

And if there was anything Roman found unappealing in a woman, it was too much weight.

He had put it from his mind. They clung to each other for companionship, and sex had never been something that either of them seemed to be interested in, so it made it easy for Roman to dispel his abhorrence of her fatness. That was until the night they had gone out to the cinema together. They usually met at the American fast-food bar that was roughly equidistant for their respective apartments, but that night they had arranged to see a film. A group of youths had spotted them and followed them, staying a few metres behind and laughing. Roaring with laughter and mocking them mercilessly, ceaselessly; making vulgar jokes and disgusting remarks about their size. The youths had tired of it eventually, but only after the damage had been done. After the film Roman and Elena had said goodbye and both knew they would never see each other again. It was obvious from the look that neither could keep from their gaze. A look of mutual disgust.

After that, Roman disengaged more and more from the real world. It had been about that time that he had given up the job in the computer store. He had despised the customers for their ignorance and stupidity and his attitude towards them had become increasingly hostile, so hostile there had been complaints; and, in any case, he was earning five times as much illegally in the evenings. If he quit his job, it meant he could spend even more time working on his fraudulent activities. It also removed the imperative to leave his flat every morning.

Roman looked at his profile page on *Virtual Dimension*. The fiction within a fiction. He had given himself an English name, Rick334, invented a completely false biography for himself, downloaded someone else's photographs from elsewhere on the web. Someone slim, handsome, blond. He had extended the fiction by basing his *Virtual Dimension* avatar on the stolen face and body. The rules were that you only allowed people to view your 'real' profile after you had known each other for some time within the virtual world of New Venice, the impossibly beautiful city at the heart of *Virtual Dimension's* fantasy universe. He had let Veronika534 see his profile and she had allowed him access to hers. They both lived in Hamburg, bringing the possibility of a real-life meeting close. Dangerously close, as far as Roman was concerned. Roman had worked out that it was no huge co-incidence that they shared the same home town: *Virtual Dimension* attracted people from around the world, but Roman had guessed that, to live up to its promise of 'consol-idation' of virtual and physical realities, it must analyse the geographical origins of your IP address, grouping people according to their real-world geography.

Of course, Roman could have circumvented this. He had a dozen ways of connecting with a region-non-specific IP address, and his illegal servers allowed him to hide behind other people's regis-tered details but, whenever he was on *Virtual Dimension*, he used the same, non-dynamic and geographically accurate IP address. It was, unbe-lievably, actually legal and registered to his real home address. He used it for *Virtual Dimension* and nothing else and, in a way, this allowed him to demonstrate a perfectly legal means of connecting with the internet that was free of any association with his fraudulent activities.

He pushed his heels against the floor and his massive bulk, supported in his custom-designed chair, glided weightlessly and settled in front of another monitor. He logged into his internet account through a telecom company in Buenos Aires, which took him to a secure online banking account in Hong Kong, which transferred euros from an account in London, which in turn were traded for dollars in New York. There were some minor difficulties, but nothing that took more than fifteen minutes to circumvent, by which time he was five thousand dollars richer. The account he had stolen from actually had a balance of more than six and a half million, and he could just as easily have emptied it as taken the humble sum of five thousand, but that was the way Roman operated. Investigators would realise that, if the transaction was fraudulent, then the account could as easily have been emptied. It therefore wouldn't make any sense to believe that it was fraud. They would spend months sorting through accounts to try to pin down what had happened to the five thousand. In the end they would decide they were spending more on the investigation than had been taken. It would be dropped and they would change the security settings and tighten their monitoring.

Roman would not hit that account again. He took a little, often, from many. Unconnected frauds that could only be linked to him if an investigator had full details of all of the unconnected accounts into which he deposited the money. And, of course, because he was working across national boundaries, it was often more than one agency, each with limited jurisdictions, that did the investigating.

Occasionally he would get a bad feeling; he would intuit that his pilfering was perhaps being seen as part of a larger-scale operation. So, every now and then, Roman would steal a second sum from the same account; a slightly larger sum to suggest a thief growing in confidence. Then, hacking into the bank or corporation's personnel files, he would deposit the graft into the account of some hapless accounting clerk. Roman never gave any thought to the personal suffering, the human injustice created by his actions. To Roman, these were not real people. They were pieces of information. An employee number and a bank account. Data floating like plankton in a cybernetic ocean.

Not real people. Not the real world.

He realised that a thread he had been following had unintentionally led him into the San Francisco headquarters of an environmental technology company. He withdrew as quickly as he could, covering his tracks as he did so. Roman never hit companies in the United States or in Russia. It was not that he had any affection for these nations, it was just that the American FBI was notoriously sophisticated – and tenacious – when it came to tracking down hackers and fraudsters. If you accidentally hacked into a company which supplied anything to the massive US military complex, then the FBI would come after you wherever you were in the world.

And the Russians . . . well, with the Russians you never knew who you were really stealing from and they had the best hacker talent of any country. Between them, the Americans and the Russians had the best cybercops and cybercrooks on the planet. It was best to stay well away from them.

He pulled out of the American company. After another fifteen minutes he had enriched himself by another six thousand. Euros this time, and from a British airline's pension fund.

Roman always moved his funds about, sometimes for months, redistributing them, consolidating them, then redistributing them again, before eventually placing small amounts into the various German bank accounts to which he had direct access. He was planning to build a new computer that would be faster than anything he had at present; probably faster and more powerful than anything any cybercop would have. He needed to transfer enough to his credit-card account to cover the purchase of two SATA-interface HyperDrive Fives. It was a much larger sum than he usually liked to transfer at any one time, but he needed the drives.

After he was finished he shut down his equipment, which took some time and was not something he always did. There was more risk of system problems on restart and, of course, it stopped him taking immediate action if one of the many possible law-enforcement agencies came knocking on his door. But he liked to let the hardware cool every now and then. And he always kept the electromagnet ready for use whenever needed.

He half shuffled, half waddled through to the kitchen and took a family-sized bag of snacks back through to the lounge, settling himself into the permanent depression his body had made on the sofa. He switched on the TV and watched an item where a woman wanting to go back to work had to get some old granny from Bavaria to teach the husband how to do the housework and keep their flat clean using environmentally friendly but traditional materials. Lemon juice, vinegar, that kind of stuff.

'Why?' snorted Roman contemptuously at the TV before muting the sound and picking up the cellphone from the coffee table.

He examined the phone. A good one. A Nokia 5800. Web-enabled, integrated satnav.

Roman didn't know why he had stolen it. He had been sitting in the café having lunch when she had come in and sat at the table next to him. He tried not to stare at her, but he couldn't help noticing how beautiful she was: dark hair, large dark eyes. Tall, slim, elegant. She was the kind of woman who would never give someone like Roman a second glance, unless it was a look of disgust. Yet she was exactly the kind of woman he desired; the *only* kind of woman he desired. The opposite of Elena.

But it wasn't her beauty that he remembered most. There had been something about the woman in the café – about the way she moved her eyes and the way she sat – that had disturbed him. He could have sworn she had been afraid. She had kept looking at the door of the café as if she was expecting someone to follow her in. Above all, it had been the way she had put the phone down on the table, placed her paper napkin over it and walked out, forgetting the phone was there. That was why he had taken the phone: not because she had forgotten it and he could return it to her, but because everything about her leaving it behind was fake. She hadn't forgotten it: she was leaving it somewhere she knew it would be stolen if found.

It was intriguing. She was intriguing. And, for a moment after she had left the café, Roman Kraxner, the obese, balding computer geek turned fraudster became his online persona of Rick334, private detective out of New Venice. After paying his bill he had squeezed his bulk past the table she'd been sitting at. He had pretended to drop the hand-held PDA he had been working on onto the table and, when he had picked it up, he had palmed the Nokia.

It was a subterfuge that had been totally

unnecessary. No one had been looking in his direction. It was one of the consolations for the fat or ugly: it was not just that people did not notice you; they made a real effort not to notice you.

Roman's curiosity had been stirred even more when he had got home and flicked through the contents of the phone. There were no contacts in the address lists and Roman got the idea that the phone had been purged shortly before being dumped. All previous destinations in the satnav had also been cleared. The text messages, too.

But one thing had been left untouched: the ringtone. And it was set for everything: incoming calls, text messages, alerts. 'Message in a Bottle' by The Police. When Roman had seen that he had known instantly that all his instincts about the woman in the café had been right. She *had* deliberately left the phone for him to find. Like a castaway tossing a bottle into the ocean, she had put something inside this phone. A message. All Roman had to do was find it.

Not that that would present a problem to Roman: the great thing about cellphones was that they were a convergent technology – a phone was a camera, an organiser, a web browser, an mp3 player. Unlike earlier models, this generation of mobile was more computer than phone and Roman had the software to retrieve the data that had been dumped.

It was then that things had become very interesting.

CHAPTER 20

Anna Wolff stood by the window of Fabel's office, looking out across the dark shapes of the trees in Winterhude Stadtpark. Outside, the light was fading but the sky, now clear of clouds, was a sheet of dark blue silk.

'That was a long coffee break . . .' She turned when Fabel came into the office.

'What's this? You our new time-and-motion monitor?' He sat down behind his desk. 'I've just had a very interesting chat with Fabian Menke of the BfV. About the Pharos Project.'

'That's what I wanted to talk to you about. That and what Technical Section have retrieved from the computers we seized this afternoon.' Anna tapped a document folder on Fabel's desk. 'Interim stuff. As we speak, geeks are burrowing deeper and deeper into silicon.' She imitated a small crawling animal, wrinkling her nose.

'Anything hopeful?'

'Absolutely nothing,' she sighed. 'It looks like these guys are clean. Weird, but clean. Of course, we *did* come up one computer short.'

'I couldn't take it away from him, Anna. If you

had been there . . .' Fabel frowned. 'Actually, no . . . if you'd been there you would have taken it. And probably confiscated his wheelchair, too.'

'We really do need to check it out,' said Anna. 'Even if he is physically unlikely to be a suspect, there may be something in his interactions with the victims that could give us something.'

'I'm well aware of that, Anna. I've arranged to send one of Kroeger's people around to Reisch's home to check the computer.' Fabel picked up the folder and flicked through the report inside. 'I guess we just have to keep plugging away. Hit the next bunch of IP addresses.'

'We could be at that for ever,' said Anna.

'It's all we've got,' said Fabel. He nodded to the chair opposite. 'Sit down, Anna.'

'I'm okay,' she said absently. 'I'd rather stand. I've been sitting all day and my leg stiffens up a bit.'

For a split second, Fabel found himself lost for words. Anna picked up on it.

'Jan,' she said. 'I'm fine. I wish we could stop dancing around this. It wasn't your fault.'

He stared at the report in front of him, more to avoid making eye contact with Anna than to study the file's contents.

'It was my fault,' he said. 'I was in command. Just like I was the night Paul was killed.'

'This is a dangerous business, Jan. I know that and Paul knew that. You can't legislate for every eventuality.'

'I dream about him all the time,' Fabel said in

a flat, quiet voice. 'Nearly every week or couple of weeks. Always the same dream. We're always in my father's study, up in my parent's house in Norddeich, and Paul talks to me. Not about anything important or significant. He just sits there and chats to me. But I know he's dead. He has the wound in his head and sometimes he explains that it's difficult for him to have an opinion or perspective on whatever it is we're talking about, because he's dead.'

'I thought all the dreams had stopped,' said Anna.

'That's what I tell Susanne. The official line. It's tough living with a psychologist. I don't know if she believes me, but that's what I tell her. The point is, I know that if I had done things differently Paul would be alive, Maria Klee wouldn't be in a mental hospital and you wouldn't have got shot.' He sighed. 'I'm sorry – can we drop it?'

'You're the boss.' Anna smiled at him. 'About the Pharos Project, if I show you mine will you show me yours?'

'Go ahead . . .' Fabel leaned back in his chair.

'I don't know why you wanted me to look into this for you, but I've been hearing some very dodgy things about Pharos. And – how you knew I won't ask – but there *is* a connection with the murders.'

Fabel looked stunned.

'You *did* ask me to look at this because there's some kind of connection?' asked Anna.

'No . . . no, not at all – like I told you, it's something unrelated.'

'Then it's quite some coincidence,' said Anna. 'It took a bit of unravelling, but Dominik Korn, who heads the Pharos Project, also heads the consortium that owns and operates *Virtual Dimension*, the simulated-reality game that all the victims were logged into. So why *were* you interested in Pharos?'

'A long shot . . . I thought there might be a link to the other body we found. The wash-up.' Fabel sighed. 'There's a woman who seems to have gone missing: Meliha Yazar. I think there may be a link to the Pharos Project. She might have been investigating them.'

'What have you got yourself into, Jan?' Anna left the window, came over to Fabel's desk and leaned on it, the concern in her expression genuine.

'Something I maybe shouldn't have,' he said, and meant it. 'I got talked into it by Berthold Müller-Voigt. This is strictly between us, Anna . . .'

She nodded.

'Müller-Voigt is involved with this woman . . .' began Fabel.

'And half the female population of Hamburg, from what I've heard,' said Anna.

'It's not like that. Müller-Voigt is nuts about this woman. And he is really concerned about her disappearance.' Fabel sketched out some of what had passed between him and the Environment Senator.

'You know,' said Anna when he was finished, 'I think I'd better sit down after all. You have no idea what I found out about Pharos. If Müller-Voigt's latest squeeze really was investigating them, then she could well have got out of her depth. The Pharos Project is the brainchild of Dominik Korn. Have you heard of him?'

'Not until Müller-Voigt mentioned him to me,' said Fabel.

'That's hardly surprising. Dominik Korn is one of the world's richest men – worth billions, as is his deputy, Peter Wiegand – but he's also one of the world's most reclusive men. No one outside Wiegand and his circle of closest advisers has had contact with him for years. Occasionally he will take part in video conferences with other key people in his business empire. He lives on a massive yacht. And I *mean* massive. It would make the average Russian oligarch feel inadequate.'

'Why is he so reclusive?'

'Apparently he had a diving accident that caused him to have some kind of cataclysmic stroke brought on by severe decompression sickness and other complications. He shouldn't be alive; it was a miracle that he survived it, but it's left him in the same kind of condition as the guy you interviewed earlier today. Since then he's needed round-the-clock care.'

'And he's also head of this cult?'

'Guru number one, apparently. He may sound like a nut-job, but he's said to be as rich in brains as he is in cash. His IQ is said to be off the scale. He studied . . .' Anna referred to her notebook '. . . oceanography, hydrology and environmental science in the United States – he has dual German and US citizenship, by the way – then did a doctoral thesis in hydrology, and then went on to become a hydrometeorologist.' She looked at her notes again. '*Studying the interaction between large bodies of water and the climate.* Korn became the world's leading expert on ecohydrology. That's what he was doing when he had his accident. He had designed this unique submersible for research work and was taking it on its maiden dive when it all went tits-up.'

'His accident?'

'And his epiphany, apparently.'

'Yes . . .' said Fabel. 'Müller-Voigt made mention of some kind of revelation at the bottom of the sea.'

'Right up until the accident, the Pharos Project had been an oceanographic research study. Korn had poured millions of his own money into it. It was examining the environmental impact of various human activities at the deepest ocean levels. Then, after his accident and the damage it did to him, Korn changed the nature of the Pharos Project. To start with it became a lobbying body, campaigning against oil exploration in deeper waters. It gained a lot of credibility after the BP thing in the Gulf of Mexico. Then Korn approved members of Pharos getting involved in protests and direct action. After that, about nine months after his accident, Korn started to talk about his epiphany and what it meant.'

'Which was?'

'All his adult life, Dominik Korn had positioned himself as a disciple of *deep ecology* – apparently that means he believed that human beings shouldn't see themselves as distinct from the ecosystem and that they should work to shape the environment sympathetically while preserving biodiversity, all that sort of stuff. But after his accident he totally rejected the concept of deep ecology and started spouting his theories of *disengagement*. He claimed his experience five thousand metres down had revealed some kind of universal truth to him.'

'Don't they all,' said Fabel. 'Going by the number of cults there are, there must be a hell of a lot of universal truths.'

'Well, Korn's particular revelation was that he had been damaged because he had been a human in an environment humans had no place being. The philosophy of the Pharos Project is that mankind should remove itself from the environment.' Anna shrugged. 'This *disengagement* he talks about.'

'Where did you get all this stuff?'

'The federal boys,' said Anna. 'I've got a contact there. An ex-boyfriend, actually. He was pretty cagey. He said this was a big thing for the BfV. The French security services and the American

FBI are all over the Pharos Project too, apparently. He doesn't know exactly what it is about it that's flipped their switches, but the Pharos Project is on all kinds of hot lists.'

'So I gather. Your sniffing around on my behalf was noticed.'

'Menke?'

'Yep. He knew all about your enquiries. Your ex-boyfriend was obviously so cagey that he felt he needed to cover his back.'

'So what did Menke tell you?' asked Anna.

'Less than you've told me, but enough for me to see that if Meliha Yazar had been snooping around Pharos, then Müller-Voigt might be right about her being in danger. Menke's promised to send me some information over later.'

'But?' Anna raised an eyebrow.

'But I think our interest is unwelcome. To be fair, I haven't confided in Menke about Müller-Voigt or his concerns about Meliha Yazar. Menke did tell me that the Pharos Project meets all the criteria of a destructive cult. Particularly its dictatorial control over its members. Menke wasn't too specific, but it seems it's the same old thing: conversion becomes indoctrination becomes brainwashing. He did say that Korn has added his own twists here and there. The other thing that distinguishes Pharos is its financial clout. The inner chamber of the Project are all board members of the various companies in the Korn business empire. And from what you've said, that includes the developers of *Virtual Dimension*.'

'Maybe we should make your unofficial snooping into Meliha Yazar an official investigation. If you think she might be the wash-up. We could get familial DNA . . .'

Fabel shook his head. 'It's not as straightforward as that . . . Anyway, I still think it might be a wild-goose chase.' He looked at his watch and saw it was eleven-thirty. 'It's late. I'm heading home. We'll pick this up in the morning.'

Fabel tried ringing Susanne's cellphone again as he came out of the elevator and crossed the Presidium's basement garage. He cursed when he once more got her answering service: he left a message, telling her that this was his temporary cell number and asking her to check in with him.

Fabel hadn't eaten since lunchtime and he didn't feel like cooking for himself so he decided to eat somewhere on the way home. Driving through the night-time city, his mind wandered and ranged over everything that had happened over the last forty-eight hours. Two bodies in the water. Two different MOs. He guessed that the press would be all over the second body by the morning and van Heiden would be on the phone to him again to state the obvious. But the strange thing was that his conversation of the night before with Müller-Voigt, and everything he had found out since about the Pharos Project, were what really haunted his thoughts.

It was only after Fabel stopped his BMW that he

realised what he had done. It had been as if he had been on autopilot. He had driven down to the harbour. He knew why he had done it and he felt a leaden sadness coalesce in his chest. He had been working late and had wanted to eat something on the way home so, as he had so many times before, he had driven down to the harbour to buy a beer and something hot to eat from Stellamanns' Schnell-Imbiss snack bar.

Dirk Stellamanns had run the harbourside snack stand since his retirement from the Polizei Hamburg. Like Fabel, Dirk was a Frisian by birth and, as the experienced officer, he had shown Fabel the ropes when he had first entered the service. He had taken him under his wing, and the two had only ever talked to each other in Frisian Low Saxon. Throughout the years, and despite Fabel's rise through the ranks, the two men had remained close. Then, after his retirement, Dirk had set up his immaculately kept snack stand – a caravan with a serving window and canopy and surrounded by parasol-topped waist-high tables – smack bang in the middle of what had been his old beat, in the shadow of the dockside cranes that loomed above it.

Fabel visited regularly to grab a beer and something to eat, particularly when something was troubling him. Seeing Dirk, and hearing his accent that was as broad and flat as the landscape they had both grown up in, had always cheered Fabel up. Stellamanns had been that kind of man: no matter what life had thrown at him, he always seemed to remain cheerily philosophical about it.

Fabel stepped out of his car, stood in an illuminated pool of cobbled road, and looked over to a vacant patch of scrub-land next to the dock road.

The summer before, on a particularly hot day, Dirk had been doing his best business of the season. He had built up a huge clientele of lorry drivers who would stop on their way into or out of the docks. He had been working over the stove when it happened: a massive heart attack that had killed him before he hit the caravan floor.

For those few minutes while his mind had been preoccupied with other things Dirk had still been alive in Fabel's subconscious, his snack stand still open for business as usual.

The world was changing around Fabel. And, like everyone else, he sometimes lost track of the changes. People he had thought of as constants, as always being there, suddenly were no longer there. It depressed and annoyed him that, for a moment, he had forgotten that Dirk had died. He had often done the same thing when he had thought of his childhood home in Norddeich; that his long-dead father was in fact still alive and sitting in his study, bent over some old map of the coast, his glasses perched precariously on the tip of his nose. It was what you did: you had an entire universe in your head, the one you grew up with, and it stayed there, unchanged.

'It's not here any more.'

Fabel turned, startled. The young woman had stepped out from nowhere and into the pool of light. He looked up and down the roadway but could see no sign of another parked car.

'I beg your pardon?'

'It's not here any more,' the young woman repeated. 'The snack stand.'

'Oh . . . yes. Yes, I know.'

'I was looking for it myself,' she said. For a moment Fabel wondered if she was a prostitute, even though this was not one of the regulated areas. But she was smartly dressed in a dark grey jacket-and-skirt business suit and court shoes, as if she worked in a bank or insurance company. She had neat, shortish blonde hair and regular features: attractive but not particularly memorable.

'It's not been here for a while,' said Fabel.

'Nor have I,' she said.

'Where are you parked?' asked Fabel. 'I didn't see . . .'

'Oh, over there . . .' She made a vague gesture with her hand, indicating further down the road towards the docks. 'Are you a policeman?'

'Why do you ask?'

'It's just that "*Where are you parked?*" is a very policeman kind of thing to ask. And the guy who ran the stand was an ex-policeman. He used to get a lot of his former colleagues as customers. And you don't look like a trucker.'

'I guess not. What brings you down here?'

'Like I said, I was looking for the Schnell-Imbiss myself. I was peckish.'

'It's a bit out of the way.'

'Nowhere is really out of the way. Did you know him well? The guy with the stall, I mean?'

'Very.'

'He was a nice man,' she said. 'He was very . . .' she struggled for the right word '. . . *avuncular*.'

Fabel realised he was feeling increasingly uneasy. There was something about the girl that disturbed him. It was almost as if she was flirting with him, but the lack of expression in her face made him think of Reisch, the man with the wheelchair and a terrifyingly clear view of his immediate future.

'I still don't really understand what you are doing here,' he said. He took out his police ID and flipped it open. 'If you don't mind, I'd like to see your card.'

'And if I do mind?'

'I'd still like to see it.'

'I don't understand why you're so concerned about me being here. I'm not the one who's living in the past, forgetting that their friend is dead.'

Fabel stiffened a little. 'Okay, let me see your ID card.'

'Certainly, officer.' She smiled, but it was an artifice, something done because it was expected. She reached into her shoulder bag and handed him her Personal Identification Card. It told Fabel that she was Julia Helling, from Eppendorf. 'I was just making conversation. Have I done something wrong?'

'No, Frau Helling. It's just that you should be more careful. This is a lonely spot at night and you shouldn't be here on your own.'

'I'm not on my own, am I? I have police protection. Or are you worried that I've made a date on the internet with the *Network Killer*?'

'Now that's a very odd thing to say.'

'Is it? It's just with your concern for my safety . . . he's very much in the news at the moment.' She sighed. 'Anyway, I won't disturb you any longer. Good night, Chief Commissar.'

'How do you know my rank?'

She shrugged. 'Your ID. It was on it. Good night. I hope you find somewhere to eat.'

Fabel watched as she walked off into the dark. Getting back into his BMW, he phoned the Police Presidium and gave the name and address in Eppendorf that the girl had given him. The control room told him the name and address checked out and she had no known record. Waiting for a moment before starting up, Fabel headed down towards the docks, in the direction she had taken, driving slowly to make sure she had got back to her car. It took him only three or four minutes to reach a dead end of closed dock gates.

No sign of her. And no car had passed him in the opposite direction.

CHAPTER 21

Fabel woke up with a start. He had been dreaming again and something in his dream had frightened him, but it ran away from his recall as soon as he awoke. He had the vague idea that the woman from the night before had figured in it.

It wasn't fully light and he switched on the bedside lamp; checking his watch, he saw it was just before six a.m. He reached over to the bedside cabinet, picked up the replacement cellphone and frowned. No call from Susanne. Not even a text to tell him which flight she would be coming back on.

He got up and showered, but still felt tired. Sluggish. He left the apartment early and called into a café for breakfast. It was somewhere he visited often enough to be recognised but not so frequently as to be considered a regular. It saved him the effort of making conversation at this time in the morning. It was quiet in the café; the only other customers were a couple who sat at a table at the back, away from the window. Both the man and woman were dressed in grey business suits and stared blankly at Fabel as he came in, before returning to the joyless consumption of their coffees.

For some reason he didn't quite understand, the café offered a choice of breakfasts, each named, in English for some reason, after a port city: *The Hamburg Breakfast, The Liverpool Breakfast, The Rotterdam Breakfast.* Fabel ordered the Rotterdam and was served with a Dutch style *Uitsmijter*: poached egg on a bed of ham, cheese and toast; served with a cup of industrial-strength coffee. He sat and pushed the food about on his plate for ten minutes, watching through the window as the faint drizzle fell without conviction on the Elbe. His cell-phone rang.

'What the hell's been going on?' Susanne said impatiently and without preliminaries.

'It's nice to talk to you, too,' said Fabel. 'I've been trying to reach you for days. Didn't you get my texts?'

'What texts? The only text I got from you was the one I picked up this morning, from your new phone. What's going on, Jan? What happened to your other phone?'

'It's been playing up. You know, the usual problems: signal failure, poor battery life, predicting by itself the location of the next victim of the Network Killer.'

'What?'

'The text I asked you about. Remember . . . *Poppenbütteler Schleuse* . . . I get the text and within a few hours a body is found floating in the Poppenbütteler Schleuse.'

'You're kidding . . .' Susanne said. 'Did you find out who really sent it?'

'This is where it gets good – the text has disappeared. Deleted itself somehow. That's why I've got this new phone. They're working on my old one to try to recover the message. You heading for Frankfurt airport?'

'Yeah . . . but my flight isn't till this afternoon. I'm going to do some shopping first. Can you pick me up?'

'Sure. When do you get in?'

She gave him the flight's scheduled arrival time. 'Listen, Jan,' she said, concern woven through her tone. 'You say you sent me some texts from that phone?'

'Yes. And a voicemail message.'

'I never got them. And, from what you are saying, you didn't get my messages either.'

'You left messages for me? No, I didn't get any.'

'But that doesn't make any sense. Voicemail messages aren't stored on your phone, they're stored on the network provider's service. Try retrieving them with your PIN from that phone. I don't like this, Jan. It's like someone's hijacked your phone. Cloned it or something.'

'I don't know, Susanne. That sounds pretty far-fetched. I've maybe deleted the messages myself by accident. Anyway, Technical Section will let me know soon enough.' He paused. 'I've missed you.'

'I've missed you, too,' said Susanne. There was still a thread of concern in her voice. 'See you at the airport.'

Leaving most of his Rotterdam Breakfast uneaten, Fabel paid and got back into his car. He felt jumpy after the too-strong coffee and, as he drove across town to the Presidium, he switched on his mp3 player to mellow his agitated mood. Lars Danielsson this time. Maybe, thought Fabel, he should have been born a Swede.

The music had the effect it usually had on him and by the time Fabel parked in the Presidium car park, despite the odd caffeine flutter, he felt able to face anything the day had to throw at him.

He could not have been more mistaken.

CHAPTER 22

As soon as he stepped out of the elevator, Fabel knew something was wrong.

He passed Anna walking in the opposite direction. She hesitated for a moment and her mouth moved to say something but she was cut off by van Heiden, who leaned out into the corridor behind her and called Fabel into the Murder Commission. Anna walked on, but not before firing Fabel a look so laden with warning that he felt a sudden sinking in his gut.

They were waiting for him in the Murder Commission's main office: van Heiden, the BfV man Fabian Menke, and Werner, who smiled at Fabel with something between sympathy, frustration and desperation. Whatever it was that had sunk in Fabel's gut when he had passed Anna sunk some more.

Over the years Fabel had become used to Criminal Director van Heiden's lugubrious greetings. He often felt that his superior was a man of very limited emotion. It seemed to Fabel that van Heiden had only two expressions: gloomily serious, and even more gloomily serious. His moroseness was usually prompted by unwelcome press or political intrusion into an investigation that was still in progress, or by some newspaper headline critical of the Polizei Hamburg. But this, Fabel knew, was something different. Whatever it was that now played across the Criminal Director's face, Fabel hadn't seen it before.

'Why do I have the feeling I've just arrived at a funeral, only to find out it's mine?' Fabel smiled at van Heiden and was reminded by his un-responsiveness that the Criminal Director's sense of humour was as limited as his emotional range. 'What's happened?'

'You had better come with us,' said van Heiden. 'You too, Senior Commissar Meyer.'

'Okay . . .' sighed Fabel as they made their way in the lift up to the fifth floor. 'Do I get some kind of clue?'

'It's Müller-Voigt—' started Werner, only to be silenced by a sharp look from van Heiden.

Fabel let his boss and the BfV man lead the way. The fifth floor of the Hamburg Police Presidium was somewhere, if you were of Fabel's rank or below, you were led. This was the management level of the Presidium and when Fabel realised they were headed for the Presidial Offices, his feeling of foreboding ratcheted up a notch or two. When they reached the reception area they were admitted immediately into the Police President's office.

Hugo Steinbach stepped around from behind a huge desk to meet Fabel and the others. Just as van Heiden could not be anything other than a policeman, Steinbach looked as though he should be anything but a policeman. Fabel had always felt the avuncular, habitually smiling Steinbach looked more like a provincial family doctor, or even a jovially hospitable rural hotel proprietor. But he was a policeman, through and through. Steinbach had entered the police as an ordinary beat patrolman and had worked his way up through every rank and every department. He prided himself on the fact that whenever he talked to one of his officers he knew exactly what it was like to do their job, to face whatever they had to face. That was even true of Fabel: Steinbach had been a lead detective in the Polizei Berlin's Murder Commission.

'Is this about my expense account?' Fabel said with a small, uncertain laugh.

'Sit down, please, Fabel,' said Steinbach with a gentleness that unnerved Fabel even more. He sat down, his unease now beginning to give way to anger.

Steinbach sat casually on the corner of his desk and picked up a file, which he examined briefly.

'Last night you rang into the Presidium for an ID check on a woman. Someone called Julia Helling.'

'Oh, yes . . . yes, I did. What about her?'

'And you confirmed to the officer on duty that she lived in Eppendorf. Why did you check out that particular name and address?'

'It was after I left the Presidium last night. I was

going to pick up something to eat and I forgot . . .' Fabel checked himself. It sounded insensitive to say the least that he had forgotten that his friend of twenty-odd years was dead. And, as he sat there feeling as if he was under interrogation, the fact itself seemed odd. '. . . I forgot that the place had closed. Then this woman sort of appeared out of nowhere. Her behaviour was, well, *odd*. I don't know why, but I got the feeling that she knew who I was.'

'What made you think that?' asked Steinbach.

'I don't know, exactly,' said Fabel honestly. 'There was just something about the things she said. She knew all about the guy who used to own the snack stand. And it was as if she knew that he had been a friend of mine.'

'Dirk Stellamanns?' asked Werner, frowning. Exactly the reaction Fabel had been concerned about. It did sound odd. Fabel nodded.

'So you asked this woman for her ID?' asked van Heiden.

'Yes. Will someone tell me what this is all about?'

'All in good time, Fabel.' Steinbach took the edge off it with a smile. 'I know this is all very unusual, but this is a very serious matter and we have to establish some of the facts and chronology of events. Could you describe this woman?'

Fabel outlined a description of the unremarkable, business-suited woman he had encountered down by the docks. As he did so, a thought struck him: the couple he had seen in the café that morning had been dressed in a very similar manner. He dismissed the thought. They all did look the same: corporate clones.

'You say she was blonde?' asked van Heiden. 'Not a brunette?'

'She was blonde. Like I said.'

'And you have had no previous contact with her, or with anyone else with the same name?' asked Steinbach.

'No, I haven't. Why do I feel like a suspect all of a sudden? What is the significance of this woman?'

'Please bear with us, Fabel,' said Steinbach. He handed Fabel a photograph from the file. Fabel knew the picture had been taken in the Butenfeld mortuary, because he recognised the dead woman instantly.

'And this is not the woman?' asked Steinbach.

'Of course it isn't. You know it isn't. This is the woman we found at the Poppenbütteler Schleuse. How could it have been her? She was long cold and in the morgue last night. The woman I spoke to was very much alive.'

'We got an ID for her, Jan,' explained Werner. 'It came through this morning.' He nodded apprehensively towards the photograph in Fabel's hands. '*This* is Julia Henning. She lived at the address in Eppendorf you phoned in with.'

'*Shit*,' Fabel said in English. 'So the woman I met must have something to do with these killings.'

'That's not our main concern at the moment,

Fabel,' said van Heiden. 'We've had a report from Chief Commissar Kroeger and Technical Section about the phone you handed in. They say there is no trace of you having received a text message that said "Poppenbütteler Schleuse".'

'Like I said, it's been deleted somehow.'

'Herr Kroeger assures me that even if it had been deleted,' said van Heiden, 'his team would have been able to retrieve it. And they have checked the records of your service provider. Again, no trace.'

'You see where this leaves us, Chief Commissar,' said Steinbach. 'You seem to have had prior knowledge of where a victim was going to be found, then you radio in the victim's name and address before we have an identity for her.'

Fabel stared at Steinbach incredulously. 'You can't seriously be saying that these coincidences make me a suspect?'

'On their own, no . . .' Menke spoke for the first time. 'But they are not on their own. We talked at length yesterday evening about the Pharos Project, and you instructed Frau Wolff to gather as much information as possible on the organisation. This is a day after Senator Müller-Voigt quizzed me persistently on the same subject.'

'So?' Fabel resented the BfV man becoming involved; this was a police matter.

'I asked you where you had been the night before last,' cut in van Heiden. 'You evaded my question. Why did you do that, Fabel?'

'Quite frankly, Herr Criminal Director, what I do in my own time is none of your affair.' Fabel was beginning to feel outnumbered and exchanged a glance with Werner.

'Quite the contrary,' said van Heiden. 'If you are using your own time to meet and discuss police matters with a member of the Hamburg Senate without my knowledge, I feel that that is very much my business.'

'If you know where I was, then why did you ask me?'

'*Did* you visit Herr Müller-Voigt at his home the night before last?' asked Steinbach.

'Yes, I did. After we finished our meeting here in the Presidium, he asked me if I would come out to his home that evening.'

'Why?'

Fabel drew a long breath before launching into the story of Müller-Voigt's missing girlfriend, the Senator's belief that someone had deliberately erased all trace of her existence in Germany, his suspicions about the Pharos Project, and how Müller-Voigt had asked Fabel to make his enquiries 'unofficial'.

'So that's why both you and he quizzed me about Pharos,' asked Menke.

Fabel nodded. 'And the more I find out about it, the more I believe that there could be a connection to this woman's disappearance.'

'Since when did you have the licence to undertake private investigations, Fabel?' Something like a storm cloud darkened Van Heiden's expression. 'What the hell did you think you were doing agreeing to snoop around for Müller-Voigt?'

Fabel held his hands up. 'Let's get one thing straight: there's a limit to how *unofficial* my enquiries were. To start with, I told Müller-Voigt that there was no way I could spare the time, but then I realised that there's a good chance that the torso that was washed up at the Fischmarkt is that of Meliha Yazar. And *that* was the only reason I agreed to look into it. And I have to say that Senator Müller-Voigt accepts that I cannot guarantee to keep his name out of the spotlight. To be honest, all he is interested in is finding out what has happened to this woman.'

There was a pause and an exchange of looks between Steinbach, van Heiden and Werner. Fabel made an exasperated face.

'Müller-Voigt is dead, Jan,' said Werner. 'He was found by his cleaner in his living room first thing this morning. That's where Anna was headed when you came in.'

Fabel sat stunned for a moment. Then, as if a current had been switched on, he stood up suddenly. 'I'm going out there . . .'

'That would be inadvisable, Fabel,' said Steinbach. 'You can see that yourself, given the circumstances.'

'You can't seriously be suggesting that I am a suspect?'

'No one is suggesting that,' said van Heiden in a vaguely offended tone that still did not convince

Fabel. 'But you are *compromised* as far as both of these murder investigations are concerned. You simply cannot be seen to be heading up an enquiry in which you feature. You must understand that.'

'So what happens? Am I suspended?'

'Of course not,' said Steinbach.

'Then I insist on leading the Müller-Voigt case.' Fabel still could not believe he was referring to the man he had sat and talked with just two nights before as a case. 'That *is* my job, after all. And I have a personal stake in this . . .'

'But that's exactly the point,' said van Heiden. 'It's precisely because of your personal involvement that we have to place the case in the hands of another officer.'

'I suggest we all head out to the crime scene,' said Menke. 'There's clearly more to this than meets the eye. And, in my opinion, Herr Fabel hasn't compromised himself: someone else has deliberately gone out of their way to remove him from the investigation.'

Fabel looked at Menke: he was surprised that the intelligence man had spoken up for him.

'I agree,' said Werner. 'This is all crap, the thing with the text messages and this woman with a victim's identity. It's all engineered to get Jan off the case. Unless you really believe that he *is* a suspect. In which case you can suspend me as well.'

Fabel shot Werner a warning look: Van Heiden, who now glowered at Werner, was by-the-book enough to take him up on his suggestion.

'You lead the investigation, Werner,' said Fabel. 'The Criminal Director is right. I'm too close to all of this.' He turned to van Heiden. 'But I still want to see the Müller-Voigt murder scene.'

Fabel sat in the back of the Mercedes that took them out to the Altes Land. Werner followed. Stuck in the back of the car next to Menke, watching a huge sky above a billiard-table landscape slide by, Fabel still felt more than a little like a suspect and found himself resenting the intelligence man's presence.

'What did Müller-Voigt say to you about this supposedly missing woman?' asked Menke.

Fabel remained quiet for a moment. Long enough to make the point that he resented Menke questioning him.

'If you don't mind me asking,' said Menke into the void.

Fabel sighed. 'She's not just supposed missing, she's a supposed woman. Müller-Voigt told me that he said that he could find no trace of her existence. He asked me to investigate because he felt that if he were to go through official channels he would look like he was losing his mind.'

'You do realise,' said Menke, 'that this all ties up. Your encounter with a woman who shows you identification that belongs to someone already dead, your problems with electronic messages disappearing.'

Van Heiden twisted around in the front seat,

edged his broad shoulders so he could turn to Menke. 'If you have some information we should know, Herr Menke,' he said, 'then I strongly suggest you share it with us.'

Menke shrugged. 'I was just making an observation, that's all.'

Holger Brauner and his team had been at the Müller-Voigt murder scene for some time and when Fabel entered the house with Menke, van Heiden and Werner, Anna Wolff was standing in the lounge, talking to a uniformed officer. She came over and spoke directly to Fabel, pointedly ignoring van Heiden.

'Müller-Voigt is over there . . .' She indicated the seating area where Fabel had talked with the politician two days earlier. Fabel could see a scattering of books and magazines on the floor next to the coffee table. Müller-Voigt's feet were just visible: he had obviously fallen between the sofa and the coffee table. There was an arc of blood spatter visible on the leather of the sofa. 'You want to see?'

Anna handed Fabel blue stretch overshoes and a pair of latex gloves but ignored van Heiden. The Criminal Director began to fume and Fabel shot Anna a warning look. She handed the Criminal Director a set. Anna was an officer of great ability and promise, but Fabel knew her very obvious problem with authority meant she would never be promoted much above her current rank. It frustrated him but somewhere deep inside he was heartened by these little displays: maybe her rebellion was not at an end after all.

'Signs of struggle?' asked Fabel as they approached the body.

'Minimal,' said Anna. 'It looks like he knew his attacker. There's no sign of forced entry and all this . . .' she indicated the scattered books and magazines '. . . could have been simply when he fell, or at the most after a very brief struggle.'

Fabel nodded a greeting to Holger Brauner. 'Can I have a look?'

'So long as you don't contaminate my crime scene,' said Brauner, with a grin.

Fabel looked down at Müller-Voigt's body and Müller-Voigt looked back at him with an unblinking stare and an expression of surprise. It was not really an expression, Fabel knew, just the slack-jawed stare of eased rigor mortis. One side of the politician's head, above the right temple, was badly deformed, as if dented, and the hair was parted by an ugly deep laceration where he had been hit with a heavy object. There was a halo of dark, thickly viscous blood around Müller-Voigt's head. Fabel felt something unpleasant flutter dark wings in his gut when he realised that Müller-Voigt was wearing the same clothes as he had been the last time Fabel had seen him.

'How long has he been dead, roughly?' Fabel asked Brauner.

'He's not fresh,' said the forensics chief. 'More than a day. Maybe two.'

Fabel tensed.

'What did you say?' asked van Heiden over Fabel's shoulder.

Brauner gave a small laugh and looked at Fabel quizzically before turning to van Heiden. 'I said the victim's been dead for more than a day. What's the problem?'

'I met with the victim the night before last,' explained Fabel in a dull voice. 'Here.'

'Ah . . .' Brauner said and frowned.

'Wait a minute.' Fabel turned to where Menke was standing. 'Didn't you say Müller-Voigt missed a meeting yesterday but got in touch to make his apologies?'

'Yes . . . that . . .' Menke said ponderously. 'The thing is, we don't have the email any more. Or, for the moment, any of our other emails. I'm afraid your concerns about email security were right, after all. You see, the message sent from Müller-Voigt's computer had corrupted our entire system. It would appear to have been infected with the Klabautermann Virus. And, of course, an email doesn't mean he was still alive. His killer could have sent it from his account.'

'Müller-Voigt told me that his computer had been infected,' said Fabel. 'But he had sent it off for cleaning and repair. He told me that the computer he had was new and clean. And that he was using a new account to send emails. So I'd say your infected emails didn't come from him.'

'Herr Meyer . . .' van Heiden called over to

Werner. 'I'd like you to take *sole* charge of this investigation.' He turned back to Fabel, 'I think you can understand, given the position we're in.'

'As far as I can see,' said Fabel, 'I'm the only one in a *position*.'

'You said you saw a picture of this mysterious missing woman when you were last here,' said van Heiden. 'Where is it?'

Fabel pointed to the digital picture frame. 'It's on that.'

Leaning over the sofa, Brauner reached and picked up the remote control, handing it to Fabel. Van Heiden took it instead, frowning at the images.

'These are all scenic photographs, as far as I can see,' said the Criminal Director.

'It's a digital picture frame,' said Fabel. 'It stores hundreds of photographs. May I?'

A new image appeared every time Fabel pressed the frame's button. Seascapes, lots of seascapes, some images of the countryside around the Altes Land, several littoral scenes, many with lighthouses. Nothing with Müller-Voigt in it. None of the other photographs he had seen when the politician had flicked through them. Before they had viewed half of the photographs, Fabel already knew that he would not find any photograph of Meliha Yazar.

'And you say that you definitely saw the woman Müller-Voigt said had gone missing on this thing?' asked van Heiden after they had gone through all the images.

'Without a doubt. Someone has deleted it. And a lot of other images.'

'Just like the text message you say you got about the location of the victim the other day.'

'Just like . . .' Fabel handed the digital frame back to Brauner. 'You'd better bag that up. Whoever did Müller-Voigt has been playing with his toys.'

Brauner nodded. 'By the way,' he said, reaching down and picking up a large plastic evidence bag from the floor, 'this would appear to be our murder weapon. Bloody ugly thing, if you ask me. Anyway, it has blood, hair and skin on the base and its weight and form seem consistent with the damage to his skull. We'll take it back for a full fingerprint check. What's up, Jan?'

Fabel stared at the evidence bag and its heavy, soiled contents in Brauner's hand. In that moment he felt his career, his life unravelling.

'It's a bronze sculpture of *Rahab*. A Hebrew sea devil.' Fabel's voice was dull. Distant. He struggled for a moment to remember Müller-Voigt's exact words. '*Rahab* was the creator of storms and the father of chaos. And I think I'd better tell you now that you will get a good set of prints from it. Mine.'

PART II

CHAPTER 23

When he was eight years old Roman Kraxner's parents had taken him to see the family doctor, who had shaken his head and frowned a lot and referred them on to a child psychiatrist who had not shaken his head or frowned at all. In fact, Roman had not noticed much of any kind of expression at all on the specialist's face. Instead of frowning and head-shaking, the psychiatrist had discussed Roman with his parents in a disjointed, almost incoherent way. Roman recalled that about him; that and the heavy, black-rimmed spectacles he had worn. To hide his eyes, Roman had thought; to hide them so he didn't have to look anyone else in the eye. And with this realisation, all Roman's anxieties had gone. And so had those of his parents: the psychiatrist had reassured Roman's parents that their son did not have any profound learning difficulty or mental instability.

'Your son has a schizotypal personality,' the doctor had said, fiddling with his black framed glasses and not engaging in eye contact. 'But he . . . it's not that . . . he doesn't suffer from schizotypal personality disorder, or schizophrenia . . . no . . . we have also ruled out Asperger's. But . . . he does . . . he's got . . . he displays blunted affect and excessive introspection.'

'What does that *mean*?' Roman's father had asked.

'Roman . . . well, he lacks a developed ability to function . . . to, erm . . . he will struggle to get on well socially. He doesn't really understand others. But all this is typical of a schizotypal personality and it does *not* mean that he cannot enjoy a full and successful life. There *are* compensations: he is clearly highly intelligent and a schizotypal personality can manifest itself in an extremely imaginative and creative mind. A great many composers, artists, writers, mathematicians, physicists . . . in many walks of life it is an advantage.'

Roman had sat there and wondered why the incoherent physician, hiding behind the heavy glasses, had not added *psychiatrist* to the list.

His parents had never fully understood the implications of what the psychiatrist had said. After a period of reassurance, the old doubts had begun to creep back into their heads: the psychiatrist had said *schizotypal*, hadn't he? And that sounded a lot like *schizophrenic*. In the meantime, Roman had blossomed from a strange child with no friends into an even stranger adolescent with no friends. It was not so much that others avoided him – although that certainly was the case – it was more that he avoided others. At school, there had been only one person with whom he had anything approaching a friendship: Niels Freese. But Niels had been even stranger than Roman and had been taken out of the school for long periods of therapy. Still, when they had spent time together, they had recognised that each, in his own way, saw the world completely differently from their peers.

After Niels had been permanently transferred to a special school, Roman had shunned any kind of intimacy or contact. Not that he had to do a lot of shunning: his classmates either ignored or avoided him. Those who did not tormented him.

When puberty had come along, Roman became aware that his rejection of intimacy was even more profound than he had guessed himself. The concomitant storm of hormones had failed to stir much in the way of sexual desire, for either gender. The idea of physical intimacy with another was not so much abhorrent as superfluous. He genuinely could not see much point in it.

Roman realised that he was not *entirely* asexual, however. He found that any tingles of arousal he felt were connected to girls and women who were totally beyond the already corpulent Roman; for the only thing that stirred anything like desire in him was true beauty. Perfect symmetry, perfect skin, perfect figure. But, even then, the level of his arousal was muted. He had often wondered if it had been their very unattainability that had drawn him to these women: the knowledge that such desires were unfulfillable and could never result in actual physical contact.

Roman had sunk deeper and deeper into a world of self-involvement. He rarely left his room and spent most of his time reading, listening to music and, most of all, daydreaming. Daydreaming played a major role in his life: fantasies in which a slimmer, happier, better-looking alter-ego Roman was popular and rich and physically attractive. It was not that he had been unhappy with his life: withdrawal into a better world of his own construction was what he wanted to do.

Then, one day, his life changed for ever.

His parents had worried about their only child. Fretted about him. They worried about his ballooning weight and they worried about him squandering his obvious intellectual gifts. He found out later that it had been his mother's idea to buy him a computer for his fourteenth birthday. Suddenly, a whole new world of possibilities opened up for him. The carefully constructed fantasy world he had built now had an environment outside his head.

His parents were, of course, devastated by his decision not to go to university. But it was also, in a way a relief: they had never been able to envisage their overweight, painfully shy, reclusive son functioning in a campus environment. And it soon became clear that he had a real and marketable talent for designing computer games; he found a job with a software design company which seemed more interested in the games Roman had devised in his bedroom than in any paper qualification.

It had not lasted. Roman's inability to relate to other people meant that, despite his clear talent, he was let go from the software company. There had been another similar job but that, too, had not lasted. Then a less well-paid job. Finally the job in the computer store, selling Macs and PCs to morons who asked continually 'How much memory does it have?' without having the slightest idea what the question, or its answer, really meant.

Stuck at home with his parents, Roman had found it impossible to cope with the weary sadness in their eyes every time they looked at him. They had been good to him, however, and whenever he needed cash for a new piece of computer equipment they seemed to find it. Then, one afternoon that had become evening that had become night as he had lost hours in idle surfing, he had found his way into a secure company site. It had been easy and he had not meant to do anything, but he found himself able to make online payments to suppliers. So he did. Not much, and it was not technically fraud, because Roman in no way benefited personally from the transaction, but he had done it because he *could* do it. He had returned the next day to find that the security settings had remained unaltered, so he put the money he had moved back to where it belonged. Roman had realised that if the discrepancy was discovered, then the IP records of people accessing the site would be examined.

Before he attempted anything like it again he would have to camouflage his presence.

It took Roman six months to set up his elaborate system of bot herders, shell accounts, proxy servers and bouncers to conceal his identity. The first theft was large: over thirty thousand dollars which he immediately transferred to the account of an environmental charity. No direct benefit yet. He was still working at the computer store and had to do his *real* work in the evenings and at night; it took him another three months to set up the elaborate web of bank and credit-card accounts around the world, through which he could channel the income from his fraud. He monitored transactions on the account from which he had stolen the money. It took the company a month to uncover the theft and another month to work out that it had been committed online; only then did they change and tighten their security.

It was then that Roman knew the course his life must take.

Of course, there was the risk of detection. Arrest. Conviction. Prison.

But, as someone whose expansive intellectual architecture was already confined by the dragging mass of his own body, there was a limit to how much a threat of confinement to a cell would be to the eremite Roman. And, of course, if he were to be sent to Billwerder prison in Hamburg he knew they ran computer training programmes. Even if they did catch him, they would never be able to track down *all* the money he had sequestered. He would leave prison a rich man. The risk was worth it. Worth it for the reward, worth it for the thrill.

His parents had been surprised when Roman announced that he was working as a freelance developer for a major virtual-reality games-design company. He showed them their website and the letters of contract they had sent. The website and the letters, of course, had been created by Roman himself. But they had satisfied his parents that all the new equipment that arrived was being supplied by his employers. They were delighted when Roman eventually announced that he had enough money to find himself a small flat some-where, but it would be best if he rented it in their name. To alleviate their concerns he had given them a deposit of eight thousand euros.

Since then, Roman had amassed a personal fortune, stashed around the world, of somewhere in the region of four million euros. He knew he would never use a fraction of that amount: he could only access his funds in small bites and, in any case, Roman knew that the health prob-lems associated with his obesity meant he would be lucky to live to see his thirtieth birthday. Setting up an automated transfer system meant that, if he were to die and could not enter the appropriate cancellation code at the end of the month, one million euros would be transferred to his parents' account. He had left a note with his other papers that would explain that he had been paid massive royalties for one of the games he had developed and that the accumulated proceeds were to go to them.

Roman sat in his custom-made computer chair and gazed absently through the window. Today, for some reason, he had opened up the blinds. The sky hung over Wilhelmsburg like a grey curtain with a pale horizontal hem broken by the angular forms of the other apartment blocks. To Roman what he was looking at was no more real than the other world he watched through the windows of his computer screens. He contemplated it for a moment before diving back into his natural environment.

One of the things he did habitually was to intrude on the lives of strangers.

There was, he felt, no harm in these intrusions: no one knew that he had been there, there was no sense of violation as he carefully peeled away the layers of their identity, tracing their past, getting to know their families, their friends, their hobbies. It allowed him, for an hour or so, to live another life. To experience vicariously the society from which he otherwise felt excluded. Roman would pick someone at random from Facebook or MySpace or any of the countless other social networking sites and he would trace their cyber-radiative signature. The phrase was one of his own invention: 'cyber-radiative signature' best described, for him, the presence – the *degree* of presence – that individuals had in cyberspace.

Roman had come up with the idea late one sleepless night. His obesity meant that he suffered from a range of problems which threatened to kill him each night as he slept. He went to bed with an oxygen mask strapped to his nose to combat sleep apnoea and to boost the blood-oxygen levels that his obesity-hypoventilation syndrome pushed so dangerously low. It was ironic that someone as disconnected from the physical world as Roman was should live with the constant threat of being smothered, literally, by his own mass as he slept.

For Roman it was like diving into water. The risk of death from cerebral hypoxia, to which he was exposed each time he slept, was exactly the same as swimmers and free-divers faced. He had read of Shallow-Water Blackout and Deep-Water Blackout, where fit, experienced free-divers would lose consciousness because the instinct to breathe when the carbon dioxide in their blood reached dangerous levels was overridden. Their brains starved of oxygen, there was no warning, no physical symptoms. They simply passed out and drowned. It would be, thought Roman, a peaceful, painless death.

There had been more than a few nights when he had considered sleeping without his oxygen mask.

But most of the time Roman purposely avoided sleep and the hazards that lay hidden in its depths. He would stay at his desk until the small hours, only going to bed when exhaustion forced him to do so. Until then, oblivious to the time or the physical world around him, Roman would work and play in his natural environment. When he wasn't stealing funds from businesses around the world, much of his time was spent reading and researching. This was often in the most arcane and abstract realms of knowledge, far removed from anything Roman would need to know as part of his criminal work. Quantum mechanics and physics, philosophy of mind and consciousness studies, biotechnology and the history of science were his favourite areas of reading. He would lose himself reading about or listening to video lectures on quantum entanglement, string theory, computer simulation. What Roman particularly liked to do was to explore every aspect of a subject, shining his searchlight into the oddest corners. For example, he liked to explore the genuine philosophical implications of quantum physics, but also the New Age wacky angles that many blogs and groups took on it. The holographic theory of the universe, for example, which solved the problem of black holes contradicting the Second Law of Thermodynamics was, at the end of the day, merely a new interpretation of the arrangement of matter, but Roman found scores of New Age-y sites and conspiracy-theory blogs that announced that we were, after all, *really* living in the Matrix.

Roman found himself totally immune to the paranoia of the conspiracy theorists and the ludicrous spiritual significance that New Agers attached to the innate beauty of some quantum theories. This, he knew, was highly unusual for his type. Schizotypes were famous for their *magical thinking*, as psychiatrists called it: beliefs in spooks and ESP; in UFOs and telepathy and telekinesis. They also had a strong tendency towards paranoia. But Roman had known that all these things were crap. There were no such things as ghosts or poltergeists or God. He found he could do all the magical thinking he needed within the realms of science. A Big Bang in the Void, not a Bump in the Night.

It was this knowledge – that physicists were now treating the universe as composed of *information* rather than matter – that led him to devise his concept of 'cyber-radiative signature'. Maybe, thought Roman, the Bostrum Hypothesis was right and the reality we experienced was not reality after all, but a highly sophisticated ancestor simulation. In which case, mankind was perhaps about to create its own simulated universe *within* a simulated universe. And the foundations of that simulation would be the internet.

This thought, in turn, brought him to the idea that people were already beginning to 'exist' on the internet to some degree or other. There were individuals who interacted with each other *exclusively* through the internet; who had never met and never would meet in real life. If a personality was the sum of other people's perceptions, then there *were* personalities that existed only in cyberspace. This was not mediated reality, it was not even virtual reality. It was the beginning of an actual and absolute – if alternate – reality.

But it was not a reality yet shared by all. If you were over fifty, then it was most likely you had little cyber-identity or none at all; the younger you were, the more likely you were to use the internet as a major social medium, and the more 'mass' your cyber-radiative signature had. He had started to think about the internet in the same way that physicists had once thought of space-time. It was a continuum and within it people and ideas had a mass that created its own radiative field. Every degree of connection was there, each person connected to a circle of others, each circle intersecting with other circles, spreading wide across cyberspace. And at the heart of each presence was a name: the quantum of identity, the smallest indivisible self. People became a scattering of facts. The nucleus was their name, the core of their identity, but they would appear elsewhere, with different usernames, existing simultaneously in several locations but never really existing in any. Exactly, Roman realised, like quantum superposition.

But no matter how diffuse or nebulous an identity, or how misleading the username at its core, Roman would seek it out and give it form. In between his wide-ranging research, his surfing and stealing, he would pick a person at random from a social network. He would seek out commonalities, shared friends, past locations. On many occasions he could access bank accounts, club memberships, charity donations. He had software that could run through a million alphanumeric password permutations a minute and, he had found, once you cracked someone's password for one site, you usually found they used it for a number of others, sometimes all of the secure sites they used. Most people would use only two passwords, both of which would be chosen for ease of recall. And that made them easy to break. It was amazing what you could find out, even without delving too deep. The web, Roman had realised, brought out the egotist in everyone. Every voice that was unheard in the real world shouted its opinions here.

But he could not find her. Anywhere.

She simply did not exist.

The first thing he had done was to disable the roaming function on the mobile phone he had picked up in the café. Roman had become more and more convinced that the beautiful woman who had left it behind had done so deliberately, and the only reason he could think of was that she had been afraid of being tracked through it. He himself had Enhanced Cell Identification software that could pinpoint a mobile to within ten metres; if what he had guessed about the woman was true, then someone, somewhere would be trying to track down her phone. Roman had been very careful about switching it on: it was not necessary for a call to be made or received for it to be traced. As soon as the Nokia was switched on, it would emit its roaming signal, seeking out a network to connect to; so the first thing he did was to dismantle it and remove its antenna.

And that was when he found it: a non-standard GPS chip. Someone had implanted an even more accurate form of tracer on the phone. Once he was into the phone, Roman removed the GPS chip, examined it and destroyed it. He felt himself sweating. More than usual. There was something going on here that was making him feel uneasy. Very uneasy.

With the tracking disabled, he was able to download the phone's contents onto his computer, decrypting any hidden or protected information.

It did not take Roman more than an hour to grow to hate the woman he had seen in the café. He hated her because she really had been in grave danger. And by leaving her phone for him to find, she had transferred that danger to him.

He stared at the computer screens before him. His portal to another universe. His element. His safe place. But even there – *especially* there – they could find him.

And Roman was in no doubt that if they did find him, they would kill him.

CHAPTER 24

The interview lasted all morning and into the afternoon. Van Heiden arranged for lunch to be brought up from the canteen. It was the strangest position for Fabel to find himself in. No one actually used the word *suspect*, but that was the noun Fabel would have attached to himself. Before they had started to discuss Müller-Voigt's death, van Heiden had actually reminded Fabel of his rights under the Basic Law of the Federal Republic.

'Just to keep things right,' van Heiden had said. Presumably that was why he had also had their conversation recorded. Menke, the BfV agent, had sat in on the discussion.

'You cannot seriously be suggesting that I had anything to do with Müller-Voigt's death?' Fabel had protested.

'Of course not,' said van Heiden. 'But we have to be seen to do this all above board.'

So they had sat and gone over every detail of every conversation Fabel had had with the Senator. When he had left to visit him, when he had arrived.

'I wouldn't have thought it would have taken you so long to get there,' said Menke.

'I lost my way a little,' explained Fabel. 'I ended up going through the centre of Stade.'

'But you'd been to Müller-Voigt's house before.'

'A couple of years ago, yes.'

Van Heiden, not the most extemporary of thinkers, had a list of questions prepared on a notepad. He worked his way through them, taking notes, asking supplementary questions. Pausing to frown every now and then. Menke contributed little, but Fabel noticed that the few questions he did ask were much more relevant than those that Fabel's boss asked. At three-thirty van Heiden switched the recorder off, indicating the end of the formal interview.

'Well?' asked Fabel. 'Do I go back to my desk or down to the holding cells?'

'This is no laughing matter,' said van Heiden.

'I do not, in the slightest, find this funny. A man has been murdered within an hour of my talking to him, from what we can gather. He also happened to be a man I rather liked. And someone, somehow, is trying to frame me for it. And implicate me in a serial-murder case I've spent the last six months of my life working on. No, Herr Criminal Director, I do not find this a laughing matter.' Fabel was aware he had started to raise his voice.

'They're not . . .' Menke did not look in Fabel's direction when he spoke.

'What?' Fabel frowned irritatedly at the security-service man.

'They're not trying to frame you,' repeated Menke. 'Or at least I don't think they are. Like I said before, they're trying to *compromise* you more than anything. Take you out of the picture. Make it impossible for you to lead the investigation into Müller-Voigt's death, and/or the Network Killer murders.'

Fabel drew a breath. For the first time in the day he felt less isolated; but the knowledge that his own boss had not voiced a belief in his innocence seethed inside him.

'It seems very elaborate,' said Fabel.

'To you or me, yes. But if you have access to the right technology and expertise, then causing this kind of confusion takes very little effort.' Menke shrugged, but held Fabel's gaze for a moment.

'So where does this all leave me?' Fabel asked van Heiden.

'Maybe it would be good if you took some leave.'

'In the middle of three major murder enquiries?' Fabel was incredulous. 'That's giving whoever is behind this exactly what they want.'

'That might not be a bad idea.' said Menke. 'For the moment . . .'

'I'm not buying it. I'm the head of this Commission and if you're telling me otherwise, then you can have my resignation this afternoon.'

'And that would be exactly what whoever is creating this mayhem would want you to do,' said

Menke. Van Heiden said nothing; it was clear he was out of his depth and Fabel's threat to resign had taken him aback.

'Listen, Fabel,' continued Menke, 'the Criminal Director is right. To put it bluntly, you simply cannot be seen to lead an investigation when you are under investigation yourself.' He turned to van Heiden. 'Why not leave Werner Meyer officially in charge of the Müller-Voigt case and put another officer in to oversee the Network Killer investigation? That will leave Herr Fabel free to investigate the firebomb killing of Daniel Föttinger in the Schanzenviertel. In the meantime, I think it's only fair that he is kept fully informed of developments in the other two investigations. He still heads the department.'

Van Heiden looked less than comfortable with the idea and said nothing.

'If you don't mind me saying, Herr Menke, you're taking a very *profound* interest in the workings of the Polizei Hamburg. And in protecting my career prospects.'

'We have areas of mutual interest, Herr Fabel,' said Menke. 'As you've already guessed.'

'These people you say have the technological expertise and resources to pull a stunt like this. The Pharos Project?'

Menke smiled. 'I suggest you read that file I gave you. Very carefully.'

After van Heiden and Menke left Fabel's office, Anna Wolff came in.

'You're in trouble,' she said bluntly.

'Tell me about it,' Fabel sighed, leaning back in his chair.

'Not with Robocop and the Spook.' She grinned. 'Susanne's been on the phone.'

'Oh, *shit* . . .' Fabel jumped up and looked at his watch. 'I was supposed to pick her up from the airport.'

'An hour ago. Don't worry – when she phoned she was pretty pissed off, but I explained that things were *serious*. I sent a car to pick her up and take her back to your flat. But I'd give her a call if I were you.'

'Thanks, Anna. You tell Susanne anything about what's been happening?'

''Course not. But I did say it was serious. Well, it's always serious, but I told her it was more serious than usual. That you'd had a rough time and I was sure you'd explain.' Anna crossed her arms and frowned. 'You okay?'

'What did the Criminal Director tell you?'

'That we were to keep you under close surveillance and not let you into the incident room in case you saw your picture at the top of the suspects board.' Anna's delivery was deadpan.

'Very funny . . .' Fabel made an impatient face.

'He told Werner and me that you would have to withdraw yourself from the Müller-Voigt and Network Killer investigations but that you were still head of the Commission. He kind of suggested that you would be taking a *break*. He also said that

243

Werner was top dog on the Müller-Voigt case and Principal Chief Commissar Brüggemann will be coming in to head up the Network Killer caseload.'

'Nicola Brüggemann?'

'We stay assigned for the meantime, but she runs the show.'

Fabel nodded. He knew Nicola Brüggemann well: she headed up a specialist child crime unit, which, inevitably, often had to work closely with the Murder Commission.

'Nicola Brüggemann is an excellent officer.' Fabel invested his tone with a warning. 'Don't be . . . don't be your usual contrary self, Anna. It's not Nicola's fault I've been . . . what have I been? . . . not suspended or reassigned . . . *reallocated*. I need you and Werner to stick to the Network Killer case like glue. And, obviously, I want to be kept fully informed of developments. In the meantime, I need to get all the information on the Schanzenviertel arson attack.'

Susanne was waiting for him when he got home. There was no anger in her expression, just concern. And she looked tired. Her concern deepened as Fabel went through everything that had happened during her absence.

'God, Jan . . . I can't leave you alone for a minute. What happens now?'

'I don't know. It's all over the place. I've been reassigned to take personal charge of this death in the Schanzenviertel: the guy who died when his car

244

was torched. Officially, I'm still running the show with the other cases, but . . .'

'Who do you think is behind all of this? I mean, it takes a lot of organisation and resources . . .'

'I've already had that conversation.' Fabel held up the file. 'My spooky pal Fabian Menke suspects the Pharos Project. What the connection between an environmental cult and a serial rapist and killer could be is beyond me, but Müller-Voigt expressed real fears about them. He reckoned that his girlfriend was investigating them and that was why she disappeared. I have to say that it is more than a coincidence that all official records – all *computerised* records – of this woman's existence in Germany seem to have disappeared into the same black hole as my text messages. It's also a hell of a coincidence that *Virtual Dimension*, this role-playing crap site that all the Network Killer's victims were logged into, is also owned by the Korn-Pharos Corporation.'

'You think this cult has targeted you as well?' Susanne frowned.

'My guess is that they suspected that Müller-Voigt knew more than he did and passed some of that on to me – enough to start me looking in places they don't want me looking. The problem is that I'm not as smart or well-informed as they suspect.'

'But you're the *police*, for God's sake. They can't take on the police or the government and get away with it.'

'From what I've found out so far, the Pharos

Project and the Korn-Pharos Corporation have between them several hundred times the budget and ten times the manpower of the Polizei Hamburg. This isn't just some commercial concern or cooky cult, Susanne – this is more like a *state* but without physical borders. There's no way I would underestimate Pharos or how far they would go to achieve their goals. I think that could be a fatal mistake.'

'If you and Menke are so sure Pharos is behind all of this, why can't you bring people in for questioning?'

'After my *interrogation* by van Heiden I talked to the State Prosecutor's Office. We just don't have enough to justify a warrant. And in any case, we're talking about a corporation and a cult – groups of people, not individuals. We're still far, far away from placing an individual at any of the murder scenes. Oh no, I forgot, we can place *one* individual at the murder scene . . . there's a bronze sculpture covered in fingerprints in the evidence store. Unfortunately those fingerprints just happen to be mine.' Fabel let go a long sigh. 'Sorry. The point is that we don't have enough to get a warrant and, even if we did, we don't know what or who we're looking for.'

Susanne came over to him and brushed a lock of blond hair back from his brow. 'You'll get there. Try not to worry. Just do what you always do and look at the big picture. No one else does it the way you do. You hungry?'

Fabel shook his head. 'I'm going to catch up with

my reading.' He dropped the file onto the kitchen table. 'Maybe you're right, but somehow I think this particular picture is too big even for me.'

As he read the BfV file, Fabel found himself being drawn deeper and deeper into something more complex and wide-ranging than he had ever imagined. And a way of perceiving the world that he really could not understand.

He read again what Anna and Müller-Voigt had already told him: that Dominik Korn, the reclusive genius billionaire with joint US/German nationality, had taken over his father's business empire and built it into the Korn-Pharos Corporation, the world's number one environmental technologies group; how he had invested millions in environmental projects, including the ill-fated *Pharos One* deep-sea exploration to discover the true impact of deep-water oil drilling. As it turned out, Korn's concerns had been proven correct with the 2010 BP Deepwater Horizon disaster in the Gulf of Mexico; but the maiden voyage of Korn's submersible had ended in its own disaster, with Korn suffering massive neurological damage as a result of his unprotected ascent.

No one saw much of Dominik Korn after that. He had been seriously ill for months and had made only one brief appearance – at a press conference, wheelchair-bound and speaking with an artificial voice through a computer – about a year after the accident. He had turned this one appearance into a clarion call for mankind to *disengage* from the environment, to reduce its impact on the natural world to zero. An impossible goal. But environmentalists around the world had been inspired by Korn's courage and commitment. Fabel could see why a young Meliha Yazar would have drawn comparisons with Mustafa Kemal Atatürk. Korn really did seem to offer a new and radical vision. He had proposed a completely new political structure for the world, where *global* concerns like the environment were dealt with at a *global* level; that no one nation should have rights or control over any given natural resource. Much of Korn's early reasoning made sense to Fabel, although he could see that even these original ideas would have been seen as dangerous to both commercial vested interests and national governments.

But after that single appearance, Korn had become more and more reclusive and his pronouncements, made through the Korn-Pharos press office, had become increasingly bizarre. He announced the foundation of the Pharos Project as an international environmental movement and his philosophy of disengagement became more and more extreme. It was once he started to call for the strict control of the human population – for euthanasia and enforced sterilisation – that alarm bells started to ring. Especially in Germany.

As the Pharos Project became quasi-religious and its attitude towards detractors more aggressive, one name pushed its way to the front with increasing frequency: Peter Wiegand. Wiegand was Korn's deputy. It had been Wiegand who had been in charge of Korn's rescue from Pharos One and who, after his boss had been incapacitated, had taken over the reins until Korn had been well enough to take control again, albeit from a motorised wheelchair and out of public view. Wiegand was a German national and the movement set up a European headquarters in the Federal Republic, while officially maintaining its main base in the United States. The truth was that the German headquarters, the architecturally innovative Pharos, on the south bank of the Elbe, was seen as the real world HQ of the Pharos Project. Korn may have been King, but Wiegand was his Prince Regent.

When the editor of a boulevard-press newspaper had compared some of the Pharos Project's policies with those of the Nazis, and had alluded to the cult's deputy as 'Pharos's Himmler', Wiegand had sued for massive damages, and won.

Fabel could see where the BfV's concerns had come from: Pharos fitted almost all the criteria for a destructive cult and an anti-democratic philosophy. There was the usual unquestioning adoration of the leader, one who was conveniently distant and aloof and whose disabilities had been turned into an expression of his particular breed of asceticism. And there was the total subjugation of the individual: when you joined Pharos your identity became subsumed into the single greater consciousness. And that meant, of course, that any personal wealth you might have would become the property of the cult. It was the first step in your *disengagement* from the physical world. Like most cults, Pharos had its Day of Judgement: The Consolidation.

An hour became two, then three. Eventually Susanne came into the kitchen and made a sandwich, placing the plate on top of the open file as Fabel was reading it. She handed him an opened bottle of Jever beer.

'Eat,' she said and sat down at the table opposite him.

'Don't tell me you're getting domesticated . . .' said Fabel, examining the sandwich suspiciously.

'I've realised my mistake in going to university and having a career and everything. I've decided to stay at home and pander to your every whim.' Susanne nodded at the sandwich. 'It's all my own recipe. Bread, butter and cheese.'

Fabel smiled and took a bite, leaned back in his chair and sipped his beer.

'I now understand why Menke has been so cooperative,' he said. 'The Bf V's Cults Unit has an entire team working on the Pharos Project. They can't get anything on them; nor can the FBI, who are equally suspicious. The Pharos Project has its European headquarters a little way along the Elbe and even the Polizei Niedersachsen has a team monitoring them.'

'So what's the Pharos Project's particular angle? A meteor that's going to take them to a different galaxy? Escape from the control of giant lizards who have disguised themselves as Freemasons? Or just that Jesus is coming in a spaceship? That's always a good one.'

'You know what the singularity is?'

'Listen, smart-ass, just because I've made you a sandwich doesn't mean my brains have turned to mush. Of course I know what the singularity is: the predicted point in history when computers and machines will be able to build other computers and machines that we can't because of the restrictions of human intelligence. God knows how many science-fiction films have been based on it.'

'The Pharos Project has a different definition,' said Fabel. 'They believe that we *will* become much more intelligent because we will become "one" with technology. That we will augment ourselves through genetic engineering and by basically adding bits to ourselves. Nanochips in our brains, microscopic machines to patrol around inside us to destroy cancer cells or dredge cholesterol from our arteries and help us live longer – that kind of thing.'

'Yep . . . I've heard that interpretation of the singularity as well. Transhumanism, posthumanism . . . kick-starting the next phase in human evolution ourselves.'

'Well, that's what Dominik Korn seems to be into.'

'Understandable when you already spend your life connected up to tubes and computers twenty-four hours a day. He has to believe there's

251

a better machine to sustain his existence just around the corner.'

'Well, from what I've read here, the Pharos Project believes that mankind will be able to disengage from the environment by "uploading itself" onto some kind of computer mainframe.'

Susanne took a bottle of white wine from the fridge and poured herself a glass. 'I've heard that hokey before,' she said. 'The concept that we'll be able to digitise human consciousness and store it on whatever computers evolve into.'

'You don't believe it?'

'I'm a psychologist, Jan. I deal with the human mind every day. There is an inherent randomness to human thought, to the electrochemical signals in the brain, the firing of dendrites, that give it a complexity that no computer could ever replicate. If I say the word "tree" to you, then your brain takes that input and generates thoughts relating to that concept. Okay, a computer can do that, have an idea of a tree. But if I say the word "tree" to you ten seconds later, although you have a central concept of what a tree is, the stimulus of that single word will fire off a thousand new thoughts, completely different from the first time. To develop a computer capable of housing the human intellect, you would have to synthesise the organic struc-ture of the brain.' She shook her head, with a dismissive laugh. 'Digitising human consciousness? It's a pile of crap, Jan. It can never be done.'

'How can you be sure? Surely in the future . . .'

'Okay, let's not even think about a computer. The brain transplant has been the stuff of horror movies since Frankenstein. The brain is the home of the mind, of the personality, right?'

'Of course.'

'So if a brain transplant were possible, the mind and personality of the brain donor would be transported to the recipient body, yes?'

'Yes.'

'Wrong. If you transplanted a brain, you would be connecting it to a completely new endocrine system, a totally different physiology. Our moods, our variations in personality derive from the enzymes, hormones and chemicals produced in our bodies. The reason men are more aggressive than women isn't complicated. It's because men have testicles and women don't, frankly. Move a man's brain into a woman's body and the mind would become feminised because it would be connected to a completely new chemistry that would actually create physical changes in the brain. So if you digitise and upload a human mind into a computer, you're not going to end up with a human mind. At best it would be a self-aware computer program. Trust me, Jan, the concept of a man-machine singularity is a crock.'

'Well, that's the crock that the Pharos Project is peddling. And the Korn-Pharos Corporation is actively researching it. Korn-Pharos lead the world in computer simulations – and I don't mean the kind of things you play on a games console.

Korn's father made his fortune developing computer models for the American military and then for NASA. These programs could create entire star systems, black holes, all that kind of thing. They started off as simple mathematical models but ended up entire hyper-realistic universes within a mainframe. According to Dominik Korn, Korn-Pharos are only a decade away from creating a hardware and software system capable of perpetually updating and repairing itself. Come the glorious day of the *Consolidation*, according to Korn, all the members of the Pharos Project will be uploaded into this super-realistic computer simulation that will allow them to live for ever in a world that seems as real as this. And by doing so they will save the real environment by being disconnected from it.'

'That's a novel twist: a cyber-afterlife.'

'Afterlife is the key word. At least as far as the BfV Bureau of Constitutional Security is concerned. You upload your consciousness and then what? Where are you really? You're mind is in two places at the one time – in the real world and in the virtual one. So as far as you're concerned after the event, nothing has changed. Unless . . .'

'Unless you cease to exist in the real world.' Susanne put her wineglass down and shook her head slowly. 'Mass suicide.'

'Mass murder-suicide, more like. Let's face it, it's the staple of all of these cults. Jonestown, Order of the Solar Temple, Heaven's Gate, Branch Davidians . . . And despite the hi-tech dress-up that the Pharos Project has given it, it's the same old promise of transition to a higher plane. All you need to do is die.'

They were interrupted by the phone ringing. Fabel was surprised to hear that it was Astrid Bremer from the forensics squad; Holger Brauner's deputy.

'You're working late,' said Fabel.

'Yeah, third week solid backshift,' said Astrid. 'My social life is to die for. You want some good news?'

'Oh yes, please,' said Fabel.

'I thought I would let you know that we have done a full fingerprint and trace analysis on the sculpture used to kill Müller-Voigt. Like you guessed, yours and Müller-Voigt's are the only fingerprints on it and there's no trace of any third-party DNA.'

'Brilliant,' sighed Fabel. 'You've got an odd sense of good news.'

'Well, actually it is. There are no other finger-prints because whoever hit Müller-Voigt with it wore gloves. There is evidence of smudging and smearing, including of your prints. It proves that you weren't the last person to handle the sculpture. Of course, it doesn't mean that you didn't pull on gloves afterwards, but you know what I mean.'

'Thanks, Astrid. It's something, anyway.'

'There's one more thing . . .'

'Yeah?'

'We found some extraneous fibres at the scene. Grey fabric. My guess is from a man's suit jacket. Were you wearing a grey jacket?'

'No. Nor was Müller-Voigt.'

'We know that. We couldn't find anything in his wardrobe that would match.'

'You can tell already?'

'Yes . . .' said Astrid. 'This fibre is highly unusual insofar as it seems to have an incredibly high polyester content. What isn't polyester is some other kind of synthetic fibre. It's the weirdest thing I've seen. I mean, I know in the seventies people went mad for synthetic materials, but nowadays . . . Anyway, I'm going to send it off to a specialist lab to get a better breakdown of its composition.'

'Thanks, Astrid,' Fabel said, and put the phone down, trying to work out why he felt what Astrid had told him was significant.

CHAPTER 25

The next morning, before making his first call, Fabel dropped by the Jensen Buchhandlung, down in the Arkaden by the Alster. Otto Jensen was Fabel's closest friend, closer even than Werner. It was a friendship unsullied by professional interests. Fabel had been at university with Otto and they had remained close, even if Otto had not, to start with, approved of Fabel's becoming a police officer. 'A waste of a fine mind,' he had said. Repeatedly. Fabel had known since he had been a boy that he was smart; that he had a good brain. But when he had met Otto Jensen at university, he had recognised a mind that worked on a completely different level. Otto was the person to whom Fabel would go to discuss anything he found confusing or arcane. Whatever it was, Otto would know something about it. But Fabel also knew that Otto was completely, spectacularly devoid of the kind of common sense needed to conduct a normal day-to-day life. The success of his bookshop was entirely due to Otto's wife, Else.

Fabel waited while Otto served a customer. From

a distance, Fabel suddenly saw a middle-aged balding man with tired eyes. It saddened Fabel, who every time he thought of his friend had the image of a tall, gangly, clumsy youth with long, lank blond hair. It was, Fabel realised, exactly the same mental mechanism that had temporarily wiped out the fact of Dirk Stellamanns's death: you kept a concept of a person in your head that never seemed to age; that was fixed at the time you first really got to know them.

'What's this?' asked Otto when Fabel came up to the counter. 'A raid?'

'Don't sweat,' said Fabel. 'There isn't a law against being a smart-arse. Yet. As soon as there is, I'll put you at the top of the most-wanted list. Actually, I wondered if you had time for a coffee? I wanted to pick your brains.'

Otto asked one of his staff to take over and led Fabel to an area set out with sofas. There was a coffee machine in the corner and, surrounded by books, the two old friends sat down and engaged in the obligatory introductory small talk. Then Fabel ran through all he knew about the Pharos Project and their ideas of Consolidation, simulated realities and the removal of mankind from the biosphere.

'I just don't get it,' said Fabel when he had finished. 'The Pharos Project is supposed to be an environmental group, yet they are obsessed with the idea of simulated reality. Other than this bizarre claim that simulated reality allows mankind to take itself out of the environment and therefore save it . . . which, by the way, I don't get: why save something that you want to escape from? Anyway, apart from that, I just don't understand the connection.'

'Well, you're wrong, Jan. The two ideas have always sort of gone together. Way back at the end of the nineteenth century, some of the world's leading geologists – Eduard Suess, Nikolai Fyodorov, Vladimir Vernadsky and a host of others – came up with both ideas and saw them as inextricably linked. A couple of them actually posited that the biosphere was itself nothing but a simulation.'

'Yeah . . .' Fabel made a sceptical face. 'Those crazy Russians . . .'

'No, Jan, you shouldn't be so dismissive. There were some ideas in there that are now part of mainstream thinking. Way back then, Vernadsky believed that the greatest force in shaping the geology of the Earth was the human intellect. Some geologists today think we should be calling this age the Anthropocene instead of the Holocene, because *we* have changed the planet so much.'

'And what about this idea of simulated reality that the Pharos Project bangs on about so much?'

'Well, going back a little further, Fyodorov, who had influenced Vernadsky, actually believed that in the distant future mankind would develop a "prosthetic society". No more ageing or death. He also thought we'd go on to achieve some kind of super-singularity – and bear in mind that he came up with this stuff in the 1890s – where we would be able to replicate absolutely *any* quantum brain state, meaning everybody who has ever lived would be brought back to life. The quantum Resurrection. All of a sudden atheist science becomes religious prophesy.'

'But it's mad,' protested Fabel. 'How could you simulate an entire world?'

'You're an old technophobe, Jan. It would scare the pants off you if you saw what games designers can do now. Hyperreal simulated worlds. And anyway, don't you realise that creating a simulated reality is the easiest thing in the world? We all do it . . . every time we dream. When we're dreaming, we *think* we're experiencing reality. How often have you had a dream and, after you've woken up, you've had to work hard at remembering what really happened and what happened in the dream?'

Fabel thought about how vivid his dreams had been over the years, when the dead would walk again and point accusing fingers at him for not catching their killers; or the nights when he sat in his father's study talking to Paul Lindemann, the young police officer who had been shot dead while on an operation organised and run by Fabel.

'Do you know that there really are quite a few respected scientists who believe that it is actually unlikely that any of this . . .' Otto indicated their surroundings with a sweep of his arms '. . . is real? That everything we experience is a highly sophisticated simulation.'

'I'd rather die than live a lie,' said Fabel.

'Why? What difference does it make? *This* is all you have ever experienced. This *is* your reality. It really doesn't matter if it's a reality outside or inside a simulation. Maybe that's who God is . . . a systems analyst. How's that for a depressing thought?'

'But this *is* real, Otto.'

'Reality is just what's in your head, Jan. You should read *Simulacra and Simulation* by Jean Baudrillard. Or get a copy of Fassbinder's *Welt am Draht*. Or even Jungian psychology – ask Susanne . . . although I always think of her as Freudian . . .' Otto said with an exaggerated leer. 'We are programmed by our surroundings, by signs and symbols. Someone says the word "cowboy" and we think of John Wayne, even though the real cowboys were small, almost jockey-like because their horses had to carry them twelve hours a day. The truth *isn't* out there.'

'You know, Otto, I could give you the Pharos Project's phone number if you want . . .'

'Yeah, very funny. I'm quite happy with my reality, thank you.' Otto suddenly became serious. 'But I do know something about the Pharos Project, Jan, and none of it's good. Terrorising the families of ex-members, harassing anyone who criticises them. You watch yourself with these people.'

Fabel drained his coffee cup. 'I'm going. You make my head hurt, do you know that, Otto?'

'Maybe that's my entire *raison d'être*. See you, copper.'

Fabel drove across town and parked over the street from the Schanzenviertel café. Before visiting Otto, he had spent the day going through all the evidence to date on the Föttinger case and had decided he was prepared enough to start talking to witnesses. It was something he always did, as a matter of course: Fabel never relied on witness statements. It was not that he did not trust the officers who took the statements to ask the right questions, it was more that reading them in a report removed the human dimension: sometimes it was not *what* a witness said, but more *how* they said it; the million little tells and tics that could reveal a doubt, an insecurity, a prejudice.

He headed into the Schanzenviertel feeling strangely upbeat. Maybe it was the weather. For the first time in weeks, it really did feel like there was a hint of spring in the early evening air. Fabel often thought about the effect the weather had on his moods and the idea reminded him of what Müller-Voigt had said about Man's connection to his environment, and how we had lost sight of it.

As he crossed the street, Fabel saw that two of the café's four large plate-glass windows had been filled in with plywood panels; the wood of the frames around the plywood was blackened.

He guessed that the intensity of the heat from the blazing car had caused the windows to shatter.

When he walked in, he noticed that only three out of the café's more than twenty tables were occupied. 'Quiet in here this evening . . .' he said to the waiter as he held up his police identification. The waiter, who had been bent over a table, made a show of being unimpressed and shrugged. The Schanzenviertel was a part of Hamburg where people were generally not impressed by the police. It was not that the quarter was populated by criminals, more that there was an instinctive disregard and distrust of the police in a part of the city famed for its alternative views. It did not bother Fabel. In fact he rather appreciated it: a touch of idiosyncrasy and a healthy disregard for authority was what made Hamburg Hamburg, after all.

'Funny, that,' said the waiter, returning to the work of tidying and wiping the recently vacated table. 'We thought that putting flambéed client on the menu would bring them in in their droves.' He straightened up wearily. Fabel saw that he was older than he had first thought. Tall and thin with a lean, deeply lined face and dressed in a way that would have looked better on him a decade before. 'I take it that's why you're here?'

'Did you know the victim?' Fabel referred to his notebook. 'Daniel Föttinger?'

'Like I told the other cops, he was a regular. He came here every Wednesday, same time and met the same woman. They would have lunch, then go off together.'

'What do you mean, go off together?'

The waiter sighed. 'They'd arrive in separate cars, but after they'd eaten they'd go off together in her car. I always noticed that the big Merc convertible sat outside for a couple of hours, then would disappear mid or late afternoon. I actually often thought that he was taking a bit of chance, with all these car-burnings around here and all. But I never imagined it would happen in broad daylight right outside our door. Or that the poor bastard would end up torched himself.'

'What do you know about him?'

'What I know about all of my customers: what they order, what they drink, what they leave as a tip. He wasn't the small-talk type.'

'Yet he came here often?'

'What can I tell you? Some customers are easy to get to know. He wasn't.'

'But you must at least have had some *impression* of him . . . the kind of person he was.'

The lanky waiter gave a small laugh. 'How can I put it? He didn't have a lot of personality going on there, and what there was was all arrogant asshole. Every time he came in and sat down was like it was the first time. You know what I mean: I'd serve him every time he came in, but he'd make out like he didn't know me from Adam. Some customers can be like that. They treat you as if you don't really exist or matter as a human being, like you simply exist for their convenience.'

'The woman?'

'She wasn't as bad. At least she talked to you; acknowledged you as a person. She's a real looker and I couldn't quite work out what she was doing with him. I mean, he seemed pretty one-dimensional to me.'

'So you had them pegged as a couple?'

'Yeah. But not married, though. And not business or colleagues. It was obvious they had some kind of regular thing going. When you've served tables as long as I have, you get to tell the nature of the visit, the agenda behind the lunch, if you know what I mean. But there was something about them didn't gel.'

Fabel raised an eyebrow.

'Oh, I don't know . . .' The waiter renewed his efforts on the tabletop and his irritation at being disturbed. 'They fitted in some ways . . . him rich, her cute . . . but it was just that he seemed so . . . I don't know . . . so *dull*. I tell you, if I had a woman who looked like that across the table from me, I wouldn't spend so much of my time playing with my electronic toys.'

'What do you mean?'

'He was always texting or taking calls on his cellphone. There was one time they were in here that he sat half the time working on his laptop. Sometimes I think it wasn't the excellence of our cuisine that brought him here. More our free WiFi.

But I tell you, his girlfriend was getting pretty pissed off with it. I reckon she was on the point of giving him the elbow.'

'And you could tell this just from waiting table?' Fabel had not intended his question to sound patronising but the lean waiter's face clouded.

'Maybe if you cops were forced to work as waiters for six months you'd be better at sizing people up. Everybody is becoming more and more detached from each other, from reality. All of this technology shit. Me, I run this place because I get to watch people. Live in the real world.' He looked at Fabel disdainfully. 'Take you . . . you're a cop but I can tell from the way you dress and the way you talk to people that you like to think you're different from the rest. That jacket you're wearing – English-cut, tweed – it's not the usual anonymous semi-corporate two-hundred-euro suit the Hamburg Kripo always seems to wear. I'd say you're not all that comfortable with being a cop and you like to think you've got a little more going on up here.' He tapped his forefinger against the side of his head. 'You're trying really hard to fit in by not fitting in. But what do I know, huh? I just wait tables.'

'Okay,' said Fabel. 'So you're the Great Observer, the ultimate people watcher. I get it. You told the officers that you noticed one of the arsonists before the attack. I don't suppose your people-watching skills could extend to giving me a decent description of him?'

'I saw him, all right. He was hanging around across the street, under that tree . . .' The waiter tutted when he realised the view of the tree was obscured by the plywood. 'Anyway,' he said philosophically, 'he was over there. To start with I thought he was a junkie. He was kinda hopping from one foot to the other, fidgeting, sort of, and checking and rechecking that big black holdall he was carrying.'

'Would you recognise him again?'

'Doubt it. He was wearing a sort of woolly hat that he pulled down as a mask when he torched the car. I did *think* I noticed something. I didn't mention it to the other cops because I only thought of it afterwards . . .'

'Yes?'

'A limp. I'm pretty sure the guy had a limp. Or at least there was something stiff about the way he walked.'

'Thanks,' said Fabel.

The skinny waiter shrugged and went back to cleaning tables.

Fabel's next visit was in Harvestehude. An impressive Wilhelmine building faced with white stucco tried to hide behind a screen of manicured shrubs and trees. Fabel found the name he was looking for and rang the bell.

'Polizei Hamburg . . .' he said into the entry system in answer to the crackling voice. 'I'd like to speak to you, Frau Kempfert.'

'Let me see your ID,' the voice said. 'There's a camera above the entryphone.'

Fabel held his card up to the bulbous electronic eye and there was a harsh buzzing and a click. He pushed open the heavy door and made his way up an ornately tiled stairwell to the apartment building's third floor. An attractive, dark-haired young woman eyed him suspiciously from her doorway as he approached.

'I told the other officers all I know.'

'You know, Frau Kempfert, everybody always says exactly that same thing. But I like to hear it all for myself. And, you never know, something might always come back to you. Do you mind?' Fabel nodded towards the apartment behind her.

'No . . .' Unsmiling, she moved to one side to admit him. 'Come in.'

The young woman led him along the long hall into a corner lounge. It was huge and bright with French windows that opened out onto a small balustraded balcony. Fabel guessed from what he had seen on the way in that the flat probably consisted of this room, one, maybe two bedrooms, a kitchen-diner and a bathroom. The architecture was typical Harvestehude: echoing a more formal and elegant age with high ceilings, huge windows and the odd bit of ostentation in the plasterwork. The flat was not big, thought Fabel, but it would still be pricey. The furnishings and artwork were brightly coloured to contrast with the white walls. It all suggested a sophisticated sense of taste.

Victoria Kempfert dropped into a huge red armchair and made a perfunctory gesture towards the sofa, indicating that Fabel should sit. I get it, he thought, I'm taking up your time. Fabel had learned to be suspicious of people who overstated how much of an inconvenience it was to have to talk to the police. Generally speaking, if someone had lost their life, witnesses were only too willing to give you their time. They were helping you make sense of an often senseless death; doing that, for most people, was a way of restoring the universe's natural balance.

'You usually came back here after your lunchtime meetings?' asked Fabel. 'You and Herr Föttinger, I mean.'

'Yes. We came back here and fucked.' She held Fabel in a defiant gaze, her eyebrows arched.

'I see,' said Fabel matter-of-factly, noting it down in his notebook. 'And where did you and Herr Föttinger fuck? In the bedroom or here, where I'm sitting?'

Victoria Kempfert's expression darkened even more. She was clearly bursting to say something but, for the moment, she could not find the words.

'Listen, Frau Kempfert,' said Fabel. 'I know that you have had a terrible experience, and you've made your distaste for police officers clear. But I've been a murder detective for a long, long time. There is very little that this world has left to throw at me that could shock me, so petulance and adolescent language isn't going to set me back on my heels. But if you want, we can keep the conversation at that level. How often did you and Herr Föttinger fuck here?'

She dropped her eyes. She was a beautiful woman. Strong features and a mane of thick, dark hair. Not unlike Susanne. And very much, he realised against his will, his type.

'Daniel and I would come here every week – every Wednesday – after lunch. We'd see each other maybe one other time during the week, depending on our schedules. He was away a lot.' She paused. 'I'm sorry if I was being . . . it's just that after seeing that, seeing what happened to him . . .' She bit her lip and something in her eyes hardened again. It was clear that she was determined not to cry.

'I do understand,' said Fabel, more gently. 'Did the police officers you spoke to give you details of victim support?'

'I don't need *counselling*, Herr Fabel. I'll get over it. Eventually.'

'Did you see the attackers?'

'No . . . yes . . . I mean I didn't know they were the attackers then. The bastards just stood and watched Daniel burn. To start with I thought they were just passers-by like everyone else, then I saw they had ski masks or something on. Over their faces. I didn't even know it had been an arson attack to start with. I didn't know what had happened.'

'Was there anything you particularly noticed about them?'

'Other than the ski masks? Nothing. I was too busy watching Daniel. And then . . . Why would someone do that?'

'What I need to establish is if they had intended to do what they did. A lot of expensive cars get torched in the Schanzenviertel. It could be that that was their sole intention.'

'I don't know . . .' Kempfert said slowly, her eyes unfocused as if replaying the scene in her head. 'It was the way they waited. Watched. One in particular.'

'That could be a sign that they were shocked by the consequences of their actions.'

Kempfert shook her head vigorously. 'That's the thing . . . You asked if there was anything I particularly noticed. Well, just before he jumped on the back of the motorbike and they made off, I could have sworn the guy in the ski mask . . . I could have sworn he was *laughing*. You don't do that if you are shocked by the consequences of your action.'

'No . . . probably not. But, believe it or not, it can be the result of shock. Or psychological conditions. Paradoxical laughter.'

'There was nothing paradoxical about it. That bastard was laughing at what he had done.'

Fabel regarded her for a moment.

'How long had you been seeing Herr Föttinger?'

'A couple of months. Maybe three. It was all coming to an end, though.'

'You knew he was married?'

'He made no secret of it. I made no secret of the fact that I didn't care. We met through business. I design websites and I'd done some work for his company. But that had stopped months before our relationship started. He hired someone else. Then, about ten, twelve weeks ago, I met him at a business event. You know, the usual rubber-chicken dinner with flow charts and Powerpoints for dessert.'

'I'm afraid I don't,' said Fabel. 'Not my natural environment, as it were. So that's when you started to see him?'

'About a week or so later he phoned me and asked me to lunch. We started to see each other each week, but it was becoming . . . *tiresome*.'

'In what way tiresome?'

'On the face of it, Daniel was charming and interesting. But there was something missing. It was like he was all veneer and nothing beneath. I know this sounds weird, but even when we were intimate it was like he was on his own. In fact, there were times it became *unpleasant*. It was like I didn't exist for him in any real way. That's mad, I know. But that's why there was no future for us.'

Fabel thought about what she had said; it was almost exactly how the waiter had described Föttinger. 'What do you know about Herr Föttinger's business?'

'Just what I found out through working on its website. Environmental technologies. Daniel was involved in all types of carbon-capture technology. He was supposed to be involved with this Global Concern Hamburg summit – you knew that, didn't you?'

'I'd heard.' Fabel paused for a moment. 'What about Frau Föttinger? Was there ever any suggestion that she knew about her husband's relationship with you?'

'What? Hell hath no fury? No, I don't think Kirstin Föttinger paid for someone to torch Daniel's car because she knew about us. Trust me, she's not that *engaged.*'

'What do you mean?'

'In some ways she was very like Daniel, but more so, if you know what I mean. Daniel's wife was the *real* environmental freak. And I mean extreme. She's a strict vegan and believes that we should make *zero* impact on the planet. She got involved in some group with weird ideas. I mean really weird ideas. Daniel was involved with them too, but not in the same way she was. I think she dragged him into it to start with. The sad thing is I think that at one time, not so long ago, Daniel really loved her. The way he put it to me was that she simply disappeared . . . faded away. I don't think he would ever have got involved with me if she hadn't gone all weird. The funny thing is I sensed the same thing happening to Daniel. He was fading away. Becoming weird.'

'Group? What kind of group?' asked Fabel,

although he was pretty sure he already knew the answer.

'More of a cult,' said Kempfert. 'They call themselves Pharos, or something.'

Fabel nodded slowly, looking down at his notebook. A deliberate movement to conceal from Victoria Kempfert the significance of what she had just told him.

'You say he was involved with this group too, but not to the same degree?'

'Well, yes. But, from what I could gather, they didn't believe in degrees of involvement. You had to give yourself totally to Pharos. It creeped me out a bit. More than a bit. Daniel was a bright guy. He had great ideas but didn't have the money to back them up. His wife was loaded, though. She bankrolled him to start with but he built up his business to become a leader in the field. The price he had to pay was to become a member of Pharos. He used to joke about it.' Kempfert frowned. 'Then he stopped. In fact, he stopped joking about anything much.'

'He changed?'

'He was changing. I told him to get out while he could. I could tell that a big part of him really wanted to, but every time I met him it was like that part of him was getting smaller. As if a little more of his personality – a little more self-will – had been sucked out of him. That's what I meant when I said it was all getting tiresome.' She paused. 'Listen, Herr Fabel, I wasn't that much into Daniel. Even at the start. It was fun – *he* was fun – to begin with, but then it all got a little tired. And the weird stuff with this group that he and his wife were involved with.'

'You wanted out?'

'I told him at lunch. Right before that happened to him. Can you imagine how that makes me feel?'

'You weren't to know, Frau Kempfert. How did he take it?'

'Well. So well, in fact, I could have let it damage my ego. It was as it he didn't care. Actually, more like he was relieved.'

As Fabel crossed the street to his car, he did not need to turn to know that Victoria Kempfert was watching him from her window. She had been all prickles; defiant to the point of hostility. It was, he knew, part of the denial process that followed a trauma such as the one she had experienced. But there was more to it. There was something she had wanted to tell Fabel but had been too unsure or afraid to voice. Instead she had ring-fenced it with verbal barbs. He took his cellphone out and hit the speed dial for the Murder Commission, before realising that this was the replacement phone and did not have the number stored. It took him a moment to recall it and key it in: the irony of technology making life easier was that you forgot how to do things for yourself. He got hold of Anna Wolff.

'Anna, I need you to run a couple of checks for me. And I need them quickly.'

'Okay, anything for our number one suspect. The last time you had someone checked they ended up dead.'

'When this is over, Commissar Wolff, I'm going to have you transferred to Buxtehude where the highlight of your week, of your month, will be a bicycle theft.'

'Oh no!' she said with mock horror. 'That's too far away from Billwerder prison. I'll never get to visit you. Who do you want checked out?'

'The guy who was burned in that arson attack in the Schanzenviertel. Daniel Föttinger. And the woman who was with him, Victoria Kempfert.'

'Okay. You heading back in?'

'I'll be in later. I've got another house call to make.' Fabel used his remote to unlock his BMW and slid in behind the driver's seat. He checked his rear-view mirror. Yes. Still there. 'Anna, there's one more thing I need you to run through the computer. And keep this to yourself. I'm being followed. A new VW four-by-four. A Tiguan, I think. It's been popping up in my rear-view mirror all day. I suspect it's either one of ours or a BfV team. I just want to make sure.'

'Shit . . . you don't think anyone really suspects . . .'

'I doubt it,' said Fabel, 'but they're maybe keeping tabs on me *just to keep things straight*, as Criminal Director van Heiden would say.'

'Index number?'

Fabel strained to make it out in the rear-view mirror and read it out to Anna.

'Give me a couple of minutes,' she said.

Hamburg's architecture tells you in a very discreet, decorous way that this is a city where some serious money is made. Daniel Föttinger's house lay where Nienstedten became Blankenese and somehow managed to scream massive wealth quietly. It was set in four hectares of some of the most expensive real estate in Germany. Given the business Föttinger had been in, Fabel had expected it to be the same kind of ultra-modern zero-carbon set-up as Müller-Voigt's house in the Altes Land. Instead it was an elegant white aristocratic nineteenth-century villa with green shuttered windows and a double-storey aviary-cum-conservatory on its east side. Its grounds were laid out like an English park, its lawns punctuated by century-matured oaks.

It was not at all what Fabel had expected. But what he had expected was that Föttinger's widow would not be alone. He was right.

At first, given the grandeur of the surroundings, Fabel assumed that the stocky, impeccably neat man with the shaven head and the goatee beard who opened the front door to him was the butler. But it was apparent from his tailoring and demeanour that this was no manservant. He showed Fabel into a huge, bright drawing room. Another, younger, man stood over by the far wall, next to a grand piano. He too was wearing a business suit, but his was grey and not of the same quality. The younger man was made distinctive by the contrast between his pale complexion and his extremely dark, short hair.

The only other person in the room was a woman of about thirty-five sitting on a rosewood settee. She was slim, with shoulder-length wavy hair of a vibrant auburn brushed back from her delicately modelled, pale and lightly freckled face. She wore a simple, black, sleeveless dress that clung to her slim figure in a way that only the most expensive fabrics could and her poise was so perfect that she gave the impression of sitting on the settee without actually touching it.

Fabel's first impression of Kirstin Föttinger was that she was made of fine china.

In terms of attractiveness she was the equal of Föttinger's mistress, but hers was a totally different type of beauty. Where Victoria Kempfert was the kind of woman men desired, Kirstin Föttinger was like a fragile, beautiful, expensive object to be collected and preserved. And there was something about her, thought Fabel, that made her seem otherworldly.

'I'm glad you could make time to meet with me, Frau Föttinger,' he said. 'I know you must be in shock after what has happened.'

She smiled a polite porcelain smile. The truth was that she did not seem to Fabel to be in a state of much shock at all, and less grief. Perhaps it was a forced composure that had temporarily robbed her of expression.

'Frau Föttinger has taken something to help. A mild sedative prescribed by her doctor,' said the older man who had led Fabel into the drawing room.

'And you are?' Fabel turned to face him fully.

'Peter Wiegand. I'm a friend of the family. I was also a business associate of Daniel's.'

'Peter Wiegand? You're the deputy leader of the Pharos Project, aren't you?'

'I have worked with Dominik Korn for close to thirty years. My principal role is Vice President and Director of Operations of the Korn-Pharos Corporation. But yes, I am also active in the Pharos Project. Both Kirstin and her husband are members of the Project, so I am here to lend my support and comfort at this difficult time.'

'I see.' Fabel looked pointedly at the other man.

'Oh, sorry . . .' said Wiegand. 'This is Herr Bädorf. He is our chief of security for the group. I felt, given the violent circumstances of Daniel's death, that I should bring him along.'

'For the group?' Fabel spoke directly to Bädorf. 'Does that mean for the Korn-Pharos Corporation or for the Pharos Project?'

'I am not a member of the Project,' said Bädorf. Fabel noticed he had a southern accent. Swabian, he reckoned. 'I work for the Korn-Pharos group of companies. Believe it or not, Principal Chief Commissar, one is not obliged or even pressured to join the Project just because one works for the Corporation.'

'I see,' said Fabel again. But he remembered what he had read in Menke's file on the Project; the rumours about the Consolidation and Compliance Office, which sounded as if it had something to do with mergers and business etiquette but which was actually the secret police of the Pharos Project. As Fabel looked at Bädorf he was pretty sure he was in the presence of a Consolidator. And a senior one at that. Fabel had had to phone ahead to arrange this meeting and he had known that, in doing so, he was giving the Project the opportunity to have someone present to coax the right responses from Kirstin Föttinger.

Fabel turned to the newly widowed redhead. 'Frau Föttinger, I wonder if I might speak with you in private . . .'

'I would rather that Herr Wiegand and Herr Bädorf remained here. Herr Wiegand has been a great support to me.'

'As you wish. May I?' Fabel indicated the armchair opposite Frau Föttinger. It had been worth the attempt, but Fabel had known there was no way he would have been allowed to question Föttinger's widow without someone from Pharos being present. She nodded and he sat down.

'I know this is a very painful subject, Frau Föttinger, but were you aware of the relationship between your husband and Victoria Kempfert?'

'I knew nothing about any such relationship until told about it after Daniel's death.' Her answer actually sounded rehearsed.

'Do you know Victoria Kempfert?'

'We have never met.'

'Do you have any idea why someone would want to harm your husband, or kill him?'

'I was led to believe Daniel's death was an accident . . .' It was Wiegand who spoke. 'Well, not an accident, but I thought the intent of the attackers had been to set fire to the car while Daniel was inside the café.'

'Frau Föttinger?' Fabel ignored Wiegand's interruption.

'No. Not on a personal level. Daniel was not the kind of person to make enemies. But it's possible that some groups would view him with some distrust, because of the company's activities.'

'Such as?'

'Föttinger Environmental Technologies is a leader in sea-based carbon-capture technology. And Daniel was a key mover and organiser behind the GlobalConcern Hamburg summit.'

'Why would anyone object to carbon capture?'

'It's the way we do it. Daniel perfected a more efficient way of iron seeding.'

'Iron seeding?'

'Perhaps I can explain,' said Wiegand. 'It was in this area that Herr Föttinger's company cooperated with the Korn Corporation. Iron seeding is exactly how it sounds: it involves seeding deep ocean with iron dust.'

'For what purpose?' asked Fabel.

'Put simply: to trap atmospheric carbon dioxide

281

at the bottom of the ocean. The theory has been around for a time and there have been trials – with mixed results. I would guess that even officers of the Polizei Hamburg are aware that the main danger we face on the planet is the increase of CO_2 in the atmosphere, leading to catastrophic global warming. The two main causes are emissions into the atmosphere and deforestation, which is reducing the Earth's biosphere's ability to process carbon dioxide. What do you know about plankton, Herr Fabel?'

'Whales eat it. That's about it.'

'There are two types of plankton: phytoplankton and zooplankton. Effectively, phytoplankton is microscopic plant life, zooplankton is microscopic animal life. The principle of iron seeding is that the iron dust seeded into the ocean acts as a fertiliser. It causes an explosion in the population of phytoplankton. And phytoplankton, because it's plant based, employs the process of photosynthesis: it absorbs carbon dioxide and releases oxygen back into the atmosphere. In fact, even as it stands, a huge percentage of the planet's "breathing" is done by phytoplankton. The theory is that by increasing the volumes of phytoplankton in the ocean, we can take up the slack created by a reduction in rainforest and other large vegetation on land. In many of the tests, there have indeed been massive increases in the levels of phytoplankton. The process of photosynthesis also creates organic materials, sugars, which cause the phytoplankton to sink out of the light and into the dark levels of the ocean, effectively locking up the carbon in the sea floor. The irony is that this dead plankton would, over geological time, eventually become mineral oil.'

'So why isn't everyone running out to do this?' asked Fabel.

'There is a problem. Put crudely, plants make oxygen, animals make carbon dioxide. Zooplankton, which *creates* CO_2, also lives in the sunlit levels of the ocean, and it feeds on phytoplankton. That has meant that in some of the iron-seeding trial areas, the zooplankton has increased in equal proportion to the phytoplankton. It threatens to neutralise the benefit of iron seeding. That is why, with some segments of the eco-protection community, iron seeding remains a controversial topic. Some see it as a danger, not a remedy.'

'Enough to earn Herr Föttinger enemies who are willing to kill?'

Wiegand shrugged. 'You're the policeman, Herr Fabel.'

'If this iron seeding is so controversial, why were you and Föttinger Environmental pursuing it?' asked Fabel. He became aware that he was not questioning the person he had come to question, but allowed himself to be deliberately diverted for the moment.

'Because if we can iron out the problems, if you'll pardon the pun, then the benefits are potentially enormous. It could literally save all our lives. The other reason is that Daniel's researchers are close to developing potential fixes. They are adding elements to the mix that would speed up the process, causing the phytoplankton to sink much faster. Zooplankton cannot survive below three hundred metres, so if we can drop greater amounts of phytoplankton below that level after photosynthesis but before the zooplankton has a chance to feed on it, then we have our solution.'

'I see. Do you have rivals . . . competitors in this area?'

Wiegand laughed. 'No one who would kill to get ahead. The environmental-technology industry does not work that way. The planet always comes before the profit.'

Fabel turned his attention back to Kirstin Föttinger. He ran through the usual questions, establishing as detailed a chronology of the dead man's movements as possible. When Fabel was finished, he went through what he had been told.

'Going by what you have told me, Frau Föttinger,' he said, 'your husband spent – in fact, both of you regularly spent – upwards of six hours an evening on the internet or otherwise using computers?'

'That's correct,' she said blankly, the porcelain face devoid of any hint that such behaviour should be considered odd. 'It was part of his work and who he was. Who I am, as well. We both liked to remain connected.'

Fabel nodded and let it go, but made a mental note to discuss with his team the possibility of getting a warrant to examine Föttinger's computers. No, it would be futile. By the time the Polizei Hamburg's experts got into the computers, the Pharos Project's even better experts would have removed anything that might have proved embarrassing for the cult.

'Your husband knew Berthold Müller-Voigt quite well, I believe.'

'Not well. Naturally, they encountered each other frequently.'

'But Herr Müller-Voigt was a director of Föttinger Environmental Technologies . . .'

'A non-executive director. Berthold's function was one of adviser.'

'I would have thought that that would create a conflict of interest for him as Environment Senator.'

'He lodged it with the Senate as a declared interest. In any case, our company does not operate in the Hamburg area. There are no contracts to be awarded or the like.'

'But you do understand that I have to examine any connections between your husband and Senator Müller-Voigt?'

'Do you really think there's a connection?' asked Wiegand. 'They died under different circumstances, didn't they? Poor Daniel's death may not even have been intended and, from what I've read, Berthold was murdered by someone he had let into his home.'

Fabel turned to Wiegand and held him in his stare for a moment. The agenda behind the last remark was clear: Wiegand knew, somehow, that Fabel had been in Müller-Voigt's house shortly before he died.

'I don't know if there is a connection or not,' said Fabel. 'Yet. I take it you knew *Berthold* too.'

'As a matter of fact, I did. Obviously our paths crossed because of our mutual involvement in environmental affairs.'

'I see,' said Fabel. 'Did you ever meet his partner? Meliha Yazar?'

'I can't say I did,' said Wiegand, with nothing to read on his face.

'Frau Föttinger?'

'The name is not familiar,' she said. 'I thought that Berthold was not exclusive with anyone. He had a reputation as a ladies' man, as I'm sure you're aware.'

Fabel thanked Kirstin Föttinger, expressed his sympathy for her loss once more, and took his leave of her. He knew he was a character leaving a stage: nothing about the interview had been natural or spontaneous. There was nothing more to find out here. As he had on the way in, Peter Wiegand made sure to act as Fabel's escort as the detective left.

'Your *society* intrigues me, Herr Wiegand,' said Fabel as they reached his car. 'Tell me, do you really believe in the Consolidation? That you can all be uploaded onto a mainframe?'

286

'Herr Fabel, every religion, every belief system, has a central tenet that is open to a multitude of interpretations. Whatever the belief system, some adherents will hold that tenet to be literal, some to be figurative. In any case, for all I know all of *this* . . .' He made a sweeping gesture with his arm to indicate the house's parklike gardens, the trees and everything beyond. 'Maybe all of this *is* the Consolidation. Maybe this isn't true reality and we're all just self-aware programs in a post-human generated environmental model. But if this is reality, and I firmly believe that it is, then it is coming to a close if we do not do something radical, and do it quickly.' He paused and looked at Fabel as if assessing him. 'You are welcome to visit us, Herr Fabel. Have you seen the Pharos, our headquarters here, out on the coast at Hörne? In fact, it's not very far away from Berthold Müller-Voigt's house. And I believe you have been there.'

'No, I can't say I have seen the Pharos,' said Fabel, refusing to take the bait.

'Then you should come! It really is an exceptional piece of architecture. The Pharos is built as an extension to an existing nineteenth-century lighthouse. The entire building projects out over the water. We even have sections of glass flooring where you can look down at the sea, twenty metres below.' He handed Fabel a card. 'Please visit us, Herr Fabel. We are open to all, even to policemen. But I would ask that you ring first so we know when to expect you. The only other thing I would ask you to bring is an open mind.'

'So you can close it?'

'Despite what your colleagues from the BfV may have told you, we are *not* a cult. We are an environmental-action group.'

'I have to say,' said Fabel, 'I don't fancy the idea of being suspended above the sea.'

'You have a fear of water, Herr Fabel?'

'No . . . not a fear. I was brought up in Norddeich. I have a healthy respect for it.'

'The only water I fear,' said Wiegand, suddenly less affable and more serious, 'is dark water. Do you know what the albedo effect is? Albedo is the reflectivity of a surface to the sun's rays. Polar ice reflects the sun's rays and prevents sea warming. The more ice, the cooler the sea, the more stable the climate. The higher the ratio of dark water to white ice, the faster the planet heats up. Every year there is less and less ice at the poles and more and more dark water. I want you to understand, Herr Fabel, that whatever you think of me or the Pharos Project I am genuinely afraid of the cataclysm that awaits us and genuinely committed to doing all I can, using every weapon at my disposal, to prevent it happening. We are not playing a game here. This is a battle to survive.'

Fabel nodded thoughtfully. He was actually thinking about how far Wiegand would go, and what weapons he was prepared to use. But Fabel had also read that Wiegand's personal wealth could be counted in billions, rather than millions; there was a profit to be made out of any apocalypse.

'Maybe I will pay you a visit, Herr Wiegand,' he said. He looked at the card Wiegand had handed him. It had the same stylised eye motif as the poster he had passed on the way to the airport. 'Sometime soon.'

Once he was in his car, Fabel switched his cellphone back on. It rang almost immediately. It was Anna Wolff.

'Okay,' she said. 'This is interesting. I ran a check on those names and I've got the details on that plate you ran . . . if that car really is following you, then it's not one of ours and it's nothing to do with the BfV. It's registered to Seamark International, which, I am told, is a private maritime security company.'

'What? Why the hell is a private security company following me?'

'Do you want me to send someone to their offices to get some answers?'

'No, not yet. I don't want them alerted to the fact that I'm onto them. If I see the same car on my tail again I'm going to have them pulled over. One thing you could do for me is to check out this Seamark International. I'd put a month's wages on it turning out to be some kind of subsidiary of the Korn-Pharos Corporation. What about the names I gave you to check?'

'Victoria Kempfert is as clean as a whistle. No

convictions or arrests, no contact of any signifi- cance with the police. But it's Daniel Föttinger who makes things much more interesting. He would appear to have been someone who didn't take "no" for an answer. An accusation of sexual harassment last year lodged by a female employee, and *two* accusations of rape. One when he was still a student and the second in 1999. All three accusations were dropped as soon as the police investigated. It would appear that Föttinger's daddy had the kind of wealth to make unpleasant- ness disappear . . . and, of course, so did Föttinger junior, later.'

'Now that *is* interesting.'

'There's more. Föttinger's parents put him in a fancy hospital in Bavaria after the student-days incident. A psychiatric hospital. I've asked for a court order to get his records. I thought you'd want them. I don't know how relevant any of this is, but I thought there might be a chance that someone was exacting revenge.'

'Well done, Anna.' Fabel thought about what she had told him. 'Get me the names and addresses of the victims, would you? I'd like to talk to them. Or at least one of them.'

'Sure, *Chef*, but you'll have to give me some time. I'm in the Commission but I'll be mobile in ten. I'm going out to see the disabled guy you talked to, Johann Reisch. Two officers are going to check out his computer, one from Tech Section, the other from Cybercrime. By the way, they're none too pleased with you. They say that the delay in examining his computer means he could have erased a lot of evidence.'

'Reisch isn't our man, Anna. And that's good old-fashioned police instinct, not technology.'

'Well, the problem is that they're out at Reisch's right now and can't get an answer. And Reisch was expecting them. They arranged a time with him on the phone.'

'That doesn't sound good, Anna. Reisch is pretty much housebound. Get a uniformed unit to go out with you. If you get no answer, force the door. I'm on my way now. In fact, hold fire until I get there. And see if you can get a number for his carer. *Shit*, I've forgotten her name . . .'

'Rössing . . . I'm already on it. See you there.'

CHAPTER 26

As it turned out, they did not need to force entry into Reisch's house. Frau Rössing, the disabled man's carer, turned up with a key just as Fabel arrived. Fabel noticed that Reisch's carer wore an expression of genuine concern.

'He was fine this morning when I left,' she said as she fumbled through her bunch of keys.

'Wait here,' Anna told her after she had unlocked the door. 'We need to go in first.'

Fabel and Anna found Reisch exactly where he had been the last time Fabel had spoken to him; sitting at the table, staring at the computer screen of his laptop. Except that today Reisch was staring at the screen through the clear polythene of the plastic bag that was pulled over his head and sealed at the neck by a drawstring. The bag was large and ballooned out as if pumped full of air; it gave Fabel the impression of an oversized space helmet, or the hood of one of those suits you saw worn by people who handled radioactive material. Reisch still sat upright, the neck brace of his wheel-chair preventing him from slumping, his blank stare aimed at the laptop screen.

Fabel pushed two fingers into the flesh at the side of Reisch's neck, just beneath where the drawstring had been pulled tight. He turned to Anna and shook his head.

'Shit . . .' Anna stared at the still-upright dead man. 'Do you think someone's killed him because of his connection to *Virtual Dimension?*'

Fabel did not answer. Instead, he flipped open his cellphone and called it in to the Presidium. He asked who was on forensics duty.

'Keep the carer out of here, Anna,' he said quietly after he hung up from his call. 'But tell her that Reisch has passed away. Holger Brauner's on his way with a team.'

After Anna and the uniformed officer left the room, Fabel took a closer look around Reisch's desk. There was a postal packet that had been untidily torn open. Next to it lay what looked to Fabel like a small oxygen canister with a length of tubing attached. Fabel took a latex glove from his jacket pocket and, without slipping it on, used it as a shield while he rolled the canister around. It had the symbol *He* on it. Not oxygen, helium.

Fabel checked the laptop's screen. When Reisch had died, he had been locked into *Virtual Dimension*. Now his avatar walked aimlessly through a surrealistically realistic world rendered by computer graphics. It had been what he had watched as he died. The last thing his dying brain would have registered. Even now, Reisch gave the impression of watching his cybernetic alter ego.

Once Brauner and his team had arrived, Fabel joined Anna and the uniformed officer outside. Brauner had only been in the house for fifteen minutes when he called Fabel back in.

'You can forget this one, if you ask me, Jan,' said Brauner. 'Of course you'll have to wait for the autopsy, but this is no murder. Well, it's self-murder, but that doesn't interest you.'

'But someone tied that bag around his neck. If he did it himself, then as soon as he started to suffocate, the survival instinct would have kicked in.'

'No it wouldn't, Jan. That's a so-called "*Exit Bag*". A suicide kit. The fastening is a drawstring you pull tight yourself. And the "survival instinct" you talk about is called the hypercapnic alarm response. It's the panic you feel when the level of carbon dioxide in your blood becomes dangerously high and your brain tells you that you've got to start breathing fast. He won't have experienced that. That's what the canister was for: you fill the bag or your lungs or both with an inert gas like nitrogen or helium. It confuses your brain and it overrides the hypercapnic alarm response. You just feel you're breathing normally, no pain, no panic, then you pass out and never wake up. Believe it or not, you can buy Exit Bags on the internet, or download instructions on how to make one yourself. We've bagged up the postal packet it came in: you might be able to find out whom he ordered it from. And I guess you'll find something about it on that . . .' Brauner nodded towards the laptop on the table.

'So you're convinced it was suicide?'

'There's no evidence to suggest it wasn't. Why was he in the wheelchair?'

'Some kind of motor neurone disease. Poor bastard.'

'Then I don't blame him. If it were me, I'd do the same before I couldn't do it for myself. And, truth be told, these Exit Bags are not the worst way to go. You don't want to be interrupted and saved, though. Pull through from an attempt with one of these and your brain'll be mush.'

The officer from Kroeger's Cybercrime Unit came in. She had been the one who had alerted Anna and had waited while the forensics had done their work. She was an unlikely-looking police officer, petite with auburn hair tied back in a pony-tail and wearing jeans and a waist-length casual jacket. She looked as if she could still have been a student on her way to a lecture. Something about her reminded Fabel of his daughter, Gabi, who had the same auburn hair and who had expressed an interest in following her father into the Polizei Hamburg. Fabel noticed that the young police-woman worked at not looking at the dead man in the wheelchair.

'You all right?' he asked her.

'Yes, Herr Chief Commissar. Sorry.' She frowned. 'I wondered if you still wanted us to take the laptop for examination?'

'Of course,' said Fabel. He looked again at the screen. *Thorsten66*, Reisch's virtual-world persona, still wandered the counterfeit world of *Virtual Dimension*'s New Venice. In one corner of the screen, beneath the photograph of the muscle-torsoed youth who Reisch had chosen because it reminded him of a younger, healthy self, were messages from other users, inviting *Thorsten66* to parties by the lagoons, or to take part in the New Venice Olympics. It was no accident that Reisch had had this on-screen, in his line of sight, as he died. Maybe he really had believed that through an effort of will he could project himself, at the moment of death, into that ersatz but infinitely preferable reality.

The young cybercrime officer bent to close the laptop and remove it.

'Leave it,' said Fabel; then, more gently, 'Leave it switched on. I'll bring it out in a minute.'

On his way back to the Presidium, Fabel kept checking his rear-view mirror. But there was no sign of a VW four-by-four following him and he started to wonder if paranoia was infectious. Fabel always found strange the things that got to him about his work. Not always the exposure to violence or horror, or the constant exposure to all that was the worst in people: as he drove towards Alsterdorf and the Presidium, it was the image of a dying Reisch sitting in front of his computer wishing himself into a lie. It was the sadness, the vulnerability, the desperation that Fabel saw in his day-to-day work that troubled him most.

The entire team was again assembled and they went through the usual recap of the caseload as well as any new information on each murder. As had been agreed with van Heiden, Nicola Brüggemann had taken over as lead investigating officer on the Network Killer case.

Brüggemann's build was what Fabel's mother would have euphemised as *mollig*. But there was very little else about the Child Crime Principal Commissar that could be described as cuddly. Brüggemann carried her plumpness on a frame that was at least one metre eighty tall and with shoulders that would have put an American Pro-footballer to shame. Her black hair was cut short at the sides and thick on top, adding to the masculinity of her look. She was, Fabel knew, a no-nonsense Holsteiner whose manner could best be described as abrasive and her wit as acerbic. It was not the same kind of prickliness that Fabel encountered on a regular basis with Anna, more an uncompromising, direct professionalism. If they were all in the business of policing, then Nicola Brüggemann was the *no-frills* offer. Fabel had a great deal of respect for her as a colleague. As she ran through the progress of the Network Killer case, Fabel appreciated the way she made a point of asking him for authority to allocate resources and people. She was making a point: Fabel was still in charge.

After Brüggemann had finished summing up,

Fabel briefly outlined what had occurred at the Reisch residence in Schiffbek. It was, he said again, unlikely that there was any relevance to any of the other enquiries.

Thomas Glasmacher and Dirk Hechtner looked an unlikely team: Glasmacher was tall, blond and burly, Hechtner was small, dark and slight; Glasmacher was reserved, Hechtner was outgoing. Fabel had recruited and paired them over a year before and he was pleased at the way they had gelled as a partnership. Dirk always did most of the talking and he confirmed that the full report on the body found at the Poppenbütteler Schleuse had come in. Like the other victims, Julia Henning had been raped and strangled, and again there was no stranger DNA or trace to be harvested by the forensics team or the pathologist.

But the autopsy had revealed something different.

'It would appear that she wasn't as fresh as we first thought,' explained Dirk.

'Meaning?' Nicola Brüggemann and Fabel asked the same question simultaneously.

'Meaning that an analysis of the victim's blood found evidence of cold storage. Not freezing, but that she had been kept at a very low temperature, like in a cold store.'

'Someone was trying to confuse us about the time of death?' asked Fabel.

'It looks like it,' said Thomas Glasmacher. 'There's no way of telling how long she was in the cold store or how long she was kept at room temperature afterwards. So yes, it looks like the killer has tried to confuse us about the time of death. And he's succeeded.'

'But why?' asked Werner. 'Why now? He's never done anything like this before.'

'Unless our guy feels he's slipped up,' said Dirk. 'Or maybe he thinks he was seen. It could be that he's trying to fudge the time of death so he can't be pinned down to the scene of crime.'

Fabel thought about what Hechtner had said. 'Possible, but it doesn't gel with what we know about his modus. I don't know, Dirk – it's an odd change of pattern, that's for sure.'

They left it for the moment and Thomas Glasmacher and Dirk Hechtner went on to provide a report on the victim. It revealed nothing other than Julia Henning had been a pretty, bright but reserved and unattached young lawyer who had worked for a commercial law office in Hamburg, dealing mainly with copyright disputes. Thomas and Dirk had spoken to Julia's parents, colleagues and friends, of whom there were comparatively few. Despite being attractive, Julia had had few boyfriends and had not been seeing anyone at the time of her disappearance. She had lived alone in the apartment at the address Fabel had been given by the woman at the docks and had not been seen since she'd left work on the Friday afternoon. She could have been killed at any time over the weekend.

One thing did stand out, however. When her

apartment had been searched, everything had been in order. It was only as they were leaving that Dirk had suddenly realised that something was missing. Something that became instantly conspicuous by its absence. A computer. And all the Network Killer's victims had connected with him on social networking sites.

'So we thought, if she didn't have a computer, maybe she had a web-enabled cell phone.'

'Let me guess,' said Fabel. 'No cellphone, either.'

'Julia Henning must have been the only twenty-seven-year-old in Hamburg without a computer or cellphone. So we pulled out of the apartment and sent in a forensics team. It's pretty obvious that someone has been in there and taken her stuff, possibly our killer.'

'The neighbours see anything?'

Thomas Glasmacher, the larger and quieter of the two answered. 'No . . . no one saw anything unusual or anyone they didn't know come in or out. We found a shoebox full of receipts and warranties and we've been going through that. Also, we've asked her bank for full details of her outgoings. I'll bet we'll find a direct debit to a phone-service provider. But proving she had a computer and a cellphone doesn't bring us any closer to actually finding them.'

Fabel grunted; they seemed to be perpetually scrabbling around in a fog.

'There's something about this one,' he said, rubbing his chin. 'It all smacks of someone trying to cover tracks and confuse times. As Werner said, why now? Why did he feel the need to make these changes with this one?'

They moved on to the Müller-Voigt inquiry. Werner ran through the progress to date. He confirmed what Astrid Bremer had already told Fabel about the fingerprints and the stray sample of grey fibre found at the scene. Fabel felt the tension in the room when Werner read from the report that only Fabel's and the dead man's fingerprints had been found on the weapon. Other than that, the investigation into the politician's death also seemed to be stalling, despite it being obvious that Werner was pulling out all the stops to remove any suspicion, no matter how slight, that his boss might have been involved in the murder.

Anna Wolff then picked up the thread.

'Müller-Voigt's mystery woman is less of a mystery,' she said. 'But not much less.'

'Oh?' said Fabel, his interest pricked.

'Müller-Voigt had a broad range of restaurants he would take women to. It would have made things easier if he had been more a creature of habit, but I have checked them all out. No one saw him with a woman fitting Meliha's description. Then I thought that maybe she called the shots and decided where they should eat. And with her being Turkish, I thought I'd check out some of the Turkish restaurants in town. Believe me, there are a *lot* of Turkish restaurants in Hamburg. I took the liberty of pulling in a favour from uniform and circulated a picture of Müller-Voigt and a description of Meliha Yazar. We struck gold in Eimsbüttel – not something you get to say every day. There's a restaurant on Schulterblatt in the Schanzenviertel and the owner swears Müller-Voigt and Meliha were regulars. He recognised Müller-Voigt's picture but didn't have any idea he was a politician, and he remembers Meliha because she spoke Turkish to him. He said she told him she was from Silviri, on the coast. She had been in a couple of times on her own, but there's no credit card transaction recorded because either Müller-Voigt paid or she paid by cash. But I'm afraid that's it – he couldn't tell me any more. Although he did say their regular waiter is on holiday at the moment. But he'll be back this week. The owner said he got the idea that the woman didn't like being asked questions. Other than that, she was very friendly and he got the impression that they were a very close couple.'

Another amateur psychologist waiting table, thought Fabel. 'Well, it's something. It's more than something – well done, Anna. At least now we can demonstrate that Meliha Yazar did exist.'

He resumed the formal procedure of the caseload recap, hoping that something would leap out at them. Usually the job of the Murder Commission was to find a commonality between cases, to establish links. The problem at the moment, thought Fabel, was that they kept tripping over commonalities and links where there should be none: the

Network Killer case was unlikely to be related to the female torso washed up at the Fischmarkt; Müller-Voigt's murder *could* be linked to the torso, but logically Daniel Föttinger's death – his possible unintentional death – should have been separate from everything else.

But there were links. There was a commonality. Or at least there was a mass of coincidences that stretched the laws of probability beyond the credible.

Müller-Voigt's missing girlfriend had been investigating the Pharos Project and the body on the Fischmarkt had been in the water for almost the same period that she had been missing. Müller-Voigt was a non-executive director of Föttinger Environmental Technologies, and both Daniel and Kirstin Föttinger were members of the Project. Even the Network Killer case had an unexpected, if coincidental, link to Pharos through the company that had developed *Virtual Dimension*. Then, of course, there was the fact that someone had done their best to implicate Fabel in both the Network Killer case and Müller-Voigt's murder; and whoever had done that had enormous technological skills and resources at their disposal. Like the Pharos Project.

'But what possible link could there be between the Pharos Project and women who have been targeted in a classic serial sex-offender way, raped and strangled?' asked Nicola Brüggemann. 'Ritual murders, I could believe. Elimination of ex-members would be probable, but we know that none of these women had any connection to the Project at all.'

'Other than *Virtual Dimension* being owned by a Korn-Pharos company,' said Werner.

'True, but that's not such a big coincidence. Between all the companies in the group, Korn-Pharos generates a hell of a lot of internet content.'

'What about this guy Reisch, Jan?' asked Werner. 'His death could be seen as another coincidence. He was involved with *Virtual Dimension* too, and we know he had contact with the dead women. Maybe his suicide was guilt over their deaths.'

'But he was physically incapable of committing the crimes,' said Fabel.

'I think Werner has a point, though,' said Brüggemann in her deep contralto. 'Because he was incapable of commission, it doesn't mean that he wasn't involved in some way. Maybe he was part of a killing team, with some kind of *folie à deux* or *folie à trois* crap going on. Maybe he got some kind of vicarious cyber hard-on by having an accomplice commit the act for him.'

'No. It doesn't fit, Nicola. But we'll explore it, anyway. Cybercrime Unit is doing a forensic search of his hard drive. Maybe we'll find something there. But I think Reisch was just a poor schmuck who had been dealt the worst hand you can imagine. He just decided to throw that hand in. Or that's my take on it, at least.'

'What about the State Prosecutor's Office? Are

they closer to budging on warrants?' asked Henk Hermann.

'We simply don't have enough on the Pharos Project. To be honest, the State Prosecutor's Office is reluctant to take on the legal might of the Korn-Pharos Corporation without being totally sure of their ground.' Fabel sighed. 'I don't blame them. We are talking about something with the resources of a small country behind it. We *have* to get more on Pharos. And something evidentially solid; not more coincidences.'

'It's odd,' said Henk. 'Usually we have an individual, a single person, at the top of our suspects list. But now, with all this, we've got a *group* of people, a pretty amorphous and anonymous group of people at that. It's more like corporate crime.'

Fabel stared at Henk. So long that the junior officer started to look uncomfortable and eventually laughed nervously and said. 'What?'

'You're right, Henk,' said Fabel, animated. He stood up and grabbed the file that Menke had given him. 'Crimes aren't committed by corporate bodies. I read somewhere in here . . .' He flicked determinedly through the pages of the BfV report. 'Here it is . . . one of the cult's philosophies stresses the importance of the *egregore*, the groupmind.'

Fabel started to read from the file: '". . . the *egregore* has been a concept in occultism and mystical thinking for more than a century, but the Pharos Project has adopted it in the more contemporary sense from current business and commercial law usage, where corporate bodies are seen to have a single mind or corporate culture, at least in terms of corporate responsibility and liability. Like all destructive cults, the Pharos Project seeks to diminish the sense of the individual and increase the concept of a singular groupmind. To achieve this, members of the Project are subjected to psychological programming over protracted periods as well as having to follow a highly disciplined, hierarchical and structured daily routine. Part of the creation of a sense of corporateness is the exclusive use of English as the principal language of communication, something the Pharos Project has borrowed from large German corporations who conduct all senior management meetings in English, even if all present are native German speakers. Another element of the Pharos Project's corporation-like culture is the wearing of uniforms by all its adherents. Because of federal restrictions on the use of uniforms by political or quasi-political groups, the Pharos Project has employed the simple device of forcing all members to wear identical business suits: pale grey for the rank and file, dark grey for Consolidators, and black for senior figures in the organisation. This avoids any difficulty with federal regulation and allows an element of anonymity, as the outfits supplied differ in no significant manner from normal business apparel . . . ."'

Fabel snapped shut the file. 'Werner, can you

get onto Astrid Bremer and ask her if she can give us a detailed background of the grey fibre she found at Müller-Voigt's place? She told me that it was particularly unusual because it was entirely synthetic. I'll bet that the Pharos Project buys its uniforms in bulk from some corporate-wear wholesaler. Anna, I need you to sweet-talk your contact in the State Prosecutor's office and tell him we need a limited search-and-seizure warrant for a couple of jackets from the Pharos Project for a comparison.' Fabel checked himself and looked across to Nicola Brüggemann.

'Go ahead,' she said without a hint of antagonism. 'It's your department.'

'Thanks,' said Fabel, then frowned, like someone trying to remember where they had left their car keys. 'That woman down by the docks – she was wearing a dark grey business suit.'

'God, Jan,' said Brüggemann, 'that's a bit of a stretch. A business suit is a business suit.'

'Maybe so. But I'm pretty convinced that she was a Consolidator. It's all beginning to come together. The Network Killer murders are linked to the Pharos Project. But I can't for the life of me work out why.' Fabel picked up his jacket from the back of the chair.

'Nicola, I'll leave you to it. I need to go out.'

'Where are you off to?'

'I'm going to take a North Sea lighthouse tour.'

CHAPTER 27

Susanne was still at the Institute for Legal Medicine when Fabel phoned her from his car as he headed out, once more, towards the Altes Land and Stade. This time he avoided the town and headed out along a ribbon of road that ran parallel to the coast but was shielded from it by the ripple of dyke that ran along close to the water's edge to Fabel's right. To his left the land was divided up into long narrow fields, pale green, dark green or muted gold; each contained by the type of Knick turf wall Müller-Voigt had talked about. It really did have the look of a patchwork quilt, but one that had been ironed impeccably flat except for the ripple of the waterside dyke at its hem.

It took Fabel another hour or so to reach the Pharos. He actually pulled over to the side of the road and got out to admire it from a distance. The light was beginning to fade and the cloud cover dulled things even more, but even with that Fabel could see that Müller-Voigt had been right: the Pharos was a truly remarkable piece of architecture. There was a lighthouse, about four or five storeys high, against the flank of the new building.

The lighthouse was the traditional North Sea German type: not slender but solid, squat and square-edged with a large lantern gallery criss-crossed with iron. It had clearly undergone a major renovation and looked bright, almost as if it had just been built rather than having stood there, resolutely planted in its landscape, for more than a century and a half.

But it was the main building attached to the original lighthouse that really impressed Fabel. It was made up of three sections; modules, almost. The section against whose side the lighthouse was set was a long two-storey block. Clearly the intention had been not to obscure the view of the original lighthouse from either direction. This section extended fifty metres or so towards the water's edge; then a five-storey block, with the profile of a massive parallelogram – a rhombohedron, Fabel suddenly remembered from school mathematics – took the Pharos to the water and jutted out over it. This section was outlined by a heavy reinforced-concrete beamed frame, but the flanks of the building were all glass. The third section was really an extension of the top floor of the building and projected out over the Elbe, supported by two rows of piles driven into the river bed. From the roof of the suspended level a pale blue needle of laser light, now visible in the twilight, pierced the clouds above. The light of the Pharos.

This, thought Fabel, was more than a building. It was a statement; a dramatic statement of power and wealth. For a supposedly environmental group, it seemed to Fabel to be an aggressive statement of human dominance over Nature. And a statement not without a tone of menace.

He drove further along the narrow coastal road until he reached the end of the drive that led up to the Pharos. It was even more breathtaking close up. The lower-level module was clad in natural materials: pale wood, glass and large blocks of stone. He turned off the road and up the drive. After a short distance, Fabel came to a closed gate. There was a small blockhouse on the other side of the fence and Fabel had to give his horn a blast before anyone came out. It did not surprise Fabel to see that the young man with short cropped blond hair who emerged from the blockhouse was wearing a grey suit, white shirt and dark grey tie. He stood behind the heavy-gauge wire, regarding Fabel impassively but without making any move to open the gate.

Fabel got out of his car. He estimated that the fence that extended on either side was three metres high and heavy-duty enough to keep out any but the most determined intruder.

'I would like to talk to Herr Wiegand.' Fabel held up his police ID. The man at the gate remained silent and impassive. 'Now . . .' said Fabel with more emphasis.

'No one is admitted without an appointment.' The gatekeeper's voice was as flat and dull as Fabel had expected. 'We do not allow anyone access to the Pharos unless it has been arranged in advance.'

'I don't need an appointment. I'm the police.' Fabel noticed that the gateman had a Bluetooth earpiece lodged in his ear.

'Then you either need an appointment or a warrant.'

'I don't think you understand,' said Fabel wearily. 'I am here by personal invitation of Herr Wiegand. Your Director General.'

The gatekeeper continued to stare at Fabel; whatever was going through his mind certainly was not breaking the surface.

After what seemed an age, the young man broke his silence. 'Wait here.'

He walked a few metres away and stood with his back to Fabel, who guessed the guard was communicating with the main building. After a while he came back out and opened the gate.

'Leave your car here,' he said. 'We don't allow vehicular traffic beyond this point.'

Fabel shrugged, used his remote to lock his car and stepped into the compound. The gateman led the way up to the main entrance to the Pharos where another unsmiling escort was waiting, again wearing an earpiece. Fabel examined the building from up close. It loomed. It was no accident that the Pharos Project used the symbolism and vocabulary of the world of international corporate commerce: this building was all about out-scaling everything human. Just like any multinational business's headquarters, the Pharos had been built to embody and glorify the corporate and diminish the individual. It was the same trick that medieval cathedral architects had used, where the scale was supposed to represent God, but really was all about the power of the Church, the great multinational corporation of the Middle Ages.

Fabel was taken into a large atrium in which the lighting had been kept low. The reason, Fabel guessed, was the atrium's centrepiece. A circle of beams, changing hue, shone upwards, illuminating what Fabel perceived as some kind of giant jellyfish, diaphanous and beautiful, with a deep red core and a skirt of transparent tentacles, suspended in mid-air. It was very well done: a holographic projection that rendered the jellyfish in three dimensions and made it pulse and change colour. But Fabel was surprised at his own reaction to the projection: for a split second it had looked so impossibly real, but Fabel had instantly, instinctively known it was an artifice.

It was as remarkable a building from the inside. As he was led through halls and corridors, and taken up to the top floor in an elevator, Fabel never lost sight of the landscape around him. No matter where he was, there was always a view through glass, even in the lift. He noticed that everyone wore the same kind of grey suit, although a minority, his escort included, were dressed in a slightly darker shade. They made their way past a host of glass-walled rooms that looked to Fabel like any other offices. Despite his escort deliberately keeping the pace up, Fabel took in as much as he could. Every room had dozens of desks with computer consoles, but of a design that Fabel had never seen before: monitors that were impossibly thin; people typing on keyboards that must have had such a low profile that Fabel could not see them. Then, as he passed a smaller office with a workstation closer to the glass wall, he realised why. The fingers of the grey-suited woman sitting at it ranged over a virtual keyboard: light projected onto the tabletop.

Fabel remembered reading about how toxic the heavy metals used in electronic hardware was to the environment. For an environmental pressure group, thought Fabel, the Pharos Project loved their gadgets. The other thing that struck him as he walked through the Pharos was how much it looked like a working office, and how the men and women he saw circulating through it did not look like cult members or mystical acolytes but more like the employees of some international bank.

Peter Wiegand was waiting for Fabel in his office; although Fabel struggled to attach the word 'office' to a space as vast as this. Wiegand conducted his business from the last room on the projecting top floor. The office stretched the full width of the building and was longer than it was wide. All three external walls were glass and offered views in every direction. This was where the Elbe began to open out to meet the sea and water was the element that dominated the view. Fabel noticed there was even a large rectangle of glass set into the floor, through which he could see the water rippling dark below. He made a point of stepping around the panel.

'Please, Herr Fabel,' said Wiegand, stepping out from behind a desk that made van Heiden's look inadequate. 'Don't concern yourself. That reinforced glass is stronger than concrete; it's entirely safe to walk on.' He shook Fabel's hand and led him to a chair, asking him to sit.

'That's a very interesting . . .' Fabel struggled for the best description. '. . . *piece* you have in your reception. The hologram, I mean. It's very beautiful, but an odd choice of subject. Is it because of Dominik Korn's sub-sea history that you've chosen a jellyfish?'

'I didn't choose it. It was Dominik Korn's inspiration. It symbolises almost everything the Pharos Project is about.'

'Oh?'

'The medium is the message, Herr Fabel. Dominik chose a hologram as a medium to reflect the holographic nature of the universe, that it is made up of bits of information. And, of course, that is Dominik's great philosophy: that almost anything can be transformed into information and transferred. Stored.'

'I wasn't aware the universe was holographic.' Fabel failed to keep the sneer from his tone.

'Then you're not acquainted with the latest discoveries in quantum physics. I'm not spouting New Age mysticism, if that's what you think. I'm talking about the latest developments in string theory.'

'And that's your *unique selling point*, isn't it? Digital immortality?'

Wiegand did not let his smile falter. 'Let me ask you something: do you believe in immortality?'

'No. Everything dies. It's a simple law of nature, of the universe. I know that you believe we can all live for ever in a computer mainframe, but that's not life. It's not even existence, because it wouldn't be real and it wouldn't be you. You would not experience it yourself. Immortality is impossible. Everything dies.'

'Again, Herr Fabel, you've only succeeded in revealing your ignorance. Immortality *does* exist. It exists right here and now in your *real* world. The holographic image in the atrium is of *Turritopsis Nutricula*. It is beautiful, but the projection in the atrium is several thousand times the size of the real creature: in reality, they are only four or five millimetres in size. But do you know why *Mister* Korn chose *Turritopsis Nutricula* as a symbol?'

Fabel shrugged. 'I have a feeling you're going to enlighten me.'

'It is, truly, really immortal. It is the only living creature on the planet that is immortal.'

'How can that be?' said Fabel, intrigued despite himself.

'All jellyfish are born, mature and mate. Normally, immediately after mating, the jellyfish dies. The Immortal Jellyfish, as *Turritopsis Nutricula* is also known, doesn't. It goes through a process called transdifferentiation, where it literally transforms the structure of its cells. And what it transforms those cells into is its juvenile state. It bypasses senescence and cheats death by becoming a polyp again. Then it matures, mates, transdifferentiates, becomes a polyp again. And it can do this for ever. So immortality *does* exist, Herr Fabel. And the hologram in the atrium represents the combination of digitisation and immortality. It also has an environmental message: *Turritopsis Nutricula* was once found only in the Caribbean, but it has been transported all around the world in the ballast tanks of ships. Our activities have caused a population explosion of this creature. A population explosion of a creature that breeds and multiplies but never dies.'

'You know something, Herr Wiegand? I know that you're the second most powerful figure in this organisation, and I'm sure the bulk of your members buy this cyberlife-eternal crap, mainly because they're brainwashed into it. But you? Somehow I doubt very much that you believe a word of it. I think that this is all a way of controlling people and generating wealth. What else you get up to is what particularly interests me. You're hiding something.'

Wiegand smiled his billionaire's smile, affable but slightly condescending. 'You'll have seen we use glass extensively throughout our buildings,' he said. 'We do this for two reasons: firstly, it reduces our dependence on artificial light and heating. All of our windows use energy-capture glass and the roof is basically one giant solar panel. Secondly, it

316

communicates to our members and to visitors such as yourself that the Pharos Project is, literally, transparent. We have nothing to hide, Herr Fabel. Nothing.'

'Maybe that's the view from here looking out,' said Fabel. 'But I'm not so sure big windows do much for those on the outside who see you as secretive and manipulative; who see you exploiting your members and intimidating anyone else who might dare to criticise you.'

'I'm glad you took me up on my invitation, Herr Chief Commissar.' Wiegand ignored Fabel's comment. 'Perhaps you will find it an enlightening experience and you'll see that there's nothing malevolent or cultish about the Pharos Project. Although I would have preferred it if you had phoned first, as I requested. I tend to be a very busy man and between my duties as vice-president of the Korn-Pharos Corporation, visits to the Americas Pharos in Maine, and involvement with various environmental programmes around the world, I am seldom here.'

'But you've spent most of your time here over the last few months, Herr Wiegand. You must have something of particular concern here at the moment.'

'Particular concern? No, I wouldn't say that. Oh . . . you mean the GlobalConcern Hamburg Summit? Of course that's taking up a lot of time.'

'No, I didn't mean that. I wondered if it perhaps had something more to do with Meliha Yazar.'

'Who? Oh yes, you mentioned her before. Someone poor Berthold was supposed to be involved with. No, I'm afraid I don't understand your question. I don't know of any Meliha Yazar.'

'Let me refresh your memory. She was the woman who breached your security here and made a startling discovery about the Pharos Project. So startling that it would be extremely harmful to you. Perhaps even personally.'

Wiegand leaned back in his chair and watched Fabel, smiling. It was not the usual affable salesman's smile that Fabel had so far experienced at every encounter with the billionaire. This was something much darker. Malevolent. 'I have to admit, Herr Fabel, you chose a good spot for a fishing expedition.' He vaguely indicated the river beyond the windows.

'You do admit that you are almost paranoid about security? I mean, the Hamburg State has prisons with more relaxed gatemen than the guy you've got doing meet-and-greet. It suggests that there is something you don't want the outside world to know. Every person you recruit into the Project isn't just brainwashed, they're checked out in advance. But somehow Meliha Yazar got round your security. She got to the heart of your big secret, didn't she?'

'I've already made it perfectly clear that I have no idea who you're talking about. And there's no "big secret" here. Naturally, we have to be mindful of security. There are a great many people and organisations who have a severe prejudice against us. It has to be said that the BfV is one of those organisations. Listen, you can accuse us of being crooks and freaks and a malicious cult, but the fact remains that the world is heading for a cataclysm. The Pharos Project is subject to all kinds of rumour and suspicion and investigation, but no one subjects companies that continue to seek out new oil reserves to bleed, to pollute and poison others while enriching themselves, to the same kind of scrutiny. I don't see the BfV devoting the same time and manpower to investigating multinationals who allow hectare after hectare of rainforest to be slashed and burned to provide grazing for cattle so that some fat teenager in Minnesota can stuff himself with a cheaper burger.'

'Is that why you work with the Guardians of Gaia?' asked Fabel. 'Or is it more that they work *for* the Pharos Project? It strikes me that you have set yourself up almost as a state. And all states have a military wing. An army. Is that the deal with the Guardians?'

Another smile; even colder than the last. 'Herr Fabel, I shouldn't have to point out to you what is happening in the world today. The fiercely held political beliefs of the past are no longer relevant. The forces that control our lives are no longer political; they are corporate. Nation states really don't hold sway as they used to. It is the multinational companies, the *corporate* states that shape the lives of every man, woman and child on the planet. The Pharos Project is the brainchild of Dominik Korn who is, first and foremost, a far-sighted, genius *businessman*. We have taken the same shape as our enemies, the global corporations. Our fighting is done in boardrooms and committees, not on any other type of battlefield. Dominik Korn is also a pacifist, as am I and everyone else involved in the Project. So no, if the Guardians of Gaia are involved in violent acts – no matter how much we understand the provocation – we condemn those acts. We have no place for violence. Everything we represent is about stopping violence, the violence being done to our ecosystem.'

'Then, if all that is true, you will have no objection to doing me a small favour. Could you ask the gentleman who conducted me here to step back in for a moment?'

Wiegand sighed, as if indulging a child. 'As you wish . . .' He hit a button and said a few words in English. The young man who had conducted Fabel from the main entrance to Wiegand's office came in.

'I take it you have a storeroom full of these suits?' asked Fabel. 'I mean, you clearly issue them to your members . . .'

'We do, yes. We take care of all of our members' material needs.'

'Then you could replace this gentleman's jacket if I were to ask him for it?'

'What on earth do you want his jacket for? I can supply an unused one from our stores.'

'Indulge me, Herr Wiegand. I want to make sure

that the jacket I take is of the kind that this gentleman wears.' He turned to the man by the door. 'I am right in assuming that you work for the Consolidation and Compliance Office?'

The Consolidator did not answer but looked to Wiegand for guidance.

'Please give the Chief Commissar your jacket. What do you need it for, Herr Fabel?'

'I'd like to compare the material of the jacket to a fibre we found at the Müller-Voigt crime scene.'

'Ah, I see.' He held up a hand to halt the Consolidator who had removed his jacket and was about to hand it to Fabel. 'Then, if there is a suggestion of some kind of accusation, you should perhaps obtain a warrant.'

'Do I need a warrant? Are you telling me that you won't cooperate?'

Wiegand said nothing for a moment, then nodded to the Consolidator, who handed Fabel the jacket.

'So I take it from this that you suspect someone from the Pharos Project of being involved in the murder of Berthold Müller-Voigt?' asked Wiegand when the Consolidator had left. 'Obviously, that is a laughable assertion, but if that is the case then you should have told me earlier. I can assure you that the Project will cooperate wholeheartedly with the police in any investigation. I have to say that it is impossible for any of our members to be involved in something like that. We have counsellors and mentors within our community who would identify anyone with violent or antisocial tendencies.'

321

'I wouldn't have thought that *any* form of individual action would be encouraged. I get the impression that the Project sees itself as operating as an egregore. A groupmind.'

'Now why would the Pharos Project have a collective will to cause Berthold Müller-Voigt harm?' Wiegand remained cool. If Fabel was getting to him, he was not about to let it show.

'Perhaps it was suspected that Meliha Yazar had told him what she had found out about the Project. Maybe it's something so big that anyone who could possibly be aware of it is in danger.'

'This is pure fantasy. And, I have to say, typical of the kind of fabrications that the authorities here in Germany seem to feel free to level against us. But I promise you, Herr Fabel, that if you repeat such accusations outside this room you had better be able to back them up in a court of law.'

'That, Herr Wiegand, is exactly my intention.'

Wiegand stood up to indicate that the discussion was at an end. Fabel remained seated.

'There is another matter I would like to discuss.' Fabel carefully folded the jacket he had been given on his lap, running his fingers over the material. He could tell that it was made from the kind of fabric that Astrid Bremer had described: there was no yield to it and it had a nylon-like feel. 'As you are no doubt aware, we have a case running at the moment concerning the murder of four young women targeted by someone they met through the internet.'

'The Network Killer case. Yes, I'm aware of it.'

'Well, a few nights ago, I was approached by a woman who was dressed in a style not unlike this . . .' Fabel indicated the jacket on his lap. 'She gave me a false identity. In fact, she gave me the identity of the next Network Killer victim – before we found the body. What makes it especially interesting is that when we did find the body, there was evidence that it had been kept in cold storage for some time.'

'And . . .?'

'Nothing . . . other than it suggests to me that the body was kept on ice long enough for me to be approached with the victim's name, and also to confuse us about the time of death. As if it was important for us to believe that the woman died some time later than she actually did.'

'And this means what to me?' asked Wiegand wearily.

'I've been thinking about it a great deal, and I think I understand its significance. And I think it tells me what it was Meliha Yazar found out.'

'Which is?'

'I think we'll save that for another time.' Fabel stood up. 'Thank you for your time, Herr Wiegand. I look forward to our next chat.' He looked around at the office, the glass walls, the dimmed view of the water around them. 'Next time we can meet in my office, I think.'

It was fully dark as Fabel drove back along the narrow road towards Stade. It was deserted of cars and he could see there were no headlights in his rear-view mirror. Anyway, he thought, Wiegand knew exactly where he had been and the road he would take back to town. So there was no need for him to pick up a tail until he had reached the main road network.

Jan Fabel was a man who liked to do the right thing in every situation; to follow the rules. It sat heavy and hard with him that he had just done something he would never have allowed one of his junior officers to do: he had deliberately exposed himself to danger. Fabel had known that there was no way that he would ever build a solid case against an organisation as sophisticated, resourceful and skilled as the Pharos Project. He needed to flush them out. Flush Wiegand out. Wiegand had said that Fabel had been on a fishing trip and he had been right; except Fabel was the bait. Fabel had hinted that he possessed the same knowledge that Meliha Yazar had, and had been abducted and more than likely murdered over. Müller-Voigt had had his skull pulped in the belief that he *might* have had the information. And now they would believe that Fabel had that knowledge. And, as someone who could do infinitely more damage than either Yazar or Müller-Voigt, they would no doubt come after him.

The truth was, he was beginning to believe that he *did* know what it was that Meliha had found out. How he could ever prove it was another matter.

He was just approaching Stade when his cellphone rang.

'Chief Commissar Fabel?' It was a male voice. Deep – too deep and faintly robotic; punctuated with deep, rasping breaths. Fabel realised that it was being electronically altered.

'Who is this?'

'Call me the Klabautermann, that seems appropriate.'

'You're joking, right?' Fabel laughed. 'You want me to call you the Klabautermann? I'm guessing you read too many comics. Or what is it they call them these days? Oh yes, *graphic novels*. Now listen, you know you are speaking to a police officer, so I suggest you stop wasting my time . . .'

'Now wait a minute . . .' The menace of the electronically altered voice dissipated as the person behind it grew flustered. 'You've got to listen to me . . .'

'Lose the Darth Vader crap and we can talk.'

There was a pause. Then something clicked on the line.

'Who is this?' asked Fabel.

'I can't tell you.' Now the voice was natural. Male, but high-pitched. Still punctuated with snorting breaths. Someone overweight, Fabel guessed.

'Then I can't talk to you.'

'They'll kill me,' the voice said and something in the tone told Fabel he believed it.

'Who will?'

'The same people who killed Meliha Yazar. I know all about Meliha Yazar, I know about Müller-Voigt. I know about Daniel Föttinger.'

325

Fabel pulled over to the side of the road, putting on his hazard-warning lights. Snatching his cell-phone from its cradle, he took the call off-speaker.

'What do you know?'

'I can't tell you yet. They're probably listening right now. Making me take the voice changer off will make it easier for them to find me, but they would have deprocessed it eventually. They can do anything with technology. Remember that, Fabel. Don't use technology.'

'Where is Meliha Yazar?' Fabel's voice was determined. 'What happened to her?'

'You already know that. It's *why* it happened that you should worry about. I've got something they're looking for. Something that Meliha left for me to find and I'll die because I found it. Now they will find me, Fabel. They'll find me and kill me. They'll kill you too and anyone else they think knows.'

'Knows? Knows what? Listen, if you really believe your life is in danger, then tell me where you are. We will protect you.'

There was a snort at the other end of the connection. 'Don't make promises you can't keep.' He paused. 'I'll be in touch later. I have to find a way of contacting you without them intercepting it. Do you understand?'

Fabel frowned, then, after a moment said: 'Yes. I understand.'

The phone went dead.

CHAPTER 28

Fabel knew he was not going to get a warm welcome. He had phoned to arrange a meeting with Tanja Ulmen, the first of Föttinger's alleged victims, and she had asked if they could do it on the telephone. She was happily married with children and living in Bad Bramstedt, a small town between Hamburg and Kiel. Her family knew nothing of the incident when she had been a student with Daniel Föttinger. This was part of a murder enquiry, Fabel had explained, so a telephone interview was not an option. The truth was that Fabel disliked anything getting between him and the reactions of the people he questioned. Tanja Ulmen reluctantly agreed to meet with him after she finished work. She was a teacher at the local high school, she explained. He had been slightly taken aback when Ulmen had insisted that he bring a female colleague.

It took forty minutes for Fabel and Anna to get to Bad Bramstedt and another ten to find the rest area off the 207 route to the west of the town. During the journey Anna had noticed Fabel checking his rear-view mirror more than usual.

'Is it there again?' she asked. 'The four-by-four?'

'No. I thought maybe it was . . . but no. Maybe I'm becoming paranoid in my old age.'

'If you really think you are being tailed, especially with all of the crap that's been going on with emails and texts going missing, then I think we should visit this Seamark International and get a few answers.'

'It's maybe nothing,' said Fabel. 'It could be coincidence or maybe I've mistaken two or three different cars as the same one. I want to be sure before we show our hand. Anyway, it's not there now.' He paused for a moment, then said uncertainly: 'There's something else, Anna. I mean, as well as the texts and stuff. I got a call last night. An anonymous call from someone who claims to know all about what happened to Meliha Yazar and Müller-Voigt.'

'And you believe them?' Anna sounded incredulous. 'I mean, after everything else that's been going on, don't you think it's likely to be the same lot playing games?'

'I thought that, too. But, I don't know, there was something about this call. He said they would find him and kill him and I believe he meant it. Maybe he is an ex-member or has some other kind of connection to them.'

'So you *are* convinced it's the Pharos Project behind this?'

'More than that, Anna, I'm beginning to get an idea about what's really happened. Look, there she is . . .'

It was the only car in the rest area: an elderly Citroen. The rest area was screened from the road by a thick curtain of trees and there was an even deeper wedge of forest to the other side. Frau Ulmen had insisted that they meet there: it was far enough out of town but close enough for her to get back home without causing too much suspicion.

'I've told my children I've got shopping to do but I'll be back in an hour,' she said bluntly in greeting as she got into the back of Fabel's car. 'You said you wanted to talk to me about Daniel Föttinger?' Fabel knew from the report that Tanja Ulmen was in her mid-thirties, but she had a weary look that would otherwise have made it difficult to guess her age on first sight. She had untidy blonde hair heaped on her head and held in place by a large wooden hair clasp patterned with a Celtic bow. Her clothes were baggy and vaguely bohemian. She looked every bit the eccentric art teacher, but Fabel knew that the subject she actually taught was information technology.

'Yes, Frau Ulmen,' said Fabel. 'We'd like to talk to you about Daniel Föttinger. You know that he's dead?'

'Yes. I read about it in the papers.'

'So you know how he died?'

'Yes. Painfully. And I was glad. I hope it took him a long, long time to die.'

'It did, I'm afraid to say,' said Fabel. 'I can't imagine a worse way to go.'

'So you're here to accuse me of having something

to do with it?' Ulmen's face was set hard. Defiant. Fabel guessed that she wished she really could feel good about Föttinger's death, but could not.

'No, Frau Ulmen. Why I asked to talk to you was because I'm trying to build up a picture of Föttinger. I wanted to ask you about what happened between you and him.'

'Nothing happened *between* us. The bastard raped me.'

'So why didn't you pursue the case?' asked Anna. 'You do know that he went on to commit at least one more alleged rape?'

'His father paid me "compensation", as he put it. But before you think I was simply bought off, Old Man Föttinger made sure he employed a stick as well as a carrot. The Föttingers were filthy rich and very well connected. He made it very clear to me that things would go badly for me, *very* badly. They were peas in a pod, father and son.'

'What do you mean, exactly?' asked Anna.

'They both thought that they could get anything they wanted, whenever they wanted. People didn't matter to either of them.'

'Please, Frau Ulmen,' said Fabel. 'It would be very helpful to me if you could tell me what happened with Föttinger.'

'Daniel asked me out when we were both students in Hamburg. He was studying philosophy . . .'

'Philosophy?' Fabel was genuinely surprised. 'I would have thought he would have studied some science or technological subject.'

'Maybe he did later, but back then he was doing philosophy. And he was really into it. Anyway, Daniel asked me out. He was very charming and handsome, but there was something about him really gave me the creeps. So I said no. He couldn't understand it. He simply could not wrap his mind around the fact that someone was denying him something he wanted. It was like it didn't compute. That's what I mean about him and his father being the same: neither of them could understand that the entire universe didn't revolve around them.'

'So he didn't take no for an answer?' asked Anna as gently as she could.

'I was sharing a flat with some friends and he called around when they were out. He tried his lethal charm again, still not able to believe that someone could resist it. When that didn't work he tried a more direct approach. A knife held to my throat.'

'I know this is very difficult for you . . .' began Anna.

'No, it's not. It was a long time ago and somehow I've managed to make it seem that it happened to someone else . . . make it a story, not part of reality. It was my way of coping and it worked. They say that every cell in your body is replaced every seven years or something like that. So I tell myself that what happened did not happen to this body, to the person I am now. But I never stopped hating him. Despising him for his arrogance.'

'What I wanted to ask was how he behaved.' Anna frowned at her own clumsiness. 'I mean, the things an attacker says or does, the *extra* things, they can tell us a great deal about their state of mind.'

'He just kept the knife at my throat. Otherwise he wasn't violent. As his father made sure to point out, I didn't have any bruises to show the police. No signs that I struggled for my virtue, as he put it, the old bastard.' Ulmen looked through the passenger window for a moment, out to the dark green of the forest. 'In a weird way, and I know this does sound *really* weird, but I don't think Daniel thought for a second that he was doing anything wrong. I've thought about it a lot, over the years – doing what I said and imagining it was something you just read about happening to someone else . . . that makes it easier to be objective about it. Anyway, when I think back to the way he was, it was as if he didn't really understand that I was there. You know, theory of mind or simulation or whatever psychologists call it. I think both father and son were sociopaths of some kind – I'm not being bitter, I really do believe that. I honestly think Daniel Föttinger didn't understand that I had the independent consciousness to truly give or withhold consent.'

'As if you weren't really there?' asked Fabel.

Tanja Ulmen stared at Fabel. 'Yes. Yes, that's exactly it,' she said, animated for the first time during the conversation. 'Like I wasn't really there.'

★   ★   ★

332

On the way back to Hamburg, Fabel asked Anna for the address of the Turkish restaurant that Müller-Voigt and Meliha Yazar had dined in regularly.

'Could you give them a ring and see if that waiter's back from holiday?' he asked her. 'And if he is, could we talk to him when we get there?'

Anna phoned and confirmed to Fabel that the waiter would be waiting for them when they arrived.

'Did you see the report that Tramberger, the Disaster Team guy, sent in?' asked Anna. 'It arrived this morning.'

'What, from his *Virtual Elbe* thing? No, I haven't had a chance yet.'

'You should. According to his model, and he says he ran it several times, that torso was dumped three kilometres upstream, but right in the middle of the river, in the deep channel.'

'From a boat?'

'Looks like. He says we should get the pathologist to check for signs that it had been weighted. He thinks that whoever dumped it there did so because it's the deepest part of the Elbe that far upstream. Fewer big vessels, more barges and less likelihood of it being churned up. His opinion is that the torso was meant to stay at the bottom and never be found. Makes sense, Jan. My guess is that the head and limbs are scattered along the bottom as well. Whoever did this really didn't want her identified.'

★   ★   ★

333

The Ottoman Palace was a lot less grand than the name suggested, but it did have a certain style to it. No clichés or walls bedecked with tourist posters of Turkey. It was a simple eatery with subtle reminders, such as the colourful kilim tapestry on the wall, of the culture behind the cuisine. While they waited for Osman, the waiter who had regularly served Müller-Voigt and his date, Fabel had a good look around the restaurant. It would not have been Müller-Voigt's normal type of place; it was a choice, whether Meliha's or Müller-Voigt's, that owed a lot to discretion.

A smallish man of about twenty-five or so, with russet-blond hair, brought his eager smile out of the kitchen. He introduced himself as Osman, and told Fabel he would happily do anything he could to help. Osman was one of those people whose exuberant good nature, no matter how hard you tried to ignore it, was infectious.

'She had an Istanbul accent,' Osman explained after Fabel had asked him what he could remember about Meliha. 'She sounded well educated and I got the idea she was quite rich. Her clothes were expensive. She was a beautiful woman.'

'But the owner here said he got the feeling that she didn't like talking about herself.'

'That's for sure. Naturally, when a customer speaks to me in such perfect, beautiful Turkish, I ask where they are from. As soon as I asked her

I really got the feeling that I'd done the wrong thing. It's funny with customers. You learn to drop a topic quick sometimes. The last thing you want is a patron to feel uncomfortable,' he said very earnestly.

'And she was particularly sensitive about where she was from?'

'I got that idea. When I asked, she said she was from Silviri, on the coast near Istanbul, but the shutters came down, if you know what I mean. So, like I said, I dropped it quick.'

'Did they seem happy?'

'Very. Especially him. They were a nice couple. Good together, if you know what I mean. There was a big age difference, of course, but they seemed to be totally into each other.'

'Was there ever any interaction between them and anyone else? Did they ever bring any friends or guests to the restaurant?'

'No. It was always just the two of them. I don't even remember any other diners coming up to them and saying hello in passing. That was their usual table . . .' Osman pointed to the furthest-away table at the back of the restaurant, at the end of the seating arc. It confirmed Fabel's theory about the restaurant being chosen because it offered an element of anonymity: no one would pass that table to leave or go to the washrooms. Meliha and Müller-Voigt would have had to endure only Osman's good-natured interruptions.

'I want you to think very hard, Osman,' said

Fabel. 'Was there anything, anything at all, out of the ordinary that you can recall about them?'

Osman frowned as he did exactly as Fabel had asked. After a moment he said: 'No, I'm really sorry, but there was nothing. They were just a happy couple who seemed very involved in each other. I was so upset when I heard about Herr Müller-Voigt. I really wish I could do more to help . . .'

'Thank you, Osman. You have been very helpful.' Fabel smiled; he knew the young waiter really had done his best to remember any useful detail. Fabel thanked the owner of the restaurant and he and Anna headed for the door.

'I was surprised she didn't come in here more often,' Osman said as they were leaving. 'With her living so near.'

Both Anna and Fabel froze in the doorway. They stepped back in, letting the door close behind them.

'You know where she lives?' asked Fabel. Something like a small electrical current tingled in the back of his neck.

'Well . . . yes. I guess. Unless she was just visiting, but it looked to me like she lived there.'

'What do you mean?' asked Anna.

'There's an apartment building about three blocks away. I was passing it one day – my cousin lives in the next building – and I saw Frau Yazar go in through the main door, carrying groceries.'

'Get your jacket . . .' Fabel said to Osman and held the door open.

★　★　★

336

It took no longer than fifteen minutes of talking to her neighbours to establish that Meliha Yazar lived on the third floor of the building. It was a modern apartment building only three blocks, as Osman had said, from the Ottoman Palace.

Once they had established that they had found the right place, Fabel had sent Osman back to the restaurant, the young waiter beaming at the thought that he really had contributed something worthwhile. Fabel had been able to dispel Osman's only concern that perhaps Meliha Yazar was in trouble with the police.

'Not at all,' Fabel had said reassuringly. 'We're trying to help Frau Yazar. *You* have helped Frau Yazar.'

Osman had gone back to work happy.

But it soon became clear that Meliha Yazar was not Meliha Yazar.

'You mean Frau Kebir . . .' said the young mother who had answered the door of the other apartment on the third floor, clutching a toddler to her flank. 'I haven't seen her for ages. Maybe a month. She does go away a lot. To do with her job, probably. I think she maybe goes back to Turkey.'

'Do you know what her job is?' asked Anna.

'Couldn't really say.'

'And there's been no one around the apartment for a month?'

'I didn't say that. *She*'s not been there for a month, but she was having some work done on the apartment. About three weeks ago there was

337

a team of workmen in, after she had gone. It was okay, though, because she slipped a note under my door a couple of days before, just to warn me.'

'I see,' said Fabel. 'Did Frau Ya— I mean Frau Kebir . . . did she leave you a key, by any chance?'

'Oh no.' The young mother bounced the restive toddler in her arms. 'She was very quiet. Very private.'

Fabel thanked her and the young mother went back into her flat.

'You know something, Anna?' said Fabel as they stood outside the door of the apartment. 'They're not as good as their PR makes out.'

'Who?'

'The Pharos Project,' said Fabel. 'All this time I thought they had wiped out all trace of Meliha Yazar. But it wasn't them all along. The phoney address she gave Müller-Voigt, her fake surname – nice move, that, I have to say: keep your first name in case someone you know from your past bumps into you in public – all that was her herself. *She* didn't want any trace of Meliha Yazar.'

'Some kind of scam? Is that what you're saying she was into?'

Fabel shook his head. 'No. Far from it. More like an undercover investigation.'

Anna stared at the solid-looking front door for a moment. 'Do you want me to get an emergency warrant to enter?' asked Anna.

In answer, Fabel swung a kick at the door. It

338

took a second kick before the wood around the lock splintered and the door yielded.

'We have reason to believe that the occupant of this dwelling is in danger,' he said. 'We don't need a warrant.'

The front door opened onto a long hall. It was bright and immaculately clean and at its far end there was a large framed poster from which a handsome middle-aged man gazed back at Fabel with piercingly light eyes. The man wore an old-fashioned suit and had his thumbs rammed into the pockets of his waistcoat. There was an incredible sense of determination in the pale eyes, one of which was slightly out of alignment because, Fabel already knew, of a First World War shrapnel wound.

'This is her apartment, all right,' said Fabel, nodding towards the poster.

'Who's that?' asked Anna.

'Her icon. Mustafa Kemal Atatürk. The father of modern Turkey. Meliha Yazar – or Kebir or whatever her real name was – was seeking a new Atatürk. An "Atatürk for the Environment", Müller-Voigt said. Come on. Let's check this out.'

They moved from room to room. The flat was filled with books in Turkish, German and English. Literary classics, environmental tracts, geological and ecological textbooks. Fabel walked into the bedroom. The bed was made, everything was in perfect order as it had been throughout the apartment. Absolutely perfect order.

339

'She was tidy, I'll give her that,' said Anna somewhere behind Fabel.

'Too tidy,' he said, picking up the three paperbacks that sat on her bedside table. 'They've been through everything. Every corner. Every nook and cranny. My bet is that they photographed everything first and then put it all back when they'd gone through it. It's nice work, I'll give them that.'

'The workmen her neighbour talked about?'

Fabel did not answer; instead he sifted through the paperbacks as if he were slowly shuffling cards. An English edition of *Nineteen Eighty-Four* by George Orwell. A German edition of *Der Richter und sein Henker* by Friederich Dürrenmatt. A copy of *Silent Spring* by Rachael Carson, again in English. He looked through them again. There was something significant about the mix of books, but he could not think what it was. He stepped out of the bedroom, the books still in his hands. By the time they had finished, the forensics team had arrived.

'You been handling anything else I should know about?' asked Holger Brauner, with a nod towards the books in Fabel's hand.

'You won't get anything here, Holger,' said Fabel. 'Have a look around. What's wrong with this picture?'

Brauner scanned the room, then turned back to Fabel and shrugged. 'You got me . . . other than it's a hell of a tidy place.'

'Someone's beaten us to it,' said Fabel. 'Real

340

professionals. They've cleaned up behind themselves.'

'I wish they'd turn over my apartment,' said Anna. 'It could really do with a spring clean.'

'But that's not all that's wrong with this picture. You too, Anna. Notice something odd?'

They both looked around the room again. Anna frowned for a moment, then a look of enlightenment swept across her face.

'Same as the last Network Killer victim?'

'Exactly,' said Fabel. Brauner made a confused face.

'No computer . . .' said Fabel. 'No computer, no cellphone, no chargers, no memory sticks, not even an electronic calculator.'

'So what are you saying?' asked Brauner. 'That the Network Killer has been here too?'

'I can guarantee you it wasn't the Network Killer, Holger. That's one thing I'm certain about. It was someone else who turned this place over and took Julia Henning's computer and cellphone. Someone who didn't want us to know who the Network Killer was and what had happened to him.'

'Now you've lost even me,' said Anna.

'All in due time,' said Fabel. 'In the meantime can you do the follow-up here? I want to get back to the Presidium. I need to talk to Fabian Menke about—'

He was interrupted by his cellphone ringing.

'Hi, Jan, it's Werner. You're not going to believe

341

this . . . we've got another body in the water. The Harbour Police have just notified us that they've fished a body out of the river near the mouth of the Peutehafen. They're transferring it to Butenfeld.' Werner used the police shorthand for the mortuary at the Institute for Legal Medicine, where the bodies of all sudden and suspicious deaths were taken.

'I'll be right there,' said Fabel.

CHAPTER 29

Fabel, Nicola Brüggemann and Werner Meyer stood without speaking and looked down at the body that had been wheeled out into the main morgue hall by the attendant. Outwardly, it looked like some token of respect: a moment's silence. The truth was that they were doing what they had learned to do as police officers. You took a moment to look, to examine, to assess. To bring your fresh perspective to someone's death.

The body on the mortuary trolley was thin and pale, the ribs showing through the pallid skin and the upper arms skinny. Despite the evidence of stubble on his chin, the dead male looked more boy than man. There were four holes, now bloodless, in his skull, two above the hairline and two below, puncturing the skin of his broad forehead. Fabel noticed dark mottling on the pale skin of his brow: powder burns from a close-quarter shot. He was on his knees, thought Fabel. Probably begging for his life.

A larger, uglier wound gaped beneath his jaw, where one of the rounds had exited. There was a dark green tattoo on his left breast, like a small inverted loop.

'These, apparently, are the mortal remains of one Harald Jaburg,' said Werner, with an expression that suggested he had just tasted something sour. 'We found his ID in his jeans pocket. Unemployed. Twenty-eight years old.'

'I thought he would be younger,' said Fabel absently. He turned to Brüggemann. 'Our workload seems to be growing exponentially. I think I'll take you up on your offer.' He ignored Werner's quizzical look.

'He has a tattoo on his chest,' said Brüggemann. 'Right above his heart. Some kind of symbol.'

'I saw that, too,' said Fabel. 'It looks to me like the lower-case version of the Greek letter gamma.' He turned the corpse's arms over to examine the inside of the forearms. 'No track marks.'

'He doesn't look the Classics type to me,' said Werner.

'No . . .' said Fabel. 'Nor me. Do we have an address for him?'

'Billbrook. We've got uniform onto that,' said Werner. 'God, Jan, if we go on like this, we're going to have to hire a fishing boat to trawl the Elbe for all the stiffs in the water.'

'It would never be allowed,' said Brüggemann. 'I think we've already exceeded our EU quota.'

'Tell me about it,' said Fabel. 'Werner, I know you're up to your eyes and I've left Anna at Meliha Yazar's place, but I'd like you and Henk to follow this one up too. Run his name through the computer and speak to Organised Crime Division. This looks like a drugs thing, but he wasn't a user as far as I can see. Ask them if there's any gang they know of that uses the symbol gamma as a tag.'

'Okay, Jan. But he looks to me even less like a gang member than he does a Classics scholar.'

'Could have been small fry,' said Brüggemann. 'Someone suspected of cheating or being a snitch. But no, I agree he doesn't look like the type.'

The mortuary attendant came back carrying a heavy-duty polythene bag. He dumped it unceremoniously on top of the dead man's chest. 'You asked for his clothes,' he said. 'They've been bagged for the forensics people. They're still wet, so they'd better get them out of that bag quickly or they'll go mouldy.'

'Cheery chap,' said Werner sarcastically after the attendant had left them alone again. 'It must be the job that brings out the optimist in him.'

Fabel read the evidence-tag list attached to the bag out loud. 'Black or dark grey hooded top. Black or dark grey jeans. Dark green T-shirt. Studded leather wrist band, right wrist. Broad leather-banded wristwatch, left wrist. Alloy metal neck chain with symbol pendant . . .' Fabel shook and tilted the clear polythene bag. There was a considerable amount of oily water trapped in it with the clothes, but he spotted the neck chain. As he suspected, the pendant was also in the form of the Greek letter gamma. '. . . Dark red ankle-length socks. Black leather engineer boots. Leather wallet containing ID, twenty-five euros in notes, further fifteen euros in coins. White boxer-style undershorts.'

'Funny, that,' said Brüggemann. 'I would have put him down as a briefs type.'

Fabel did not respond but instead took out his notebook and flicked back a couple of pages. When he found what he was looking for, he leaned across the body and handed the open notebook to Werner, who frowned as he read Fabel's notes.

'No . . .' Werner said, handing the notebook back. 'You don't think . . . ?' He nodded towards the corpse between them.

'His clothing exactly matches the description of what the rider of the motorbike was seen wearing.'

'It's a common enough look, *Chef.*'

'Are you talking about the arson killing?' asked Brüggemann.

'We need to get a time of death for this guy,' said Fabel. 'My money is on it being *after* the Schanzenviertel attack.'

'You still want me to check with Organised Crime?' asked Werner.

Fabel nodded. 'It could still be something else. But I have a line of enquiry I want to follow up myself . . .'

There was no doubt in his mind this time. Fabel had only driven fifty metres from Meliha Yazar's apartment when he had thought that he had seen the large VW Tiguan pull out from behind a parked van and into traffic four or five cars back. But then he had lost sight of it and there had been no sign of it behind him as he had driven up to the Butenfeld mortuary in Eppendorf. But when he had left the morgue he had seen it again, once more keeping a distance of four or five cars back. Sometimes it was as if the VW did not need to keep him in view at all. A couple of times, when the four-by-four was out of sight behind a corner, he had taken a sudden turn off the road and followed a new route, only to see the VW appear a few blocks later.

He continued to head towards his destination, the docks. There was much less traffic now and the VW found it difficult to find cover in the thinning camouflage of other cars. It was now only two cars behind him. Fabel used his cellphone to contact the Presidium. Anna Wolff, who was now back from Meliha Yazar's apartment, took his call.

'I've got good news and bad news, Anna. The good news is that I'm not growing paranoid in my old age.'

'The tail? Are you sure?'

'Positive this time. I've just passed the Fischmarkt. Could you contact Ops Room and ask for a marked car to be on standby down at the junction of Grosse Elbestrasse and Kaistrasse? It's quiet enough down there for us to pull them over and have a chat.'

'I'll do it now. But I'm coming down too.' She hung up before Fabel had a chance to answer. He continued to head west. Again there was no sign of the VW on his tail. They had been stopped at the traffic lights and had obviously decided to use the opportunity to open up a little space between them and Fabel's car.

He was on St Pauli Hafenstrasse when he saw it again, three or four cars back. These guys were good. Or they had help. Fabel began to wonder about what could have been attached to his car during his guided tour of the Pharos.

Anna called him on his cellphone. 'The uniform guys are in position.'

'Good. Chummy is still on my tail. I'm on Hafenstrasse – could you tell the uniform unit to be ready to pull him over?'

'Sure. I'll be there myself in a couple of minutes.'

Fabel hung up and checked his mirror. There was only one car now between him and the big VW. He thought he could see the outlines of two men through the darkened glass.

'Let's make this interesting,' he said to himself under his breath. He spotted a narrow cobbled roadway off the main carriageway. It led to the other side of the riverside buildings and the water's edge. This was an access way that no normal traffic would use. The opposite lane was clear of oncoming traffic, so Fabel swung across to the left without indicating and slammed on his brakes, pulling into a parking bay at the edge of the water.

The car behind drove past, the driver blasting his horn at Fabel's failure to indicate. He saw the VW thunder past the road end too: either the driver felt he could not make the sudden turn or was trying to convince Fabel that he was not really following him.

Fabel called Anna. 'The Tiguan has just passed me. I didn't give him an alternative. Tell the uniform unit he's heading their way and to pull him over. I'll be right behind him. If he's pulled over or double-backed, I'll let you know.'

He had just begun to twist around in his seat to start reversing back out onto the main road when he saw a four-by-four hurtling towards him. The car had only just registered in Fabel's brain when it slammed into the back of Fabel's BMW. He was thrown violently forward, only to be caught painfully by the inertia reel of his seat belt.

'Bastard!' he shouted into the rear-view mirror. He slammed on the brakes and undid his seat belt. He tried to work out what had happened. He was not sure, but he thought that the four-by-four was another make. Not the same car that had been following him. Two cars?

At least that made things easier in one way: he could detain the driver for careless driving, or on suspicion of drunk driving. He twisted round to see the four-by-four reversing back from the impact. There was the ugly sound of grinding metal as it did so and a tinny clang as something from the rear of Fabel's car hit the cobbles of the wharf-side roadway. He could see it was not the VW: this vehicle was a Land Rover.

Fabel had just reached for his door handle when the Land Rover smashed into the back of his car again. This time he was thrown forward without the restraint of his seat belt and his chest slammed painfully against the steering wheel, forcing a pulse of air from his lungs. Winded, he gasped for breath, his body screaming for oxygen. Between desperate gasps, he fumbled to free his service automatic from its holster. Another impact. The SIG-Sauer automatic jumped from his tremulous fingers and fell into the footwell. He turned again in his seat. The Land Rover was reversing away fast. Fabel felt faint and sick from lack of oxygen and his chest hurt with every breath, but he desperately sought to make sense of his situation. He reached for his phone. In the rear-view mirror he saw the car's huge dark bulk loom at him as it slammed once more into the rear of his BMW. But this impact was different. This time the engine of the Land Rover screamed as the driver floored the accelerator.

Fabel realised what was happening. The bastard was trying to push him off the wharf and into the river.

He instinctively pushed the footbrake to the floor. A useless exercise, he realised immediately, so he slammed the BMW into reverse and pushed back against the four-by-four. It was an unequal struggle and his tyres squealed and smoked as they spun impotently on the smooth cobbles.

He had to get out. He had to get out before the car went over the edge. But he was on the wrong side of the car, the water side. He stared wildly at the grille of the Land Rover, which completely filled his rear-view mirror. Filled Fabel's universe. Fabel had just decided to risk making the jump when he felt suddenly weightless, and realised that his car had gone over the edge.

There was another impact, this time as the car hit the surface of the water and Fabel was thrown around in the metal confines of his car. Everything went dark and for a moment he thought he had passed out, until he realised, as the passenger cabin of his car filled with cold, oily, dark water, that he was sinking to the bottom of the River Elbe.

CHAPTER 30

He had found out her name remarkably easily. Getting around the encryption had not been difficult. It had taken Roman less than half a day to decode and transfer the information.

Meliha Yazar.

The woman he had seen in the café had been Meliha Yazar. Roman felt a profound sadness at the idea that such a beautiful woman would now be dead. So would he be, soon.

He had stopped hating Meliha for leaving the phone for him to find. With that act – which he now felt was not as random as it had first seemed, maybe she had seen him, recognised something in him – she had given him a great gift, for now Roman knew something about himself that he had not known before. He was brave. He had always thought of himself as cowardly, but now he realised that he was not afraid of dying. They would kill him, but before they did he would make sure that the information he had, that she had entrusted to him with that simple act in the café, would be passed on to the policeman Fabel and others. Roman realised that sending the information by email would never work. He recognised the sophistication of their expertise and the scope of their technical resources. He genuinely admired some of their work. Truly creative.

But they were dangerous. The first thing they would do when they traced Roman would be to wipe out his email traffic and blogging presence. To silence his electronic singing.

He also knew that he could not simply rely on Fabel, because the chances were he would soon be dead too. Roman and Fabel both represented the outer radiations of a spidering spread of knowledge that had to be contained. A circle that had to be closed.

But that was in the real world. And Roman existed in more than the real world. He knew the truth and the falsity of their fantasy of a digital otherworld. It existed, but it was not somewhere you could go unless you accepted the total death of the ego. A soulless shadow of reality. He knew. He had spent so much of his young life there.

He finished decrypting the files. And there it was: he had found the secret about the Pharos Project that they could never allow to be known. They had been mad to think that they could keep something like that hidden from the world. But, there again, the Big Lie was always the most enduring, the easiest to sustain.

As soon as he had finished transferring the file to the various formats he wanted, Roman went around his apartment, opening the curtains. He struggled with a couple of the half-light windows but managed to get them open and allow some air into the apartment.

Then he went out.

It was sunny. The first really sunny day of the year. The Wilhelmsburg street was full of noise after the quiet of his apartment. He thought about the Albanians who lived below him who had not really been noisy; it had been Roman who had been intolerant simply because he had been unable to remove himself that one step further from mankind and the real world. There had, Roman realised, been people just like him throughout history. The medieval monks who chose the austerity of a monastic cell and the virtual reality of religion; the ancient philosophers who hid in caves or barrels and commented on the human condition from which they had disconnected.

It took him a long time to walk into town. But he had been determined to walk. It meant that every now and then he had to lean against a wall to catch his breath, and he sat down every time the opportunity presented itself on a municipal bench or, on one occasion, even on a lidded waste bin.

He saw the way others looked at him. But today Roman did not care. Today he had a mission to fulfil, a purpose that was, for once, not all about him. He went to the DeutschePost office first and bought five padded envelopes, dropped a memory stick and a handwritten note into each. He paused for a moment before he let the envelopes slip from his grasp and into the mail chute; in that moment, he thought of Meliha, the woman in the café, the woman behind the truth. He hoped that somehow, somewhere, she would be aware of what he was doing for her.

After the post office, Roman went to an ATM and withdrew five hundred euros, folded the notes neatly and placed them in a sixth envelope. On the way home he visited two more ATMs, using a different card each time; each time removing five hundred euros. By the time he reached the main door of his apartment building, Roman was wheezing and sweating profusely. He leaned against the wall and looked up at the sky. High above him, the distant glint of a passenger jet left a trail of vapour, like a needle running white thread through blue silk. There is never just one reality, he thought as he watched the jet, wondering what the passengers saw of Wilhelmsburg from that altitude. There are as many realities as there are people on the planet: reality is what lives in each person's head. When they kill me, he thought, my reality will end, but I will have no sense of it ending. Just as I was not aware before my birth, I will not be aware after my death, so all time only exists as I perceive it. Time began with me and will end with me. I am immortal.

When he had recovered enough, he entered his

apartment building and started the slow, painful climb up the stairs. His breathing was even more laboured by the time he reached the door of the apartment beneath his. When the Albanian opened the door and recognised Roman, his face darkened with dull anger; then he seemed to notice the state Roman was in and the anger was replaced by concern.

'Are you all right? You no look so good . . .'

'Jetmir . . .' Roman spat the words out between rheumy wheezes. 'That's your name, isn't it . . . Jetmir?'

The Albanian nodded and moved out to help Roman. Roman nearly laughed: Jetmir was a small, wiry, dark man whom Roman reckoned would be crushed to death if he fell on him.

'You come in. You not well man. I get doctor, maybe.'

'No doctor, Jetmir. I'm sorry. I'm the one who kept calling the police. You knew that anyway, but I'm telling you now, it was me and I'm sorry.' He pushed the envelope containing the fifteen hundred euros into the Albanian's hands. 'Take it. I want you to have it. I know you don't have a lot of money.'

The Albanian stared at the cash. 'Why?' he asked. But he made no attempt to return it.

'Because I've been a bad neighbour. And because I want you to do something for me. It's payment in advance.' Roman paused. A pain started to shoot across his chest and down his

356

right arm. He grabbed the Albanian's shirt front and pulled him close. With his other hand he shoved a second envelope against his chest. 'This is for the police,' he said. 'It's very important that they get this. There are bad men coming, Jetmir. They're coming for me.'

'Then I get police now . . .'

'No!' Roman shouted and tightened his grip on the small Albanian. 'No. That could be dangerous for you and your family. Listen, if anything happens to me, you've got to give that envelope to the police. But only to a policeman called Fabel. Jan Fabel. His name's on the front. Have you got that? Don't give it to anyone else.'

The Albanian nodded vigorously. 'You wait here, I get you some water.'

It took a full fifteen minutes for the pain to ease and for Roman, sipping slowly at the water, to get something of his breath back. While they sat together on the stairs, Roman and the Albanian talked. They chatted about the most inconsequential things, about Jetmir's home in Albania, about his children and how they sounded just like Germans. But throughout the whole conversation the earnest expression of concern never left the Albanian's face. Roman remembered how the Albanian had tried to talk to him when the family first moved in, how they had made an effort to befriend him. He felt bad when he thought about that. They were people, after all; not just a noise, an annoyance, on the periphery of Roman's existence.

'Don't worry about me,' said Roman, slowly and painfully easing himself up from the stairs. 'I'll be fine. Just don't forget your promise.'

'I won't forget. We is good neighbours now. You are my *fqinj*. We look after each other.'

The Albanian helped Roman up the rest of the stairs to his front door.

'I'll be fine now. Thanks for your help, Jetmir.' Roman unlocked his door, smiled and waited until he heard the Albanian shut his own door one floor down. Only then did Roman step into his apartment.

Roman looked around. It really was a nice place, if only he had kept it tidier. He regretted that now. There was a lot he regretted now. He stood leaning against the door, still struggling with his breathing.

There were three of them in the flat. None of them spoke. They all wore identical grey suits and had Bluetooth earpieces jammed into their ears as if fused there. One was sitting at Roman's computers, another held Meliha's cellphone in his hand. The third stood directly in front of Roman, staring at him with nothing in his face.

Roman had known they would be there. Before he had left to carry out his chores he had reassembled Meliha's phone, including the tracer, and had left it switched on. A beacon. A digital lighthouse. They were big on that kind of metaphor, he thought.

He started to laugh at the absurdity of it all just

as the Consolidator closest to him stepped forward, slipped the large plastic bag he had in his gloved hands over Roman's head and pulled the drawstring tight.

CHAPTER 31

Fabel knew that it would be panic that would kill him. He forced the thought to the front of his mind. He had been winded by the first impact and his lungs were still depleted of oxygen; a primal instinct screamed within him to open his mouth and breathe: to suck in the filthy river water; to fill his lungs with something, anything.

The natural buoyancy of his body was pushing him up against the fabric roof of the car as it sank and he knew he was being dragged deeper into the Elbe. The wharf had originally been intended as a shipping berth, meaning the water was deep enough to accommodate a large ship's draught. Deep and dark.

Now Fabel could see nothing. This was the car he had owned for ten years but suddenly its interior was totally alien to him. A strange and toxic environment. One window, he knew, was open and offered a quick exit. The other was intact. A simple choice: one direction or the other. He pushed himself toward what he thought was the right side of the car. No steering wheel. He found the edge of the passenger window and pushed himself through. He was out of the car. And rising. His lungs screamed and a searing pain he had never felt before sliced through his chest. He could now see the surface above him but it did not seem to get any nearer. The light above started to dim, the water around him growing darker again. He felt renewed panic when he realised he was going to black out. He was going to lose consciousness and he would never regain it. His arms and legs became leaden and he knew he was sinking again.

All fear left him and he let his held breath go in an explosion of bubbles.

Something closed over his mouth and pinched his nose shut. A hand. There was someone in the water with him. Another arm looped under his armpit and around his chest. Fabel instinctively fought against the hand bruisingly clamped over his nose and mouth: the logic that it was preventing him breathing in the filthy dock water lost in primal panic.

He knew they must be rising, but the water became even darker. Black. He no longer felt his limbs, the chill of the water, the hammering in his chest.

Fabel found himself sitting again in his father's study in Norddeich. It was dark and the study was illuminated by only one desk light. Somewhere outside the window, on the other side of the dyke, there was the sound of a storm. As Fabel listened to the wind and the rain he noticed that Paul Lindemann was sitting opposite him, the bullet wound in the centre of his forehead crusted with a circle of long-dried black-red blood.

'Does it hurt?' Fabel asked.

'Not any more.'

'I'm sorry.'

'It wasn't your fault. It wasn't anybody's fault. It happened. It was my time.'

'It's my time now. Is this real?'

'It's not your time,' said Paul and smiled. 'I don't know if this is real. Do you remember that case you investigated, the one where the murderer thought he was made up, that everything, including himself, was all part of a fairy tale?'

'I remember him.'

'Maybe he was right after all. Maybe there is no such thing as reality.' Paul paused. 'Did you see the books?'

'What books?'

'The books she kept beside her bed.'

'Yes, I saw them.'

'Are they with you now? Do you have them in the water?'

'I'm not in the water. I'm here.'

'You're in the water, Jan. Do you have the books with you?'

'No. Anna took them. In a bag.'

'Remember the books.' Paul frowned, creasing the punctured skin around the bullet wound. 'Don't forget about the books.'

362

Fabel wanted to answer Paul but found himself becoming sleepy. The room went dark and the sound of the storm faded.

Something seared through him; penetrated every millimetre of his being. There was a great roar, like the crashing of waves but too fast, one after the other. The pain surged with each roar and Fabel realised it was his own breathing. There was something still clamped over his nose and mouth and he grabbed at it. A hand caught him by the wrist.

'Take it easy.' A female voice mixed authority and reassurance. 'It's just an oxygen mask.'

He tried to get up but more hands gently restrained him.

'It's Anna, *Chef*. You're going to be okay. You're in an ambulance. We're taking you to the hospital.'

Fabel's vision cleared and he saw Anna and a female paramedic leaning over him. Full consciousness returned like an electric shock.

'Did you get them?' He tried to sit upright but again was restrained. Pain throbbed nauseatingly in his head. 'They pushed me into the water. They tried to kill me.' He saw there was someone else in the ambulance. A figure sitting on the bench seat next to Anna; hair wet-black and plastered to his brow, a blanket wrapped around hunched shoulders.

'This is Herr Flemming, Jan,' said Anna. 'It was Herr Flemming who pulled you out of the water.

He saw your car go in and he jumped in to save you.'

Fabel remembered the hand over his nose and mouth, the arm looped around him, pulling him upwards.

'You saved my life?'

Flemming shrugged underneath the blanket. 'Right place, right time.'

'It was more than that. You risked your life to come in for me.'

'Jan . . .' Fabel thought he sensed something tentative in Anna's tone. 'Herr Flemming works for Seamark International.'

'But I thought . . .'

'You were right, Herr Fabel,' said Flemming. 'We were following you. But we're on the same side, so to speak. But rest now. They're taking me to the hospital, too. We can talk later.'

'Was it you who phoned me last night? Are you *Klabautermann*?'

Flemming laughed. 'Maybe I was the Klabautermann today, but no, I didn't phone you.'

Fabel lay back on the gurney. The oxygen eased his breathing. He closed his eyes and tried to fight back the nausea that washed over him in great, welling waves. The ambulance started to move, jolting over some obstacle as it got under way. Fabel tore off the oxygen mask and twisted sideways, vomiting over the edge of the gurney. The paramedic held him while he finished retching, before asking him if he felt better and

364

easing him back into a lying position. As he lay there, feeling the pressure of the paramedic's fingertips on his wrist as she checked his pulse, Fabel felt a dull surprise as his eyelids closed. He was going to sleep.

Susanne arrived at the hospital in St Georg about half an hour after Fabel had been admitted. She looked shaken and Fabel found himself worrying more about her than himself as she sat at his bedside. She stayed there while he was re-examined on the hour. The frown on her face refused to dissipate, no matter how often he reassured her that he was all right, or the doctors told her that there was nothing to be concerned about.

'I didn't take in much water,' he said. 'That guy Flemming made sure of that. He got me out really quickly, Susanne. I'm fine, honest.' He placed his hand on her cheek and smiled. She placed her hand over his.

'They tried to kill you, Jan,' she said incredulously. 'These maniacs actually believe they can get away with trying to kill a senior Hamburg police officer.'

'Truth is, as far as I can see, they *are* getting away with it. We have nothing to tie the vehicle that rammed into me with the Pharos Project or the Guardians of Gaia. Or anyone else for that matter. They could claim it was a random road-rage attack. I don't know. But we'll get them, don't worry Susanne. We *will* get them.'

Anna Wolff came in. She clearly saw Susanne clasping Fabel's hand and looked awkward for a moment.

'It's all right, Anna,' said Susanne. Fabel thought he detected a little frost in her smile. She stood up, leaned over and kissed him proprietarily on the forehead. 'I'll go and get a coffee. I'll be back in a minute.'

'Sorry, *Chef*,' said Anna. 'I didn't mean to . . .'

'It's fine, Anna. What's up?'

'Flemming has been given the all-clear to go, but he's hanging around because he thought you'd want to talk to him. If you're up to it, that is.'

'Damned right I want to talk to him. Did he tell you why he was following me?'

'You're better getting all the details from him, but I gather that Seamark International works for a company called Demeril Importing. It's a Turkish carpet and textile importer, down in the Speicherstadt. Seamark work for a lot of companies like that, providing security for imported and exported goods, even with men on ships safeguarding the cargo. They even have their own investigative branch, apparently. Mainly because the cargo and shipping they look after passes through so many jurisdictions and shades of legislation.'

'What the hell has that got to do with anything?'

'The owner of Demeril is a Herr Mustafa Kebir. His brother is a well-known Turkish archaeologist and environmental campaigner, Burhan Kebir, who happens to be very concerned about the whereabouts of his daughter . . .'

'Meliha?'

'Meliha Kebir – our Meliha Yazar – is an environmental campaigner and "underground" investigative journalist. The reason we could find no record of her is that she doesn't write as either Meliha Kebir or Meliha Yazar. All her work appears on the internet on activist and environmental sites under the tag *Mermaid*. She's already done several exposés on various companies who have shafted the environment. In two cases the internet shit-storm she's created has spilled over into the mainstream media to such an extent that charges have been brought against the companies she's named.'

Fabel eased himself up in the bed. His head still hurt like hell and he winced at the effort. 'Exactly the kind of person the Pharos Project wouldn't want anywhere near.'

'I've been in touch with the mental health sanatorium in Bavaria where Föttinger was placed by his parents. I managed to get a federal warrant for their records on him and guess what?'

'They've had some kind of computer glitch and the records have been mysteriously erased?'

Anna looked disappointed that she had not had a chance to drop her bombshell. 'Lucky guess?'

'Educated one. Anything else?'

'Yes – Nicola Brüggemann is here to see you.'

'How are you getting on with her?'

'Fine. She's a good cop, like you said.'

'That it?'

Anna shrugged. 'Oh no, there was one more thing. Fabian Menke called to cancel. He said he'd arranged to meet you but something had come up and could you reschedule for same time, same place tomorrow?'

Fabel frowned. 'That's who I was going to meet when I got shunted into the river.'

'Will you be up to seeing him tomorrow?'

'All I've had is a needle in my ass for tetanus. I'm fine. A little shaken, that's all.'

'They want to keep you in overnight, just for observation.'

'They can observe me remotely. Will you get my clothes for me while I talk to Nicola? Susanne brought in a fresh change of clothes for me. And you better get them here before Susanne comes back. She'll want me to stay in.'

'How's it going, Jan?' Brüggemann asked in her low contralto as she sat down on the edge of the bed. 'Do you have a moment for a chat? I mean, you don't have anything planned, do you? A swim or . . .'

'Very funny, Nicola. Have you been taking sarcasm lessons from Anna Wolff?'

'There are a few things young Anna could teach me, Jan. That's not one of them.'

Anna came back in and handed Fabel his clothes. 'You'd better be quick,' she said. 'I think they've told the chief nurse and she's steaming this way. I'll leave you to it.'

As Anna left, Fabel made a face at Brüggemann who turned her back to him as he stood up and dressed. He found his head still hurt and he was a little unsteady on his feet.

'All of this crap about me being in charge of the Network Killer case because you've been *compromised* . . .' said Brüggemann. 'I've had a word with Criminal Director van Heiden and he agrees that the attempt on your life makes it all a crock of shit.'

'"Crock of shit"?' Fabel grinned. 'I take it you didn't actually use that phrase to Horst van Heiden? It's okay, by the way, I'm decent.'

She turned to face him. 'As a matter of fact, I did. You know, for a police officer with a service as long as his, and who's bound to have seen his fair share, he certainly does shock easy. Anyway, he agrees that whoever tried to compromise you has clearly decided to take a more direct approach, so he's agreed that you should head up the enquiry again.'

'You want out?' asked Fabel.

'Not necessarily. I'm quite into the case and would like to stick with it. Under your supervision, that is. If you're comfortable with that. I mean, that's really what's been happening anyway. Unofficially.'

'How has the team been with you?'

'Great. You've put together some squad there, Jan. Werner's been a star, Dirk, Henk, Thomas

369

and the others have been really good. Anna can be a little . . . *feisty*.' Brüggemann grinned as she said the word.

'Nicola, is this a job application?'

'Could be, Jan. I know you're a senior down since Maria Klee . . .' She faltered. Everybody had learned to tiptoe around the subject of what had happened to Maria. 'It's just that you and I have always worked well together and I think it would be a good challenge for me. And I do know you could do with the support. Unless you don't think I'm up to it . . .'

'Don't be silly, Nicola, you know how highly I think of you. It's just that you have your own unit. You sure you want to be second fiddle again?'

'Your team has a Republic-wide reputation, Jan. No one is going to see it as a backward step for me. And there's a limit to how long you can work in the Child Crime Unit before it starts to *really* get to you.'

Fabel nodded; he could imagine. The Child Crime Unit was on the same floor as the Murder Commission and Fabel passed it often. There was a room set aside, incongruously bright and colourful against the rest of the Presidium's tonal decor, as a playroom, with toys, children's books and games. The intention was to put the children brought there at their ease; a place where it was safe to be a child. Every time he passed it, Fabel thought of the price each child must have paid before they could play in that room.

'The other thing is that I have experience with dealing with that geek Kroeger. I sense you and he don't hit it off too well. I've worked with him closely through the Child Crime Unit. He's been invaluable at times and we get on. If I stick with the Network Killer case, I could maybe provide a more constructive liaison with the Cybercrime Unit.'

'Oh, yes . . . I need you for your *people* skills.' Fabel smiled. 'Okay, Nicola, let me talk it over with the Criminal Director. I'm not going to pretend I wouldn't want your experience and skills on board, but Herr van Heiden is going to want to find a replacement for you.'

'My deputy is ready to take over, but of course there will have to be a replacement for her.'

'So apart from pitching your CV, I take it there was something else?'

'Yes. While you were taking a constitutional dip in the Elbe, I was reading through the autopsy report on Julia Helling, the Network Killer's most recent victim. I don't get this thing with the killer keeping her in cold storage. Like you said, it just doesn't fit. Why would he try to confuse us about time of death?'

'He wasn't. It wasn't the killer who put her in cold storage. Listen, Nicola, I think I've got it all straight in my head. But I can't prove a thing. I'll get the team together and go through what I *think* is going on. But first I need to talk to Flemming, the guy who pulled me out of the river.'

Susanne came back into the room and said hello to Nicola. They had known each other for some time, Susanne providing psych assessments on both victims and suspects for the Child Crime Unit. But her greeting was muted by the frown that darkened her expression when she saw that Fabel was dressed. He held up his hands in apology and they argued for a minute or two over the rights and wrongs of him discharging himself. Eventually Susanne gave up.

'I suppose we'd better take my car,' she said, her tone still conveying her displeasure.

'My car . . .' Fabel suddenly looked taken aback, as if he had only just realised that his BMW convertible was lying at the bottom of the Elbe.

'Make sure you drive, Susanne. Unless you stopped off at home to pick up your swimming cozzie . . .'When neither Fabel nor Susanne laughed, Brüggemann moved on. 'They've got a crane down there at the moment,' said Brüggemann. 'Lars Kreysig has taken personal charge of getting your car out, but it's going to be a write-off.'

'I loved that car,' said Fabel melancholically.

'Well, you shouldn't have tried to drive on water,' said Brüggemann. 'I know everybody at the Presidium thinks you can walk on it, but . . .'

Fabel smiled sarcastically at Brüggemann, then turned to Susanne. 'I think, given what's happened, we'd better arrange an escort back. I want the apartment checked out, too. I'll be with you in a minute, Susanne. I just need to talk to the guy who saved my neck.'

Flemming was waiting for Fabel in the reception area. He was dressed in dark blue overalls and sipped coffee from a Styrofoam cup.

'I begged these from the hospital,' he explained, plucking at the blue overalls. He grinned. 'I'll send you a dry-cleaning bill for my suit.'

'You can send me the bill for a new one. I thought I was a goner for sure. I don't know how I can begin to thank you for what you did.'

'Armani would be a start.' Flemming's grin widened. He was a big man with huge shoulders but otherwise slim. Fabel reckoned that he was someone who was more than a hobby-fitness fan. He estimated Flemming's age to be somewhere in his mid-forties. Beneath the dark, curling hair a scar traced its way to the corner of his eyebrow.

'What's your background?' he asked Flemming. 'I mean, before Seamark International?'

'Polizei Kiel Harbour Police for ten years. Before that Kampfschwimmer Kompanie.'

Fabel raised an eyebrow. 'Then it was my lucky day.' The Kampfschwimmer Kompanie was the special-forces unit of the German Navy. Commando frogmen. 'How long?'

'Twelve years. So taking a dip to pull you out of the water was nothing. To join the Kompanie you have to be able to swim at least thirty metres underwater without scuba and be able to stay

373

underwater for at least sixty seconds without breathing. So today really was no big deal.'

'Trust me,' said Fabel. 'It was a big deal to me. Can I get you another coffee?'

'I'm fine, thanks.'

Pleasantries over, Fabel's tone became more businesslike. 'What exactly have you been doing tailing me for the last couple of weeks?'

'You spotted me that long ago?' Flemming gave a small laugh. 'I must be slipping.'

'Well?'

'Mustafa Kebir is more than a client, he's a friend. He knows about my background, so when his niece went missing he came to me. Obviously the first thing I did was tell him to go to the police, but he said that Meliha would resent that. She's very anti-establishment.'

'You do know that impersonating a police officer is a serious offence?'

'I don't know what you're talking about, Herr Fabel.' Flemming's expression remained open and frank. He was good, thought Fabel.

'Someone had the brass balls to walk into Butenfeld, flash a Polizei Schleswig-Holstein badge and ask to see the torso that had been washed up at the Fischmarkt after the storm. I put it down to the Pharos Project, but now . . .'

Flemming shrugged and took a sip of his coffee.

'Isn't it a huge coincidence that "Commissar Höner" showed a Kiel division ID? You know, where you served . . . Listen, Flemming,' Fabel turned in his chair to face the big man square on. 'After what you did for me today, I don't want to make any trouble for you. But I *could* get someone up here from the morgue to see if they can spot anyone who looks a little like the Schleswig-Holstein detective who turned up to view the torso . . .'

'Okay. It *was* me. I wanted to see if it was Meliha.'

'And?'

'You saw that torso. The only way to get a positive ID is to check against familial DNA, which I'll leave to you, now that you know where to find a family member.'

'But your instinct?'

'I don't have one. When I saw the torso it had been degassed – you know, to stop it exploding – but it was still quite bulked up. It could be Meliha. But it could be anyone. As you can imagine, I've seen a lot of floaters over the years and they're always very difficult to age and size up. Your Fischmarkt torso had certainly been in the water for a long time. And the longer the immersion, the more difficult it is to age them accurately. For all my subterfuge, it really didn't do me any good.'

'Okay. I'll arrange for a DNA comparison with Herr Kebir. In the meantime, you keep your nose clean and out of official police business.'

Flemming sighed and leaned forward, resting his elbows on his knees. 'Okay. But if there's anything

I can do – and I mean *anything* – then I want you to let me know.'

'I appreciate it,' said Fabel. 'You can start by going through everything you know about Meliha Kebir . . .'

The next day, Fabel was in the Presidium early. He had woken up with a start and had known that something bad had happened the day before but, for a few seconds, had forgotten what it was. He had sat upright in bed, a cold sweat on his brow, until it fell into place.

Susanne had always worried about the stress Fabel's job placed him under. There had been a time when, driven by the bad dreams that he experienced almost nightly, he had himself considered giving up the Polizei Hamburg. But the look on Susanne's face that morning had been far beyond anything that he had seen before; more like fear than worry. Someone had made a pretty good stab at killing him.

She clung to him as they said goodbye in the morning. She was working out of the Institute for Legal Medicine and, in a reversal of the normal routine, she had dropped him off at the Presidium first. And she had been punctual, which worried Fabel most of all.

When he entered the Murder Commission Fabel was confronted with grim determination. The full team was there, including the officers who were not slated for duty. It was clear that Nicola

Brüggemann had called them all in and had given them an informal briefing on what had happened; several of them came up to Fabel, asked if he was okay and expressed their support, each with appropriate gravity. Fabel noticed that there was a Kevlar bulletproof waistcoat sitting upright on the desk behind Nicola Brüggemann.

'We've talked it through, *Chef*,' said Brüggemann, her face set hard, using the informal title to identify Fabel as her commanding officer, 'and we feel you need some extra protection. Werner . . . ?' She stood to one side to let Fabel have a view of the body armour. Werner grabbed the vest and pulled it to one side, like a stage magician whipping the cover from a cage of freshly disappeared pigeons. The room exploded into laughter: on the desk, until now hidden by the bulletproof vest, was a pair of bright yellow inflatable water wings, each complete with the neck, head, and bright red bill of a duckling.

Laughing, Fabel slipped off his jacket and slid the water wings onto his shirt-sleeved arms. He became aware of a sudden sobriety in the room and turned to see Criminal Director van Heiden standing framed in the door.

'Fabel . . . a word.'

Fabel self-consciously slipped the water wings off, ignoring the smirks of his team, and guided van Heiden into his office.

It was a brief meeting, and Fabel realised it was van Heiden's way of making his support for his junior officer clear. The Criminal Director confirmed what Brüggemann had told Fabel in the hospital: that he was now fully back in charge of all investigations and that he was to take whatever measures necessary and could request whatever resources he needed. It was clear that van Heiden was still out of his depth, even more so than before, but someone had tried to kill one of his own and that had fired up every policeman's instinct that van Heiden possessed.

'I just don't understand what is going on,' said van Heiden, genuinely perplexed.

'I do,' said Fabel. 'That's why I was pushed into the river. I can't prove any of it yet. And I doubt that we will ever be able to prove all of it, or any of it. But there's clearly a danger that someone is going to make another attempt on my life because of it, so I'm going to tell you.'

It took Fabel ten minutes to explain. Van Heiden sat silent, taking it all in but never looking any less perplexed.

'I'll get it written up,' said Fabel. 'But if you don't mind I won't email it. I'll have it hand-delivered to your office. I don't know how much our email system is compromised.'

'So you believe all this?' asked van Heiden.

'Yes, but like I say, I can't prove it. I've called Herr Menke to discuss it with him. We need all the help we can get with this one.'

★   ★   ★

For some reason, Fabian Menke had responded to Fabel's call by asking that they should meet, neither at the Presidium nor the BfV's office. Instead, he suggested a venue on the south side of the river, down by the docks. Fabel took a pool car and parked behind Menke's BMW 3 series. A very corporate car, thought Fabel and wondered if the security agent sold insurance policies in his own time. When he got out of his car, Fabel realised he was on another quayside, parked next to the water's edge. The sudden frisson he felt surprised him and he realised he was afraid of the water.

'Are you okay?' Menke asked as the two men shook hands.

'I'm fine. Just a bit shaken up after my last trip to the waterfront.'

'Oh God, yes,' said Menke. 'I should have thought. A pretty insensitive venue. Sorry. Do you want to go somewhere else?'

'No, it's fine.'

Menke led the way along the quayside. From here Fabel could see the arc of Hamburg on the far shore, from the Köhlbrandbrücke bridge to the Speicherstadt and HafenCity. This side of the Elbe, the south shore, was the working heart of the city. Huge cranes behind them arranged freight containers in piled-high rows, like children's building blocks.

'Before we start,' said Menke, 'do you have a cellphone with you?'

'Of course. But it's switched off and I left it in the car.'

'I see,' said Menke. 'You clearly recognise what we're dealing with here.'

'We're dealing with an idea,' said Fabel. 'Not a reality. I know that these people have massive technological resources and skills at their disposal, but I still think they're not as omniscient as their PR makes out.'

'No?' said Menke. 'I work in the business of watching others, Fabel. And *I* have technology at my disposal that you couldn't begin to imagine. I can sit outside someone's home and see what they're seeing on their computer monitor. I'm not talking about hacking into their WiFi or anything like that. They don't have to be connected to a hub or a network at all. We even have keystroke analysis where we can tell what's being typed into a computer without breaking into the hard drive . . . all done purely externally. Or take where we're standing now . . . there are at least five national intelligence agencies who have access to satellite technology so sophisticated that they could have a good stab at deciphering what we're saying to each other right now. You've read the material I sent you on the Pharos Project?' he asked when they reached the pier's end.

'I have, yes. And the more I've read, the more I'm convinced the Pharos Project is connected to the death of Berthold Müller-Voigt and the disappearance of Meliha Yazar. I am also pretty certain they are directly or indirectly behind the murder of Daniel Föttinger, and I think I know why. I wanted to talk to you because I think you can help me put the pieces together with the Föttinger case.'

'I'll do anything I can, Herr Fabel.'

Fabel gave an appreciative nod. 'We fished a body out of the river and I believe he's the motorcycle rider involved in the attack on Föttinger. He's the guy I sent you a note about: Harald Jaburg.'

'I know,' said Menke. 'You're right that Föttinger's death was arranged indirectly.' He paused, looking out over the water for a moment before turning back to Fabel. 'Do you know anything about quantum physics – superposition, unified string theory, holographic principle, that kind of thing?'

'In a word, no.'

'Quantum theory is throwing up ideas that would make your head hurt. And every cult, street-corner messiah, New Age guru and nut-job is giving these theories a spin to try to give their loopy philosophies some kind of credibility. And they're using them to snare the more vulnerable in our society.' Menke took a packet of cigarettes out of his pocket and offered one to Fabel, who shook his head. 'Harald Jaburg is indeed a person of interest for the Bureau. As soon as the name went into the system I was alerted. He's red-flagged: a known member of the Guardians of Gaia, an extreme environmental group.'

'One of the extreme environmental groups

you didn't want to go into details about with Müller-Voigt?' asked Fabel.

'Exactly. This job has made me paranoid. The Guardians of Gaia believe in direct action against any individual, group or organisation they believe is endangering the environment. So far it's been more protests and minor vandalism.'

'Setting cars on fire?' asked Fabel.

'Among other things. Our intelligence is that they're becoming more and more militant.'

'There's nothing more militant than four bullets in the head,' said Fabel.

Menke shook his head emphatically. 'No, that doesn't seem right. As far as we're aware, they haven't yet injured anyone they see as the enemy, far less carried out internal executions. This is a weird one, all right. You mentioned in your message that Jaburg had a distinctive tattoo. The green gamma on the chest is their symbol for Gaia.'

'The Greek goddess of the Earth?'

'In name, yes. But their interpretation is more in the sense of the Gaia Hypothesis, formulated way back in the seventies. Back then it was considered weird and New Age-y, but now mainstream science is buying into it. It's the belief that the Earth's biosphere, of which we are part, is actually a single, integrated, living system. An organism in its own right.'

'Sounds harmless enough,' said Fabel.

'Yes, well, the Guardians of Gaia has a distinctly

paramilitary structure. They believe that "Gaia" is dying and that mankind is the infection that's killing her. So I'm sure you understand our interest in the group. They see themselves as soldiers. Soldiers engaged in a war against the forces of globalisation and industrialisation. And in some ways against mankind itself.'

Fabel thought back to the pale, skinny corpse of a young man lying on a mortuary trolley. 'I think someone may have just fired the first shot.'

'Harald Jaburg was the most minor of minor players in the Guardians. A gofer. And definitely not an assassin type.'

'A getaway rider?'

'Entirely possible. Our intel tells us that Jaburg worked on several occasions with one Niels Freese, an entirely different kettle of fish. I know even more about Herr Freese than I do about Jaburg.'

'In what way different?'

'Freese is the one with the skewed perception of the world. He's unpredictable, violent. History of severe mental disorders.'

'Unlikely to have planned and executed the Schanzenviertel attack, then?'

'I'm not saying that. Not by a long chalk. Freese is disabled, officially. Brain damage at birth, but that doesn't seem to have blunted his intelligence. And he *can* function normally in many ways, but he does have all kinds of other problems, mainly neurological, and some that have made him outright delusional on occasion. But he's smart enough, all right. He is, however, highly susceptible to manipulation, to suggestion. His mental state means he could be convinced of almost anything, if it's articulated right and gels with his odd perception of the world.'

'What is his problem?' asked Fabel. 'I mean specifically?'

'It's tragic, really. He really does experience reality differently from the rest of us: he suffers from almost constant promnesia, a highly disconcerting condition which is like having permanent déjà vu. And he has frequent episodes of what the quacks call reduplicative paramnesia. When he's in that state, the poor bastard thinks someone's abducted him from the real world and built a perfect but counterfeit copy around him.'

'I'll ask my partner about it. She's a *quack*, by the way.'

'Is she?' Menke looked only remotely embarrassed. 'Ah, well, no doubt she can tell you more about the condition than I can. In any case, his condition has made Freese someone who can be influenced by feeding his paranoid beliefs. Not *controlled*, but influenced. The nature of his condition makes him easy meat for all kinds of mumbo-jumbo about quantum realities and environmental singularities.'

'The kind of thing the Guardians of Gaia spout?'

'And the Pharos Project.'

'There's a connection?'

384

'Not that we can prove,' said Menke. He paused as the two men watched a freighter, stacked impossibly high with containers, drift silently by. 'But there *has* been a suggestion that the Guardians of Gaia are actually just a directly controlled arm of the Pharos Project.'

'But surely their philosophies are totally different.'

Menke handed Fabel a sheet of paper with a handwritten note on it.

'This is the last known address we have for Niels Freese. The second name is one that no one knows outside the BfV . . . except now you know. That is the name of the man we now believe to be the Hamburg commander of the Guardians of Gaia. If Freese carried out the attack that killed Föttinger – and it's a big "if" – then that is the name of the man who ordered it.'

'Jens Markull . . .' Fabel read the name out loud. 'Why the big secret about his name?'

'He is . . . he *was* one of ours. You implied we must have infiltrators, undercover people working for us. Well, we do. He was one of them.'

'He's a BfV officer?'

'No. Markull is simply someone whose principles were for sale. But it looks like something's happened to make him shut up shop. We were getting really good intelligence from him, then it dried up. The last thing we heard was that he had met with some people from the Pharos Project. Then suddenly he's promoted to

Commander of the Hamburg division of the Guardians of Gaia and doesn't seem to want to talk to us any more.'

Fabel put the note into his pocket and the two men started walking back to their cars.

'There's one thing I'd like to ask you about Niels Freese,' said Fabel.

'Go ahead.'

'These neurological problems he has. Do they include a limp?'

Menke stopped and turned to Fabel, a look of surprise on his face. 'Yes. As a matter of fact he does have a limp. The result of mild palsy caused by the oxygen deprivation at birth.'

CHAPTER 32

Heiner Goetz was a burly man just on the right side of sixty. He had thinning grey hair brushed back from a broad heavy forehead and large wiry eyebrows. A pair of wire-framed reading glasses had permanent residence on his heavy nose, balanced almost at the tip. Fabel always felt the glasses were a deliberate affectation: something to mitigate the fact that Goetz looked as if he worked on a building site. But Heiner Goetz was no bricklayer; he was the Chief State Prosecutor for Hamburg.

He sat and stared out of the window of his office on Georg-Fock-Wall as Fabel ran through, for the third time that day, his suspicions about the Pharos Project and its role in the disappearance and probable murder of Meliha Kebir, as well as the killings of Berthold Müller-Voigt, Daniel Föttinger and Harald Jaburg.

Fabel did his best, but knew that he had no hard evidence on which to base his claims. Securing any kind of warrant was a distant hope. He looked at his watch and glanced across at Werner Meyer whom he'd brought along with him. They had been talking it through for the best part of the morning and Fabel wanted to get back to the Presidium. After his conversation with Menke the previous day, Fabel had initiated a major manhunt for Niels Freese.

Goetz did not turn from the window when Fabel had finished speaking and gave no indication that he had heard what the Chief Commissar had said. Fabel remained patiently quiet: he had dealt with Goetz on countless occasions before and knew that the Chief State Prosecutor always took his time to think things through. Either that, or he enjoyed making police officers desperate to close in on a suspect sweat.

'So all of these deaths have been sanctioned to keep a secret?'

'That's what I believe.'

'But you have no substantiating evidence?'

'None, Herr Goetz. We need the warrants to seize computers and compel testimony. It's the only way we're going to get to the bottom of this.'

'Herr Fabel, you have been a police officer long enough to know that if I granted warrants on this kind of speculation, and the execution of said warrants yielded nothing material, then you and I would both be looking for another line of work before long. Now, if you had asked for surveillance warrants – wiretaps, email interception, that kind of thing, through which we could gradually harvest more convincing evidence – then I would have given that more credence.'

'But don't you see, Herr Goetz,' said Fabel, trying to keep the frustration out of his tone, 'such measures are futile against an opponent who is infinitely better resourced in terms of technology than we are. There is no form of electronic surveillance that they would not immediately spot and counter.'

Another silence as Goetz continued to stare out of the window.

'All this internet business,' he said eventually. 'It's a whole new environment for crime and we don't have the laws or even the basic understanding to combat it. About six months ago there was a case put up to me, not by your commission but by one of the child protection agencies. This girl – fifteen, if I remember right – threw herself under an S-Bahn train. She'd been a victim of so-called cyber bullying. She couldn't get away from it. It was relentless – vicious, vile stuff sent constantly to her computer, to her phone . . . it was a real campaign to destroy the spirit of a human being and it was facilitated by all of this technology that's supposed to make our lives better. She felt she couldn't escape it so she threw herself in front of a train. Fifteen. A life over before it had properly begun. I really wanted to go after the girls who had driven her to it, but the laws aren't there. The understanding isn't there. That poor girl, driven to that . . .'

Turning suddenly from the window, he leaned forward onto his desk, the heavy shoulders hunching.

'We've got four dead victims – and from what you've told me, these people have the arrogance to believe that they can go on killing whoever they feel is in their way, including a Hamburg State Senator, and attempting to murder a senior Hamburg police officer. If there's one thing that really gets me fired up, gentlemen, it's when someone thinks they're beyond the reach of the law.' Goetz slammed his open hands down on the desktop. 'I'll grant your warrants. Search, seizure and arrest. I'll try to get them ready for this evening, but there's a jurisdictional crossover because of the location of the Pharos or whatever they call this cult commune. I need to speak to the Lower Saxony Prosecutor's office.'

Fabel stood up, beaming. 'Thank you, Herr Prosecutor . . .'

'When do we execute the warrants?' asked Werner once they were back in the pool car Fabel had been given.

'Tomorrow morning. When we get back I need you to do the liaison with the Polizei Niedersachsen.'

'No problem.'

Fabel took his cellphone from his pocket and rang Susanne at her office in the Institute for Legal Medicine.

'You okay?' he asked. 'You were a bit shaken up this morning.'

'Can you blame me? Are *you* okay?'

'I'm fine, like I told you. Still a bit shaken up too, but I've got a job to do. Have you finished going through the psych assessment and history I got on Niels Freese?'

'Yes. It's an interesting one, I'll give you that. According to his records, Freese suffered brain damage at birth that's left him prone to Delusional Misidentification Syndrome.'

'In layman's terms?'

'We all suffer from a mild form of it every time we experience déjà vu. Just as we experience the delusion of having experienced something before, patients with full-blown DMS have more florid and specific delusions.'

'What kind of delusions?'

'Take your pick. Fregoli's Delusion makes you think that everyone around you is actually the same person in disguise . . . if you've got Capgras Delusion you believe your family members or friends have been replaced by identical impostors . . . and if you've got Cotard's Delusion you don't believe you're even alive. What Freese seems to have is Reduplicative Paramnesia. The poor bastard thinks he's been transported to an exact copy of the world.'

'Well, I have to say, that makes him sound pretty mad to me.'

'The sad thing is that these delusions are never the result of a mental illness. The root always lies in neurological damage: a brain injury, stroke, Alzheimer's or something like that. Poor Freese has had this since birth. His reality is one that's almost impossible for us to imagine, Jan. Just think of it: almost continuous déjà vu, constant feelings of deep significance provoked by the most ordinary object, person or event. And then the long periods of short-circuited memories and the belief that everything around you is a fake, a conspiracy. All the trappings of paranoia without the schizophrenia. Niels Freese is a sane man who lives in an insane reality.'

'But he's a killer; and from what you're saying, these people are not dangerous . . .'

'Anyone who's delusional is dangerous. There are instances of people suffering from Capgras Delusion slicing open their spouse to look for the mechanical workings or the robotic circuitry inside. People with Cotard's Delusion frequently kill themselves or others, believing it doesn't matter because no one is alive anyway. If you want my professional opinion, Jan, then I suggest you find Freese quick. Before he harms himself or others.'

'I need to find him quick, all right,' said Fabel. 'Freese *is* the key to reality as far as I'm concerned. He ties everything together.'

After he hung up from his call to Susanne, Fabel dialled Anna's number.

'Did you get the information I asked for?'

'Yep, *Chef*. Tim Flemming is exactly who he claims to be and his background is what he said.

No disciplinary or other problems, either while in the Kiel harbour police or as a naval frogman. But something interesting did come up. His younger sister became involved with an extreme religious group that later became a focus for the attention of the BfV. Flemming apparently removed her from this group against her will and held her at a secret address in Denmark, where he worked with established deprogrammers to undo the brainwashing. It worked, so no charges were ever brought.'

'But – let me guess – Flemming is known on the bush telegraph as the go-to guy for getting your nearest and dearest out of the clutches of a cult?'

'That's about it. But there are rumours of Flemming and his helpers being rather *forceful* in extracting cult members. The word is that you don't get in his way. Tough guy. Other than that, everything else he said about his business is true. They really do provide security advice and personnel for importers and shipping lines.'

'Thanks, Anna.'

'What now?' asked Werner after Fabel had ended his call.

'Let's go and pay Herr Flemming a call . . .'

People had an idea, a stereotype, of what a model-train enthusiast should look like. Frank Lesing was aware of that and often laughed at the reactions he got when he told people about his hobby.

Frank was thirty-two, tall, with a handsome face and thick dark hair. His looks, he knew, had been an advantage in building up his business. In business, people liked to deal with the good-looking. It was superficial, but it was true. His looks and his easygoing personality had made him popular at school and university and had eased his speedy progress through the international bank that employed him. It had all been so easy for Frank; so easy that sometimes it just did not seem real. As a senior member of the team, he was generally expected to make his lunches working ones: eating a sandwich while tied up in meetings or taking clients out to lunch. But whenever he did have a lunchtime to himself, this was where he would come: to the model-railway museum in the city's Speicherstadt. What had started off as a large model-railway display now stretched over nearly twelve thousand metres of track. The largest model railway in the world. But it had become much more than that: there were motorways, roads and streets with moving traffic; offices, churches, theatres; two hundred thousand models of people doing every possible human activity, and a perfect duplication of central Hamburg. Container ships, trains, buses, cars, fire engines – perfect scale models, regulated by computers in the central control room – moved around the miniaturised landscape, creating the illusion of looking down from a great height on a real, living city.

It had been quiet for a lunchtime and Frank did

not have to wait long to get in: the exhibition controlled the numbers passing through at any one time. He stood for a full five minutes looking down on a section of the Elbe while a container ship sailed through real water before reaching the crane-forested docks. It was then that Frank became aware of the young man standing at his side. There was something about the man that concerned Frank. He was dressed in dark clothes that looked old and grubby and Frank could smell the rancid odour of stale sweat coming from him. His hair was matted and he had the look of someone who had slept rough. But it was not that aspect of the man's appearance that troubled Frank, it was his eyes. There was a look of excited desperation in those eyes. The young man stared at the massive model of the Köhlbrandbrücke, the bridge that spanned the river where the South Elbe became the North Elbe again. It was one of Hamburg's most striking landmarks and even the model of it was impressive: six metres long and one and a half metres high.

'Are you all right?' asked Frank tentatively. He knew it was a bad idea – the guy was probably a junkie – but Frank had always found the imperative to help someone in need irresistible.

'I thought they didn't let you on it,' said the young man, without taking his wild eyes from the model of the Köhlbrandbrücke.

'What?'

'The bridge. I thought it was only for cars. There are people walking on it. Cycling.'

'Oh, that . . .' Frank smiled. 'It's supposed to be the cycle race. They open it for that once a year. And the people on foot are supposed to be environmentalists protesting.'

The young man moved a little further along, to change the angle of his view. Frank noticed that he limped a little as he did so. He frowned as he examined the replica structure.

'Are you sure you're all right?' asked Frank.

'Is it real?'

'Is what real? I think I should get you some help.' Frank looked around for an attendant.

'Is it real?' the man asked again, his voice dull.

'What? The bridge? Of course the bridge is real. Everything here is a copy of the real thing.'

'A copy? Everything here is a copy?' The young man looked up suddenly and Frank saw, for the first time, the full turmoil in the eyes. A storm of anger and fear and confusion. Frank now felt very uneasy. He walked away from the young man, moving as casually as he could, while desperately trying to locate an official.

'IS IT REAL?' the young man screamed at Frank's back. Everyone else in the museum stopped and turned to see who was shouting. When Frank turned around, he found himself facing the barrel of an automatic. It shook in the young man's outstretched hands. Frank could see that he was crying now, thick rivulets of tears streaking his cheeks. 'I . . . want . . . you . . . to . . . tell . . . me . . . IS IT REAL?'

'Is what real?' asked Frank, through his panic. He saw a member of staff over the young man's shoulder, speaking into a walkie-talkie. 'Do you mean the bridge? Do you mean everything here?'

'Is it real?' he repeated, calmer this time but taking deliberate aim along the gun's barrel.

'Of course it's not real!' Frank was shouting now. 'It's just a model. It's just make-believe.'

The young man's eyes widened and Frank waited for the sound of the gun. Time had slowed down, each second adrenalin-stretched, and he found himself wondering if he *would* hear the gun, or whether he would be dead before his brain could register the sound.

'It's not real?' asked the young man, sobbing.

'No. Of course it's not.'

Frank flinched as the young man surged forward at him, shoving him to one side and pushing his way through the screams of the crowd and out through the exit.

Suddenly Frank felt his legs give way under him and steadied himself on the handrail. He found himself looking at the Köhlbrandbrücke at the level of the roadway and a hand-painted environmental protester stared back at him defiantly.

Quite appropriately, the offices of Seamark International were in the HafenCity. It was, on the face of it, a modest outfit. The offices were new and, like the rest of the HafenCity, were all about the new century and its promises. They were not, however, particularly big: just a reception and three offices.

'I've been expecting you,' said Flemming when Fabel and Werner arrived. 'You better take a seat.'

'So which is the biggest part of your operation?' asked Fabel after the receptionist had brought in a tray with coffees. 'The maritime security or the cult-member deprogramming?'

Flemming smiled. 'I take it you've found out about my hobby?'

'Rescuing and deprogramming cult members? Yes, I have. An interesting sideline.'

'I don't do it for money. If my expenses are covered that's all I care about. And in some cases not even that. I hate cults. I hate what they do to people.'

'And is the Pharos Project your particular focus of interest, Herr Flemming?'

'Of late, probably. We live in strange times, Herr Fabel. Most of the religious and spiritual certainties have fallen by the wayside. Christianity, Marxism, Nationalism . . . Everything is changing, becoming more technological, globalised, faster. People feel overwhelmed and they're looking to more and more abstract concepts for some kind of guidance. The Pharos Project is very clever with its pitch, particularly to the vulnerable. My personal belief is that it is the most dangerous cult on the planet.'

'So Herr Kebir believes Meliha has been recruited and brainwashed?'

'No, I'm afraid we're all pretty sure that Meliha has been murdered. She wasn't an acolyte, she was an infiltrator. But I won't stop searching for her until we are sure one way or the other. There is always the chance that they have kept her alive somewhere.'

'Berthold Müller-Voigt was her lover. He was convinced she'd uncovered a secret that would have done massive damage to the Pharos Project. Do you think she was onto something big?'

'I don't know,' Flemming shrugged. 'It could be. I only came into this after the fact, as it were. But I think it's entirely possible that she found out something about either the Korn-Pharos Corporation or the Pharos Project. She was totally dedicated to exposing false environmental prophets, from what I've been told.'

'But you've had experience of dealing with people who have been involved with the Project?' asked Werner.

'We've liberated four former members so far. Technically, we've broken the law each time but after the rescued member has been "deprogrammed" they have been grateful rather than wanting to press charges. You asked me why I'm so secretive about what we do. I think you are beginning to get an idea of how ruthless Pharos can be. They don't like losing members; not just because they resent the loss of a revenue stream, but because ex-members are likely to talk about what goes on in the cult.'

'And the ones you've liberated – have they talked?'

'Yes, but the cult is structured in such a way that each member has a very restricted view of the whole organisation. But, by piecing things together, we've built up an idea of some of the more secret aspects of the Project.'

'Such as?'

'Such as unregulated experiments in Brain Computer Interface – a branch of neuroscience that just happens to fit in with Dominik Korn's weird ideas. It's all about micro-thin sensors implanted in the brains of people with disabilities to connect them to external technology – blind subjects being able to see again through an external artificial eye, amputees having full sensory control over robotic prostheses, that kind of thing. There are even complex versions already developed to help people with specific kinds of paralysis. I'm sure you can see why Dominik Korn, given his condition, has a vested personal interest in funding development of this area.'

Fabel found himself thinking of Johann Reisch, a man desperate for exactly that type of technology. But it had been too late for him.

'So are you really suggesting that the Pharos Project is carrying out illegal surgery on members in pursuit of a better class of electric wheelchair for Korn?' he asked.

'You have to remember that many of the cult's members are only too willing to take part.

"Enhancement" is seen as a step on the path to realising singularity.'

'God . . .' said Fabel. 'These people are really taken in by this stuff?'

'No matter how sophisticated their technology or how much cash they've got in the pot, the Pharos Project is just another destructive loony cult like any other. And that means the same old tricks. They restrict the calorie intake and the amount of sleep of their members to dull their mental responses. Sometimes even sedate them slightly. It all makes new subjects more amenable to indoctrination. The problem we have is that when we "liberate" one of them, it is, to all intents and purposes, abduction. We hold them against their will in a secret location and use the same kind of brainwashing techniques as the cults we've freed them from, except in reverse. Then we introduce them back to their families. That's usually the end of it, except some cults make an effort to track down ex-members. In the case of the Pharos Project, they use Consolidators – officers of the Consolidation and Compliance Office.'

'And that's who you think pushed my car into the Elbe?'

'I'm certain of it. There are even rumours that some Consolidators have been "augmented" – taken that extra step on the path to becoming consolidated. Special implants to boost hearing, improve sight by giving them infrared vision, that type of crap. Personally I think it's all cult hype.

Even the Pharos Project doesn't have that kind of technology at its disposal. Yet.'

'Well,' said Fabel. 'I have to say your intelligence gathering is excellent. I mean, you seem to be *extremely* well informed . . .'

'We have to be. We're up against sophisticated enemies.'

'Mmm . . .' said Fabel thoughtfully. 'Do you happen to know someone called Fabian Menke? He works for the BfV.'

'No. Can't say I do,' said Flemming, and there was nothing in his expression for Fabel to read. 'Should I?'

'No. It's just that I thought your paths might have crossed.'

They had just left Flemming's office when Anna Wolff called Fabel on his cellphone.

'Jan, I think we've found Freese.'

'That was quick.'

'To be honest, he's made it pretty easy for us. There's a guy walking across the Köhlbrandbrücke bridge. He's taken potshots at passing motorists. It sounds like the same guy who was reported to have waved a gun around at the model-railway museum in the Speicherstadt. From the description, it sounds like Freese.'

CHAPTER 33

The Köhlbrandbrücke was a sweeping arc of road bridge suspended from two 135-metre-high stanchions that gave the impression of inverted giant tuning forks. By the time Fabel got there with Werner, the uniformed branch had sealed off the bridge to traffic. He could see that about seven hundred metres beyond the police barricade a Thyssen TM 170 armoured car of the Polizei Hamburg's MEK Mobile Deployment Commando was parked at an angle across the carriageway. A team of MEK officers, clad in black helmets and body armour, used the TM 170 for cover while training their weapons on the figure who stood on the parapet, looking down at the river. Fabel estimated that the armed man was roughly at the centre of the bridge, which meant there was a fifty-metre drop beneath him to the water.

'I need to get up there,' Fabel said to the uniformed Senior Commissar at the barrier, pointing to the armoured car. 'With a bullhorn.'

Once Fabel and Werner were kitted out with body armour and helmets, two MEK officers led their crouching half-run to the TM 170, shielding them from the armed man on the bridge with Kevlar shields.

'That's all we need . . . tourists,' said the senior MEK officer when the two murder detectives reached the TM 170.

'How's it going, Bastian?' Fabel asked. 'Shoot anyone I know recently?'

Bastian Schwager nodded towards the figure on the bridge. 'What's the Murder Commission's interest in this bozo?'

'We think he topped the guy fished out of the water yesterday. He's some kind of eco-terrorist. But he's also got some pretty major mental health issues. He's potentially suicidal.'

'If he waves that handgun in our direction once more, Jan, I'm going to have to save him the trouble.'

'Listen, Bastian, this guy is a key witness,' said Fabel. 'I really need to talk to him. Can we get closer?'

'And give him an easier target? I don't think so. From what you've said, mental illness or no, he represents a threat to more than himself.' Schwager sighed and pointed to the bullhorn. 'Okay, use that and tell him we're moving the armoured car closer so that you can hear what he has to say.'

'Niels . . .' There was a feedback whine and Fabel held the bullhorn a little further from his mouth. 'Niels . . . this is Principal Chief Commissar Fabel of the Polizei Hamburg. I want to talk to you. I want to hear what you have to say, but I can't from over here. I'm too far away. We're going to move the armoured vehicle closer to you. No one is going to shoot you or try to grab you. I just want to talk. If you are agreeable, please raise your right hand.'

Niels shouted back something indistinguishable.

'I can't hear you, Niels. Raise your arm if it's okay to move closer.'

The figure on the bridge remained motionless, the gun hanging loosely at his side, his gaze cast down towards the water fifty metres below.

'Niels?'

The figure on the bridge parapet still did not move for what seemed an age. Then it half-heartedly raised its arm.

Bastian Schwager barked orders at those of his men within earshot, then into the radio. The TM 170 growled and rolled slowly forward, straightening up and moving slowly, the MEK team and Fabel and the other officers shielded by its flank. When it stopped, the sharpshooters took aim again at Niels, now only twenty metres distant.

'Niels . . .' Fabel called across to him once the armoured car's engine had been cut. 'I need you to come down from there. I want to talk to you about what has happened.'

Niels did not answer for a moment, his back still to Fabel and his gaze still downwards onto the river below.

'Do you want to know something funny?' Niels said at last. 'I used to be afraid of the water. And of heights. That's funny, isn't it?'

'Niels . . .' Fabel kept his voice calm and even. 'You need to put the gun down. You're placing yourself in danger by having that thing in your hand. I want you to put it down.'

'This?' Niels raised the automatic and looked at it as if he had never seen a gun before. Fabel sensed the MEK team preparing to fire and held up a restraining hand. 'I thought I'd already thrown it away. And that I'd thought I'd already thrown it away when I threw it away the last time. I don't know if this is a gun. Maybe the first one was . . . Anyway, I don't need it any more.' Niels opened his hand and let the gun tumble from his grasp. It clanked against the parapet and disappeared over the edge.

'It did that the last time, too,' he said.

Now that Niels represented a danger to no one other than himself, Fabel and the other officers moved around from behind the cover of the TM 170. Bastian Schwager ordered all but one of his sharpshooters to lower their weapons.

'Okay, Niels, that was good,' said Fabel. 'Now I need you to step down from the parapet before you fall.'

'No. I'm not going to do that. I'm going to stay here. You can see so much more from up high. I mean in every way. Don't you think it's funny? You know, what I said about how I used to be

406

afraid of water and heights. Isn't it funny that I'm up here, so high up, and above water? But I'm not afraid. How high up do you think I am?'

'I don't know. Fifty, fifty-five metres. Enough to make sure that you're dead if you slip, so why don't you come down from the parapet?'

Niels looked up from the water and out across to the city. 'You know, it's a crime that this bridge is closed to pedestrians. You get such a great view from here. But that's the world we live in. The car is God.' He paused, as if perturbed. 'Or at least I *think* that's the world we live in. I get confused. Maybe that's the other place. I had it all straightened out in my head, but now it's all muddled again about which is which.'

'You've got muddled about a lot of things, Niels. You're tired and confused. Why don't you come with me and we can talk it all over? Get it all straightened out.'

'I'm not going anywhere I don't want to. And you would take me somewhere I don't want to go, where I couldn't see things I want to see or go places I want to go.'

'Niels, why did you kill Daniel Föttinger?'

'Who?'

'The man who burned to death in the Schanzenviertel.'

'Oh, him. I was told to. He was an enemy of Gaia.'

'But he was working on projects, on technology to *protect* the planet.'

'That doesn't matter,' Niels said absently and shrugged his shoulders as he continued to take in the view from his vantage point. 'He did things. Bad things. Things that would look bad for the movement.'

'What kind of things, Niels?'

'Oh, I don't know.' He turned his attention back to the river below. 'Do you think that the water is like a mirror? That there is actually an exact copy of our world underneath?'

'No, Niels, I don't. Who told you to kill Föttinger?'

'The Commander. But he was told by the grey suits, I think. I do *think* that that's the truth of it all.' Niels sounded suddenly animated, as if he had solved some great puzzle. 'No . . . it makes sense. All the feelings I have, about all of this not being real. Don't you see? It isn't real. The real world is on the other side of the water. It's us who are under the surface.' He nodded down towards the river. 'The real world is down – I mean *up* – there . . .'

'Niels, I need you to focus. Who are the grey suits? Who was it who gave your commander the order to kill Föttinger?'

It was as if Niels had not heard a word Fabel had said. He kept his focus on the distant surface of the water. 'I didn't see it before, but now it all makes sense. I always knew that this was just some kind of copy. That I'm just some kind of copy. The real world and the real me is there . . .'

Fabel sensed that Niels had tilted forward a little and something lurched in his gut. 'Niels, listen to me . . . *this* is the real world. There's nothing down there for you except death, trust me. Now, please, will you come with me so we can get this all straightened out?'

For the first time Niels turned his head to look directly at Fabel.

'No, I think you're wrong. I don't blame you, because it is all very convincing, all very well recreated, but I don't believe this is the real world. I do believe it's on the other side of the water. I'll just go and look . . .'

With that, Niels Freese took a step forward and disappeared from Fabel's view.

The other officers ran to the parapet and leaned over. Fabel remained where he stood. He didn't want to see Freese's smashed body floating on the oily dark water of the Elbe. That way, part of him could believe that Freese's wish had been fulfilled, and he was now in some other reality.

One that would be more kind to him. One where he could see things the way they really were.

CHAPTER 34

Fabel looked up at the seven a.m. sky. It had been like waiting in for an overdue package to be delivered but here, at last, was a sign that spring had arrived. It was a bright, warm morning and the sky was cloudless.

'Great, isn't it?' said Anna.

'Long overdue.' Fabel fastened the straps of the Kevlar body armour at his sides. 'We all set?'

His team nodded: Anna, Werner, Henk, Dirk and Thomas. Nicola Brüggemann was still struggling with the body armour.

'Am I the only person in the Polizei Hamburg with TITS . . . ?' She shouted the final word in the direction of the MEK team leader who had provided the armour. Then back to Fabel, 'This shit is clearly designed by men.' After some more struggling and cursing, she had the armour fastened.

In addition to Fabel's team there was a squad of eight MEK special-tactics commandos, Fabian Menke and two other BfV men. A large custody wagon with three uniformed officers was parked behind the cars. They had parked around the corner from the squat, but Fabel knew they would have to move quickly. Even at this time in the morning, news of a police presence in the Schanzenviertel would spread fast.

'Any movement?' Fabel asked the team leader. There had been a single unmarked surveillance unit outside the squat since Niels Freese had taken a dive off the Köhlbrandbrücke the afternoon before. Fabel had managed to keep the story away from the press, despite the heavy police presence on the bridge and it being closed to traffic. There was an unofficial arrangement with the press that suicides from the Köhlbrandbrücke should be played down, in case it became an even more popular suicide spot.

'Nothing much. A woman arrived about half an hour ago and let herself in. Odd thing – she was smartly dressed, not the usual type you would associate with a mob like this.'

'Has she come out yet?' asked Fabel.

'No, she's still in there.'

'We're all clear on what we're doing?' asked Fabel. More nods.

'We shouldn't have too much trouble,' said Menke. 'So far the Guardians have been all talk. We've no reason to believe they have weapons but, given their increased militancy of late, it's best to be safe.'

Fabel nodded. 'Right,' he said, addressing the whole team. 'When we go in, we arrest anyone we come across. Prone them, cuff them, search them,

411

and then it's a pass-the-parcel chain out to the custody guys. You've all seen the photograph of Jens Markull. He's our main target. He is the link between Niels Freese and whoever ordered the murder of Daniel Föttinger. Nicola, I want you to take Thomas and Dirk and go round the back of the house with a couple of the MEK boys. The rest of us will go in the front door. Anna, you stay with the custody guys.'

'You're kidding me?'

'I am not kidding anyone, Commissar Wolff. I've given you your post.'

'Jan, I'm not going to get shot again. I'm *definitely* not going to get shot here. The worst thing these bozos are going to do is chuck lentils at us.'

'Anna, humour me.'

'Okay.' She made a resigned face.

'Remember, I want everyone out as fast as possible,' Fabel spoke again to the whole team, repeating what he had said at the briefing. 'It's not so much them I'm interested in as any evidence we can seize. Since Freese took a high dive, we need to get evidence to tie the Guardians and the Pharos Project to Föttinger's murder. Don't give anyone a chance to delete data or destroy paperwork. And remember that Jens Markull gets priority.'

Menke had told Fabel that the house would normally have someone on lookout, so they decided not to approach on foot. Instead, on Fabel's radioed signal, the cars drove around the corner and pulled up directly outside the building. The custody van followed seconds later, giving the officers enough time to leap from the cars and race to the door, led by the MEK men. Two carried a door ram and the heavy wooden door yielded with surprising ease.

Fabel followed the black-uniformed commandos into the house, yelling 'Polizei Hamburg.' He heard a splintering smash from the rear of the house and knew that the other team had gained entry. There were four grubby rooms on the ground floor. No lookout, just three men and one woman who had been sleeping on scattered mattresses, rudely awakened, hauled to their feet and handcuffed. They looked unwashed, underfed and overwhelmed by the sudden violence of the raid. Fabel swiftly took in the faces: all too young to be Jens Markull.

'Where's Markull?' he barked at the girl, who responded by spitting at him.

There was a sound from upstairs.

'Henk, you come with me. You too,' Fabel called to one of the MEK men. They took the stairs three at a time. Four more rooms upstairs. Fabel nodded to Henk and he and the MEK commando kicked open the door closest to the landing. Nothing. Another sound.

'Here!' shouted Fabel and kicked open the second door.

It took him less than a second to take in the room, but for that sliver of time his brain could

413

not process it all. This room did not look like it belonged to the rest of the house. It was spotlessly clean and contained banks of expensive-looking computer hardware that filled the room with a quiet hum. The windows had been completely boarded up but the room was brightly lit. Fabel recognised Jens Markull instantly. He sat behind a large desk, staring directly at Fabel, but it was clear that the activist was incapable of seeing anyone. The side of his skull was smashed in, his dark curly hair matted with deep red blood and brain matter. He looked like he had been killed and then sat back up in his chair.

And there was a woman in the centre of the room. Fabel recognised her instantly too. She was wearing exactly the same grey business-style suit that she had on the night when she had approached him down at the docks and given her identity as a woman already dead and waiting to be found.

'Stay exactly where you are!' Fabel aimed his SIG-Sauer at the woman but there was no hint of alarm or aggression or fear in her expression. She simply stood still in the centre of the room, staring at Fabel with eyes that were almost as dead as Markull's. She had something in her hand. Not a gun. Something smaller. Like a TV remote control.

Fabel was aware of the MEK officer at his shoulder. Then, suddenly, the commando grabbed the collar of Fabel's Kevlar vest and tugged him violently out of the door frame and back onto the landing. Fabel was about to protest when he heard the MEK officer scream 'Bomb!' at Henk Hermann and anyone else who could hear.

The three police officers had only got halfway down the stairs when the device detonated. Fabel felt simultaneously that someone had stabbed him in his left ear with something hot and sharp and that the world had disappeared from beneath his feet.

Fabel, Henk and the MEK officer plunged together with the shattered staircase into the ground floor. Suddenly Fabel was aware that Werner was leaning over him, then Anna. It felt as if someone was blowing a high-pitched whistle in his ear and he had had the wind knocked out of him. Apart from that he and the other two seemed to be in one piece.

'Thanks for that,' he said to the young MEK officer when they had both been helped to their feet.

'We had better get out of here,' the MEK man said. 'There could be other devices and we'll need the bomb squad here. We have to get everyone out.'

'Sure,' said Fabel. But he knew there would be no other bomb in the squat. The one upstairs had only been big enough to do the job it had been intended for: to destroy all the computer equipment and any data stored on it.

As he made his way outside, Fabel could not

get the face of the young woman who had detonated the device out of his head. She had not come there to die.

'I take back my lentils crack,' said Anna, once they were a safe distance away from the building. Black smoke billowed from the upper floor. Fabel guessed there must have been an incendiary element to the bomb. 'You sure you're okay?'

'I'll get checked out.'

'God, Jan,' said Anna. 'A suicide bomber. These people are as bad as radical Islamists.'

'It wasn't meant to be a suicide bombing, Anna. It was the same woman who approached me down at the docks. She wasn't meant to die. She was there to shut Markull up, permanently . . . and to destroy evidence. Get out and detonate the bomb from a distance.' Fabel tentatively pressed his fingers to his ear, then checked his fingertips. No blood. His eardrum was intact.

'You should have seen the computer hardware in that room,' he said. 'A shit-heel outfit like the Guardians of Gaia couldn't stretch to that. Markull had someone behind him and that someone was severing their partnership. I reckon she smashed his head in, then propped him up to make his injuries look consistent with a bomb blast. It was all supposed to look like the increasingly militant Guardians of Gaia had decided to go into the bomb-making business and that Markull had been clumsy when assembling a device.'

Fabel stared at the burning building for a moment.

'Get the team reassembled.' His voice was hard. Determined. 'We can't let this hold us up.'

'We're going ahead as planned?' asked Werner.

'Yes. We hit the Pharos now.'

Fabel knew that they would be spotted well in advance. There were only two ways to approach the Pharos: the river and the shoreside road. Both offered no cover and the approaching police would be spotted from half a kilometre away. This was a raid where speed was everything; each second would mean more data lost, and that meant less evidence to bring before a court.

He had briefed and rebriefed the teams. But five valuable hours had passed since the botched storming of the Guardians' squat and Fabel was afraid that the Pharos People would now be expecting a police raid. His own people were backed up by MEK officers of both the Polizei Hamburg and the Polizei Niedersachsen. The Harbour Police were leading the water-based assault. Fabel had no reason to believe the police would be resisted, and he had no evidence that the so-called Consolidators who took care of security would be armed but, as he had pointed out at the briefing, recent history was full of cults resorting to murder-suicide. He did not want this operation to turn into a German Waco.

Menke was there with his whole Pharos Project

investigation team and Fabel had even roped in Kroeger and other officers from Cybercrime. It would be up to them to retrieve as much data as quickly as possible. Fabel knew that the Pharos Project would no doubt have some kind of self-destruct software for exactly this kind of situation.

Fabel, Werner and Brüggemann went on the lead Harbour Police boat. It was a fast rigid-hulled inflatable craft that tore through the river, lifting its nose out of the water and bouncing over any hint of a wave. The small flotilla stayed tight in to the shore to delay being spotted for as long as possible.

'You all right, Jan?' Werner shouted over the whine of the engine. Fabel sat crouched over, his jaw set rigid, clutching the sides of his seat tight.

'I'm fine. Just not good on water.'

The Pharos was even more impressive from the water. The boat arced out a little into the river and swept between two of the twelve support pillars and under the projecting floor where Fabel knew Peter Wiegand had his office.

There was a jetty set centrally under the cover of the building. Two grey-suited Consolidators watched the approach of the police boats. One of them was talking – but not to his companion – and Fabel guessed that their arrival was being announced to the main building.

As they reached the jetty, Fabel received a radio message from Anna that her team was through the main gate and heading for the principal entrance.

The MEK officers secured the jetty, spinning the Consolidators around against the wall and checking them for weapons. Nothing.

'That doesn't mean the others aren't armed,' said Fabel. 'Take no chances.'

A police raid has a contained violence, a force that is intended to dominate and establish control. For the innocent bystander caught up in it, and for most criminals, it is a traumatic experience; yet, as Fabel marched through the building, forcibly subduing any Consolidator they came across in the process, the cult members they encountered watched the police advance room by room with an absolute passivity. There was no panic. What concerned Fabel more was that there was no sign of anyone hunched over a monitor, desperately trying to delete data.

Peter Wiegand was waiting for them, as he had the last time they had spoken, in his office. He sat behind his vast desk with a studied serenity. His chief of security, Bädorf, stood beside him, hands folded, like a butler waiting for instructions.

'I take it you would like to have that chat you mentioned the last time you were here, Herr Fabel,' said Wiegand, with a small polite smile that suggested he found Fabel slightly tedious. 'The one at your office . . .'

Peter Wiegand somehow managed to convey a sense of authority, that he was a master of his environment, even though that environment was now one of the interrogation rooms in the Hamburg police Presidium. He sat composed as always, and neat. Wiegand's neatness extended far beyond his tailoring. The beard was immaculately trimmed, his shaven head burnished. He was a shortish heavyset man, yet there was a compactness about him and a physical efficiency in the way he moved.

Sitting next to Wiegand was an attractive woman in her early forties. She had butter-coloured hair combed back into a French pleat and she was wearing a business suit that certainly had not a single synthetic thread in it and probably, thought Fabel, cost more than he earned in a month. Fabel had recognised her right away: Amelie Harmsen was not the kind of legal representative he was used to coming up against. She was one of the Hanseatic City's most high-profile lawyers, known more for winning punitive damages for her celebrity clients than fighting criminal cases. Harmsen was certainly not an indoctrinated member of the Pharos Project. She was here representing Wiegand the billionaire, not Wiegand the cult leader.

'I want to know how long you intend to detain my client, Principal Chief Commissar,' she asked. 'And if you have something of which you wish to accuse Herr Wiegand, then I would like to hear it. Now.'

'As would I, Herr Fabel,' added Wiegand, with the same hint of bored disinterest.

Fabel smiled politely. Werner handed Fabel a folder, which he placed squarely on the table before him. He started leafing through the file's pages.

'You know, this is very interesting reading,' he said conversationally. 'Did you know that Daniel Föttinger studied philosophy at Hamburg University?'

'No, Herr Fabel. I did not.'

'Really? I would have thought you and he would have discussed such things. After all, the Pharos Project trades heavily on the philosophy of mind, wouldn't you say?'

Wiegand said nothing, instead keeping Fabel locked in a cold, contemptuous glare.

'He didn't do too well with his studies,' continued Fabel. 'From what we've been able to find out, he had a tendency to become too fixed on one particular aspect of philosophy. Obsessive, almost. He lacked intellectual discipline, apparently. Not enough *rigour*. His dissertations were considered to be too narrow and ill-researched. Take this one: it was supposed to be a general exploration of Plato's Theory of Forms, but it turns into a very, very discursive piece on Platonic Simulation.' Fabel flicked further through the document. 'But where it really gets interesting is when he gets into a discussion about *qualia*. Now, I'm no philosopher, but *qualia* seem to me the sensory experiences we have of the world, how we perceive our environment.'

'Does tedium fall under that description, Herr Fabel?' said Wiegand wearily. 'I really do hope that you intend to make some kind of point.'

'Well, let me put it this way. Daniel Föttinger's personality, I feel, is revealed through these notes. Philosophy is, after all, all about making sense of the individual's experience of the world. Föttinger was interested in a very specific concept related to *qualia*: the concept of the "philosophical zombie". That is the idea held in some fields of philosophy that there is only a minority of people in the world who are real; that some people – most people, in fact – don't really exist at all in the real sense of the word. They react to stimuli the way you would expect them to – they express feelings of sorrow, pain, anger, love . . . but they don't really *feel* these things, because they have no real sentience.'

'Point?' asked Wiegand's lawyer.

'Simply that it's interesting that these notes suggest that Daniel Föttinger was obsessed with the concept. Now, I've spoken to a lot of people about Herr Föttinger, and I've gained a bit of an insight into his personality. And I have to say it's not a very pleasant personality. I believe that, as a young student, he was obsessed with these ideas because they fitted pretty much with his experience of the world.'

'Which was?' asked Wiegand.

'That people didn't really matter. Daniel Föttinger was a person completely devoid of empathy. He simply could not imagine that others had any kind of consciousness in the same way that he did.' Fabel closed over the file. 'Daniel Föttinger was, quite simply, a sociopath.'

'And what does this have to do with my client?' asked Harmsen.

'Let me get to that. Sociopathy, as a personality disorder, is much more common than one would think. A mildly sociopathic personality is probably something of an advantage in the corporate world; the "ruthless businessman" is very often someone who is supremely egocentric and blind to the feelings of others. Daniel Föttinger was certainly such a businessman, as was his father before him, from what I can see. Daniel must not have seemed the ideal candidate for you to recruit into the Project, but you already had his independently wealthy wife and you needed Föttinger's business to work in harmony with the Korn-Pharos Corporation. I don't know, but it was probably your intention that, when you had him brainwashed sufficiently, Föttinger Environmental Technologies would become absorbed into the Korn empire.'

'I still don't see—' began Wiegand's lawyer.

'Your brainwashing techniques started to work on Föttinger, mainly because the concept of a virtual world peopled with self-aware programs appealed to his already skewed ideas. But he was a bit of a thorn in the side, wasn't he, Herr Wiegand? My guess is that his behaviour became increasingly erratic. I would also guess that you perhaps started to encounter problems with how he interacted with the female members of your little group.' Fabel paused. 'So how does that have anything to do with you, Herr Wiegand? I'll tell you. A young environmental activist and web-journalist calling herself Meliha Yazar infiltrated your organisation. Somehow she gained access to the deepest levels of the Project. She discovered something big. Something so big that it could bring the Project down. And because she gained that knowledge, you had her killed. Then, because you thought she had passed that information on to her lover, Berthold Müller-Voigt, you had him killed too. You even arranged for me to be shoved off a pier and into the Elbe because you thought I was getting close to the truth, which I was.'

'Are you going to enlighten us?' asked Wiegand. Fabel could see the billionaire did not feel threatened. He knew that accusations were one thing; having the evidence to back them up was another. His counsel remained quiet.

'First of all, let's talk about the death of Daniel Föttinger. You arranged that, too. Your Consolidators actually run the Guardians of Gaia and you used poor, confused Niels Freese to kill Föttinger.'

'And why,' asked Harmsen, 'would my client do that?'

'Because of the big secret that Meliha Yazar discovered, the knowledge that Herr Wiegand here has tried so hard to wipe off the face of the planet.'

'And what is this "big secret"?' asked Harmsen.

'That Daniel Föttinger was the Network Killer.'

There was a pause. Nothing to read on Wiegand's face. Less certainty on Harmsen's.

Fabel turned to Wiegand again. 'As Föttinger got more and more drawn into your wacky ideas – ideas that actually made sense of his experience, just as they did with Niels Freese – he became more and more out of control. He spent up to six hours a night logged into *Virtual Dimension*, leading a substitute life that spilled out into the real world. He arranged to meet these women online, then raped and strangled them, dumping their bodies in the waterways around the city. You found out about it but couldn't get to him before he got to his last victim. In fact, I suspect you didn't find out about it until you caught Meliha Yazar. Am I right?'

Wiegand remained impassive and silent.

'So your Consolidators did a clean-up operation,' continued Fabel, 'wiping out all trace of any online contact between Julia Henning and all the other victims and Föttinger. You even cold-stored her body until after Föttinger's death so that he would not be connected to the murders.'

Wiegand remained silent for a split second, then burst into laughter. His lawyer, however, did not even break a smile.

'You know something, Fabel?' Wiegand leaned forward, his shaven head gleaming in the artificial light of the interview room, his eyes hard and cold.

'You're the one with the problem with reality. Everything you've said is absurd. Pure, unadulterated fantasy.'

'Is it? It certainly was embarrassing enough for you. You messed with Föttinger's mind just that little too much, too quickly. He had sociopathic tendencies. Not immediately apparent, and the type that make for ruthlessness in business. But what you didn't know was that he had a history of sexual assaults, all covered up by Daddy. Your crackpot theories started to appeal to his sense of superiority; his belief that there were people out there who weren't real people. That maybe all of this isn't reality at all, but some kind of simulation. A game. He probably convinced himself that the women he raped and strangled didn't even feel what he was doing to them. That they were *philosophical zombies* programmed to simulate fear and pain.'

'Do you have any actual proof with which to back up these allegations?' asked the lawyer.

'That was the object of this morning's raids. Our first was less than successful. There was a young woman at the headquarters of the Guardians of Gaia, the same young woman who had tried to compromise me by giving me the identity of Julia Henning before her body was discovered. Anyway, this young woman was dressed a lot like one of your Consolidators and she detonated a bomb that wiped out the evidence we needed. Wiped herself out, too. But we've got material from the

426

Pharos and Technical Section is taking that apart, bit by bit, at the moment. I'm afraid you'll be our guest until they're finished.'

'Then I wish you luck,' said Wiegand. 'Because if you don't find anything with which to substantiate these outrageous claims, then I'll be having a very long conversation with Frau Harmsen here about our options.'

After Fabel suspended the interview, he went back up to the Murder Commission. He sat for a moment at his desk, gazing absently at the three books that Anna had left there for him. The books that they had found on Meliha Kebir's bedside table. *Nineteen Eighty-Four. Silent Spring. The Judge and His Hangman.*

Werner came in and slumped in the seat opposite.

'We're fucked, aren't we?'

'All in all, I think that sums up our situation quite well. We'll keep him overnight and hope that the tech boys turn something up. How did Anna and Henk get on with Bädorf?'

'They didn't. Bädorf's keeping his mouth shut, except to demand that someone produces some evidence against him. They're a pretty confident bunch, Jan. By the way, there's a complete "infirmary" on the second floor of the Pharos. The guys doing the search say that, given the size of this infirmary, Pharos members must be very accident-prone or a pretty unhealthy bunch.'

'Operating theatre?'

'Looks like there has been one, but it's been cleared out. Again, no proof we can present in court. You thinking about catching up on your reading?' He nodded towards the books on the desk.

'Do you think you should listen to dreams?' asked Fabel.

Werner frowned. 'You're not coming apart on me, are you, Jan?'

'I dreamt about Paul Lindemann again. He told me to remember these books.'

'No, Jan,' said Werner. '*You told yourself* to remember these books. That's the way dreams work. The people in them aren't real, you know. They're just there to tell you what you already know; what's locked up somewhere in your subconscious, or some shit like that.'

'I know that, Werner. But it's odd. It was so like Paul.'

There was a knock and Kroeger stuck his head around the door and asked if he could join them.

'Well?' Fabel asked once the Cybercrime Unit officer had sat down next to Werner.

'Nothing so far. I've got half a dozen of my best people out at the Pharos going through every file, every piece of data, and I've had a dozen hard drives brought back here. We've focused on Wiegand's and Bädorf's computers, just as you suggested, as well as the hardware used by the Office of Consolidation and Compliance, but we've come up empty. Sorry.'

'So they obviously wiped anything incriminating when they saw us coming?'

'To tell the truth, I just don't know.' Kroeger's long face looked greyer and grimmer that usual. 'I'm sorry. Normally we can tell when data's been wiped and more often than not, unless the hard disk's been truly trashed – and I mean physically damaged – we can usually retrieve erased files. But it's not that they've dumped what we're looking for, it's more that it wasn't there to begin with.'

'I can't believe there isn't *anything* on their mainframe or whatever the hell you call it.' Fabel's frustration was beginning to boil over into anger. 'I thought you and your geeks were supposed to be the best in the business. I think you've met your match. The Pharos Project has simply outgunned and outsmarted you.'

Kroeger seemed to consider Fabel's words; there was no hint of him having taken offence at what Fabel had said.

'No . . .' he said contemplatively. 'No, I don't think that's it at all. We *would* have found something. You can't wipe all trace of previous data from computers. The only anomaly we can find is that a lot of the data we are looking at has been updated within the last few hours. New files. And some of them have had update times manipulated. But I think it ties in with what happened with your cellphone.'

'What do you mean?' asked Werner.

'We're looking for a high-tech solution to these problems,' said Kroeger, creasing his high forehead with a frown. 'Maybe it's a lot simpler than that. I think that the Pharos Project has *physically* dumped all of its data. I think that several of the computers we are examining have been brought in from elsewhere, or at least the hard drives have been swapped over. The original drives are at the bottom of the Elbe or have been crushed in some waste plant. That would explain there being so many new files on some of the key computers, particularly in the Office of Consolidation and Compliance. The server in there looks brand new. My thinking is that they've brought these computers in from their other operations, loaded with harmless data, and then added some Pharos-specific stuff to make it look like they've been there for months.'

'What's that got to do with my cellphone?'

'I think they did the same with that. I think the phone I've been examining isn't yours at all. It's a substitute. A clone. And your network isn't your network. They've faked it all so that you've been connected to their network and the whole time they were monitoring you through it.'

Fabel thought about what the Cybercrime officer had said. 'So you're saying that you're not going to find *anything* on their system? Wiegand's going to walk if you don't, Kroeger, you do realise that?'

'I can't find what's not there,' replied Kroeger,

'And I honestly think we're looking in the wrong place at the wrong time. If only we had got into the network *before* they swapped drives . . . If you're right and Meliha Yazar did get something on them, then you've got to find it, if it still exists.'

There was a perfunctory knock on the door and Anna stepped in.

'Sorry to disturb you, *Chef*, but there's something I think you might want to see.'

'What?'

'What looks like a suicide, over in Wilhelmsburg.'

'And what makes it interesting?'

'Two things. Firstly it would appear the guy committed suicide using an Exit Bag, just like the invalid, Reisch. The second thing is that the dead man's neighbour insists he speak to you. He asked for you by name . . .'

'This isn't the same,' said Fabel as soon as he walked into the apartment. 'We need a forensics team up here.'

He walked over to where the massive bulk of the dead man lay slumped over the computer desk. From a distance, Fabel had had difficulty identifying the shape as human. It had appeared more like a large, formless dark mass. Unlike Reisch's Exit Bag, ballooned up with helium, the plastic bag over this man's face was sucked in tight.

'You don't think this is suicide?' asked Anna, who had accompanied Fabel to the scene.

'He's got a plastic bag over his head, but there's

no helium canister or other inert gas. This guy's gone out with every instinct screaming for breath. It would take an enormous effort of will to sit there without your hands tied and not tear the plastic bag off your head.'

'I don't see him as the willpower type, somehow,' said Anna gravely. 'Especially around pastry. Whatever it was that killed him, it wasn't anorexia . . .'

'You're all heart, Commissar Wolff.'

'If there's anyone with an enlarged heart around here, it's not me. How much do you think this guy weighed?'

'God knows. Close on two hundred kilos.'

'What's up?' Anna read the frown on Fabel's face.

'Do you see all this computer equipment? There must be thousands of euros' worth here.'

'I'm guessing he didn't get out much,' said Anna.

'No, this is more that that. There's something professional about this set-up. I can't help but think this could be tied in with the whole Pharos Project thing.'

'Could be a coincidence. By the way, do you really think Daniel Föttinger was the Network Killer?'

'I'm convinced of it. Kroeger and his boffins have seized Föttinger's computer, not that they'll find anything there, but they've also got a court order to get his records from his internet service provider, as well as his cellphone accounts. Even if I can't prove it, I'd put a year's pay on us not seeing another victim.' Fabel nodded towards the slumped body. 'What did the police surgeon say about this?'

'That he's been dead for a while, that he clearly had a history of breathing problems, going by the gear in the bedroom and some of the medication. It would have been quick and easy with the bag. Maybe that's why there's no helium.'

'Where's this neighbour who insists on seeing me?' asked Fabel.

'Downstairs.'

Jetmir Dallaku was agitated. Impatient. It was clear that he had been waiting for some time for Fabel to call.

'Are you Principal Chief Commissar Jan Fabel of the Polizei Hamburg?' The small, wiry Albanian posed the question with such earnestness and formality that Fabel had to suppress a grin.

'I am, yes. You wanted to see me?'

'Do you have badge? Card? With name on?'

Fabel glanced at a smirking Anna, then reached into his jacket pocket and held out his police ID. Dallaku studied it with a frown.

'Herr Kraxner, upstairs. He knew someone come to do something bad.'

'He told you this?' asked Fabel.

'Yes. He said that if anything bad happen to him, I am to speak to you. Only you, and give you this ...' He reached into his pocket and took out a carefully folded envelope. 'Herr Kraxner . . . he was sad man. Lonely man. Why anybody hurt him?'

Fabel stared at the envelope for a moment, seeing his own name written on it, then looked up at the ceiling as if he could see through it and into the dead man's apartment.

'Klabautermann . . .'

'What?' said Anna.

Fabel snapped his attention back to her. 'Get on to Kroeger. I've got more work for him. Tell him I want every piece of hardware taken out of that apartment and subjected to the same scrutiny as the Pharos Project stuff.'

'He was the guy who phoned you?' Anna asked. 'The guy who said he had something to tell you?'

Fabel looked again at the envelope in his hands. 'I think he probably still has.'

CHAPTER 35

'I trust you slept well?' asked Fabel, taking his seat opposite Wiegand. The truth was that the billionaire looked as fresh as if he had spent the night in the Hotel Vier Jahreszeiten. A complete change of clothes had been brought in for him by Korn-Pharos staff. Amelie Harmsen looked similarly composed and fresh.

'The accommodation was tolerable,' said Wiegand. 'But let's put it this way, I intend checking out today. Within the hour, in fact. And my stay is going to prove an expensive one. For the Polizei Hamburg, that is.'

Fabel smiled. 'I wouldn't count on it, if I were you.'

Werner Meyer and Nicola Brüggemann came in and sat on either side of Fabel. Werner had a pile of newspapers, which he laid on the floor next to his chair.

'I see you're coming mob-handed today, Principal Chief Commissar,' said Harmsen.

'Oh? Not really. It's just that this is the main event, Frau Harmsen.' Fabel pointed to the wall-mounted camera in the corner of the room. 'I have to tell you

435

that the rest of my team are all next door, watching us on the monitors. No one wants to miss this.'

Wiegand remained impossible to read. But Fabel knew that, even though she swept the expression from her face almost as soon as it had appeared, Harmsen was concerned.

'If you're suggesting that you found evidence of wrongdoing at the Pharos,' said Wiegand, 'then I know you are bluffing.'

Fabel smiled. 'You're very sure of that, aren't you, Wiegand? My mistake was to forget that today we live in a world where everything we do, every communication we make, sends out ripples across this ocean of electronic noise. Just preparing for yesterday's raid on the Pharos, for example. Or the raid on the Guardians of Gaia safe house. Yes, I'm sure we made enough ripples for you to have had sufficient warning to clear out the odd piece of hardware.'

'If what you say is true, then you have no evidence. Not that there ever was any. But, let's say there was: it sounds to me that the only way to access it would be to travel back in time . . .' Wiegand smiled. A self-satisfied smile that made Fabel feel the impulse to smack it off his face. Instead, he smiled back.

'I find the whole premise of your cult—' he began.

'The Pharos Project is not a cult, Herr Fabel. I resent the use of the word,' said Wiegand.

'I find the whole premise of your *organisation*

intriguing,' said Fabel. 'And at the head of it is the mysterious Dominik Korn. I placed a call to him yesterday, by the way.'

Wiegand snorted. 'And what did he say to you, Herr Fabel?'

'Nothing. He wouldn't speak to me. But, there again, you already knew that. I just thought that, given all of this trouble you're having here in Germany, *Mister* Korn would maybe be interested in discussing it with me. But . . .' Fabel shrugged.

'What particularly interests me about the Pharos Project is its central belief system,' continued Fabel. 'This concept of the Singularity, or the Consolidation as you call it, providing the salvation of the environment. I didn't realise that there were so many similar theories in the world of science. I mean, that some quantum physicists believe that *this* could all be a simulation – that reality lies somewhere distant on the edge of the universe. If you ask me, it's all tosh. All of this Singularity, or Omega Point, or Consolidation, or whatever you want to call it. But there are people out there, vulnerable people, some even with mental illnesses, who desperately want to believe in it. It's no different from the promise of the afterlife that religion has touted for millennia. People want some justification for believing that the lives they lead and hate aren't all there is. That there's some great transformational truth awaiting them. In your case, one that is based on pseudo-science and cod philosophy. Too much science fiction and not enough common sense.'

'Everyone's entitled to their opinion,' said Wiegand. 'But I'll tell you this – and it's the truth: I happen to believe that we are entering the next great stage in human evolution, and we ourselves will be the drivers of that evolution. Not Nature. Have you ever thought about how fast things are changing, Fabel? I mean, do you remember when you were a teenager, for example? Think about all of the massive leaps forward we have made in that time – more than in the rest of human history put together. This is the Great Acceleration, Fabel. Think about the differences in technology and population growth between, say, 1200 and 1500. So little advance in three hundred years. Then think of the massive changes between 1800 and 1900, when the industrial revolution changed everything about the way we lived. But when you look at the twentieth century, at the incredible advances in technology and the explosion in human population, then think about the period between 1975 and today – unbelievable change. It's getting faster and faster. Cybernetic technologies, genetics, genomics, nanotechnology, femtotechnology, even our basic understanding of how the universe around us works – we are now squeezing into a decade what used to take us a century to achieve. Soon it will be compressed into five years, a year . . . The Great Acceleration, as I said.'

'Let me guess, only the Pharos Project understands

the implications of this,' said Fabel. 'Only you can be trusted to steer mankind in the right direction. If that means carrying out vendettas against anyone who criticises or leaves your cult, infiltrating government bodies, even committing cold-blooded murder . . . then all of that is justified, is that it?'

'We don't commit murder. We are a peaceful group.' Wiegand's tone was controlled, even. 'But yes, sometimes it's almost as if everyone else is blind to what's happening. As a species we *are* moving towards something. Our destiny. But there is a very good chance that before we reach that point the damage we are doing to the environment will kill us.'

'And if we do make it, what does this brave new world of yours hold for us?' asked Fabel.

'The time will come – and it will come soon – when we *will* be building self-aware, intelligent machines capable of accelerating the Acceleration. Technology you're incapable of imagining. Nanotechnology and femtotechnology will allow us to build inconceivably powerful computers on a microscopic scale: computers built molecule by molecule. And the new science of synthetic genomics has already resulted in the creation of the first purely artificial life . . . the computers of the future may be as organic as we are. It's the only hope we have: to disengage from the environment and use technology to offer a higher level of existence, of consciousness. You seem to think that I don't believe in what the Pharos Project stands for. Well, you're wrong. I believe it all. I believe it's the future of mankind.'

Fabel looked at Harmsen, who kept her gaze fixed on the tabletop.

'But you don't want to save mankind, Wiegand. You want to save the chosen few. You're just one more rich guy with a messiah complex,' said Fabel. 'People as wealthy as you become so removed from the way everyone else lives their lives that you become totally detached from reality. God knows I can understand how that would affect poor *Mister* Korn, stuck there in international waters on his luxury yacht, plugged into all kinds of technology just to keep him alive. But what you're talking about isn't *enhanced* humanity. It isn't even humanity. It's something less. A diminishment.'

'You are a man of limited intellect, Fabel. And less imagination. I have no interest in continuing this conversation further.' Wiegand started to stand up but Werner placed a persuasive hand on his shoulder.

'You're not going anywhere, Wiegand,' said Fabel.

'Then I think you need to make some specific charges,' said Harmsen. Fabel could sense that she wished she had stuck to representing TV actresses with botched cosmetic surgery.

'Do you believe in the afterlife?' Fabel asked Wiegand, conversationally. 'You know that Nikolai Fyodorov, way back in the nineteenth century,

440

predicted that we would develop such computational power that we could bring almost anyone back to life?'

'I do, yes.'

Fabel placed a grey USB memory stick on the table.

'Do you know, I believe that there is someone alive in there. In that piece of plastic and silicon.' He paused. Neither Wiegand nor Harmsen said anything, but Wiegand's cold, hard little eyes remained fixed on the USB stick.

'The person alive in here was a big man in our world. Literally. According to the pathologist, he weighed one hundred and eighty kilos. He was called Roman Kraxner and he was a deeply flawed individual. Like someone else I met – Niels Freese. But Roman's main flaw was that he was a genius. And his particular talent was with computer technology. Do you know the name, Herr Wiegand?'

'No, I don't.'

'That's strange, because I believe you ordered his death. Or maybe you didn't know his name, just that he was the person with Meliha Yazar's cellphone. And whoever had that had to die, didn't they? Anyway, Roman Kraxner lived more in the virtual world than in this. I have to admit that, had he lived, we would have wanted to talk to him about certain transactions of his, as well as the Klabautermann Virus, which, we believe, was Herr Kraxner's creation.'

Fabel leaned forward, resting his elbows on the

table. 'You were right, Wiegand. I can't go back in time to retrieve the sensitive files you had stored on certain computers and in your secret data-vault. All that noise and drama . . . the police raid, I mean . . . I admit that it's all very crude. Now Roman was different. Roman was a lumbering mountain of a man in our world, but he could move gracefully and silently through networks and systems and firewalls. He paid the Pharos a visit, you know. You're so proud of your technology and knowledge, but, compared to Roman, you're a pedestrian. He passed through your security and copied file after file, incriminating document after incriminating document.'

Wiegand's smile was more of a sneer. 'Incriminating who?' he asked. 'If anyone at the Pharos Project has broken the law, then I condemn it wholeheartedly. But I wish you luck, a lot of luck, if you think you can pin anything on me personally.'

'Yes, I admit that might be difficult. But we could have a pretty good try, and I've got enough evidence here to bring charges. Oh, by the way, I forgot to mention: Roman has sent copies of this to all the major national newspapers, television and, of course, to a dozen websites. My guess is that, as we speak, the word is spreading around the world. The Pharos Project is finished.'

'I doubt that very much,' said Wiegand. 'And, like I say, you and I will be old men before you can get enough out of that . . .' he pointed to the data stick, '. . . to get me anywhere near a prison.'

'Maybe you're right,' said Fabel. He opened the folder again and placed a paperback book on the table next to the memory stick. It was the copy of *The Judge and His Hangman* by Friedrich Dürrenmatt that they had found beside Meliha Yazar's bed.

'Have you ever read this?' asked Fabel. Wiegand ignored him.

'It's a favourite of mine,' said Fabel. 'Philosophy for a policeman. The question being that if you can't bring a criminal to justice for a crime they have committed, is it moral that they should be punished for a crime they did not commit?'

'Again, Herr Fabel,' said Harmsen, 'if you have a point . . .'

'I got it all wrong, yesterday, didn't I? I was so sure I knew what it was that Meliha Yazar had found out,' Fabel continued. 'But I got it completely wrong. Well, not completely . . . I was right about the fact that she uncovered that Föttinger was the Network Killer. But, bad as that was – and it was potentially devastating to the Project – it still wasn't the *big* secret Meliha had found out. Was it, Wiegand?'

Wiegand sat with his arms folded, his face set hard.

'It wasn't because of Föttinger she was killed, or at least that wasn't the main reason. You did order that Daniel Föttinger should die because his

443

activities would, sooner or later, lead back to the Project. You *did* arrange that Meliha Yazar and Müller-Voigt were murdered because you thought they might know about it. But that *wasn't* the secret that they really had to die for. That was a much bigger secret, one that you had to make sure never saw the light of day. You were so paranoid about it that you bugged my communications and tried to compromise me out of the investigation, and when that didn't work you arranged for me to take a dip in the Elbe. You probably realised that Müller-Voigt didn't know anything specific but might have passed something on to me that could have led to the truth, maybe without either of us realising it.'

'What secret?' asked Harmsen. Wiegand remained silent, his face stone.

'All this crap you spout, it actually did get me thinking . . . wondering if it is possible already for someone to exist purely as data . . . cybernetically, rather than physically. I don't mean for them to have any real consciousness, or to be in any way real, but to *seem* to exist to the rest of us, when in fact they don't exist at all.' Fabel picked up the memory stick and turned it over and over in his fingers as he examined it contemplatively.

'The funny thing about cults is that, no matter how different the central beliefs or where they operate in the world, they all share common features. And the thing that's number one on the list is that they always have some kind of charismatic leader. An inspirational figurehead. And nothing fits the

444

cock-eyed philosophies of the Pharos Project more than Dominik Korn. After all, he's halfway there to *consolidation* . . . someone totally dependent on technology to sustain his existence. Add to that his heroic survival of a tragic accident, from the depths of the ocean . . .'

'Trust me, Fabel,' said Wiegand, 'Dominik Korn is an intellect and a force of will that someone like you can't begin to understand.'

'Is that so?' Fabel placed the memory stick back down. He half stood and planted his hands flat on the interview-room table and leaned forward, bringing his face close to Wiegand's. 'I know what the secret is, Wiegand. I know the real reason all those people had to die.'

'What?' asked Harmsen, her voice quiet. Wiegand said nothing.

'Do you know, Frau Harmsen, that Meliha Yazar discovered that Dominik Korn really was, after all, her "Atatürk for the Environment"; that he hadn't converted to these bizarre ideas about the "Consolidation", and that his will and instructions for the future of both the Korn-Pharos Corporation and the Pharos Project have been subverted by Herr Wiegand here?'

'So what are you saying?' asked Harmsen. 'That Herr Wiegand is holding Dominik Korn against his will and is forcing him to comply with his wishes?'

'Oh no. You see, that's the big secret, the Big Lie, at the heart of the Pharos Project. There is no invalid in a wheelchair out there on his luxury yacht. There are no bedside summits with Korn-Pharos vice-presidents. There is no font of Pharos philosophy.' Fabel fixed his gaze on Wiegand. 'There is no Dominik Korn.'

'You're talking nonsense, Fabel,' said Wiegand, but without anger.

'Dominik Korn is dead and my guess is that he's been dead for nearly fifteen years. I believe he survived the accident, but not for long. And he died before Herr Wiegand had the opportunity to alter all of the documents left behind. You see, Korn recognised Wiegand's megalomania and greed. He suspected that he had been siphoning off funds from the Project. After the accident, he became convinced that Wiegand had sabotaged the *Pharos One* in an attempt to gain sole control of the Corporation. In the months following the accident, for as long as he survived, Korn made sure that Wiegand was shut out. Of course, Herr Wiegand could have launched a legal challenge, but, at the end of the day, the Korn-Pharos Corporation was all about one man: Dominik Korn. So when Korn eventually succumbed to his injuries, he was reinvented as a *virtual* person. A phoney leader of a cult with phoney philosophies. As he seemed to become more reclusive and his pronouncements, generated by you, became more bizarre, it fitted that he became a remote figure, a recluse seen only by a close inner-circle entourage. And – surprise, surprise – he invested Wiegand with almost total power of attorney.'

Wiegand laughed. 'You know something, Fabel? You're going to have a hell of a time proving any of this in a court of law. Whatever you have on that thing . . .' he pointed derisively at the data stick '. . . you have no original documents or testimony. And as for these other murders, I'm saddened to find that Bädorf, a trusted employee, has turned out to be a psychopath and has used the Office of Consolidation and Compliance for his own ends. You'll never prove that I had any connection at all with any of this. And as for Dominik's accident? That is something that's well outside your jurisdiction. As is Dominik, for that matter.' Wiegand stood up, his posture and gaze defiant. 'And trust me, you will never, ever be able to prove that Dominik does not exist.'

'True,' said Fabel. 'That's why you're free to go. But there are some people waiting for you downstairs. They've travelled overnight from the US Embassy in Berlin. I believe one is from the State Department and the other is a young lady from the Federal Bureau of Investigation. After all, Dominik Korn is, or was, a US citizen. They're really keen to discuss *Mister* Korn's whereabouts with you. In fact, I believe they have a writ of *habeas corpus* with them.'

Wiegand stared at Fabel, lost for words.

'You see,' said Fabel, drumming his fingers on the copy of *The Judge and His Hangman*, 'maybe I can't prove that Dominik Korn *doesn't* exist. But, for your sake, I hope you can prove that he *does*.'

447

EPILOGUE

In the months that followed, Fabel watched with interest as Peter Wiegand made the headlines. He actually found himself using the internet to follow events on American news channels. Wiegand fought extradition vigorously but lost, and when the Korn luxury yacht finally docked in Portland, Maine, the American authorities established that there was no Dominik Korn on board.

As Fabel had guessed would happen, the FBI charged Wiegand with the murder of an American citizen outside the US. Fabel did not believe that Wiegand had caused Korn's death and he also knew that the US authorities would also struggle to put a murder case together. But, as the investigation progressed, more and more revelations about Wiegand's dealings came to light. Corporate crime, Fabel realised, made bigger headlines in the US than murder, and he knew that Wiegand was unlikely to see the light of day again.

The German press also had a lot to report: Frank Bädorf, Wiegand's head of the Consolidation and Compliance Office, made a full confession about organising the murders of Berthold Müller-Voigt, Daniel Föttinger and Jens Markull. He would not, however, make any statement incriminating his boss, nor about Meliha Kebir – or Yazar, as she had called herself. Which was a pity, because the night before his trial Bädorf committed suicide by suffocating himself with a smuggled-in plastic bag.

There were three more things that happened almost coincidentally, about a week after Wiegand's arrest. The first was that the familial DNA test proved that the torso found washed up at the Fischmarkt was not related to Mustafa Kebir. The second was that the Polizei Niedersachsen found the bodies of two men in a remote disused farmhouse near Cuxhaven. Both men had had their necks broken. Very professionally.

The third occurrence was the strangest. A butcher from Wilhelmsburg walked into the local police station and, in floods of remorseful tears, admitted the murder and dismemberment of his nagging wife, whose neatly cut-up remains he had dumped in the middle of the river.

The GlobalConcern Hamburg summit launched with the minimum of protest. At the opening plenary session, a minute's silence was held for Berthold Müller-Voigt. No mention was made of Daniel Föttinger.

Fabel attended Berthold Müller-Voigt's funeral, on a sunny day under a cloudless sky, along with a host of Hamburg's great and good. Fabel was unsure why he had felt so compelled to attend; he had just been aware that there had been some connection between him and the politician that he needed to acknowledge. While he was at the graveside in Osdorf, he was surprised to see Tim Flemming there, hanging well back from the crowd, accompanied by a young woman whose face was hidden by her hat as she bowed her head, her shaking shoulder revealing that she was weeping. But what Fabel could see of her face reminded him of a photograph that he had once been shown.

He watched them leave before everyone else and thought of intercepting them with questions about two consolidators found with broken necks.

Instead Fabel decided to ignore them. As if they didn't exist.